THE TALE OF MURASAKI

Liza Dalby is an anthropologist specialising in Japanese culture, and the only Westerner to have become a geisha, resulting in the definitive guide *Geisha* (2000). She is a consultant on Steven Spielberg's film of *Memoirs of a Geisha*, and lives in California with her husband and three children. This is her first novel.

D0969333

ALSO BY LIZA DALBY
Geisha

Liza Dalby

THE TALE OF MURASAKI

VINTAGE

Published by Vintage 2001

2 4 6 8 10 9 7 5 3

Copyright © Liza Dalby 2000

Liza Dalby has asserted her right under the Copyright,
Designs and Patents Act 1988 to be identified as the
author of this work

This book is sold subject to the condition that it shall
not, by way of trade or otherwise, be lent, resold, hired
out, or otherwise circulated without the publisher's
prior consent in any form of binding or cover other than
that in which it is published and without a similar
condition including this condition being imposed on the
subsequent purchaser

First published in Great Britain by
Chatto & Windus 2000

Vintage
Random House, 20 Vauxhall Bridge Road, London SW1V 2SA

Random House Australia (Pty) Limited
20 Alfred Street, Milsons Point, Sydney,
New South Wales 2061, Australia

Random House New Zealand Limited
18 Poland Road, Glenfield,
Auckland 10, New Zealand

Random House (Pty) Limited
Endulini, 5A Jubilee Road, Parktown 2193, South Africa

The Random House Group Limited Reg. No. 954009

www.randomhouse.co.uk

A CIP catalogue record for this book
is available from the British Library

ISBN 0 09 928464 2

Papers used by Random House are natural, recyclable products
made from wood grown in sustainable forests. The
manufacturing processes conform to the environmental
regulations of the country of origin

Set in 10½/12 Sabon by SX Composing DTP, Rayleigh, Essex
Printed and bound in Great Britain by
Bookmarque Limited, Croydon, Surrey

For Michael
and Marie, Owen, and Chloe

MURASAKI'S
JAPAN

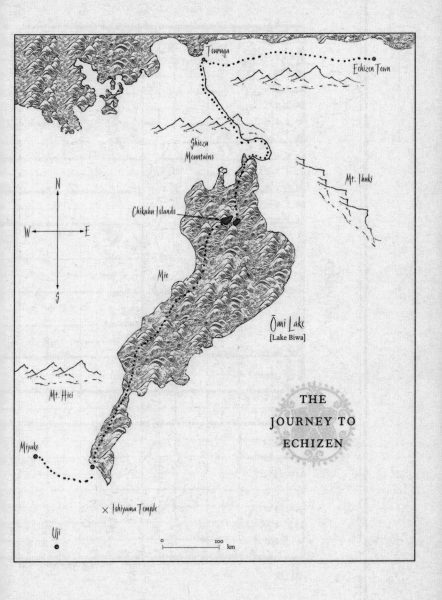

Tsuruga

Echizen Town

Shiozu
Mountains

Mt. Ibuki

Chikubu Islands

N

W   E

S

Mie

Ōmi Lake
[Lake Biwa]

Mt. Hiei

THE
JOURNEY TO
ECHIZEN

Miyako

× Ishiyama Temple

Uji

0   100
km

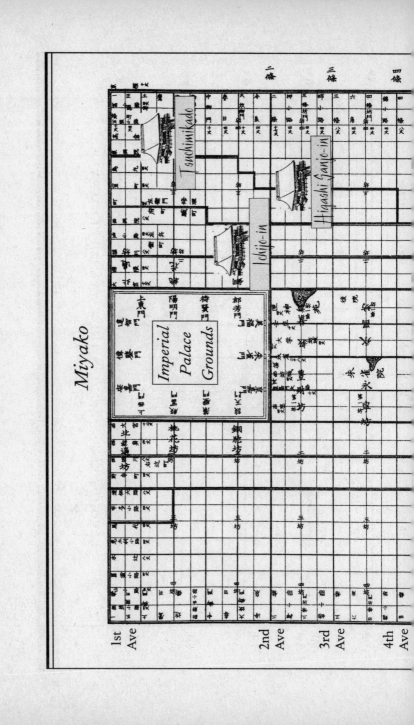

Miyako

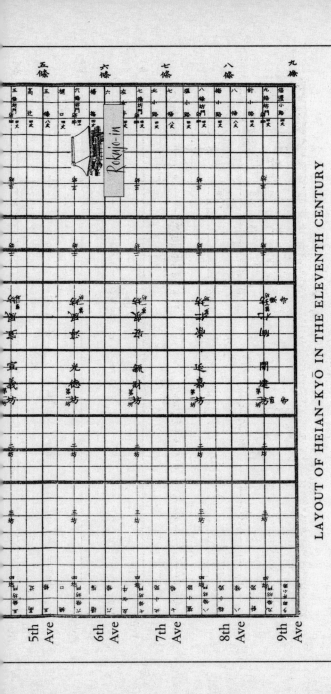

LAYOUT OF HEIAN-KYŌ IN THE ELEVENTH CENTURY

CONTENTS

FOREWORD

In Japanese a tale, *monogatari*, means a story – literally a telling of things. There may be stout threads of fact woven into a tale, but as a genre it is considered fiction. The most famous tale in all Japanese literature is the lengthy, eleventh-century *Tale of Genji* (*Genji Monogatari*) by the court lady Murasaki Shikibu.

The author of this extraordinary work is the subject of *The Tale of Murasaki*. I have pieced the existing historical fragment of her diary into an imagined reminiscence, much as an ancient vase might be reconstructed by setting the original fragments into a vessel of modern clay – a sort of literary archaeology. The shape of the shards dictates the structure of the vessel, so my tale is in the form of a poetic diary, a literary genre well established in Murasaki's day. And while the material of reconstruction is new, I have blended into it eleventh-century sensibilities, beliefs, and preoccupations.

The poems are all Murasaki's or those of the people she engaged in poetic dialogue. Poetry, in the fixed form called *waka* (precursor of the *haiku*), was a primary mode of communication for men and women in Murasaki's circle. The *waka* in the existing collection of her poems often carry brief headings giving a hint of the circumstances under which they were composed. From such hints I built my tale.

I imagined Murasaki writing this memoir at the end of her life, and that it was found, after her death, by her daughter, Katako.

LIZA DALBY

DRAMATIS PERSONAE

AMIDA BUDDHA The Buddha of the Pure Land Paradise, where people could hope to be reborn through their faith in Amida.

ATSUHIRA, PRINCE (1008–1036) Reigned as Emperor Go-Ichijō from 1016 to 1036. Son of Ichijō and Shōshi; grandson of Michinaga.

ATSUYASU, PRINCE (999–1018) Son of Emperor Ichijō and his first empress, Teishi. Prevented from becoming crown prince by Michinaga in favor of Shōshi's sons.

"AUNTIE" Author of the *Gossamer Diary*, distantly related to Murasaki.

BISHI, PRINCESS (1000–1008) Daughter of Emperor Ichijō and Teishi, who died giving birth to her.

CHIFURU Murasaki's childhood friend.

DAINAGON, LADY Niece of Rinshi, in service to Empress Shōshi. Known to be a mistress of Michinaga.

FUJI Murasaki's childhood nickname.

FUYUTSUGU, FUJIWARA (775–826) Important minister during the reign of Emperor Ninmyō, influential in developing the canon of incense. Ancestor of all the prominent Fujiwaras.

GENSHI (891?–1002) Consort of Crown Prince Okisada; sister of Korechika.

ICHIJŌ, EMPEROR (980–1011) The sixty-sixth sovereign of Japan and the reigning emperor for most of Murasaki's lifetime.

IZUMI SHIKIBU A renowned poet and contemporary of Murasaki Shikibu.

JYO, MASTER (*Jyo Shichang*) A Chinese official who led a

delegation to Echizen to escort a number of shipwrecked sailors back to China in 997.

KANE'IE, FUJIWARA (929–990) Powerful consolidator of the Fujiwara family's hegemony over the regency. Father of Empress Senshi and three sons who all became regent: Michitaka, Michikane, and Michinaga. Philandering husband of the author of the *Gossamer Diary*.

KANETAKA, FUJIWARA (985–1053) Son of Michikane. Patron of Murasaki's daughter, Katako.

KATAKO (999–1083) Murasaki's only child.

KAZAN, RETIRED EMPEROR (968–1008) Reigned as the sixty-fifth sovereign for only two years before being tricked into taking the tonsure by Michikane.

KENSHI, EMPRESS (994–1027) Second daughter of Michinaga and Rinshi; younger sister of Shōshi. Became empress when her husband ascended the throne upon the death of Emperor Ichijō in 1012.

KERRIA ROSE Murasaki's friend from girlhood who becomes a nun.

KINTŌ, FUJIWARA (966–1041) One of the most influential arbiters of the cultural life of the court in Murasaki's day. Known as a scholar, musician, literary critic, and poet in both Japanese and Chinese.

KODAYŪ, LADY Famous poet contemporary and companion in court service with Murasaki.

KORECHIKA, FUJIWARA (973–1010) Son of Regent Michitaka; brother of Empress Teishi.

KOSHŌSHŌ, LADY (?–1013) A lady-in-waiting to Empress Shōshi; close friend of Murasaki; longtime mistress of Michinaga.

MICHINAGA, FUJIWARA (966–1027) Son of Kane'ie, assumed regency on death of his brother Michikane. The most powerful of the Fujiwara regents. Father of Empress Shōshi and two other empresses.

MICHITAKA, FUJIWARA (953–995) Son of Kane'ie; father of Empress Teishi and Korechika. Regent between 990 and 995.

MING-GWOK Murasaki's Chinese friend and the son of Master Jyo.

MURAKAMI, EMPEROR (926–967) The sixty-second sovereign.

His twenty-year reign was considered an age when the arts flourished.

MURASAKI (MURASAKI NO UE) Character in the *Tale of Genji*.

MURASAKI SHIKIBU (973?–?) Author of the *Tale of Genji*.

NOBUNORI, FUJIWARA (980?–1011) Murasaki's younger full brother.

NOBUTAKA, FUJIWARA (950?–1001) Murasaki's husband.

NORIMICHI, FUJIWARA (996–1075) Michinaga and Rinshi's second son.

OKISADA, CROWN PRINCE (976–1017) Became Emperor Sanjō upon Ichijō's death.

RINSHI, MINAMOTO (964–1053) Michinaga's principal wife and mother of six attractive and intelligent children – two sons and four daughters.

RURI Murasaki's unconventional girlhood friend.

SAEMON NO NAISHI, LADY A lady-in-waiting from the palace.

SAISHŌ, LADY A high-ranking lady-in-waiting to Empress Shōshi.

SANENARI, FUJIWARA (975–1044) Assistant master of Her Majesty's household. Murasaki appears to have been rather fond of him, judging from several incidents in her diary.

SEI SHŌNAGON (966?–?) Author of a collection of brilliant short essays known as the *Pillow Book (Makura no Sōshi)*, in which she etched her mordant observations of people, life at court, and the aesthetics of nature.

SENSHI, DOWAGER EMPRESS (962–1001) Daughter of Kane'ie; sister of Michinaga; mother of Emperor Ichijō. A major political figure after her son's accession in 986.

SHŌSHI, EMPRESS (988–1074) Eldest daughter of Michinaga and Rinshi. Married to Emperor Ichijō at age thirteen, mother of two emperors.

TAKA'IE, FUJIWARA (979–996) Son of Michitaka; brother of Korechika, with whom he was exiled for crossing Michinaga.

TAKAKO Murasaki's older sister.

TAMETOKI, FUJIWARA (945–1020) Murasaki's father.

TEISHI, EMPRESS (976–1000) Daughter of Michitaka; sister of Korechika. First empress of Ichijō.

YORIMICHI, FUJIWARA (992–1074) Eldest son of Michinaga and Rinshi.

KATAKO'S LETTER

I was pregnant with you when my mother died, but my condition was far from normal. I was often overwhelmed by waves of nausea. The only thing that held them at bay was a fresh citron. Scratching the bumpy yellow *yuzu* skin released a tiny vapor of citrus essence to inhale and quell my rising gorge. But most of the time I simply surrendered to queasy lassitude. I had to tuck emergency drafts of *yuzu* and tangerine peel in my sleeves to get through my mother's funeral. She had been living in seclusion for some time. Some people, on hearing of her death, were surprised that she had still been alive.

Your grandmother was well known as the lady who wrote the *Tale of Genji*. That novel of romance and poignant observation appeared like a bright full moon floating out of a dark sky. No one had read anything like it before. It brought my mother fame and notoriety in her day. Still, I was surprised at the crowd that gathered for her final rites. At least a dozen ladies endured the inconvenient all-day trip to Ishiyama Temple. They must have been *Genji* readers who preferred the life they found in my mother's stories to their own dull husbands or difficult situations.

I'm sure my mother became a recluse in order to disentangle herself from Genji. The work had come to envelop her life. Yet Genji was also her child. She had created and nurtured it, but then, as children do, it grew up and eventually slipped from her control. I was a much more compliant child than the book. I never gave her as much cause for concern as did Genji.

Perhaps because people were infatuated with the heroine of her novel, they confused my mother with that character. She was nicknamed Murasaki when she entered Her Majesty's service. Readers of the tale seemed to think they knew her because they knew Genji's Murasaki. I think my mother grew tired of the letters and visits from people of all ranks, including imperial personages, whom, of course, she could not ignore. It had gotten to the point where readers became so involved with her characters that they importuned my mother to create particular scenes to satisfy their imaginations. They came to expect things of Genji, and my mother grew equally tired, I'm convinced, of meeting their expectations and thwarting them.

She had even been invited to join the empress's entourage because of Genji. It must have seemed a miracle to her, a bookish widow, to have been lifted out of obscurity into the conspicuous brilliance of that imperial salon. Genji writing brought her to the attention of the regent Michinaga, the man who controlled emperors and ruled the country in fact if not in name. Whatever my mother's relationship to Michinaga may have been, Genji was largely responsible.

One bears children and eventually launches them into society, praying they will make a favorable impression, attain a suitable status, or at least not be an embarrassment. Perhaps one has taught them something that will give them the strength to suffer the karma they were born with. Yet eventually children will do as they will. The influence of previous existence will play out in ways we cannot possibly know. As a parent, one accepts this. But a work of fiction is a perverse child. Once treated, it makes its own way without apology, brooking no influence, making friends and enemies on its own.

Perhaps it's not so different from a flesh-and-blood child, after all.

The Genji tale was like an elder brother to me from the time I was born. It was always taking up my mother's time, demanding her attention like any selfish boy. It never went away or lessened its demand. As jealous as I was when I was young, eventually I, too, fell under Genji's spell.

We did not meet often during the years my mother lived as a nun. My own career at court was developing moderately well, and I was then under the protection of Counselor Kanetaka, a nephew of Regent Michinaga. It was his child – you – I carried at the time of Murasaki's death.

I thought I should probably never marry. How was I to know the fated connections and promotions that were to come my way? I was not worried about my future, because my mother was not. She would not have abandoned me at sixteen unless she felt my prospects were secure.

The faint scent of cherry blossoms will always remind me of my mother's departing this world. As we left the sand-strewn funerary plain at dawn, we passed stands of blooming cherries in the morning fog. Then, as the sun warmed the earth and the fog melted away, a soft smell filled the air. No one thinks of *sakura* for its scent – it hasn't the strong honey odor of plum – but out in the countryside, in such masses, *sakura* seemed to have a subtle fragrance.

I was carrying the urn with Murasaki's ashes to take back to our family temple. My grandfather Tametoki should have been in charge, but, mortified at seventy-four to have outlived his children, he shrank from taking an official part in the ceremony. Shaking his gray head like one of the querulous macaque monkeys we saw on the mountain roads, my grandfather lamented the fortune of his continued good health as much as his daughter's death.

The following month I journeyed for the last time to my mother's retreat near Kiyomizu Temple to gather her things. I knew there would not be very much because she had already given away her musical instruments, her books, and – of course, long since – all of the fine silk clothing she had worn at court. There were some good padded winter robes, which I donated to the temple, as well as the sutras she had been copying in her graceful calligraphy. I managed to find the only things I wanted – her dark purple inkstone, a set of writing brushes, and a Chinese celadon brush rest in the form of five mountains. As I knelt at her low writing table, I noticed another bundle of papers, rolled tightly and wrapped in a scrap of chartreuse silk. Thinking these to be old letters she had kept for the paper on which to copy more sutras, I decided to take them with me for my own writing practice. Paper is not cheap, and I thought I might as well put it to the use my mother intended. The priest was disappointed. These people are always on the lookout for extra paper.

What with one thing and another, and the weather turning hot after I returned to court, and the fact that my nausea did not pass as the older woman said it would, I didn't happen to look at my mother's papers until the twelfth month, after you were born.

You must keep in mind what a fuss your grandmother's writing used to cause. It seemed that Murasaki was discussed after her death as much as when she had lived at court. Because people were still eagerly reading the story of Prince Genji, I would often be asked to arbitrate between two readers who had obtained different versions, usually because the court ladies had made mistakes in copying. I don't know how it happened, but entire chapters would get shuffled and occasionally be missing altogether from some texts. I tried to keep a full set of my own in proper order, letting people refer to it when questions arose. Then, too, there were my mother's poems, some of which had been selected for inclusion in imperial anthologies. I suppose it was not surprising that Murasaki should have continued to maintain a literary following, yet her reputation could not have rested on her poems. They are respectable, of course, but it was really Genji that set her apart from the others.

After giving birth I felt like myself again. You were a healthy infant, and I insisted on nursing you alongside the imperial prince I had been awarded the privilege of wet-nursing. With your birth, the torpor of pregnancy evaporated like a heavy cloud chased by a crisp autumn day. I felt the urge to pick up my brush and get back to my own diary again. I added my mother's fine old brushes to my collection and arranged them all in a large mottled-bamboo holder. The one I selected to use rested on the five-mountain brush rest Murasaki had kept until the end of her life.

My writing hand was stale, and as I looked around my

4

room for some scrap paper to copy poems for exercise, I came upon the bundle of pale green silk that I had shoved into a chest during the nauseous days of pregnancy. I untied the knot and smoothed out the tightly rolled sheets. Some of it was old, some fresh. Much consisted of copies of the Lotus Sutra. I recognized my mother's handwriting and at first thought these were letters. Some indeed were letters, as it turned out, and other bits were from a journal. On the back of every sheet of paper was writing in Murasaki's hand. It was all a jumble and I could see no sense or order at first. Finally I found the scrap that made it clear. Near the end of her life, my mother seems to have rummaged through her diary, her poems, her Genji drafts, and her letters, and composed a reminiscence. Yet rather than put her thoughts down on fresh paper, she inscribed her last work upon the backs of the very journals upon which it was based. Now that I had the key, I began to read.

Over the following months I divided my time between milk and paper – your greedy little plum-bud mouth and my voracious eyes. You sucked sustenance from me and I from those texts, so I am truly surprised at your lack of interest in literature now, since you must have absorbed so much of its savor in infancy.

Publicly I was the conservator of the true version of the *Tale of Genji*, my copy being the standard. Privately I became the guardian of my mother's reminiscences. I have already told you that Genji was like an older sibling. He received preferential treatment while I was growing up, but then helped me later, just as an older brother watches out for his sister. When she renounced the world, Murasaki let go of Genji even as she let go of her aging father. It fell to me to take care of both. If she resides now in Amida Buddha's paradise, I trust her soul is untroubled. I have done my best to watch over those she left behind.

People commended me for caring for my grandfather. Some thought it must have been onerous to be tied to an elderly relative, but I never felt that way. Tametoki was always a source of wisdom for me, never a trial. Always courteous, never presuming, he seemed anchored by a melancholy so deep it had, in a curious way, stabilized his life. In fact he always assumed that he was taking care of me.

Now that you are grown, you should read your grandmother's memoir in order to understand who you are by virtue of what you have come from. I suggest you keep it to yourself until you give it to your own literary descendant someday. In the future, if the *Tale of Genji* is still being read, sensitive people may find Murasaki's private thoughts of interest, and the gossip will be too old to do any harm.

A poem she once wrote for someone else comes unbidden to mind:

Tare ka yo ni   nagaraete mimu   kakitomeshi   ato wa kiesenu   katami naredomo
As life flows on, who ever will read it – this keepsake to her
** whose memory will never die?**

I can't help but think someone will.

MY GOSSAMER HERMITAGE
Kagerō-an

At this point in my life I look back and am appalled at the amount of paper I have used. Surely there must be a place in hell for people who have scribbled as much as I. Next to me sits a box of my old journals; here is a bound collection of my poems; here is a set of Genji stories from the time the empress had a number of them copied; and here a chestful of letters. When I think of the countless drafts I later burned or made into dollhouses for Katako, the amount of paper would far exceed that which surrounds me now. I have redeemed some small portion of it by copying the Lotus Sutra on the reverse, but I'm sure there is not enough time remaining in my life to atone for it all.

For some reason deep in my karma, I have always felt

6

compelled to set down a vision of things I have heard and seen. Life itself has never been enough. It only became real for me when I fashioned it into stories. Yet, somehow, despite all I've written, the true nature of things I've tried to grasp in my fiction still manages to drift through the words and sit, like little piles of dust, between the lines. The histories are even more unsatisfactory than tales in capturing the essence of things. As I look back through the diaries I've kept over the years, I realize that although they jog many memories for me, they are likely to be utterly flat to anyone else.

Why do I persist in thinking there must be another way to grasp the elusive existence of things? My auntie's notorious *Gossamer Diary* comes closest to anything I've ever read in capturing it, although she concentrated only on life's bitterness. I have thought to rummage back through my journals and set down my life, including my long relationship with Prince Genji. Perhaps by engaging the fact of my fiction I will at last be able to come to some sort of truth.

Can it possibly atone for all the paper, though?

THE EARLY JOURNAL

Nikki no hajime

My mother died when I was fifteen. I remember the black wave of chanting clergy that swept into my grandmother's house as my mother lay groaning in her last fevered agony, her smooth round face sunk and stretched into sharp sallow planes. The chanting monks hunkered in the main hall, bellowing and rattling their sutra beads, but their mantras were as useless as the furious sea foam. It was clear she was dead, and my father ordered them to stop the clamor. The clerics receded to the temples whence they had been summoned by my distraught grandmother.

My mother had been beautiful, but her corpse was not. I

7

closed my eyes and felt I was in a dream from which I would awake to find her sitting in front of her mirror, staining her teeth or sampling the scent of a jar of incense she had unearthed from the garden where it had been ripening by the stream. Over the next few days this unhappy dream turned solid, and the realities of my childhood became tenuous. I remember her cremation vividly, for it was there that I suddenly awoke to the change.

I watched the plume of smoke rising from the pyre as dawn slowly seeped into an overcast sky. People had begun to leave, but my father, brother, sister, and I stayed on in our carriage. Our bearers had rested its poles on stones set in the moist, odorous earth while they were off attending the ox. Earlier, the pyre had produced deep orange flames and clouds of smoke, but for the past few hours there had been no flames, just smoke trails and finally a single plume. I held it in my eye, breathing lightly, afraid if I exhaled the plume would vanish. When it died, she would be completely gone. I held my breath as I had at her sickbed.

There. The filmy ribbon of gray ceased. My heart beat faster and I felt a hot coal choking the back of my throat. I couldn't bear the end. Then the plume appeared again, stronger, as if lifted out of the pyre by the power of my will. I glanced at my younger brother. He had fallen asleep with his mouth open, his head resting awkwardly on the carriage strut. My father sat straight, deliberately not looking at the pyre, fingering a string of sandalwood prayer beads. He made no sign that he saw the smoke disappear or resurge.

I watched the new plume of smoke as dawn turned into the morning. Sounds of people stirring and stretching their limbs in other cramped carriages caught my attention and the plume wavered. Panicked, I turned the full force of my will upon the smoke.

—Stay, I silently commanded. As long as the smoke endured, she had not yet left this world. The gates of the Western Paradise opened, and Amida Buddha himself may have reached down to pull her soul up to his resplendent lotus throne – but she had not gone yet. I became dizzy from my effort, then afraid.

—This is too much, I wanted to cry out. I can't hold it any longer. I wanted the smoke to die now, but by itself, without my willing it.

And then it ceased. And so my mother ceased to be my mother. She was something else. I let my breath out cautiously and for a few minutes felt the air pass in and out of my lungs.

The marshy plain where bodies are burned was as a damp, acrid, permanently melancholy place where creatures dressed in rags, with filthy matted hair, tended the fires. They appeared partly human. I remembered being somewhat surprised that they lived in families. Children crept about like shy foxes, and I thought I saw a woman standing behind a thatched hovel. The men at least could speak our language, for I noticed one of our officials giving directions and handing a parcel to one of them. But I could not understand their chattering to one another. On our way back to the city, my father confirmed that they were human, but beyond the pale.

—They make their living from dead things, he said. Someone must build the great pyres which free the souls of the deceased.

It was a privilege to be released into the air in smoke. Commoners were simply dumped in the moors, left to decompose and tumble along their karmic journey. I marveled at this level of existence, human fading into beast, and was not surprised to hear that these are the creatures who tan animal hides for leather.

Father insisted I compose a commemorative poem, but, to my disgrace, I simply could not. My emotions refused to borrow an image. My brother was young enough to be excused from composition, and my older sister was simple. So Father was disappointed by all his children.

I did, however, resolve to begin keeping a journal, for I saw that I had the power to affect things – if only a wisp of smoke. Yet, even so, this was something to keep track of. I had awakened, suddenly clear-eyed, from a disturbing dream with the ability to concentrate my will and influence something of the world. It became desperately important to me to keep this awareness, and I sensed words would be the key.

In the spring of the following year we moved out of my grandmother's house to my father's official residence near the western bank of the Kamo River. My father began teaching my brother, Nobunori, the Chinese classics. Nobu had just turned ten, so his coming-of-age ceremony was on Father's mind. The idea of my brother having his hair cut and putting on a man's trousers made me laugh, yet my father was merely being prudent, figuring it would take his son several years to master the texts for the ritual. My brother was not a bad-looking boy, but, to Father's deep chagrin, he was slow.

Nobu was forced to sit and memorize Chinese every morning. I found I could easily recite all his lessons by heart just from listening to the droning repetition issuing from his room. If I glanced at a text, the Chinese characters wrote themselves on my mind, and I had little trouble reproducing them when I sat at my writing table. Because it was so easy for me, I became impatient with Nobunori. He could not remember, let alone understand, anything he was taught. I found him mumbling his lessons in the garden as he looked for stag beetles under the iris leaves. Each time he stumbled on a line, I gritted my teeth. Finally I recited the section he muddled. He looked up at me, his dirty face crumpling most unattractively.

—It's not fair, he burst out. I'm telling Father!

—Just my luck, Father sighed. What a pity this daughter was not born a boy. She is the one who seems to have inherited the family talent.

Yet when he realized I had overheard his remark, he quickly added,

—It's not a bad thing at all – a girl born into a scholarly family – despite what people say . . .

And he gave me the task of drilling Nobunori in Chinese. In this way I obtained a thorough education in the classics.

Nobu and I went out to buy *ayame* plants for the Sweet Flag Festival at the beginning of the fifth month. We came home with a bundle of fragrant leaves for making pomanders and several roots for Father to use as specimens in a competition

10

that he was planning for his academic friends. He inspected the long pale yellow tubers with faint pink swellings and trailing rootlets. We had been excited to find one almost six feet long. Father approved our pick. Long roots foretell long life. Even when I was a child, people grew the sweet flag iris for profit and brought it into the city around the first of the fifth month.

—It is not as interesting as it used to be, Father complained. There's hardly any point in comparing roots when you've gone out and bought them. Still, you've managed to find longer ones from the peddlers than we ever found in the swamps. We'll see how they compare to what the others bring.

Coming from a family of scholars, Father's upbringing had been strict, requiring him to study most of the time. Once a year, right before the monsoon rains came sweeping through, the family took an excursion into the countryside to collect sweet flag roots for competitive games back in the capital. Our family owned some land, and the farmers who tilled it had a patch of *ayame* growing by the side of a stream. The younger children were allowed to wade through the slippery streambed with the peasants to dig the rhizomes out of the mud. They rooted about excitedly, searching for the good ones, for whoever found the longest won a prize back home. They took their trove into the farmer's house, decorated with flowers for this special visit from the master living in the capital. There the peasants washed the mud from the roots and arranged them on planks.

Contests of poetry were played by courtier and scholar, but competitions for the prettiest painting, the sweetest songbird, the best tray landscape – or the longest *ayame* root – were enjoyed by everyone. This was clearly a rare treat for the young bookish child my father had been. As he told us this story, his eyes drifted with the pleasure of memory lovingly fondled over the years.

This was the first time we plaited the fragrant leaves into pomanders without my mother. We hung the eaves with fresh sweet flags to keep us safe from noxious summer vapors.

That year the typhoons swept through in one fierce storm

after another. In the eighth month we had to evacuate our house abruptly because the Kamo River overflowed its banks. The entire eastern part of the low basin of Miyako* was inundated. Father didn't let us return until the servants had swabbed out the mud and river debris, although he himself had gone back even before the water had receded to salvage what he could of his precious Chinese books. Standing in bright sunlight in our sorry, mud-bedraggled garden, I noticed something huddled by the pillar stone. I had been afraid to ask the servants if they had seen either of the cats since the flood.

Squeezing my eyes shut, I told myself that what I noticed was a clump of river weed. When I opened them again, the clot of weed still had matted fur and tiny clenched white teeth. As I stared, the gardener emerged from the back of the house with the other cat struggling in his arms. It was yowling and scratching wildly, but he seemed not to mind. He dangled the animal in one hand, holding it stiffly away from his body.

—Look here, young mistress, he called to me, his thick lips split in a wide grin. Look who I found in the pomegranate tree!

The cat twisted free of his dirty brown hand, leaped to the muddy ground, and dashed toward me. It was the male. Both were white Chinese cats, indistinguishable at a distance. I picked him up, wondering how he managed to stay so white, and pointed to the wretched tangle by the pillar.

—Over there, I said to the gardener.

I recall standing there numb as joy and grief simply canceled the other out.

*Miyako, meaning "capital," is an old word for the city of Kyoto, which was officially called Heian-kyō in Murasaki's day.

CHIFURU

Chifuru

By the first anniversary of my mother's death I had learned to supervise the household. We still visited Grandmother almost every other day, but Father had come to depend on me to direct the servants and take care of practical matters. Certainly my older sister, Takako, could not have managed it. Mentally she was a child. With luck, Nobunori might someday be launched in a court career, but for the time being he needed a great deal of attention. I was seventeen, and though people were undoubtedly starting to wonder when Tametoki's daughter would marry, I pushed the thought from my mind. It's not that I had decided I didn't like men, but I already had the responsibilities of a household. I wasn't interested in romance.

Autumn began with the usual heat wave. I put away my white summer underrobes and changed to a blue-green chemise but did not feel cooler as a result. I could hardly bear to move. I moonbathed in the garden at night and slept during the day in the dark inner rooms of the house. Father cautioned about absorbing too much yin by moonlight – it induces melancholy, he warned – but I didn't care. My mother had suffered spells of despondence, he pointed out, yet he stopped short of forbidding me, so I continued to sit out in the garden at night. Privately I suspected that he considered my nature to be overly yang in the first place and felt that a dose of moon essence might make me more feminine.

Since the seventh month is called the Poem-Composing month, I decided to take a break from Chinese and memorize the entire *Kokin Wakashū* in order to surprise my grandmother. She had been needling me about the unladylike way I studied Chinese, and gently but constantly tried to steer me toward *waka** instead. And so, immersed in our native classic

*The *waka* consists of five lines of a set number of syllables in the pattern 5,7,5,7,7. The *haiku* is a later development, a truncated *waka*, in effect, in the pattern of 5,7,5.

13

poetry collection, I discovered that the more *waka* I learned, the easier it became to compose my own. Soon my thoughts naturally fell into that form, and I hardly had to think about it. Every occasion now, every natural phenomenon, every emotion, sparked a *waka* in my mind. Sometimes I even wrote them down.

During this hot early autumn Chifuru and her family came back to the capital and stayed with us for five days. Chifuru was one year older than I. We had played together as children before her father was posted to the provinces. It was strange to meet after so many years, but perhaps that's why we became close so quickly. At the time, I remembered her as a chubby girl, as active and loud as I was shy. Her hair was thick as a pony's mane, and short wisps bristled around her face when the weather was humid. Now she was tall and beautiful, but even at eighteen I could still see the phantom of the active little girl who once played with me, a mere year sanctioning her unquestioned authority in every game.

Chifuru had an extra tooth in her mouth. It overlapped an incisor and peeked out below her upper lip. When she smiled, I said,

—The moon emerges from the clouds.

It was our childhood joke about her extra tooth. At once I became afraid she might be angry, but she laughed and raised her wide sleeve to her face.

—Mother says I am always to conceal my mouth. At least the moon now has some cloud cover, she said, referring to her elegantly blackened tooth. I became conscious of my own artlessly white mouth.

She lowered her sleeve and looked me over slowly, as if searching for the shadow of my seven-year-old self who had once obeyed her every eight-year-old command, even under the bedclothes we shared at night. We had nicknames for each other. I called her Oborozuki, Hazy Moon, and she called me Kara-no-ko because even then I had been drawn to things Chinese. Ten years had passed since we played "going to court," as if that were a serious possibility for either of us.

When you see someone every day, the changes wrought by the passage of time are quite imperceptible. The person seems

14

not to change, or perhaps you both change together and so don't notice. This may be why it is difficult to fall in love with a person who has grown up living next door all one's life. Of course, when you meet total strangers, everything about them is new and you have no memories to connect. You spend time casting out threads to fasten on to some shared sensibility or experience, but really, it is such an effort. I found it far more interesting to look for glimmers of the child I once knew in this exotically beautiful young woman who came to stay with us.

Chifuru shared my room. As we powdered our faces with white Chinese earth, I brushed away the sidelocks of her hair. I recall that I was suddenly struck by a strong memory of the Chifuru of my childhood. It had been a quiet afternoon during the long rains of spring and we were sitting on the fragrant new mats in my mother's room, combing rice water into each other's hair. I was overcome with a pang of piercing awareness at the beauty caught in the invisible web connecting the two of us over that span of time.

For years afterward, every time I dusted my face with Chinese powder, I experienced a fleeting glimpse of that moment. It is astonishing when you consider that these connections must exist for every living thing, since every moment necessarily grows out of its past along a path directed by its karma. Perhaps this is even true for nonliving things as well – even a stone has a past, I suppose. But it's more poignant with things that live, because time works such changes upon them, even though these connections are rarely recognized. What was the power that evoked the exquisite sad sense of beauty that I felt so keenly that day? I have decided that it must be memory. This is why we will never find something totally new to be beautiful.

Lying next to Chifuru in the still-cool morning, I could tell her of my shame. My father had mentioned to some of his friends that I memorized the Chinese classics my brother was supposed to be learning. He said it with a touch of pride, for he saw nothing wrong with a woman being learned, but he should have realized that it wasn't something to brag about. Many people found it odd if not humorous, and I was naive

15

enough to be stung. My friend Sakiko, who had served at court and was extremely well connected as a gossip, told me she heard Yoshinari's eligible sons laughing about "the girl who knows Chinese."

—So your reputation is ruined, said Chifuru, stroking my elbow with the back of her fingernails. Now you will never find a decent husband.

She shook her crumpled, slightly damp chemise and smoothed it over both of us.

—If learning Chinese could prevent marriage, I would study too, she said. Unfortunately it wouldn't do any good. She laughed with a touch of bitterness.

I thought she was mocking, but should have known better. Her knowledge of Chinese characters was shaky, yet she never made fun of reading. Chifuru's mother had spent a few years as a lesser serving lady to a royal princess before her marriage. She cherished her time at court as the high point of her life, and when she had a daughter herself, all she could think of was how to educate Chifuru so that she might have the same experience. Chifuru's father had been an ambitious scribe when her parents met. He turned out to be an uncommonly able administrator, so he was sent out of Miyako repeatedly during his career to one troublesome province after another. However, the court was not particularly keen on taking girls brought up in the provinces into service.

As a scholar's daughter, I came to realize, I didn't have much chance, either. My mother and grandmother had filled my head with tales of court life when I was a child, so I had quite unrealistic notions about imperial life that were at least a generation out of date. All their talk was largely fantasy in any case, for neither of them had actually served. Their anecdotes were mostly hearsay.

How pathetically innocent Chifuru and I were, with the secret desire to serve at court burning in both our hearts. During the next few days Chifuru and I began a game of making up stories about court life – spinning out fantasies that were really just a variation on our childhood make-believe, but this time with a sensitive hero who became erotically involved with every lady he met.

We took turns pretending to be the prince or the lady. Neither of us had had any experience with men, but we used our imaginations and experimented with what we had heard from our friends.

I was devastated when Chifuru had to leave. We exchanged fans. I gave her my water-blue one with black-lacquered ribs, decorated with lines of Chinese poetry, and she gave me her pale pink three-ply cherry – antique and rather valuable. Her family was traveling, after all, and they left as if racing the moon.

Alone in my room, I wrote down this poem, which I copied and sent off to her by messenger the next day.

Meguriaite   mishi ya sore tomo   wakanu ma ni   kumogakurenishi   yowa no tsukikage
Chancing to meet again, did I truly see you or, before I could tell, had you disappeared behind the clouds – face of the midnight moon?

In that short time I discovered love and was transformed. Yet at the very moment I found it, she was taken away.

At the end of autumn Chifuru came again with her family for a last visit. In the space of one season everything changed. Sun-warmed afternoons contracted and turned chill. Maples and sumacs exploded in their annual brocade splendor, and fashionable ladies rivaled the trees in the colors of their layered gowns. Insects sang in the grass. Chifuru's family was traveling again, en route to her father's new posting in the faraway southern province of Tsukushi. It was all very sudden and not a proper appointment, but he could hardly have refused. The governor had died, the provincial office was in disarray, and Chifuru's father was summoned to straighten things out as soon as possible. Tsukushi was not what you would call a plum – people were *banished* to Tsukushi.

Before they arrived, father had taken me aside to tell me the circumstances, yet even so I was not prepared for Chifuru's misery. Her face was hidden by the veiled hat of her traveling costume that she did not remove until we were alone. Her

17

eyelids were swollen as if she had been crying for a long time and only recently stopped.

—This must be punishment for a sin I committed in a previous life, she whispered, her hands folding and refolding the veils of the hat she removed. When I offered to comb her hair out, she reached back to untie the cord that held it in a long tail where it had lain under her coat. The cord caught and refused to come undone, so she yanked mercilessly, bringing tears to her eyes as she exclaimed,

—Oh stupid cord! Why does nothing ever work right?

I caught her angry hand and held it to my cheek. Chifuru slumped against me and began to cry.

—I know, I said. Father told me. But it's only temporary . . .

I tried to soothe her with the rationales Father had used. He knew I would be upset at the thought of a friend's disappearing into the crude, uncivilized west. Chifuru was quiet as I smoothed out her long tangled hair with my comb.

—I'm not going to Tsukushi, she whispered in a husky voice.

—What do you mean? I asked, suddenly afraid.

—I'm to be married along the way, she said bitterly. My father felt it would ruin my prospects entirely if I went and rotted in Tsukushi for several years. It's not likely that I would find a husband there, so we will stop in Bizen.

—Bizen? I asked dumbly. In fact I was relieved. When she said she wasn't going to Tsukushi, I feared that she was considering something much more desperate.

—The governor recently lost his wife and is looking to marry a woman from the capital. My father thought it would be the perfect solution.

The evening air was crisp, and clouds hurried across the moon. The stars were dimmed by the moon's bright light, and the insects in the garden thrummed in full force. We sat huddled close on the verandah talking softly. As we fell quiet, the insects filled our silence, so we listened, distinguishing four different voices – the bell cricket, pine cricket, weaver-bug, and *kirigirisu*. My brother had been catching samples of these and more all month, making bamboo cages for them and feeding them cucumber and melon rinds. I had learned which insect made what kind of noise by watching his specimens. Some only sang during the day, some only at night.

As we pondered her upcoming marriage, I realized that Chifuru was the only person I could truly open my heart to.

—At least you will come back to live in Miyako when his tour of duty is over, I ventured.

But she would be a married woman then, and what my own status would be I could not even guess. Chifuru's fate had thrown a sudden dark cloud on my own situation. It was not reasonable to assume that I would simply be able to go on as I was, either.

We were wearing identical dark russet trousers of silk twill over padded white chemises. Chifuru's layered cloak was maroon, lined in pale turquoise-green; mine was tan with a dusty-pink lining. It was old, and the bright pink dye had long since faded to the color of a pale mushroom. We tried to imagine each other as married ladies. We would have to cut our sidelocks, and our long loose trousers would be scarlet instead of russet. We would get our own wardrobes of co-ordinated kimono sets rather than putting together our mothers' hand-me-down robes. We vowed always to pay attention to the fashionable color combinations, even if we had to live in the provinces.

Chifuru had mixed the evil-smelling ferrous solution to stain her teeth when she stayed with us before, and I was eager to have her do mine as well. When she left, I followed her recipe, mixing the iron filings with saké rather than vinegar as some people do, and by reapplying the mixture every three days, now my mouth matched her refined dark one. Laughing, we made up a story about our imaginary hero visiting the house of a provincial governor and seducing his beautiful young wife.

Before we knew it, the moon hovered over the western hills and we crept inside and slept as the voices of the night-singing insects faded. I wondered drowsily whether they had a premonition of the briefness of their lives. In their plaintive shrilling I heard farewell to autumn, farewell to the clouded moon, farewell to Chifuru. When she was gone, I wrote this poem:

19

Nakiyowaru   magaki no mushi mo   tomegataki   aki no wakare ya   kanashikaru kana

*As the song of the crickets fades in the hedge, it is
impossible to stop autumn's farewell; how sad they must
be too . . .*

About a month after Chifuru and her family left for the western
provinces, Father summoned his three children to his study to
announce a change in the family's living arrangements. My
brother hadn't a clue, but I grasped what was going on at once.
Father's intended was a woman in her twenties whose grandfather and father were provincial officials. Being fond of
Chinese poetry, her father was delighted at this connection to
our family. It was really rather funny to see poor Father
struggling with the attempt to break the news. A few days
earlier I noticed that he had taken his old lacquer comb case
out, and I guessed what was up. This was the comb he had used
while staying at my mother's mansion. Her family returned it
when she died, and he had kept it, cords tightly wrapped, in a
special drawer in the chest in the corner of his study. I wondered if he kept his memories of her tightly wrapped as well.

I was familiar with every corner of the house, including his
study, for he always said I had free access to his books and
papers, and I took him at his word. Surreptitiously I saw the
drafts of his attempts at love poems, and I sensed that at least
once he had been refused. Of course he never talked of these
affairs with us, but by the time an agreement had been
reached I was not surprised.

It had been three years since our mother died. Father was
forty-three but still manly. No one thought it strange that he
should take another wife. Many men kept several wives at the
same time and found it impossible to imagine life without the
support of wifely attentions. Some men couldn't even dress
themselves without a woman's help in choosing the right
colors and finding clean underrobes. My father was unusually
self-sufficient. His friends could hardly believe he didn't keep
a mistress during those years. Even so, it was unrealistic for
me to have thought that I could have gone on managing the
household for him.

I was touched to see that he seemed to worry what his

20

children would think. I understood him so well that, for me at least, there was no need for him to speak in such a formal manner. Yet this announcement marked a change, and I suspected that I would be the one most affected. Unlike the arrangement that attended his marriage to my mother, when he moved to her parents' mansion, where we children were born and grew up, this time his bride would come to live here, in his official residence.

It is now more fashionable for a wife to go live in a new house with her husband rather than stay home, but at the time I thought the prospect terrifying. If I had to marry, I much preferred the idea of staying in my own house and having a husband visit. The thought of leaving my family and moving into a new house with a stranger seemed quite awful. Though I was apprehensive, I felt sorry for Father's new bride.

To his credit, Father did his best to make arrangements that would promote domestic harmony. He had a new wing built on to the house to minimize the effect on the rest of us. My older sister, Takako, was given the luxury of moving into Father's old room overlooking the river, since he would be moving his things to the new wing. I stayed in my cozy dim room by the front garden pond next to Father's study, but received a new set of matching curtain stands and cushions. Nobunori pouted because Takako got more than he did, stubbornly refusing to recognize that Father favored Takako with treats because she was simple.

My older sister's greatest pleasure was eating, and she was always begging snacks from the maids. She was so fond of beans in sweet vine syrup that whenever the cook made this dish, it tended to disappear before other members of the family got any. Takako was very fat, but her disposition was sweet and forgiving – except with Nobunori. He enjoyed tormenting her, and she was always suspicious in his presence. She scowled and her eyes disappeared into the folds of her face the minute she saw him, for she had no ability whatever to dissemble her emotions. Of course she could never marry.

My brother was jealous of the affection Father showed her. Nobunori was treated so sternly. I was always having to come between my brother and sister to make peace. One reason Father gave Takako the riverside room was to put some distance between them. Nobunori incorporated Takako's old room into his on one side of Father's study, gaining more space to put his various collections. The only thing I requested was that, after the marriage, Father's bride not be allowed in his study.

My stepmother was three years older than I, but meek as a wordless gardenia. Despite her father's interest in the Chinese classics, she had no particular literary ability, and she kept to herself in the new part of the house. Privately my nickname for her was Kuchinashi.* I spent most of my time in the study. From there I gazed out into the garden at the fading chrysanthemums.

I was thinking about how the seasons change yet stay the same, whereas people pass irrevocably from the spring of their youth, never to experience it again. I dreaded the thought that I might soon have to leave home myself. Chifuru was gone, torn away like a leaf in autumn. Could I avoid a similar fate? Even if I managed to postpone marriage, I still ached every day with loneliness for her. I was resigned to the fact that I would never have a chance to go to court. Father once had a position that might have made it possible, but when Emperor Kazan abdicated, he had to retire from his post in the Bureau of Ceremonial. He had managed to find philosophical comfort in the Chinese classics, and now I turned to these writings myself, looking for guidance. I was convinced the answer to life's enigmas must lie in connecting our emotional yearnings to nature.

I discovered the ancient Chinese calendrical *Monthly Ordinances*† and studied to see what the Chinese sages had divined. They treated the year as if it were a stalk of bamboo, with alternating sections of shank and node: every month

Kuchinashi, "mouthless," is a gardenia. The name comes from the fact that the narrow, ribbed red fruit does not open till it is completely dried out.

†The *Yue Ling*, a first-century B.C. Chinese text.

22

contained one pair, each named to reflect changes in nature. As I contemplated the chrysanthemums in the garden, we had just entered the fortnight node called Cold Dews. Our own calendar makes use of these divisions as well, but I found that the ancient Chinese made even finer seasonal discriminations. Each stem and shank contained three smaller units of five days each. These were the "seasonals," I suppose I should call them. Altogether there were seventy-two of them in a year. With such precise depiction of the season, I felt the Chinese must have had the key to understanding the connection between human emotion and nature. So every day I paused to consider precisely what the season was.

I found that the fortnight of Cold Dews began with a seasonal called *Wild Geese Come as Guests*. This was followed by *Sparrows Dive into the Water Turning into Clams*, and then *Chrysanthemums Are Tinged Yellow* – exactly what I happened to be observing in our garden. Twelve months divided among four seasons, and the months themselves split like bamboo and then chopped even finer into seasonals. I marveled at how observant the Chinese were.

Now, it is fashionable to disparage Chinese things as gaudy and overwrought, but I have never shared that feeling. Always, the more I learned of the Chinese classics, the more humble I became. After all, were it not for the technique of writing Chinese, our own Japanese words could never have been written down. Yet at the same time, I began to think there was something deeply different about the way Chinese think. For all its erudition, Chinese was both mysterious and overly precise.

The order of this calendar appealed. The phenomena of nature were recorded like an exact string of seventy-two beads interspersed evenly with twenty-four bamboo sections. Their names were fascinating yet puzzling. How did sparrows become clams? They were poetic, too, in a rustic sort of way, but in the end I could not find the connections I sought. The Chinese calendar was an excellent way for the mind to follow nature, but it left the heart behind.

I had come to feel that there are moments when our hearts latch on to some aspect of nature with special intensity. The burning hue of the sky when the sun sets behind a bare-branched tree in autumn resonates in our hearts with the lonely resplendence of dying beauty. This is why a poet uses the image of sunset to burn autumn into his poem – sunset is the essence of autumn. Each season has its own images that express its essence reflected by poetic sensibility.

I began to compile a list of images and the seasons they represented.

After Father married, I must have withdrawn into myself, for someone accused me of being melancholy by nature. I was surprised and thought it quite unfair. It's true I didn't simper, and that may be why some people chose to label me melancholic, yet when I was with Chifuru, for example, I was infused with a radiant spirit and could talk on and on. So I knew it was not in my nature to be melancholy but only circumstances that made it so. My grandmother warned me that pensiveness was not attractive to eligible men.

—You ought to try to be a bit more vivacious, she said.

Yet, I thought, if a man were to marry me for false sociability, wouldn't he be put off all the more to discover my solemn bent? Surely there must be some suitable men who looked beyond superficial accomplishments? I was eighteen. Most of my friends were already married or entertaining serious suitors. A few whose fathers held respectable rank had gone into court service. "The girl who knew Chinese" did not receive many inquiries aside from one low-ranking student of Father's who, I suspected, only ventured his case because he thought I would be a useful study aide. To be honest, I was relieved not to have to fend off suitors, for none of them could possibly have compared to Genji, the imaginary lover Chifuru and I had invented.

We exchanged letters as rapidly as messengers could deliver them. When her family reached Bizen, the governor found her quite satisfactory, but the marriage was postponed until the official period of mourning for his wife ended. Chifuru was to go along to Tsukushi and return to Bizen at that time. I received this poem from her:

Nishi no umi wo   omoiyaritsutsu   tsuki mireba   tada ni nakaruru   koro ni mo aru kana

*Fretting and longing, gazing at the moon across the western
sea, it is a time of nothing but tears.*

She begged me to send her news of the capital, and so my
letters were full of gossip from friends in court service. I
replied to her poem:

Nishi e yuku   tsuki no tayori ni   tamazusa no   kikitaeme ya wa   kumo no kayoiji
*Westward-traveling letters with the moon, could I forget to
send news along with the drifting clouds?*

She was in my thoughts constantly, especially when I gazed
at the changing moon. It was not only her nickname, Hazy
Moon, but the very nature of the moon itself upon which I
reflected in her absence.

The moon is more interesting than the unchanging sun.
That is surely why it is used in poetry and the sun is not –
unless one talks of dawn or dusk, when the sun briefly hovers
on the edge of day. In my mind Chifuru shone as beautifully
as the moon in all its aspects. The three-day new moon
reminded me of her eyebrows. From there the moon changed
into the archer's bent bow and then on to its full roundness
that is most dramatic when veiled by a wisp of hazy cloud.
Just after full, the moon looks calm and ripe, floating in the
morning in the western sky. That, too, reminded me of
Chifuru. For the next few nights the moon waits longer and
longer to enter the sky so that the late night seems brighter
when it finally appears, especially in autumn. Then it is the
brightness-holding moon, the one Chifuru and I beheld our
last time together. I ached when the moon came around to this
stage, for I thought of her and knew that no matter how long
I waited now, the hazy moon would never reappear.

My stepmother must have become conscious of the periods
of the moon, too, for hers ceased and she was pregnant.

At the beginning of winter I wrote to Chifuru on each new
seasonal from my Chinese calendar. *The Water Begins to
Freeze* opened one letter, and five days later, *The Earth Begins
to Freeze*. We approached the fortnight called Lesser Snow.

Although there had been no snow yet, I was always deeply chilled. *Pheasants Enter the Water Turning into Monster Clams*, I wrote, beginning another letter. But what did it mean? The uncanny metamorphosis set my teeth on edge. I realized I dreaded the thought of Chifuru being intimate with a man.

She wrote back asking me to transcribe some of the stories we had invented. It was an interesting challenge, and this was how I began to write down tales of the Shining Prince Genji. The first one was inspired by my musings on the moon. It was a story for Chifuru in which Genji met a lady in the palace and was so overcome with passion that he made love to her in a very dangerous place. He did not know the lady's name, but called her Oborozukiyo, Night of the Hazy Moon.

Writing about Genji took my mind off my loneliness. As I attempted to write out the stories for Chifuru, Genji seemed to come alive inside me and pull me through a dream world of palaces and gardens. He would push out a chamber door and surprise me at what lay within. Of course I wanted to send everything I wrote to Chifuru right away, but a curious thing happened each time I thought I had finished.

Before I was satisfied with Genji's adventure, I found myself writing backward. I began with his meeting a mysterious girl in the empress's chambers, but then I had to give him a reason for being there, so I threaded my way back to describe a late night moon that inspired his amorous longings. Then I felt I had to set the story in the spring instead of fall because a hazed-over moon is a spring topic by poetic rule. I described Genji's abduction of the girl, but when I reread it, it made him sound awful – as if he simply violated her while she let him just because he was Genji. I had to work back from the part about the moonlight and try to describe why Genji was so special that he could just pluck someone up and persuade her to make love.

I worried whether or not all this was realistic. The stories we had made up were fantasy, of course, but I felt they had to be believable. In any case, writing a story down by oneself was different from spinning it out with Chifuru. This was my first tale.

NIGHT OF THE HAZY MOON

Oborozukiyo

AN ADVENTURE OF THE SHINING PRINCE GENJI

It was a perfect spring day with clear sky and singing birds. Poets and princes, scholars and courtiers, gathered in the grand hall of the palace for the Cherry Blossom Festival. The emperor was keen on composing poems in the Chinese manner and had picked out a number of rhyme topics to be distributed to guests by lot. Genji was among those present, and amid the murmuring and grumbling as people drew their subjects, his fine resonant voice stood out.

—Mine is "Spring," Genji stated.

As the order of presentation was discussed, people were reluctant to follow Genji, fearing they would be eclipsed or appear ridiculous in comparison. Producing a Chinese poem should not be such a difficult task, but even the better poets seemed gloomy and ill at ease. Meanwhile, the great professors appeared eager to show off their learning. As usual, they were so lacking in any sense of style that no one remembered their poems, only their shabbiness. The emperor couldn't help but smile at their stiff, graceless way of approaching his person.

Even in the crowd of elegant courtiers, Genji stood out. At eighteen his boyish handsomeness was charming, his clothing impeccable, but it was his quietly confident attitude that drew people to him. He radiated cool mastery, from his facility with literary Chinese (when Genji alluded to some Chinese poet, it didn't seem stuffy) to his way of drinking liquor. Genji did not refuse to drink, but stopped when his elegantly pale face colored to an attractive flush. He never allowed himself to reach the maudlin or stuporous state in which many men ended their nights.

Yet poetry was only a prelude to the highlight of the festival. On this occasion the emperor himself had gone to great lengths to plan a music and dance program. A series of outstanding performances culminated in a fine rendition of *Spring Warbler* at dusk. Since he had danced the previous autumn, Genji was not officially on the program, yet the memory of his appearance among the maple leaves was so compelling it seemed only natural that he should dance again. Genji modestly demurred until the crown prince himself presented him with a spray of cherry blossoms and a request. Genji rose and moved deliberately into the slow section of the *Dance of the Waves*. The restless jostling of the crowd immediately ceased.

His excerpt was short and exquisite. The casual virtuosity of Genji's impromptu performance made the perfection of the earlier choreographed pieces seem contrived in comparison. Genji's freshness, in the minds of some, spoiled in retrospect their enjoyment of dances that had seemed captivating at the time. But for his genuine modesty, Genji would undoubtedly have aroused animosity.

After Genji, there were a few more dances, but most people had begun to turn their attention to drinking. The festivities went on until late in the night. Gradually people slipped away until the empress and crown prince departed. At that point most of those who had lingered also took their leave. Yet the late-rising moon had only begun to shine its brightest. Genji, alone and restless, felt such a moon deserved suitable appreciation. He wandered toward the palace, vaguely imagining a lady of similar opinion lying awake and sighing as the cool moonlight poured over her robes through the shutters.

He slipped up through the gallery leading to the women's quarters. The empress was with the emperor that evening, thus her rooms were almost deserted. In the bright moonlight, however, Genji noticed that the third door in the corridor was unlatched. Interpreting this as an invitation from some visible lady, he stealthily tried it. The door opened without resistance. Encouraged, he stepped across the balustrade into the main hall and peeked through the curtains of the common room. Scattered about the space were numerous prostrate forms, islands of colored silk robes. Everyone appeared to be asleep. He was deliberating what to do when a soft voice reached his ears. It was such a delicate voice that Genji was sure it could be no common serving girl. He caught the lines of a poem:

Oborozukiyo ni niru mono zo naki . . .
  When the hazy moon shines dimly, there is nothing that can
    compare . . .

A woman's figure came toward the door. Delighted, Genji
perceived she was drawn by the same moonlight prompting
his own restlessness. He stretched out his hand and touched
her sleeve. He could feel her shudder of surprise as she gasped,
  —Who are you? You frighten me!
  —Do not be afraid, Genji said softly. It is clear that the
same hazy moon of spring has led us both here.
  She relaxed slightly at the cultured sound of his voice – this
was not a night demon, as she had feared at first. Yet timidly
she shrank back towards the main hall just as Genji, stepping
closer, lifted her off her feet in one swift move. He pressed her
face into his robes as he carried her out on to the verandah.
She wriggled in protest, and Genji found her struggle more
exciting than the simple complaisance ladies more often
displayed.
  —Hush, he said. I am no stranger here, and I am used to
having my way.
  He was captivated by her innocent air of surprise.
  —But there are people here, she whispered tremulously.
  Genji smoothed her hair, stroking her face as he continued
to speak softly. By now, the girl had recognized him. Screaming or calling for help became unthinkable. She was still upset,
and everything was happening too fast, but she didn't want
Genji to think she was naive. His hands were slipping under
her robes now, and still he spoke so quietly, soothingly, she
wasn't sure whether she was dreaming a particularly vivid
dream or whether this could really be happening. Had she
been a bit more knowledgeable about these things, she might
not have succumbed so easily, but her emotions were now
thoroughly confused. As much as she had fantasized being
alone with a handsome stranger (even Genji himself had been
the object of some of her dreams), she was terrified when
suddenly swept off her feet into exactly such a situation. At
the same time, the fragrance of the expensive scent Genji wore
seemed to soften the edge of danger. She liked some of what

he was doing with his hands – it was even more intense than any sensation she had ever aroused in herself. The combination of Genji, still a little bit drunk from the earlier banquet, the moonlight, and the fact that this adventure had gotten so far was irresistible. The girl did not resist.

—You must tell me your name, Genji pressed as dawn began to brighten the corridor. He had to leave soon or risk being found in a compromising situation. Please – how can I write to you if I don't know who you are?

The girl was in nervous agony lest they be discovered, but she mustered the presence of mind to quote in a low voice,

Uki mi yo ni   yagate kienaba   tazunetemo   kusa no hara o ba   towaji to ya omou
If I were to vanish away, would you come seeking my name
*   even unto the grave?*

Despite her youth and apprehension, she had a deep streak, thought Genji. He liked a woman who was not afraid to show her learning.

—Surely you don't regret our meeting, he said, glancing down at her cowering form. Please, tell me your name!

A shutter creaked open as the ladies in the chamber began to move around. There was barely enough time to exchange fans before Genji was forced to flee the gallery.

Back in his own room, Genji examined the fan. It was three-ply cherry, with a painting of the moon reflected through mist over water. He had fallen in love with the Lady of the Night of the Hazy Moon. What else could he call her?

I sent Genji's adventure to Chifuru in Tsukushi but did not get any response from her for almost a month. Fretting, I heard a rumor that she had married. Of course I knew this was to happen, and I expected her to change, but such abrupt silence made me uneasy. I did not know what to think. Finally I received a letter from Bizen Province. It was accompanied by a branch of maple, still fresh despite its two-day journey. In fact she had married and was worrying whether or not to travel back to visit Miyako now with her new husband.

"I wander the hills of our mountain retreat and my sleeves

30

are soaked in the heavy dew," she wrote. And this poem:

Tsuyu fukaku   okuyamazato no   momijiba ni   kayoeru sode no   iro o misebaya
Deep in the dew of these faraway hills maple leaves turn scarlet; I wish I could show you the color of my sleeves.

Sleeves soaked in scarlet tears of blood, she meant. I was disappointed. The image is one I have always disliked, even though it is originally Chinese – red tears as the ultimate mark of sincerity. It is so extravagant it gives me exactly the opposite feeling. When one has cried for days and in fact soaked one's sleeves with tears, calling them blood seems ridiculous.

The poem drove me to picture how her husband would sweep away our love like a storm tearing maple leaves from their branches. But how could I blame Chifuru? It was all quite beyond her control. She herself had been swept away from Miyako like an autumn leaf helpless before a storm. In my agitation, I wrote the following and sent it off quickly, folded in dark blue paper, wrapped round by a knotted kuzu vine:

Arashi fuku   touyamazato no   momijiba wa   tsuyu mo tomaran   koto no katasa yo
Raging in faraway hills, the storm sweeps away both scarlet leaves and dew, leaving no trace.

Yet as soon as the packet had left my hand I regretted sending such a sharp response, even though I did believe that all traces of our love had been obliterated. What good would it do to see Chifuru back in the capital now? I had lost her. Her metamorphosis was as complete and as strange as sparrows into clams. She was married.

A few days later she responded contritely to my outburst, but by then I was resigned. What choice do the fragile maple leaves have, after all? This was her poem:

Momijiba wo   sasou arashi wa   hayakeredo   ko no shita narade   yuku kokoro ka wa
Scarlet leaves, seduced insistently by the storm, had no desire to fall anywhere save underneath the tree.

31

Had she been free to follow her desire, after all, she would have stayed in Miyako and tried to go to court.

When my jealousy abated, however, I realized that I was no longer entirely alone. Now I had Genji.

MORNING GLORY

Asagao

After Chifuru married, I stopped writing Genji stories for her, but I continued to write them for myself. By the following summer I decided to read some to my grandmother, who was beginning to lose her eyesight. She was frustrated because she couldn't enjoy the picture scrolls she loved, so it occurred to me that she might appreciate being read something new. I collected the five or six tales I had done by that time, not bothering to recopy them, since Grandmother couldn't see my scribbled hand. I remember I had the papers packed up, along with a basket of pears from our garden and a dish of fried Chinese dumplings. Just as I was ready to leave, I noticed that my horoscope indicated I should not travel in a southeasterly direction. My mind on Genji, I had stupidly forgotten to check the directional taboos* until that morning. The dumplings wouldn't keep, so Takako got them. I could always pick more pears.

Grandmother loved the old tales. When we were growing up in her house, she told me well-known ones and obscure ones and countless variations. Since my mother was usually

*Murasaki's world was penetrated by ghosts and spirits from the nether realms, and also by sacred beings called *kami* whose physical world humans shared. It was believed that these *kami* regularly changed their abodes, and humans had to be careful of their own movements according to a system of taboos that prohibited traveling in the direction in which an important *kami* had moved.

busy with my baby brother, I crept off to Grandmother. She bundled me up in one of her old silk robes and kept me by her side, relating a constant stream of the classic fables into my eager ears. By the time I was five I could impersonate the coldhearted princesses from the *Tale of the Bamboo Cutter* or the *Tale of the Hollow Tree* and make up outrageous demands for my make-believe suitors. Grandmother also told me about life during the glorious reign of Emperor Murakami – which, I realized later, could only have been second-hand, since she had never been to court.

From that summer when I turned nineteen, our roles switched. I became the storyteller, reading Grandmother my Genji tales. After the first one, she said Genji reminded her of Narihira, the hero of the *Tales of Ise*. She also thought that my stories did not contain enough poetry.

—It is odd, she remarked, that your Genji is not more lyrical. Yet I do find myself caught up in your description, wondering what your young man will do next. It is almost as if, Fuji dear, you were painting a story with words instead of pictures. Maybe you're doing that for the sake of my old eyes. They seem to have dark mists floating in front of them these days.

I was not consciously trying to substitute words for pictures, but that was a good way of putting it. In fact I was a terrible painter. Rather than waste paper trying to draw Prince Genji, I preferred to let Chifuru, or Grandmother, each imagine him as she desired. Very quickly I discovered that Genji, as I thought of him, and the character Grandmother imagined were not the same. Chifuru's ideal lover was not mine. Grandmother always saw Genji as a variation of Narihira.

—More poems, dear, she would say. It needs more poetry.

I tried padding the text with poems, but it did not feel right. Overloaded with *waka*, the story becomes too brittle. In my opinion, Grandmother's beloved *Tales of Ise* is really a pile of poems with a fragile thread of story holding them together. I became aware of this as I tried to evoke a scene rather than simply repeat a character's poetic reflection of it.

*

33

Originally I was doing a favor for Grandmother by reading her my tales, but I found that the very process of speaking them aloud to an audience helped me to write them. Father's house echoed with the noise of a newborn baby, so I spent a great deal of time at Grandmother's. When I had a new tale ready for her, my cousin who lived there brought her sewing and came in the room to listen. Even the serving girls found excuses to bring rice cakes or sweets or something, and then stayed on. I was embarrassed at first, as if I were exposing myself, but soon I was able to feel more detached about Genji. Of course he arose from my sensibilities, but he was not me, after all. In time, Genji came into his own, and I felt that his actions grew out of his own karma, not mine. This made it easier, too.

I was so absorbed in thinking about Genji that summer I practically forgot myself. Yet Father had not forgotten he now had a fruit in his garden that was ripe and would soon be overly so. By coincidence, it seemed, just as the weather turned hot and we had all been dragging around without much energy, a lieutenant captain of the imperial archers turned up at our door. He had been traveling, he said, but had to stay in our quarter of the city for one night because of a directional taboo. He could have chosen one of the neighbors' homes, but he came to ours. I did not think too much about it, presuming he knew my father's reputation as a Chinese poet. Probably he thought it would be more interesting to drink with a congenial soul and compose some Chinese rhymes.

The air was so oppressive that the doors opening from the study on to the garden had all been latched open to coax an evening breeze from the river. From my room next to the study I could hear my father and the lieutenant laughing and declaiming poetry. Before the moon rose, my father retired to the new wing of the house, but the young man continued to move about in the room where his bedding had been laid out. He was humming, and I could hear him reciting what seemed to be lines of Chinese verse by Bai Juyi.

Pretty soon, I heard a tapping on the wall separating the study from my little room. It was not hard to guess that he

34

was somewhat drunk, and clearly he knew that my father had daughters. My heart started to pound, but for a ridiculous reason – this was like something out of Genji! In a case like this a young man, especially one who had spent time at court, would do the obvious thing and attempt to meet the young woman. Although I had imagined variations on this scene dozens of times, in reality it had never happened to me.

Yet precisely because of Genji, it also felt eerily familiar. I moved closer to the verandah and could see that the lieutenant was sitting on the edge, one leg casually dangling above the ferns. Hoping my voice wouldn't come out in a nervous croak, I quoted some lines from the same poem I thought I heard him recite. I hardly had my wits about me to plan what I would do next. I probably thought he would respond with another poem, and we might begin a conversation. I was definitely not prepared for what happened.

Almost as soon as I spoke, he jumped down to the garden and strode around the decorative gate separating the verandah of my room from that of the study. He appeared directly at the edge of my room. I could not see his face too well in the shadows, but he was athletic, as might be expected of an archer, and moved confidently. I quickly crawled to the back corner, but that meant I was trapped there as he lurched toward me. I shrank back as he lunged for the hems of my dress.

I was so shocked I was paralyzed. My voice died in my throat. Although everything was happening quickly, time seemed to slow down, as if I were watching all this happen to someone else. He was saying things like "such a treasure hidden away in a scholar's garden" and "the most beautiful long black tresses I've ever encountered" and one thing after another as if he'd rehearsed. It would have been ludicrous if it had not actually been happening. All the time his hands were busy, pulling open my thin silk robe, undoing the sashes of my long trousers – clearly he was experienced.

He was very strong. I had never before been pulled about and pinioned that way. I tried to say "Wait! Stop!" but my breath was pushed out of my body. He was on top of me forcing my legs open with one hand and holding my head by the hair with the other. He kept on talking, breathing harshly into my ear, as if he would distract me from the violent activity his hips were perpetrating below while his mouth wheezed lines of poetry into my ear. I discovered it was less painful when I stopped struggling. Soon he gave a moan and relaxed his grip. I felt a wetness welling over my thigh and thought I was bleeding.

I lay still. The lieutenant lifted himself up and pulled at his trousers. Unbelievably he continued to talk, pledging everlasting love and quoting five or six poems about lovers' regrets at parting. He did not seem to notice that I said nothing. After he had collected his things he fell silent. Then he coughed rather self-consciously and exited my room the same way he had entered. I heard him jump on to the verandah of the study and lie down heavily on his bedding. Some mumbling, slapping of mosquitoes, then deep snoring issued from the room.

My senses were reeling. Had I invited this attack by replying to the Chinese poem? For a while I just lay there with my legs drawn up to my chin, shivering in the muggy heat. My clothing was wet and smelled strangely of earth and chestnut flowers. I was sure I must be covered with blood. My hipbones felt bruised and there was a dull ache between my legs. Peeling off my damp smelly robes, I rolled the whole lot into a bundle in the corner. I lit the oil lamp and examined myself. There was a little blood, but I began to feel less like I was dying. I lit a coal to start a pinch of incense, and the thin straight ribbon of smoke in the still air calmed my spirits. I pulled a fresh white chemise from my clothing chest and spread a clean robe on the mat.

By now the sky was beginning to lighten, and, glancing into the garden, I perceived the gray shapes of trees and bushes emerging from the mist of early morning. Water-blue morning glories in a wooden tub grew over a trellis at the side of the house. The buds of those flowers destined to open that day were already starting to unfold. Before lying down, I carefully closed the heavy wooden rain doors on the side of my room overlooking the garden. Then I lay down and slept.

I was awakened much later that morning by Umé, the maid,

noisily raising the wooden shutters. The lieutenant had gone, and the usual household routines seemed to be occurring on schedule. Umé asked if I wished breakfast. How strange normal life felt! I said I wished to be left alone. Eventually I got up and dressed. In a peculiar way the events of the night floated in my mind like the remnants of a bridge in a dream. The experience had been terrifying, but I had crossed it and was now feeling oddly elated. One thing I knew with certainty – it would never happen to me like that again. I had been foolish and innocent, but now I would be wary.

What of the poet lieutenant? Surely, given all the poetry he had spouted, he would at least send a morning-after letter. I waited all day, but again things did not go as expected. There was no message. I found myself resenting the many romances I had read over the years. In those books, heroes always sent a morning-after poem. I was annoyed at how poorly reading prepares one for real life. One comes to expect things to occur in a particular way and then they do not. I was still fuming by evening and spent a restless night.

By the following morning I was resolved. A poem must be sent, or else my experience of the night before last would mean nothing. All night I had considered this issue of the morning-after poem, concluding that the important thing was for a poem to be created and delivered, no matter who sent it. If he would not send one, then I would. I climbed down into the dawn garden and snipped a morning glory vine. Attaching it to the following poem, I summoned a messenger to take it to the lieutenant.

Obotsukana   sore ka aranu ka   akegure no   sora obore suru   asagao no hana
Uncertain if it happened or not, gray dawning, dimly perceived morning glory flowers.

Sending it gave me satisfaction, no matter whether or not he replied. I suspected he would not. That afternoon I was surprised when a messenger came to our gate with a letter for me. Nobunori made as if to snatch it out of my hands, shouting "Sister's got a love letter" in a most obnoxious way. My father looked at me – I'm sure he suspected. I took the packet from the messenger saying I hoped it was a letter from Chifuru and immediately retired to my room. I was almost disappointed to have received a reply.

At every twist my expectations were overturned. Anticipating a most banal verse, I found instead:

Izure zo to   irowaku hodo ni   asagao no   aru ka naki ka   naru zo wabishiki
Where did it come from? As I was wondering, the morning glory flower faded into pitiful nothingness.

Was he trying to say he did not recognize my handwriting? I doubted it. He must have been angry that I challenged his right to initiate the exchange. I could feel my cheeks getting hot as I read. And then I felt perversely glad to have been able to provoke his displeasure. He had been able physically to overpower me that night, and he seemed to think it was also in his power to shape my response. How shocked he must have been to receive my poem first. Instead of acting, he had to react. It was odd that in the face of his rejection I felt nothing so much as triumph.

I decided that Genji would never reject a woman he loved. Ever.

WILLOWS

Yanagi

That summer there were no further visits from the archery lieutenant or any other young bachelor. My father may have been disappointed, but he did not reproach me. I was very much my father's daughter in the way our minds worked, and except for the question of my marriage, we were able to talk about most things. This one issue, however, was so vexatious that neither of us mentioned it for long periods. I felt bad that I was the one shadow of worry at a time when things in general were looking much brighter for him.

The following spring my stepmother went back to her family's house to give birth again. The older child was by this time two. It was very quiet and lovely at home while they were away, right when the willow trees were beginning to show their leaves. The willow doesn't flower, exactly, but it launches the first green into winter's dull brown landscape. I found that fresh green to be even sweeter to the eye than the pink, white, and red plums blooming immediately after.

Father told me that in spring the ladies at court wore a set of white robes with green linings in a color combination called *Willow*. He said he saw it done once where the green in each layer was dyed progressively darker. The edge of lining showing at the innermost layer was an etiolated, sun-starved paleness that could only be recognized as green because it lay next to white. The linings of each robe became successively greener, like a new shoot reaching out from the shadows into the spring sun. I was enchanted, wondering if I would ever have the chance to see something like that.

With my stepmother away I took charge of the house again and luxuriated in the quiet rhythm of the days, shuddering to think how tranquillity would be ruptured after she returned with the little boy and the infant. Luckily her parents were eager to have their daughter back at home for a while, so I knew they would extend the birth visit as long as possible. I predicted the two-year-old would be utterly spoiled by the time he returned.

At the time, I had a very low opinion of children. I truly did not understand how mothers could be so charmed by them, blithely ignoring the depredations of small gooey fingers into anything left on a low table or shelf. Was one supposed to laugh when one's best writing brush had been used to paint the cat? I began to worry that there was something wrong with me because I was not drawn to children. I was unable to prolong a conversation with my stepmother, though she was only three years older than I, because the conversation sooner or later inevitably turned to bowel movements or erupting teeth. I felt myself fading away. I had nothing to contribute, and of course could not reveal my feelings of distaste.

Sometimes I wondered whether my friends who had become mothers were only pretending to be enthralled by their offspring. Perhaps if I let my secret sympathy show, they would crack their masks of contentment and reveal their true feelings of dread and boredom. My stepmother brought the first child to my room several times in an effort to ingratiate herself. I believe she was sincere in her offer to include me in her state of domestic contentment, but it was awkward. I did not dislike her – I would not have minded sharing a meal or a stroll in the garden with her alone, for she was not ignorant – but with the child, everything became strained.

We were talking about a delicate subject – Father's early retirement from court service the year before my mother died – when suddenly the baby began to cry. My stepmother's attention immediately shifted to the infant, and the mood of tenuous confidentiality was shattered. She may have thought me cold, but I was not inclined to return to the subject after such an interruption. It was always like this. The fact is that women with babies cannot sustain a discussion on any subject. Their thoughts scatter like cherry blossoms in a puff of breeze.

I took heart that I was not an irredeemable monster mainly by the fact that even I could admit that a sleeping child is dear. And, of course, what my friends all said turned out to be true: it was different when I had my own.

That spring my father was a happy man. Having received an invitation to a poetry banquet at the palace, he had been told he could wear the official green robes of court service to the event. He had not worn his court uniform since he resigned his post as imperial secretary nine years before.

I retrieved the garments from their mothproof chest and aired them. By now I had gained a better appreciation of what the past decade had been like for him. On the heels of his giving up his court position, my mother sickened and, within months, died. So in the middle of his life, just when he should have been attaining the peak of his ambitions, Father instead entered a dark valley. He spent most of his time coaching Nobunori for a career in court service – an endeavor steeped in frustration because of my brother's obtuseness. But now Father had a new wife, new sons, and an invitation to revisit the court. There were still people who appreciated his skills, so who knew? Perhaps his career wasn't over, after all. I shared the excitement of his rising hopes.

Father visited the private palaces of nobles who wanted tutoring in Chinese composition, returning home on each occasion with his mind preoccupied by politics. His old patron, Retired Emperor Kazan, had taken Buddhist orders but preferred living in his aunt's luxurious mansion to austere religious quarters. Kazan liked the company of women far too much to be happy as a priest. He was an enthusiastic patron of poetry, frequently inviting Father to his parties. My father's reputation as a Chinese scholar had not suffered during the years he was out of court service.

When he came home late from a banquet, it was I, not my stepmother, who waited up to help remove his formal hat and bring his soft house clothes. He allowed me to share a night-cap of saké as he told me about who had attended, what foods had been served, what poems composed.

—You would appreciate this, Fuji, he might say, and recount how some ranking courtier would misquote a line of Chinese and how he, Tametoki, had been hard-pressed to keep a straight face even though nobody else noticed.

—If you could have been a moth on the wall, Fuji, how you would have enjoyed listening.

He told me gossip from the palace about those people who "live above the clouds" from the point of view of lesser beings such as ourselves. This was how I came to hear about Retired Emperor Kazan's peccadilloes.

—This will sound terrible, Father said once, but those who dwell within the ninefold enclosure really aren't superior to us so much as they are simply larger – in the scale of their follies as well as their virtues.

Father was rather scandalized by Kazan's behavior. He confided everything that had come to his ears, with no idea I was putting his tales of court life to use in my stories about Genji. In fact he was largely unaware of the writing that now consumed me, until one day he overheard my grandmother and cousin talking. That same evening he came to my room.

—Who is this Prince Genji, and what is this about seducing the empress's sister? he inquired sternly.

Father had always encouraged me to compose *waka*, but he did not approve of the romances that circulated among ladies at the court and from them to the houses of the lesser nobility. Even serving girls who couldn't read pored over the pictures whenever they got a chance. I was careful to keep hidden from his view the ones lent me by friends. Now he had caught me. I don't think he would have minded so much to find me reading them on the sly, but writing them was a different matter. What if he forbade me to continue?

Father had been indulgent in allowing me to ignore marriage so far. Would he be as understanding about Genji? I could only trust the fact that we were attracted by the same kinds of literature. He demanded to read something I had written. Knowing protest would make it worse, I meekly took out the clean copy of one of Genji's adventures I had been planning to present to a friend who was about to enter court service. He slipped it in his sleeve and took it away, leaving me in a state of uncertainty. What would I do if I lost Genji now?

The next day I found the manuscript in the hallway outside my room, carefully wrapped in a square of brown silk. There was a note.

"I'm glad to see your young gentleman likes Chinese poetry," he had written. "He shows excellent taste. You should follow his example and practice your poetry."

That summer a plague of smallpox swept the city. I kept to my room, although I did not write much. Too many people were afflicted, and it was hard to think about Genji. The court sponsored a citywide purification ceremony in the eighth month, but the demons of pestilence were unmoved. Neither did they seem to notice the cold when winter came, for people continued to fall sick and die.

I decided not to regard Father's comments on Genji as a prohibition, and so, on the rare occasion when inspiration stuck, I wrote. A year passed during which once in a while he

42

said things like, "What is your Prince Genji up to these days?" Or "I met a woman at the palace who would have interested your hero." But I thought it unwise to show him more stories and tried even harder to be discreet.

I turned twenty-one and feared the subject of marriage would come up again. As it turned out, the smallpox demons rampaged more fiercely than ever, so people were not thinking about match-making. It got so bad Father decided to send me, with a driver and two retainers, to stay with my auntie at her mountain retreat. I remembered this auntie from my childhood at Grandmother's house, where she often visited when I was growing up.

RURI, BLUE LIKE LAPIS LAZULI

Ruri

Excited to be traveling out of the city, I was unprepared for the horror of the journey itself. We left before dawn so as to be past the crowded center of Miyako by morning. Even so, the air was heavy, and when we were out of sight of our house, I ordered the ox driver to raise the blinds on the carriage, despite the bad smells. As it grew light, I saw with dismay that the bundles heaped at the street corner were not cordwood as I first thought, but human bodies. Our carriage rumbled past, dispersing monstrous crows shrieking into the air, angry at being disturbed from their ghoulish feast. I saw two heavy mongrel dogs fighting and tearing at an arm one of them had dragged from a pile of corpses. Shaken, I lowered the blinds and fell back into the compartment. The squeaking and groaning of the wooden wheels set up a relentless mantra occasionally punctuated by the driver's shouts to the ox.

Earlier in the year more than sixty people of rank had succumbed to the plague of boils. As I heard of their deaths, name after name, I grew steadily numb. The name of the archery lieutenant joined the list of the dead, and even that made me sad. Yet I saw even greater misery amidst the nameless throngs we passed by. Their noisy suffering issued from the houses, but their mute deaths were dignified by neither ceremony nor sutra. They seemed like fish trapped in a weir, dredged up to die.

In my shock at what I saw around me I realized that at least we have poetry to console our spirits and holy orders to salve our souls. Learned men say the misery of the poor is less painful than ours because they are uncultivated, and that being at a less developed stage, they do not understand suffering the way we do. I tried to believe that, for it was unbearable to imagine the pitifulness of their lives otherwise.

I recalled a line from the Nirvana Sutra: "There is but difference of degree between man and beast – both love life and dread death alike." With each turn of the cartwheel as inexorable as karma, I found myself mesmerized into murmuring an invocation to Kannon, Bodhisattva of Mercy.

By midday we had left the city streets behind, following a path to the eastern hills. My stepmother had taken the children away from the capital the month before, seeking refuge with her parents in the hills north of the city. My father, Takako, and Nobunori remained behind. Takako did not adapt well to change, and Father did not want to stop cultivating his contacts at court. Nobunori was put in charge of the house.

Auntie's mountain retreat was not what I had imagined. I expected a cottage such as the great Chinese poet Bai Juyi described during his exile in the south – someplace deep in the mountains with a "fence of woven bamboo, pillars of pine, and stepping stairs of stone." There was a rough fence, and the pines grew tall, but it was hardly a rustic retreat. The natural aspect of the garden was more artfully arranged than the most contrived landscape. The materials used to construct the house were countrified thatch and wattle, but the dwelling itself was more on the scale of a small palace. A central hall stood flanked by two detached wings with shrubbery and trees arranged so as to disguise the extent of the building from the outside. It was a mansion disguised as a cottage, and it reminded me of the elegant rusticity of a royal dancer dressed in a costume for a farmer's dance. The air was fresh, smelling of cedar – altogether a different world from the oppressive, pox-plagued city.

My aunt had transformed the main hall into a sanctuary for her Buddhist devotions. She was a devotee of Kannon and had placed the gilded wooden image of the elegant bodhisattva in the center, with smaller statues of Amida Buddha off to the side. Though this arrangement raised a few clerical eyebrows, she was the sort of person who managed to do things her own way. I immediately felt the appeal of the serene Kannon, who postponed entering Nirvana to remain in the world as a guide and solace to all suffering souls. When, after an eternity, the myriad sentient beings all attained enlightenment, then Kannon would enter Nirvana – as a woman, Auntie believed. I took everything she said quite seriously at the time, although I learned later that her theology was rather idiosyncratic.

To gain merit and improve her karma, Auntie spent hours meditating on and making copies of the Lotus Sutra. Of course I had heard this scripture chanted all my life, but for the first time, I actually read it. Auntie's image of Kannon had come from China. It was very feminine, without a hint of mustache, and its graceful limbs curved voluptuously. Whereas the famous Kannon figure at Ishiyama Temple had eleven faces and a crown of heads pointed in all directions, Auntie's statue had but one head and held a willow branch and a vessel of water.

Besides my aunt and all her servants, a distant cousin – a young woman called Ruri – like me, had taken refuge here. Her mother had named her after the exotic blue *ruri* glass from faraway lands that she saw used in the palace. Except for the guards posted outside, the mansion was entirely inhabited by women that summer.

How delightful the place was. Ruri and I had leave to go anywhere we liked. Since there were no men around, we dispensed with curtains, blinds, and screens, and opened all the rooms to the mountain breezes. We became so cavalier about our appearance that I neglected to reblacken my teeth, and they began fading to pale grey. Soon they would revert to white, and I would look like a child again. Except for some summer clothes, writing brushes and paper, I had brought along only my thirteen-string koto. I had planned to use this time to rewrite the Genji stories and also ask my aunt to coach me on koto fingering technique. She had once been an excellent musician before taking up religion.

Plucking the instrument's silk strings in the sweltering heat back home in Miyako, I had tried to imagine how the music would sound drifting out from wild pine-clad hills. I imagined Genji hearing it faintly as he rode home from some pilgrimage, turning his horse to follow the sound to its source. As a bee to nectar, Genji would be lured to my house and, taking out his flute, begin to play a melody in the same mode. The koto player would hesitate as she heard the flute, raise her hand to her breast, and peer anxiously outside to see who was there. Her dreamy and desultory playing would change to something more challenging. Would the flute keep up? Her fingers danced over the strings; her long black hair spilled over her shoulder as she reached for the dramatic vibrato of a very low note. Unseen himself, Genji could glimpse her from the low hill where he had reined in his horse. His flute joined her playing with complete confidence.

Auntie had a reputation as a writer. She had once been married to Fujiwara Kane'ie, the statesman who became regent for Emperor Enyu. Their marriage was exceedingly prickly, and they were completely estranged by the time I was born. Auntie wrote and circulated a diary of her suffering as the secondary wife of a man who philandered. Her complaint became something of a scandal, but far from wounding Kane'ie with its reproachful barbs, the *Gossamer Diary*, as it came to be known, rather enhanced his reputation as a ladies' man. Auntie seemed to fall into and climb out of deep depressions. She embarked on a series of pilgrimages lasting five years, after which she built her retreat and stopped writing. Her opinion was of grave importance to me – so much so that I was afraid to show her my stories.

At first, I thought Ruri rather fierce-looking. She never did blacken her teeth when her friends started to do so, nor did she pluck her eyebrows. They remained full, each hair left just as it grew on her brow. I offered to pluck them for her, but after tweezing out the first few hairs, Ruri pulled her face away, tears springing to her eyes.

—That smarts so much! she complained. I can't bear it!

I guess I was lucky that my natural eyebrows were not nearly so thick as hers. I hardly noticed the pain anymore. Although she refused to do her own, Ruri was happy to help me pluck mine. I lay with my head in her lap in a sunlit corner of the room open to the garden, and she gently stretched my skin between two fingers.

—It hurts less when the skin is taut, she murmured, concentrating the silver tweezers hair by hair.

An entire morning could fly by in this way. I knew Ruri didn't scent her robes, but she seemed to have a natural sweet fragrance of her own. Lying there in the drowsy warmth, I gazed up at Ruri's plump bosom almost brushing my face. Through her diaphanous white summer singlet, her nipples were dark like the centers of poppy flowers. Most of the time she kept her hair trussed back, but when I convinced her to let me comb it out, I was overwhelmed by the rich black river that spread over her shoulders, rippled down her back, collecting in a pool at her feet. Her hair was a good six inches longer than her height. Were a young man to catch a glimpse of Ruri from behind, he would grow faint with longing to touch that lustrous spill. She would frighten him when she turned around, however, exposing her gleaming white teeth and bushy brows! Ruri utterly lacked the coy manner one would expect of someone whose mother spent so much time in the palace.

Because her mother had been a lady-in-waiting, Ruri had heard many tales of life at court. Her stories were utterly different from those my father had related over the years, and the contrast was fascinating. My father analyzed everything in terms of its political implications or, when it concerned Chinese, its scholarly purity. Listening to Ruri, I was struck most by her convoluted stories of rival groups of noble ladies, all with too much pride and time on their hands. It was helpful to be able to talk with her as I thought about Genji's background.

For some time I had been feeling that the episodes I had written were drifting. Although they seemed to have substance at first, after reading several in a row, they ran together like a rack of cloud. Genji needed a past to anchor his adventures. I planned to take all the stories and redo them with a new beginning, the story of Genji's origins.

It was clear that Genji must be of royal blood but not an imperial prince, because then his actions would be constrained by his high rank. Also, people might think I was writing about some imperial prince in particular. That could be awkward. I decided to make him the son of a vague emperor of long ago, summoning up a picture of court life that stemmed from Grandmother's stories about the days of Emperor Murakami.

A girl whose head was full of reading the usual romances might think it wonderful to be loved by the emperor. In none of the tales I ever read or heard did anyone stop to consider what a catastrophe this could be. I made Genji's mother perfect in every respect save one. She was beautiful, refined, blessed with personal grace and sensibility – but she was not of high birth. Despite this, the emperor favored her above all others, to the point where people compared the royal couple to the Chinese emperor Xuanjung, who was infatuated with the beautiful Yang Gueifei.

In the Chinese story the emperor neglects his duties, so besotted is he, and finally the army threatens to rebel unless he orders Gueifei's death. Tearfully he does so, and she is strangled with a silken rope. Ruri was horrified when I read her the ballad.

—The Chinese are so barbaric! she exclaimed. Such a thing would never happen in our civilized country!

I consulted with her, trying to imagine how someone beloved of an emperor might be treated at our own court. Ruri assured me it could be nasty. From her mother she had heard a story about a lower-ranked palace lady summoned from her quarters to visit the emperor's bedchamber at night. The hapless woman had managed to arouse the jealousy of higher-ranking imperial ladies who plotted to make her life miserable. One night they had their maidservants lock the doors of the connecting passageways between her room and the imperial bedchamber to trap her in between. When dawn came, she was found weeping in humiliation in the corridors. Another time, they planted piles of dog droppings and garbage along the connecting bridges and walkways in order to foul her attendants' skirts as they passed by.

—Imagine being bothered by a nasty smell that seemed to cling no matter where you went and then discover that it was dog excrement smeared on your hems! Can there be a more disgusting odor?

We wrinkled our noses, and I used it in my story. In my version the sensitive lady is brought low by malicious treatment that even the emperor cannot stop, since it is all so underhanded. She begins to waste away.

Ruri suggested I position Genji's mother as the lady of the Kiritsubo Pavilion. Each imperial concubine has her own suite of rooms, and the Kiritsubo suite is farthest away from the Hall of Cool Breezes, where the emperor resides. This gives the other ladies plenty of leeway to torment her as she passes through the corridors on imperial summons. Even when the emperor moves her to the pavilion directly across from his own, the situation doesn't improve – for then the Kiritsubo Lady earns the enmity of the woman she displaces. If the emperor loved his chief consort best, but the other ladies also received their due recognition – no more, no less – such problems would not arise. Yet, as Ruri pointed out, life at court conceals a constant tension between ideas of how things are supposed to be and how they are. Besides, the fact that the Kiritsubo Lady has no political advantage in her background makes the emperor's passion for her all the more outrageous.

Genji, I thought, must be the pearl of a child born to the Kiritsubo Lady, adored by his father, the emperor. But the child Genji inherits his mother's flaw. If the world were just, she would be empress. But it is not and she cannot be. Neither will Genji become crown prince. In a standard tale this situation would be remedied in the end. But I wasn't interested in that. There had to be something uneven about

Genji, something unbalanced about his life, to give it momentum. Perfect people are rather boring. As I told Ruri about my plans for Genji's early years, she listened politely for a long time, then made an odd remark.

—This character Genji is really you yourself, it seems to me. Even though you are plotting out the reasons for this and that, I think deep down you portray him as motherless because you think of this gap in Genji's life as a dark wheel, constantly turning. Or perhaps he's like a waterbird that seems to glide without effort on the surface, while, underneath, its feet are madly churning.

Ruri's comment brought me up short. I supposed she meant that I was like that waterbird. I would have said people found me even-tempered, shy, and probably dull, hardly a brilliant conversationalist, one who kept to herself. Yet Ruri recognized something that others did not. I often wondered what propelled me to write about Genji. Certainly my life would have been easier if I weren't obsessed with his stories. Ruri had identified something I was as yet only vaguely aware of – a dark wheel churning my restless preoccupations. There were times I wished I could simply go for a walk in the garden without Genji in the back of my mind, commenting on the plants.

It was helpful to be able to confide in Ruri. She did not say much, but she was sensible. My jumbled thoughts were clarified by the simple process of speaking them aloud to her. What a perfect wife she would be, I thought. But she was no more interested in marriage than I was, and given her unladylike features and manner, even less likely to be wooed.

Ruri had the most amazingly sharp eye for things in nature. She particularly liked butterflies and cordoned off one section of the garden to cultivate the caterpillars she found. The kitchen maid could not understand why the radishes and cabbage growing in Ruri's garden were to be left undisturbed for the tiny pale green worms that, in most gardens, are brushed off and crushed. Ruri explained to her that the lovely black-tipped white butterflies with sulfur-yellow underwings grow from those little green worms. I knew that, but I didn't know that the male of this species has a deep yellow spot on its body and that it emits a scent of citrus.

—Always fragrant, just like your pungent prince, Ruri observed.

In one of my stories I had portrayed Genji as a master blender of incense. The fragrance of his robes whispered his presence even in the dark.

When it came time for the caterpillars to fashion their little metamorphosis huts, Ruri gathered them in a cage by the open verandah to be able to observe them when they emerged. We had a long spell of rain followed by a clearing, and several butterflies hatched out at once. Could they sense the weather? It would have been extremely inconvenient for them to have emerged in the rain. Such a struggle it was, even so, for them to wriggle out. We could tell they were ready because the gold-flecked brown case seemed to fade and the outline of head and wings became visible. Yet they still had to crack through a transparent casing and shrug violently this way and that to break free. How beautiful their eyes were, like jewels.

—Look what we miss when we see them flitting about the garden and only notice their wings, said Ruri.

We talked endlessly about the seasons. I wrote out for her the Chinese calendar of seventy-two season units, and because she was so sensitive to the changes of nature, she thought it marvelous.

We entered upon the fortnight called Greater Heat, the first five-day unit of which is *Rotted Weeds Metamorphose into Fireflies*. I was hardly surprised to hear that catching fireflies was one of Ruri's favorite activities and that summer was her favorite season.

—Too bad we don't have fireflies up here in the mountains, Ruri remarked.

Fireflies, it seemed, like open areas adjoining the woods, or else marshy places near the water's edge. There in the mountains we were much closer to nature than back in Miyako, but the gentle fireflies appeared to prefer the tamer environment back home.

Ruri had once played a trick on her older sister as the girl was receiving a suitor. Things had progressed fairly far, but, of course, the man had not yet been permitted a glimpse of Ruri's sister's face. He was visiting on a moonless summer night when Ruri suddenly released an enormous number of fireflies into her sister's room, illuminating her surprised countenance.

—After they'd been married a while they laughed about it. Ruri grinned. But my sister was really furious at the time.

I told Ruri about my theory of things that epitomize each season, and she offered to help. We made lists of natural phenomena according to season and then compared them with the classic images from the old tales and the imperial poetry anthologies. Ruri was peeved that the classics scant summer, concentrating more on spring and especially autumn. Of course it is fashionable to like autumn best, but when she pressed me as to my favorite, I chose spring.

Nevertheless, enveloped in summer, we started our lists with this season. We agreed that fireflies express the quintessence of summer. Ruri then argued for butterflies on the same grounds: although a few appear in the spring, they are most prolific in summer and die off by fall. I tended to agree with her, although for some reason butterflies seemed slightly gaudy. Before I met Ruri, most of my experience with butterflies had been from Chinese paintings on screens, cavorting amidst peony flowers.

In general, I observed to Ruri, insects are more associated with the sounds they make, so one tends to think of them as autumnal.

—But what about cicadas? Ruri reminded me.

How could I forget? Just thinking of the deafening sound of shrilling cicadas brought back the lethargic summer heat of Miyako. Ringed by mountains, the city holds steamy humidity as a bowl holds water. Nobunori liked to catch a cicada and tie a thread around its body so he could let it fly up and buzz around his head and then rein it in. It was quite disgusting.

We considered rain. Rain was hard to ignore, since that summer had been so wet – one of the reasons we spent so much time sitting around making lists. The sudden shower, a cloudburst that rumbles up darkly, crashes with thunder and lightning, and then blows over like a temper tantrum – that was a summer rain, we decided. So were the monsoon rains of the fifth month when the plums begin to ripen, mottling from green to red, and a warm darkness infuses everything, ruining the walls.

But rain was hardly limited to summer. There are the violent typhoon rainstorms of autumn, when the temperature suddenly drops, the wind slashing the rain about in a frenzy. At the end of fall, quiet dark rains gradually turn chill. For me, however, the true essence of rain was the long rains of spring. In fact, simply to say "long rains" conjures up the smoky, soundless, threadlike rain that continues without break as the earth warms in spring. One opens the window and gazes on the hazy garden in a languid, melancholy, yearning sort of way. All these feelings are wrapped up in the words "long rains."

Ruri thought dew ought to evoke summer, but I agreed with convention and found it more autumnal. The same for lightning. Although we experience it occasionally in summer, its fierceness spoke of fall to me. For summer plants, we settled on the tree peony, paulownia, bamboo, fringed dianthus, iris, mock orange, and evening gourdflower. I relented to include rice plants, at Ruri's passionate insistence, although they did not have much poetic resonance for me. For birds, we came up only with the moorhen and cuckoo. Some things, we decided, transcended any particular season – the moon, the wind, the evening, for example. Such things had separate manifestations throughout the year. Spring's characteristic moon is a hazy crescent; summer's is full, a pale loquat above the western hills at dawn; the autumn moon is the clear bright harvest moon; and winter's is cold, gibbous, brilliant.

We argued quite a while over the phrase "summer pelt," meaning the hide of a fawn in later summer as it turns golden tan and the spots become distinct. This is the time when its fur makes the best writing brushes. For Ruri, summer pelt was unquestionably a summer thing – summer is part of its name. But, I argued, that didn't make it poetic. Still less did a pelt evoke qualities of nature and human feeling – apart from pity for the deer, downed by the hunter's bow in the summer simply because its pelt was prime.

In a way summer was the easiest season to start with. Our list for spring turned out not only to be lengthy but also to provoke many disagreements. It's a good thing it stopped raining so we could put our lists aside for a while. Autumn would have been even more contentious than spring.

I read my favorite Bai Juyi poem, "The Song of Everlasting Sorrow," to Ruri in its entirety, translating as I went. Of course everyone knows the story about the tragedy of Yang Gueifei, but not so many people actually read it in Chinese. If we had had more time, I could have taught Ruri to read Chinese, but summer was ending, and we would soon have to return to Miyako.

My mind was brimming with Bai Juyi. As I worked on my Genji story, I imagined the emperor mourning the death of the Kiritsubo Lady while gazing at pictures on a screen illustrating "Everlasting Sorrow." The Chinese emperor sent wizards to visit the spirit of Yang Gueifei on an enchanted island, and she gave them a golden hairpin to take back as a memento. How the emperor in my story would have liked to do the same for his departed love! Ruri suggested I write a similar scene in which the dead Kiritsubo Lady could be described dwelling in Paradise, sending a physical remembrance and reassurance to the living. I confess the thought shocked me.

I was surprised at my own reaction. Why did I find the idea of copying that scene repugnant? I was a great admirer of Bai Juyi, after all. I realized that Ruri's understanding of the poem and my own were at odds. Perhaps in China there were wizards with miraculous powers permitting them to visit the dead – although even Confucius said that there is nothing to be gained by speculating about the dead and spirits. In any case, such things were quite outside my experience, and I felt sure no such wizards existed in our country except in fairy tales. I never considered my Genji stories to be fairy tales, so I had never considered putting in magic tricks. The very thought went violently against the grain. I was surprised that

Ruri could even imagine such a scene, and I had the uneasy feeling that I had misjudged her.

We were about to part and were quarreling. It was very upsetting. I was sure Ruri would understand what I was trying to do once I explained the reason for keeping to real life. But she did not. She persisted in saying she saw no reason why I couldn't bring in anything my imagination could invent.

—It's your story, she kept repeating. You can write whatever you want. Why would you want to limit yourself?

I was so upset, and upset at the fact of being upset, that I'm afraid I was rather inarticulate. At the very least, I could not convince Ruri.

Writing was easier when I didn't think about what I was doing – I just did it. I could sit down with my brush, think of Genji in some situation, and describe what unfolded in my mind. But now I had become unhappily aware. I was losing my footing. I would write a line, then immediately scribble it out. I could no longer trust my judgment. Should I remove all reference to Bai Juyi?

Ruri had me questioning my entire approach. Something that once felt natural now was queer. The story of Genji's origins turned out to be much more difficult than I had imagined.

I had been very influenced by my auntie's *Gossamer Diary*. What struck me most when I first read it was a statement early in the text. She had been depressed, and, seeking to distract herself by reading the old romances, found none that could speak to her situation. "They were," she wrote, "masses of the rankest fabrication." So she decided to record a real life, dreary as it was, rather than a fairy tale.

Of course some people dismissed the result as the ravings of a demented harpy. Others found the *Gossamer Diary* embarrassing in its frank admission of jealousy, despair, depression, and other such emotions one prefers not to acknowledge publicly. But I have always thought it extremely brave of her to bare her soul to the world, no matter what her other motives may have been. It remains the most moving piece of writing I have ever encountered.

As part of her religious vows, Auntie renounced all writing. She says she once had something to say but then said it and had nothing more to add. I think her writing allowed her to congeal and expel some of the poisons that were making her sick. Her tranquillity now was enviable. I longed to show her my Genji stories, yet hesitated, afraid of her opinion. If she was too critical, I might not be able to bear it. I thought I might leave behind something for her to read after I returned to the city, but to my later regret, I was too cowardly to do even that.

After returning to the capital I still saw Ruri occasionally, yet we were no longer "two birds sharing one wing," as I had thought at one point during the summer. I was restless and moody. Ruri tried hard to be understanding. She asked if she could borrow my koto for a while, perhaps to revive the carefree mood of the summer. She then asked if I would teach her to play. Feeling slightly callous, I wrote her this poem:

Tsuyu shigeki   yomogi ga naku no   mushi no ne wo   oboroke nite ya   hito no tazunemu
You come asking to hear the sound of an insect indistinctly crying in the wormwood grass, bristling with dew.

But I consented to her request. By that time I was so knotted up about writing that I put my brush down in disgust. Ruri meant to be encouraging when she inquired about how it was going, but I didn't even want to think about it. At least playing koto gave us something else to focus on.

When my concentration was just right, the words flowed. Sometimes it was like a fast-moving brook, and my mind only lingered in a still pool for a few moments, dipping about for the right word. Then, moving into the current again, I sailed like a leaf carried along by an effort not really my own. Whenever I had a morning like this, I was cheerful for the rest of the day. I could even play with my little half brothers out in the garden. Unfortunately such days were rare. More often than not, I was stuck in dreary mud, thankful if I could produce even a trickle of thought. There were also days when

I had nothing to show for an entire morning sitting at my writing table.

My family learned to leave me alone when I was prickly, but it was harder with Ruri. When you have been intimate with someone and then discover wide areas where your thoughts do not mesh, gradually you begin to be irritated by all sorts of little things that would never have bothered you before. Habits you once found charming now are tiresome.

Ruri sensed that my feelings had changed. It was not her fault. She responded to my silences by trying harder to fill them, yet that only made me withdraw further. It became so unbearable I finally wrote to her that I was ill and would not receive visitors.

Sometime in the eleventh month she wrote to me in distress, and I replied as follows:

Shimo kouri   tojitaru koro no   mizukuki wa   e mo kakiyaranu   kokochi nomi shite
Frosted stiff by ice, my writing brush cannot begin to draw you a picture of my feelings.

Ruri replied:

Yukazu tomo   nao kakitsume yo   shimo kouri   mizu no ue nite   omoinagasamu
Though it flows not, continue to write; your pain will float away like frost and ice on the water.

I am ashamed now when I think back how she had faith in me even though I had none myself.

That winter I played the koto alone. Music was an excellent way to pass the time, although I became annoyed that my technical skill didn't seem to improve. I mentioned this to Father, who said he thought I could benefit from playing with someone better than I. Perhaps a lesson or two would be a good idea.

—I know just the person, he said. A princess, no less. She has been living in somewhat straitened circumstances since her father died, but I've heard she is a fine musician. Perhaps I can arrange something.

Father sent the lady a note and a present of dried abalone

and seaweed, and shortly afterward her reply came on a sheet of thickly furrowed mulberry-bark paper. I was surprised at the straightforward, rather unfeminine handwriting, but the message was cordial. While politely disparaging her own musical skill, the princess said she'd be willing to play koto with me. She suggested a time five days hence.

The night before we were to have our lesson it snowed heavily, but anxious for the diversion of meeting someone new, I packed up my instrument regardless of the weather. My carriage plowed through the snowy streets, off to find her house in the western outskirts of the city. Father had said not to be surprised, but I couldn't help being somewhat shocked at the dilapidated mansion where we ended up. This was hardly my idea of the dwelling of a princess. A shabbily dressed old man slowly pulled the gate open with great effort, and our driver urged the ox inside. He unloaded my koto, heavily wrapped against the cold. I carried the box containing its bridges and my bamboo finger picks.

A shivering servant let us in and showed us to the drafty main chamber where the princess was waiting. The mansion was freezing. I wondered why she hadn't chosen some smaller, cozier room for our lesson. At this rate, I was sure my fingers would be too stiff to play a note. But if the princess could play in this cold, I decided, I would force myself to play as well. Father had suggested I dress formally, adding extra layers of robes. I was certainly glad I had done so. The princess was sitting behind a faded purple curtain stand, the edge of an old sable jacket protruding slightly at the side. She welcomed me in a thin, nasal voice.

She inquired what piece I would like to play, but deferring to her rank, I asked her to choose. She suggested one I had never heard of, and, embarrassed, I had to ask her to play it through for me once. She began to pluck the strings. Every so often, the music was accented by a loud snuffle, as if her nose were dripping but she could not stop to wipe it. Despite myself, I was more caught up by the rhythm of her sniffing and gulping than by the tones of the uninspired piece. She finished with a deeply reverberating low note that vied with the wind echoing through the mansion.

—Shall we try a duet? suggested the princess, after I had praised her playing in the most flowery terms I could muster.

I suggested a popular piece. She didn't know it. I tried another. She was not familiar with that either.

—How about "Etenraku"? I said, feeling safe with a classic.

But she demurred, claiming to have forgotten the fingering for the middle section.

—I know, said the nasal voice brightly. Let's take a break.

Removing her finger picks, the princess clapped for a serving woman and whispered something to me. Another servant moved the dingy curtain stand, and I caught a glimpse of a long pale face with a bulging forehead. Peeking dramatically over the top of an ancient fan was the most amazing nose I had ever seen, bright pink at the tip, as if it had been dyed with safflower.

Soon the first woman returned balancing imported celadon dishes on antique lacquered trays. She placed one tray in front of me, one before the princess. I assumed this meant our lesson was over. Inside the covered bowls were a few slices of steamed turnip, once hot in the kitchen where they had been prepared, but now as tepid and unappetizing as the princess's koto playing.

To myself I wondered, whatever could Father have been thinking? He had certainly made some unusual contacts while at court.

THE CUCKOO

Hototogisu

Father was invited to a flower-viewing banquet at the private mansion where Michikane, the minister of the Right, had recently moved his entire establishment, on doctor's orders, in an attempt to improve his health. Michikane had been suffering from dizzy spells and unsettling dreams. The change of residence was prescribed to shake off any wandering ghost who might be causing this malaise, although some people suspected the minister's debility was the result of black magic secretly commissioned by his nephew Korechika.

The regency itself was at stake. It was not clear who stood to inherit the position of major adviser to the emperor, and until the Great Council had confirmed its choice, charges and counter-charges of spirit-tampering were rife. My father, for one, didn't trust Korechika. He was perfectly ready to believe the rumors, and he approved Michikane's steps to thwart his nephew. Father was beginning to allow himself to dream that he might be asked back to court if Michikane's fortunes rose. He pinned his hopes on the minister's interest in Chinese poetry.

Were Father to receive a post, there was even a glimmer of a chance that I might have an opportunity myself. Twenty-two was not unthinkably late – there were all manner of positions, after all. Father could not discuss his ambitions with my dullard brother, let alone his distractible wife. Instead, he talked to me. He even started letting me accompany him to poetry gatherings so that I might gain some practical experience of the way courtiers behave at banquets.

I was completely charmed by the beauty of the buildings and, even more, the garden at Michikane's temporary residence. The waters of the Nakagawa River had been diverted into the grounds to create a lake and a stream, flowing under and alongside the verandahs of the connected buildings. The centerpiece of the cultivated area was a hill fashioned to look like a Chinese fairy mountain. I was told the landscape had been hand-built. When you looked at it, it was hard to imagine the vista did not always exist just as it was – it seemed so perfectly right. Yet before workmen carted in a thousand loads of earth, there had not been so much as an ant mound there.

The irises were blooming, and I could happily have wandered along the streambed for hours gazing at each new clump that came into view along the meander. By late in the day the garden was quite overrun with courtiers jostling like butterflies among peonies. Rush mats had been set out under the late-blossoming cherry trees. Silk panels, dyed in umbered chartreuse, screened off the women's area, each panel hung with a pair of pink streamers, fading from deep to pale. I thought I had never seen anything so elegant.

Were Michikane to become regent, Father was hopeful he himself would receive a favorable post. All the people attending this event had similar aspirations. Like my father, most of them had been sitting on the margins of court life for some time. The regency had been in the hands of the eldest brother, Michitaka, for five years. When he died that spring, the question of his successor had awakened many hopes. Would it go to his own son Korechika or his brother Michikane? Both were eligible, as descendants of Kane'ie, the powerful former regent. At this point Michikane, as minister of the Right, was warily confident. The mood at this gathering of his supporters was tense, yet hopeful, and the bright blue skies and spectacular clouds of cherry blossoms seemed to bode well.

My father wrote a Chinese poem comparing Michikane to a late-flowering bloom finally coming into its own. Every other poet was likewise on his mettle, leaving no rhyme to chance. I watched Father write his poem in a smooth, casual hand when paper and brush were passed to him, knowing that he had struggled for days to choose the images he would present as if springing to mind in spontaneous inspiration. Saké was poured into shallow cups and, balanced on bird-shaped rafts, sent bobbing down the rivulet. Each guest endeavored to finish his poem by the time the cup reached the end of the stream. The first to finish would win the drink and the right to have his poem recited before the others. Father was very conscious of the fact that a person's appearance is paramount at these flower-viewings. He even premeditated his inebriation, wishing to appear neither a teetotaler nor a drunk.

—Drinking allows things to be said that need to be said, but are too uncomfortable in normal situations, he told me.

The more banquets I saw, however, the plainer it was that not everyone had my father's understanding of drink. He also warned me to retire inside the building after a certain point at these parties because invariably some men lose all sense of shame.

—It's easy enough to fend off a drunk if he is truly drunk and you have your wits about you, Father admonished me. But it's the sly pretenders I worry about – hiding their lechery under a wine cup. I would hate to see you cornered.

I let this pass. I never said a word to him about the archery lieutenant.

According to Father, it was outside under the cherry blossoms on occasions like these where matters of importance were decided. More often than not, court ceremony merely confirmed decisions made among the lacquer trays and wine cups, under the flowery clouds.

The political situation affected everyone at home. Father was tightlipped and easily irritated by the small children. Nobunori got on everyone's nerves by nattering on about what appointment he might expect should this or that happen. I told him to be quiet and go play with his beetles, and he made a sour face at me.

To escape this tense atmosphere, I took our carriage to the Kamo Shrine at dawn to pray. The early morning sky was clear and beautiful, and the quiet surroundings gradually calmed my agitated mind. Nearby in Kataoka I noticed an interesting grove of trees, exactly the sort of place where you would expect to hear the haunting call of the little gray-blue cuckoo called *hototogisu*. I was reminded of Ruri.

In Chinese poetry this is the "can't go home" bird – *fujo kigyo* it calls, like a poet in exile. In our language we give this little *cuculus* many names: the grove bird, the forest eaves dweller, the boot-footed bird, the May bird. It is also "the bird of obscure plumage" as in the poem; *haru no yo no yami wa ayanashi*, "the obscure pattern of the darkness of a spring night." The Chinese also call it something (I'm not sure how they pronounce it) that means "the sound of wings in the rain."

As I thought about the cuckoo and its names and images in poetry, I recalled how Ruri always looked past poetry because she was more interested in what she herself could observe about things in nature. Another famous poem about the cuckoo speaks of the hats of the farmers going to plant their fields in the spring while the birds' voices call *asana, asana.* No doubt Ruri would have said,

—That's stupid. The cuckoo goes *teppen kaketaka, hotchon kaketaka,* like that.

I remembered, too, that the cuckoo is the bird that meets dead souls as they toil their way to the netherworld. It's the "evening face" bird, the bird that "restores the night." Yet one of the earliest poems in our own language mentions the voice of the cuckoo at dawn. Again, I could hear Ruri saying,

—Well, there's no contradiction there, because the cuckoo sings in the morning and the evening both.

Ruri liked the *hototogisu.* I remember she wanted to include it in our list of summer birds. She mentioned that it also has the name *shokkon,* "soul of the green caterpillar."

—Probably because it eats so many of those poor worms, she said. Its belly is full of their little green souls.

Ultimately this was the problem with Ruri. She was very observant, but too liberal-minded.

—You want to know something really interesting about this bird? she had said as we were debating our lists.

I could never tell what she would come up with.

—It doesn't make a nest.

She waited for me to say, "Then how does it hatch its eggs?" so she could smile and tell me that cuckoos lay their eggs in other birds' nests and let those birds bring up the hatchlings.

—Remind you of anyone? she asked archly.

I probably replied that I didn't know anyone of the sort, but later I did think about what she said, and it gave me an idea for Genji.

Lost in thought and loath to return home just then from the shrine, I hardly noticed the sky beginning to cloud over. I did compose a poem:

Hototogisu   koe matsu hodo wa   kataoka no   mori no shizuka ni   tachi ya nuremashi
Hototogisu, as I wait for its voice standing in the quiet woods of Kataoka, I will probably get drenched.

During this period when the Great Council was deciding who should be named regent, Father went every day to attend Michikane at the Nakagawa Mansion. He was there on the third day of the fifth month when the imperial messenger arrived with the edict naming Michikane the new regent. Crowds of nobles swarmed to the residence with their congratulations, and it seemed that all the oxen and carriages of the entire city must have converged at that place. When Father came home late that night, he was strangely quiet. I helped him off with his stiff court hat.

—This is the beginning of our new life, isn't it? I ventured.

He smiled wearily.

—I hope so, Fuji. I've been on the edge of things for so long, I'm finding it hard to imagine actually being in a position of responsibility again.

—But I thought that's what you've been dreaming about all these years since Mother died, I protested.

It was odd he was not more cheerful. He stretched his legs out on the mat and gave me a thoughtful look. I could tell he was deciding how much to say. He didn't realize how transparent he had become to me.

—I'm concerned about Michikane. He's putting on a great show of energy, but I fear he is not well. I overheard his physicians discussing the merits of magnolia-bark tea. This leads me to think he may have some sort of nervous disorder.

Father yawned.

—Perhaps it's just the strain of the past few weeks, though. We should see how things go for the past few days. I'm tired. At least the matter of the regency has been decided, and we can stop worrying about Korechika.

I could never have said this to Father, but I was rather fascinated by Korechika. He was twenty-one, and from what I had heard from my friends at court, unusually handsome. Some of Genji's adventures had even been inspired by what they told me about his exploits. Yet it was true that he had stepped on a lot of toes. He was clever but not very alert to the effect he had on others. Several years ago his father had promoted him up the ranks over the heads of his kinsmen – in

64

particular, his two uncles – and they had not forgotten the slight. Then he had been appointed interim regent upon his father's death. If only he had been more diplomatic, he might have been able to retain the position.

Korechika's peremptory style was apparent after only a month in power, and it made people like my father uneasy. Even during the period of mourning for his father, Korechika couldn't resist issuing orders regarding little details of court life he felt could use improvement – niggling things like the proper length of officials' trousers. People bristled. Not surprisingly, they did not like being told how to handle the details of their posts by one so inexperienced. Korechika must have realized that his hold upon the regency was weak, so he took steps to try to undercut his rivals – primarily his uncle. Still, I found it hard to believe that he actually hired monks to hex Michikane. I think Michikane was probably jealous.

Like Father, I was apprehensive about Michikane – although it was not his health that worried me. My feelings stemmed from what I had heard over the years and observed of him myself at banquets. He was an exceedingly ugly man, short and squat with a pocked complexion. His eyebrows grew together in front like a long caterpillar, and even his arms were hairy. While it is not impossible for an ugly person to have a beautiful soul, in general it is unlikely.

In Michikane's case, physiognomy reflected personality like a mirror. His manner was domineering and shrewd, and people were intimidated by him. Father pointed to the fact that Michikane was faithful to his wife as an indication of his rectitude. Certainly no one would have accused Michikane of frivolity, yet, somehow, it seemed to me he merely used his own disinterest in romance to cast a cold eye on others' affairs. I felt he was not virtuous so much as he was simply a prude. Father wanted so badly to think well of Michikane that his vision of him was warped, I feared, by the fact that Michikane favored Chinese poetry.

People say "to know the son, look at the father," but it works the other way, too. Michikane's firstborn had the reputation of a fiend. At his grandfather Kane'ie's longevity celebration, for instance, when he and his brother were

65

supposed to perform a dance, the boy threw such a temper tantrum that, to this day, that's all anyone remembers from the ceremony. Apparently he also liked to torture small animals. Some say a curse from the spirit of a snake he skinned alive caused his death when he was just eleven.

I could imagine the horrified feelings of that boy's mother. Michikane might be faithful, but it was evident he blamed her for not producing a daughter he could use as future imperial spouse. The poor woman continued to provide sons, yet they were monsters. To top it all, his brothers, Michinaga and Michitaka, were rich in daughters. Michikane's wife was pregnant at the time, praying furiously no doubt for a girl. In any case, that this was the man upon whom my father's fortune depended made me uneasy.

Father's worry about Michikane's health was well founded. The late-flowering blossom was doomed to fall after a mere seven days. Three days after Michikane's sudden death, a new regent was appointed. Power passed, not to young Korechika as he himself expected, but to his other uncle, Michinaga.

Along with a few others, my father stayed on at Michikane's house to help with funeral arrangements, even though the great crowds of a few days before had all moved on to the new locus of influence centered on Michinaga. My father was not the sort of person to curry favor in such a way. He discharged his last duty to Michikane, then quietly came home. The appointments for the new regime would not be announced until the following new year in any case. He took a bit of comfort in the fact that the new regent, Michinaga, had been fond of his ugly brother and shared some of his scholarly interests.

Now there was nothing to occupy Father's mind until the appointments of Michinaga's regency got sorted out. I could tell he was thinking again about finding me a husband. My stepmother had just had another baby, a girl this time. She seemed so content. Father probably assumed that domestic bliss would solve my problems as well.

It's true I wasn't happy. I was stalled in my writing, and

since I had stopped seeing Ruri I had no one to talk to. One koto lesson with the red-nosed princess had been quite enough. I wished Chifuru were not so far away. But then she, too, had had a child and become preoccupied with domesticity. Still, I doubted whether marriage was the answer for me. I didn't think I liked men all that much – at least not the men who would have me.

Finally I felt the time had come to inform Father of my decision not to marry. I hoped he would feel relieved to be absolved of the need to find me a husband, when in truth the relief would have been all mine. So I told him I would like to speak to him about a matter of some importance. He responded to my request for a talk in surprisingly buoyant fashion.

—Why, yes, of course, he said. I have a matter of some importance to discuss with you as well.

So there we were, both unnaturally cheerful, ready to have our discussion. That should have made us suspicious. He spoke first.

—You know I have been concerned about your future, he began. Just because we have all been upset about the current political situation, and there has been a lot going on, doesn't mean I haven't been planning for you.

Perhaps my eyes were too bright. He looked away.

—At one point it seemed as if there might be a possibility of sending you to court, but I don't think we ought to count on that as being terribly likely now.

I could hardly keep myself from blurting out.

—I know you've been worried, Father, and you can set your mind at ease.

But of course I held my tongue and waited for him to finish.

He started talking about his distant relative and friend Nobutaka, who had been responsible for getting him a position in Emperor Kazan's court back at the beginning of his career. Nobutaka was, I suppose, five years or so younger than Father. I'd been hearing about him all of my life, and how indebted Father was to his goodwill, and what a marvelous person he was, so I wasn't paying the closest attention to Father going on about Nobutaka until I heard the words "and he's agreed that he will marry you."

I listened, stunned, as Father continued about Nobutaka's prestigious position as governor of Chikuzen, and the large fortune he had amassed at this and his previous posts. I remembered that Nobutaka had a son exactly my age. Perhaps I had missed something – maybe Father was saying that Nobutaka's son had agreed to join our two families by marriage.

But no. He was talking about Nobutaka – Nobutaka, who was divorced from his first wife but had two other wives, not to mention how many concubines, not to mention how many children by all of them.

—And so, Father concluded, we have agreed that there is no need to rush things. He will be returning to the capital early in the winter, and you can meet then.

He gazed thoughtfully at me. I couldn't speak.

—I really believe this is an excellent solution, he said after a moment. I want nothing but your happiness, Fuji.

Then,

—Now, what was it you wished to speak to me about?

—Oh, I croaked. It was nothing that important.

I excused myself and fled to my room. Of course, when my panic subsided, I thought of Auntie's failed marriage to a man with other wives. All her tart remarks I had overheard as a child flooded to mind. Rather than be a subsidiary wife to the most powerful man in the country, she once declared, she would have preferred an ordinary husband who was hers alone thirty nights a month.

Auntie had been a great beauty when she was young, clever and skilled in poetry as well, yet even she did not attain happiness in marriage. My prospects seemed to me all the dimmer in comparison. I was not beautiful and had a reputation for erudition, not charm. So, I thought bitterly, now I get what I deserve – a husband old enough to be my father, with wives and children to spare. I wondered why Nobutaka agreed to my father's scheme – and concluded that he was doing him another of those favors I had heard about all my life. Now it was the favor of rescuing the spinster daughter. Why couldn't I just be left alone? I felt betrayed.

We've all written about tear-drenched sleeves, but for the first time in my life it literally happened. Tears dripped on to my inkstone, turning my journals into gray puddles.

For the rest of the summer I sulked in despair but finally, tired of moping, decided not to give in so easily. I was oddly quiet, which unnerved my father. I didn't tell him directly that I refused his plan, of course, but he could tell that I was not delighted. Every day I pondered how best to present my case. I still could not understand why he felt he had to marry me off.

Yet this development did serve to put my previous dissatisfaction in perspective. I had thought I was unhappy as I struggled with Genji writing, but that was nothing compared to the unhappiness looming ahead now. Why did I not appreciate my life there in my father's house when it seemed as though it would continue indefinitely? Now that it was coming to an end, the time at home, in my room, in our garden, felt almost unbearably precious.

I had in fact answered my own question. We don't appreciate things until they begin to change and die. The twinge of evanescence in the gossamer floating in a summer sky causes us to look at it; the short span of the brocade of maple leaves makes us celebrate them; and the pitiful briefness of a person's life ultimately moves us. Why should my life be different? I had been lulled into thinking I could escape change, that I could exist like the garden pond, fed just enough water to maintain a certain depth and shape. Perhaps I had become stagnant as a result.

WORMS

Mimizu

Winter solstice passed with little ceremony. The weather was cold, but I still found it possible to crawl out of the warm bedclothes in the morning without flinching. According to my Chinese chart, on those days *Earthworms Twist into Knots*. Not sure what that meant, I asked the gardener if he had ever observed something of this sort. He squeezed one eye shut to show he was thinking and said,

—Earthworms, miss? Why, you never find earthworms this time of year! They're all sleeping, they are. Their bodies are mostly water, so they'd freeze if they weren't tucked down deep in the earth. They'll be back in the spring.

I checked my chart and, sure enough, the entry for the middle part of the fourth month was *Earthworms Come Out*. Maybe if we dug down deep enough into the earth, we would find the places where the worms sleep through the winter. Maybe we would find them all twisted up together in knots! I asked the gardener to dig some deep holes in the garden, but, predictably, he didn't want to because the ground was so hard. I tried to interest Nobunori in the project, but he had become fastidious of late and wouldn't dirty his hands. He was more interested in metaphysical worms than earthworms.

We had been looking forward to the cold weather to bring relief from the plague demons, so it was ironic that they struck most harshly just then. My older sister, Takako, died. She had been sick for less than a week. At first she was just cranky, but then she took to her bed. Perhaps because of her weak mind, Takako had always been vulnerable to spirit infection, so we were not especially worried until a raging fever made it clear that the disease had taken hold. Father summoned an exorcist, but his efforts were in vain. The house reeked of poppy seed burned in the attempt to flush out evil spirits, yet still Takako moaned and tossed in feverish sleep.

Then, as she neared her life's end, she became infused with a quiet lucidity. Kneeling by her side, I forgot that Takako was a simpleton. It was as if all her earthly resentments had been burned off by the fever. Her round face seemed like a living mask, her eyes looking into another world. Takako had never shown much interest in religion that I'd been aware of, but now she began to speak of the Amida Buddha, and a vision of purple clouds and golden skies peopled with heavenly *apsaras* waving silken scarves. As I listened to her rambling speech, it occurred to me that she was describing the scene on an embroidered banner in our family temple. Her maidservants treated her with the awe usually reserved for a sacred being. Naturally they thought Takako was looking directly at Paradise and that her innocent soul was preparing for its final flight. I kept my observation to myself. To me it didn't matter whether she was remembering a temple banner in her delirium or actually looking at Paradise. After all, the reason we know what Paradise looks like is that holy objects like the banner describe them for us.

Takako brought tears to my eyes as she spoke of seeing our mother seated on an open lotus flower, smiling and beckoning. Of course Father had commissioned more priests to come to the house and chant for Takako's recovery, but it became evident that they would soon need to switch to the liturgy for the deceased. The death of a young person should be tragic, yet Takako's death did not seem so. She was utterly absorbed in her personal vision and seemed more complete on this occasion than I had ever seen her.

And then the end of the year was upon us. I was wearing layers of mourning for Takako. Just glancing at my dark clothing reminded me of what a dolorous year it had been overall – both the large public bereavements like those of Michitaka and Michikane, and the small private ones, like Takako's. Death seemed to have hovered over our lives that year.

A *kōshin** day occurred and we stayed up all night as usual. Because of Takako's funeral rites, lots of relatives were staying at the house, including my grandmother. At her age she rarely ventured out of her own house, especially in cold weather. It was possible for a *kōshin* night to turn into a rather jolly affair, with people thinking up more and more bizarre ways to keep one another from falling asleep. Despite

*Originally a Daoist concept of heavenly retribution, *kōshin* was based on the notion that a person's body houses three "worms" whose job is to monitor sins and report them to Heaven every sixty days. One's life span would be shortened in atonement. But the worms could not leave unless a person fell asleep; thus one tried to stay awake so they would be unable to make their report.

71

our bereavement, that night was no exception. I was surprised to hear Grandmother say that she believed the only reason we preserve the *kōshin* custom of staying up is that it's so much fun. No one with any sense could really believe that our bodies house three malevolent worms.

Well, my brother, Nobunori, believed in the worms, and he wouldn't let Grandmother's comment go unchallenged. He even got into an argument with her – a sure sign of his lack of sense. Nobunori had always taken seriously everything people said about the *kōshin* worms. Even as a young child he made heroic efforts to keep himself from falling asleep. It was a good thing *kōshin* occurred only every sixty days, or else the poor boy would have broken down in a nervous fit. Perhaps his interest in bugs in general drove him to such a strong identification with supernatural worms. He insisted he could actually feel them stirring in his body as *kōshin* approached.

I have noticed that people will do all kinds of things to thwart their karma. For instance, it is popular to concoct a selection of herbal supplements to one's diet to prevent lassitude. Some people swear that eating wild boar meat twice a week will fortify the constitution and prolong life. Still others partake of ginkgo leaf extract to enhance their memories. I could be persuaded that these sorts of actions might enhance longevity, but it was hard to take the *kōshin* worms seriously.

It is also said that a child conceived on a *kōshin* night will grow up to be a thief, and there are cases where this actually happened. Perhaps this is the real reason we shouldn't go to bed on *kōshin* nights. The story of the tattling worms is just embroidery. People must somehow be kept from doing that which leads to pregnancy on this night.

As we were all participating in this lively argument, Grandmother told the story of a macabre event during a *kōshin* vigil some thirteen years before. She had heard it from Auntie, who was told by Kane'ie himself.

It was the first *kōshin* night of the new year. Kane'ie's daughters, the Empress Senshi and her sister, Chōshi, who was chief consort to the crown prince, wanted to make a grand party of it at the palace. Their three brothers,

Michitaka, Michikane, and Michinaga, promised to visit and keep things lively. The royal ladies composed poems and made elegant jokes, and their attendants competed in rounds of *go* and backgammon. Splendid prizes were awarded the winners of the play-offs, and excitement remained high throughout the night.

Finally the first cock crow was heard just before dawn. Princess Chōshi was seen to doze off, leaning on her armrest. One of her ladies called out,

—You mustn't fall asleep now, madam!

And another lady said,

—Shush. The cock has already crowed. Leave the princess alone.

But Michitaka wanted his sister to listen to an impromptu poem and insisted on waking her. Chōshi seemed deeply asleep and didn't respond. Calling her name, he drew close and tried to pull her to her feet. Imagine his shock to find Chōshi's flesh cold. He grabbed a lamp and held it to her face – she was dead!

Such a tragedy! And Chōshi's three little sons, aged seven, six, and two, left motherless. How Kane'ie grieved. Although they had long been separated by this time, even Auntie felt sorry for him.

A shiver ran down everyone's spine on hearing Grand-mother tell this story.

—Who killed her? someone asked, breaking the silence.

—Oh, it was a ghost, clearly, responded Grandmother. But there was never any evidence as to whose. Kane'ie always suspected it was one of his political enemies, but it is hard to tell in these cases.

At this point my brother spoke up.

—Isn't it obvious? he sneered in a superior way. This is clear proof of the power of the *kōshin* worms all of you are so irreverent about. If you ask me, it just proves what I've been saying all along.

That served to shut everyone up. Nobunori took advantage of his victory to sweep out of the room in a dignified huff. As soon as he was down the corridor, the rest of us looked at each other and broke into giggles.

Thus did we spend the last *kōshin* of the year and the beginning of Takako's mourning. Perhaps our unseemly levity came from the feeling that the year was finished, that we had weathered death and uncertainty, and that there was nothing more that could happen. The sad year was over and done. The new year would be different, and we would have the energy to face it afresh.

The day before the end of the year a messenger arrived at the house, bearing the news that Auntie had passed away of the pox in her mountain retreat two days before. We had all been thinking of her on the *kōshin* night when Grandmother related her tale of Princess Chōshi's mysterious death. Of course we had no idea – and to think that she had died just at the very time we were speaking of her! I have always wondered whether it could have been her spirit passing over us that prompted Grandmother to tell the story.

I regretted that I did not have the courage to show her my Genji stories while she was alive. Quailing at imagined criticism, I lost a precious chance to learn from her. What a coward I was. I blanched as I recalled our foolishness in presuming that the misfortunes of the year had ended. A mere day is time enough for death to sweep another frail life to oblivion.

THE NEW YEAR

Shōgatsu

Set the tone for the new year by your actions of the first few days. Even if you are distracted, vaguely uneasy, and unable to concentrate, force yourself to pay attention to the round of new year ceremonies. If you go through the motions, it is amazing how often your mental state will be coaxed into line by these mindless actions. In the new year that dawned after my sister died I had to discipline myself strongly to follow my own advice. In the end it worked, and there I was, humming happily almost despite myself.

I did love the feeling of newness that attended even the simplest activities. We took down all the paper amulets grown limp and dusty over the course of the year and replaced them with fresh ones – just seeing their crisp folds lifted my spirits. For health, we ate radishes, salted trout, and other tooth-hardening foods with brand-new willow chopsticks, and, as usual, we went picnicking on the hills to gather young herbs. We brought back pine seedlings we plucked there, festooning them about the house for good luck.

Of course much more elaborate rituals were going on at the palace, especially that particular year. The persistence of the plague meant that efforts to promote the emperor's health and longevity were doubled. Infusions of ginkgo leaf were added to His Majesty's menu, and imperial family members were enjoined to drink three cups of cow's milk a day. Father had to attend many of the imperial ceremonies for the new year.

—If you don't show your face at these functions, it's a fact that people tend to forget about you, he said.

At the great banquet of the first night, the young emperor was presented with the new calendar by officials from the Bureau of Divination, who also reported on the status of the ice in storage. Mercifully they proclaimed the ice to be thick that year, a good omen. On the second day, Father attended the official banquet given by Dowager Empress Senshi. Then he put in an appearance at the crown prince's banquet and finally the banquet given by Michinaga, the new regent. On the third day, he had to spend all afternoon at the party in the Courtiers' Hall, drinking and fraternizing with his colleagues. After this, he was able to slip away and come home. The ceremonies at the palace continued until the middle of the month. He would have to present himself again from time to time.

We were all anxiously awaiting the twenty-fifth, the day when new appointments would be announced. Father talked modestly, but I knew he was expecting a promotion. The fact that Michinaga was a cultured man who seemed to share his deceased brother's regard for the Chinese classics gave Father reason to hope that he might still be in line for something decent. He had been without official position for ten years.*

The fifteenth, the first full moon of the year, was cold and clear. I helped our cook prepare the seven-herb gruel. I rather enjoyed tying my hair back, tucking up my long trousers, and venturing into the kitchen once a year. As the ingredients simmered, I was reminded with a pang of how Takako would always turn up her nose at this stew. We made it with two kinds of rice, three varieties of millet, red beans, sesame, and herbs. Several years before, I had tried to tempt her by adding chestnuts and dried persimmons, but she only picked those items out and left the rest. Still, everyone else in the family liked the additions enough that we incorporated them afterward into our own family version of the dish.

The next ten days dragged by as we waited for the imperial announcements. At last, on the day itself, my father joined the throng of hopefuls crowding the palace courtyard waiting to hear, while the rest of us fidgeted with anticipation at home. At midday we gathered in the main hall to await his return, hoping for news that would bring a joyful end to this long period of uncertainty. To our dismay Father came storming home and, bypassing the main hall, proceeded directly to his study. I feared the worst. Luckily one of my cousins, concerned by Father's reaction to the outcome, followed him home and told us what happened.

Bad news. He had been appointed governor of Awaji Island – the lowest, meanest, most insignificant, poorest imaginable posting. My brother swore and blustered, stomping about indignantly. I tried to hush him up as my mind spun in chagrin. What could I say to Father? His disappointment would be boundless.

*Tametoki's small but secure niche in history is mainly due to the fact that he fathered Murasaki Shikibu. This would doubtless have surprised his contemporaries – to whom Tametoki was famous for his Chinese scholarship and poems in that language. A passing familiarity with the art of Chinese composition was required for all educated males in the Heian period, but by Murasaki's day Chinese studies had become quite academicized. Tametoki seems to have been somewhat rare in his serious interest in Chinese.

In the late afternoon Father burst out of his study with a folio of paper under his arm. He was still in court costume, although his hair had become badly ruffled. My stepmother exclaimed and quickly moved to tidy his appearance. Although he hardly noticed her, he did stand still to let her straighten his sash and retuck his robes and hair. I stood wordless, looking at him from the doorway. Finally his attention, which seemed to be fixed on some distant point, came to rest on me, and he said,

—It's not over yet. I'm going to give something to the emperor.

Then Father was out the gate, his manservant scrambling behind to keep up with his determined stride. My stepmother started to cry. The children took up her wails and so did the servants. I retreated to the study to escape the commotion.

The state of the room gave me a shock. My father was normally fastidious to a fault. I tend to be fairly neat, but he would occasionally chide me for a misplaced brush or unevenly worn inkstick. I had never seen his desk in such disarray. Chinese volumes were left open, scattered about the floor like abandoned children. Pieces of paper with scraps of poetry written on them were everywhere. His brush, unrinsed, lay on its dragon-shaped porcelain brush rest. I felt as if I were looking directly at the state of Father's heart. Numb, I began to straighten things out.

This line of Chinese caught my eye: "Suffering, studying, freezing, nights." And then this: "Scarlet tears soaking my sleeve." I realized that Father was struggling to compose a Chinese poem to express the deep disappointment of this day. I looked around for the rest, perhaps even a draft copy of the whole thing. I found some more lines: "On the spring morning when investitures are given." There had to be one more to complete the quatrain. Perhaps the image of tears of blood was his concluding line? No, the prosody didn't work. There must be something else.

'Clear, blue, empty sky." Could that be it? Yes, there it was: "Staring at the clear, blue, empty sky."

I shuddered. Father was going to give this poem to the

emperor? He must truly have felt that things could not possibly get worse.

This lament certainly made him appear ungrateful at best. I could only hope Emperor Ichijō would be understanding. He was just sixteen. I wondered whether he could possibly sympathize with the feelings of an old man like my father, a man facing his last chance to make a mark in his career.

I sat in front of the small votive statue of Kannon which Auntie had given me as a farewell present the last time I had seen her. I placed a pinch of aloeswood in a small censer and prayed for divine compassion to flow into the emperor's heart.

Father returned from the palace. He had passed his composition to a lady with whom he had kept in touch with his earlier days in imperial service, trusting her to bring the poem to the emperor's attention at a suitable moment. I think the enormity of his action didn't quite sink in until the next day. He woke late, having slept off a hangover resulting from the uncharacteristic drinking binge with which he concluded that awful day.

We were already a house in mourning because of Takako's death. Now we had so many other reasons to be mournful that the lugubrious air was suffocating. I found myself resenting the cheerful little pine seedlings decorating the rooms. Their message of felicity and promise of growth seemed cruel.

On the third day after the provincial appointments had been announced, an imperial messenger appeared at our gate. Father had expected some sort of reaction to his impetuously ungrateful lament, and was prepared to receive his reprimand with dignity. The messenger was ushered into the main hall where several hibachi had been set out to heat the room. Father was ready before the man had a chance to even warm his hands, and they left for the palace.

Soft clumpy snow was falling when Father returned in the early evening. It stuck to the bamboo leaves in the garden, looking just like the Chinese masters paint it – rather than snow, they painted the not-snow. We were all huddled on the verandah, shivering, listening for the sounds of the carriage. Father stepped out briskly and, shaking the snow from his shoulders, directed us to wait for him in the main hall. The room was still warm, and Umé was lighting oil lamps in the dusk. We were all seated there when Father came in. Because of the shadows, it was hard to read the expression on his face.

His cheek muscle was twitching, as it did whenever his emotions were strong. No one spoke for what seemed like a long time, and then Father coughed, and the cough turned into a spasm, and the spasm began to sound like laughter. My stepmother thought he was having a stroke, and she fluttered to his side. He brushed her away. Indeed, he was laughing, but at first none of us was at all sure that he was not ill or hadn't lost his mind. In fact, he was happy – ecstatic – and this was a condition that none of us in the room had ever before seen in my father. It took us a moment to recognize the emotion.

Finally the paroxysm died down. In retrospect, I can understand the relief of what had been, after all, a decade of mental strain brought to almost unbearable pitch by the events of the last few days. Father wiped his eyes, cleared his throat, and announced solemnly,

—The emperor has seen fit to appoint me governor of Echizen Province.

Nobunori gave a whoop like a barbarian Emishi, and my stepmother uttered a small cry of surprise and joy.

—Echizen is one of the Great Provinces, so there will be a bountiful stipend accompanying this appointment, continued my father. At least the financial underpinnings of this family will be secure, and you can all set your minds at ease. It is also a very great honor to be entrusted with the stewardship of this important province. Our family needn't ever again feel ashamed by lack of official position.

Nobunori jumped up to grab a bottle of saké from Umé, who had just entered the room bringing food.

—A toast! he bellowed, proffering a cup to my father. It was all on account of your terrific Chinese poem!

Father gave me a sharp glance, and I felt myself blush like a camellia.

—Fuji explained it to me, my brother continued, deepening my guilt.

—I never studied enough, I know, but now I really see why

it's important. That's so amazing, what the emperor did!

Nobunori went on in this vein.

My stepmother was looking thoughtful.

—My dear, she ventured. When you said "take charge of this important province," surely you meant "supervise the person who will actually be in residence in Echizen"?

She looked at him anxiously.

—No, wife, I meant take charge, and yes, this means we shall live in Echizen and direct the activities befitting the emperor's representative.

My father spoke softly, but my stepmother was struck by his words as if they had been physical blows. She lifted her wide sleeve to her face.

—You mean we must move to Echizen? she quavered. Leave the capital to go live on the frontier?

Father took her hand.

—I've been told it's very beautiful there, he said gently. And it will be interesting and new for us.

—What about the children's education? What about my parents?

The idea of being torn from the center of the civilized world and flung to the edge of barbarism took hold of my stepmother's imagination, and she began to sob. Nobunori, on the other hand, was so excited at the prospect of living in the wild north that he began to whoop some more. This had the effect of breaking the tension. My little half siblings began to tumble about the room excitedly, infected by Nobunori's noisy enthusiasm. As for me, amidst this pandemonium, a wonderful plan began to take shape.

As much as my stepmother resisted the idea of moving to Echizen, I knew that my father would eventually prevail and that she and the children would go. And as much as Father insisted that my marriage to Nobutaka should take place and I should be settled before the family left, I was certain I could convince him to take me to Echizen instead.

On the third day of the third month I went by myself to the Kamo riverbank just below the sacred shrine. I had with me a bouquet of grass orchids I had plucked from the wilder back part of our garden. When my brother discovered me there and asked what I was doing, I told him I was gathering models for brush practice. I had some Chinese sketches that included orchid, bamboo, and plum as demonstrations of various types of basic brush strokes. The grass orchids were the easiest. Nobunori made his usual insulting comments about my drawing abilities.

But I was not planning to draw these plants. The day before, I had fasted and prayed for the success of my plan to escape marriage by going to Echizen. I brushed my body with the bouquet, concentrating on letting my distractions, selfish thoughts, and disobedient impulses flow out and adhere to the leaves. The next day I went to the Kamo River, and, standing on its bank, I offered more prayers and flung the bundle of my sins into the fast-flowing water.

Of course I was not the only person performing this purification on the riverbank that day. I could feel my mood brightening as I watched the grasses tumble, break apart, mix with others, and be swept away by the rain-swelled rolling current of water. Unfortunately the carriage next to mine was full of Buddhist priests with their ears pinned back by the stupid little paper hats they wear when pretending to be doctors of divination. They looked so undignified it quite ruined the transcendent atmosphere of the place. I tried not to be distracted, but a poem crept into my mind anyway:

Haraedo no   kami no kazari no   mitegura ni   utate mo magau   mimi basami kana
Hallowed paper streamers, pure and sacred offerings to the gods – what a profane parody, these priests in paper hats.

Father was spending a great deal of time at the palace in preparation for his transferal to Echizen. My stepmother had acquiesced to the move, as I expected, although she didn't pretend to be happy. Her parents were at our house all the time, ostensibly to help plan for moving household effects, but really just using the excuse to cling to their daughter and grandchildren. They were not happy, either. They could never say anything against their son-in-law's promotion, but you could see the reproach in their eyes. No wonder my father preferred to spend his days at the palace.

I had begun my campaign to accompany the family to Echizen. Father said it was unheard-of for a woman my age to leave the capital unmarried. Poor Chifuru. This was what she went through – rushed into marriage when her father was transferred to Tsukushi. Nobutaka happened to be in Miyako on leave for a few months, and Father pressed for a meeting to plan the date. I prayed that in his innermost heart Father wouldn't be able to bear leaving me behind. With whom would he share his thoughts in rustic Echizen? His stoically suffering wife? My goose of a brother? There wouldn't be much society there, I pointed out. He remained unmoved.

Finally I put on a great exhibition, threatening to cut off my hair and become a nun if left behind. Having established an extreme, I agreed to a compromise. If allowed to come along to Echizen, I promised to maintain correspondence with Nobutaka, and go through with the marriage when we eventually returned to the capital. That was years away, I figured, and perhaps Nobutaka would no longer be interested. I could hardly worry about something so far in the uncertain future.

I was so absorbed in seeing to the success of my scheme to leave the capital with the family that I paid little attention to the scandal that had commanded everyone else's attention since early in the year. Father's appointment to Echizen may have loomed large for us, but to the world it was but a topic of gossip for a single afternoon. That the emperor would be so moved by my father's lament as to intercede with Michinaga was remarkable. It was even more amazing that Michinaga would revoke an appointment already announced to one of his own kinsmen to bestow it on Father! I'm sure this occasioned buzzing in official circles. It was lucky for us that the scandal surrounding Korechika bubbled up when it did. Otherwise the fog of malice that perennially hovers over the court might have condensed into envy and settled on Father's good fortune.

What happened was this. Dowager Empress Senshi, Michinaga's sister, had not been feeling well, so the doctors of divination prescribed a change of residence for her. She took over the Ichijō Palace with her retinue, displacing its residents to their suburban mansion. There were two daughters in the family that was obliged to move – a beautiful one and a not-so-beautiful one. Korechika had been visiting the beautiful one for some time. Presumably he was happy because it was much easier to get across to his lady in a private house than it had been when she was living at the Ichijō Palace.

But then Retired Emperor Kazan started sending love notes to the second daughter. When she refused to respond to his letters, Kazan began visiting the house in person, attempting to press his suit. Korechika could hardly believe that Kazan was really interested in the unlovely sister, and came to the conclusion that the ex-emperor must have his eye on his own lady. My father found this sort of behavior very off-putting, but he tried not to let his disapproval show.

In truth, Korechika should have been more discreet. He had suffered a major defeat when the regency was passed to his uncles Michikane and then Michinaga instead of to him. This was hardly a time to draw attention to himself. Yet what did he do but physically attack Kazan one bright moonlit night as the ex-emperor was leaving the mansion of the two sisters.

"Just to give him a scare," was his lame defense after this all came out. Kazan had been scared, all right – an arrow had actually pierced his sleeve. Although the circumstances were hardly flattering to his reputation, and Kazan himself tried to keep the matter quiet, the affair leaked out to Michinaga and the emperor. Korechika was accused of lèse-majesté. No matter that his behavior was hardly appropriate for an imperial personage, Kazan was still, in rank, a retired emperor. Everyone wondered how Michinaga would punish Korechika.

Many commemorative services took place early that summer for all those who had died the year before. During a span of ten days I attended a different service every single day, and on one day, two ceremonies. Some of the bereaved had changed back to colored clothing, but most remained in shades of gray. I found that a girl whom I had considered attractive in bright russets and pine green looked even more beautiful in ash gray. Somehow the color that is no color was more affecting.

She asked me for whom I mourned. When I told her it was my elder sister who had died, she exclaimed that she was in mourning for her younger sister who had passed away at about the same time. She suggested we think of each other as the lost relation. We began to correspond in this way, as younger and older sister, even though I was about to leave for a faraway land.

Even at these death-anniversary services, gossip about Korechika was rampant.

—He is, after all, a palace minister, and his sister is empress. They won't flush him out like a common thief, some argued.

Others weren't so sure he wouldn't be banished for those very reasons. I was curious as to what Michinaga would do. Our family was greatly indebted to the new regent, but I didn't know very much about him. Earlier this year, our fate lay in his palm like a quail's egg. He chose to coddle it by providing a nest in Echizen – but he could just as easily have smashed it. I was looking for some clues to his character in what he did about Korechika.

Not long after, Father came home from the palace with the news that Korechika and his brother Taka'ie had been banished to opposite ends of the empire. As we expected, they were found guilty of attacking an imperial personage, but they had also been convicted of directing evil magic toward Dowager Empress Senshi and, most damning, of performing rituals reserved for the imperial family.

Supposing these charges had merit, the court was assuredly justified in sending the brothers away. But I wondered whether, in fact, the charges were true. Korechika was ambitious, and certainly he was amorously hotheaded, but I couldn't believe he was stupid. From the first time I glimpsed him in public I had followed his career, pumping Father for snatches of gossip about him. I confess I thought him most attractive. In the end, I decided he had been banished more for who he was than what he'd done. From what I had experienced of young Emperor Ichijō's compassion, I was sure he couldn't be responsible for that harsh sentence. It had to have been due to Michinaga.

Korechika was temporarily installed in the regent's seat after his father passed away. That he couldn't maintain it was due to immaturity more than anything. And since time is the one thing that corrects immaturity, I suppose it was not strange that Michinaga should perceive him as a challenge. Korechika's sister the empress was pregnant. If she were to bear a son, he would become crown prince, strengthening Korechika's claims to the regency. Although Michinaga had daughters to place in Ichijō's collection of consorts, they were not quite old enough. All in all, it was not hard to understand why he might feel more comfortable with Korechika out of the capital. Yet, what a cold and calculating thing to exile one's own nephew!

Father was very keen on Michinaga's virtue as a statesman. I regarded my father as astute in many ways, but it was peculiar how much his view of people could be swayed by their professed love of Chinese poetry. It seemed to me that a regard for the classics, while admirable, could easily coexist with a beastly nature. Out of regard for my father's opinion, I tried to reserve judgment about Michinaga.

I was also curious about what really lay behind the switch of Father's appointment from lowly Awaji to coveted Echizen. People said the emperor was so moved by Father's poem that he ordered Michinaga to make the change. My brother went around bragging and telling this tale to everyone he met. Yet I knew deep down that Father's poem wasn't all that good, as Chinese verses go. I also was beginning to realize that although formally the regent carries out the wishes of the emperor, in substance it is quite the opposite. Ichijō could do nothing without Michinaga's approval. So perhaps Michinaga was humoring the young emperor – if in fact it had been Ichijō's desire to show his respect for classical learning by promoting a serious scholar like my father. Or, conceivably, it was the other way around, such that Ichijō rescinded the original appointment in my father's favor at Michinaga's request. Why would Michinaga have done that, though? There would have to be a political reason, and my father was so apolitical as to be useless, I thought.

The preparations for our Echizen journey were almost complete. I was only able to steal a few brief meetings with my new elder sister, but we wrote to each other several times a day. I was almost regretting my campaign to leave Miyako. But then I remembered that had I stayed I would have been married, and it would have been impossible to meet her anyway. Just the fact that we knew we hadn't much time seemed to make our relationship more intense.

In order to meet alone, we planned for our visits to a newly built temple called Jitokuji to coincide. For a few precious hours we were able to be together in a little room overlooking the craggy hillside. Sprays of golden-yellow kerria rose seemed to burst out of the rocks like fountains, reflected in the still waters of the garden pond below.

I felt I was experiencing true love for the first time. Of course I had loved Chifuru, but our intimacy was born of familiarity. Ruri had been a summer's infatuation gone stale after we left an idyllic retreat to return to our real lives in the capital. Now I discovered passion and I absorbed every detail of my elder sister's smooth, pale face, lilting voice, and voluptuous body. Rejoicing in her love, I panicked inside at the thought that we were about to part. She was as bold and beautiful as the kerria rose flower, and this was the nickname I gave her. I told her someday I wished to see her in those colors, the robes of russet lined in yellow, with gowns of red – a combination called *Kerria Rose*. The hues were exotic *à la Chinoise*, and to me they expressed her personality perfectly.

Meekly, as befitted a younger sister, I allowed her to teach me about love.

It would have been better to make our departure before the weather got so hot, but there was no help for it, with all of the details that had to be attended to. I wouldn't say my stepmother actually undermined the arrangements, but she surely dragged her feet. She seemed almost happy when the baby took sick, requiring us to postpone our leaving for another five days. I tried to make myself indispensable to Father. Preferring not to think about the move, my stepmother welcomed my taking over the practical arrangements.

Finally we were ready to leave. Everything was packed into bundles and loaded on to the carts. My father brought his entire Chinese library, so my stepmother insisted that she needed all of her wedding silks. Father pointed out that she would not have to dress according to the fashions of Miyako when we were in Echizen, but her trembling lip made him quickly change his mind. He allowed her to bring along anything she and the children wanted if they felt it would make life easier. The little boys were in tears that the pet cats had to be left behind, but Father mollified them by promising that they could keep a puppy in Echizen. Nobunori had been packed and ready to leave since the beginning of the month. He became very impatient with the dithering. I couldn't believe he was bringing his entire assortment of insect cages. He was convinced he would find all kinds of new specimens in Echizen.

At the last possible moment I packed up my inkstone and brushes. The last thing before we left – a poem to my Kerria Rose:

Kita e yuku   kari no tsubasa ni   kotozute yo   kumo no uwagaki   kakitaezu shite
> *Write to me as often as their wings inscribe the clouds, the wings of the wild geese heading north, never stop writing.*

A TRAVEL JOURNAL

Tabi no kiroku

TRAVEL RECORD, DAY ONE
The night before we left, Father lectured us sternly on the necessity of maintaining our composure. An imperial

representative would come to see us off, and Father said he did not relish the thought of his wife sniffling and his in-laws wailing as if at a funeral. Although our entourage left very early in the morning, at the last minute a messenger came panting up to our gate with a packet for me. Not wishing to open it under those rushed circumstances, I tucked it into the breast of my robe. The air was sweet and still in the gray, cool summer dawn. How beautiful Miyako was at this time of day! I began to think that I had made a grave mistake.

I was sharing a carriage with my stepmother and the baby girl. Nobunori rode in the other carriage with the two little boys, now aged five and three. They loved to be with their big brother because he played rough with them. With Nobunori in charge, they all acted like puppies. I was just as glad not to have to share the cramped space with juvenile males, even though my stepmother's quiet sobs and her dolor slowly darkened my spirits. I thought I should be happy on this day. Father was on horseback, as were the two guides, and he would switch places with Nobunori at some point. The trip was scheduled to take five days, but in fact it took eight.

We spent the first night in Otsu, on the southern edge of Omi Lake.* The first day's journey was mentally painful, but not really physically arduous. I had made the trip to Otsu before. The traffic was heavy along the Awada Highway in the morning. We passed carts loaded with vegetables, logs, and hay, all going into the city. There were also many farmers weighed down with bamboo frames bulging with eggplants and cucumbers. Not many groups were traveling our direction, at least not at that early hour. I supposed that in the evening the crush would be reversed, with most of the travelers heading back to the countryside.

As we crossed Ausaka Pass just after noon, my stepmother cried bitterly. I felt my throat tighten as well. This is the place where you really feel you are leaving the capital behind. It was one thing if you were just going to Otsu or to Ishiyama Temple for a few days, but quite another to be leaving civilization indefinitely. My fingers tightened around the

*Modern Lake Biwa.

packet I had privately examined when we stopped to stretch.

—A little token from Nobutaka? Father had probed.

I just smiled. He seemed to think I had agreed, and, looking gratified, he went over to comfort his wife. The gift turned out to be a deerskin traveling case containing a small inkstone, brush, and miniature inkstick the size of a twig. The whole thing was wrapped in several reams of thin writing paper. It was a charming gift, and had it in fact been from Nobutaka, I would have been impressed. But of course it was from Kerria Rose, along with this poem:

Yukimeguri   tare mo miyako ni   Kaeruyama   Itsuhata to kiku   hodo no harukesa
All who wend their way away, eventually to Miyako return.
But when? They sound so far – Kaeruyama and Itsuhata.

She was so clever, working the names of those places in Echizen into her poem. I missed her very much already.

That night, in our lodging in Otsu, I wrote the first installment of my travel record in tiny letters with the tiny brush from Kerria Rose.

TRAVEL RECORD, DAY TWO
We embarked early, for this was a long day, all on water. Shifting our luggage on to a boat in Otsu, we proceeded to trace the coastline northward with a fair wind and good speed. It was strange to realize that Mount Hiei lay to the west, since in Miyako we are so used to feeling its looming presence guarding the northeast. Clouds scudded overhead, casting shadows that danced across the green mountains below. One often sees such mountains painted on screens, and I felt as if we were passing by the most magnificent screen created in Paradise. Looking east across the lake, the gray shapes of mountains rose dreamily out of the haze – one an almost perfect cone, like a miniature of faraway Mount Fuji.

Five dignified herons flew by, and hawks chased one another near an inlet as we passed. A rather large cloud obscured the sun, turning the water from green to deepest indigo; then the light broke through, looking for all the world like the rays streaming from Amida Buddha's nimbus. In my whole life I had never experienced such a wide and open space as the expanse of Omi Lake. I was trembling with awe and amazement. Some fishermen rowed alongside our boat offering local food. Father was in a fine humor and gave them a bit of rice in exchange for the things they handed up. It was mostly fish, needless to say, including the tiniest clams I had ever seen. They had been removed from their shells and pickled. I would have loved to see the shells – they could have made a doll-size set for the shell matching game.

Perhaps I shouldn't have eaten so many. Something about the constant swaying of the boat and the slap of the waves started to make me feel unwell. In the late afternoon a squall arose, and I began to wish I had stayed home, even if it meant marrying Nobutaka. The sky grew dark, broken by flashes of lightning. Finally our boat drew up to the island of Chikubushima, where we settled for the night. Even now, when I look at the poem I concentrated on composing, I recall the sea sickness it did not quell:

Kakikumori   yuudatsu nami no   arakereba   ukitaru fune zo   shizugokoro naki
The clouds pile up darkly, waves rise up fiercely in a sudden storm; I am like this floating boat, ill at ease.

At least we were almost finished with the water part of the journey.

How odd it was to be carried off the boat. As soon as my feet were on land the queasy feeling ceased – even though my legs were still wobbly, as though they couldn't quite believe they were no longer standing on that itching surface. The previous day, all I could think about was what I was leaving behind in the capital in my stubborn resistance to marriage. My stepmother could go ahead and weep, because it was no secret how she felt about moving to Echizen. I didn't have that luxury and was grateful for the cover of illness as an excuse for tears.

Just before the heavy clouds gathered, we passed a place called Miogasaki, where we saw people pulling in fishing nets. Men and women together, their rough garments hitched up to their waists, pulled, hand over hand, to draw in the heavy

90

nets. Their arms and legs were brown and hard-looking. The image stuck in my mind and I composed a poem to send to Kerria Rose:

Mio no umi ni   ami hiku tami ni   tema mo naku   tachii ni tsukete   Miyako koishi mo

On the lake at Mio dragging their nets without cease; ceaselessly, too, I think of the one I left behind in Miyako.

TRAVEL RECORD, DAY THREE

I rose before the rest of the family to watch the sunrise. The air was fresh and the sky clear after the storm. The waters of Omi Lake were smooth as lacquer – it hardly seemed possible they had tossed us about so mercilessly. Black pines arched dramatically over the tiny harbor. I resolved to try to re-create this scene for Father on a tray arrangement someday, and gathered a bit of the golden sand and some pebbles from the beach for that purpose.

The day before, I had heartily regretted carrying through my scheme to leave Miyako. Such effort to avoid one's karma must inevitably bring distress, and I was sure I was suffering for that reason. But on this clear limpid morning standing on that tiny island, my regrets began to evaporate. A white butterfly darted about, though there were no flowers on the shore, and to my wonder made its erratic way out over the waves and disappeared from sight.

My feelings ebbed and surged like the waves in the storm. Which could I trust? I thought of Miyako, and immediately Kerria Rose came to mind. I wondered what she was doing. Was she thinking about colored robes yet, or was she still wearing mourning gray? I told myself we'd known each other for such a short time that the kerria rose flowers we saw in bloom our first tryst were only just beginning to wither. I'm sure we were close in a previous life. That's the only thing that could explain our sudden, intense passion.

I heard the children stirring and went back to help get them ready. We bundled ourselves back into the boat and made our way easily to the northern tip of the lake. Porters awaited us there to pack our baggage on to their animals. Uneasily I examined the uncouth conveyances we were expected to ride in. There were horses for my father and Nobunori, but we women and the children had to fold ourselves into bamboo-framed boxes hanging from two poles that were shouldered by pairs of unbelievably rough-looking farmers.

TRAVEL RECORD, DAYS FOUR, FIVE, AND SIX
We arrived in Itsuhata* and stayed in a guesthouse there for a few days to recover from the passage over the Shiozu Mountains. To think I rejoiced when our water journey was over! Had I known what was in store, I would have been only too happy to get back on the wretched boat and return to Otsu. How I preferred being ferried by gentle oxen than either waves or men – not that oxen could ever have negotiated those steep mountain paths and narrow ledges hewn from the rocky slopes. When I dared peek out through the blind that swung wildly at every lurch, the sight of the precipices below was enough to make me squeeze my eyes shut in terror.

At one point we were surprised to hear the sound of voices approaching from the opposite direction. The path was so narrow I wondered what we would do if we met another party. Suddenly a trio of burly men, naked but for loincloths, and shouldering great wet baskets, appeared in front of our entourage. They made faces of great disgust and shouted at our porters to make way. Then they caught sight of Father and our official guide, and sullenly backed down. It was quite impossible for our retinue to back up in any case, so, grumbling, the three runners turned around to a place where the path widened just enough for us to squeeze by. They were fish runners, Father explained, bringing mackerel packed in wet leaves from the seacoast all the way to the capital.

We didn't make it as far as the village we had hoped to reach by nightfall and so had to make camp at a woodcutter's clearing. The porters complained about being slowed down by our enormous amounts of luggage. As darkness approached, my stepmother became hysterical at the idea of sleeping in the open, so Father fashioned a tent for us out of

*The modern city of Tsuruga.

some of the clothing that had been carefully crated up. The fine silken Miyako robes looked quite incongruous pitched among the cedars on the mountainside.

My stepmother was babbling in her fatigue and fear. Finally I understood what was bothering her – it was the fact that the porters kept staring. She had had a most sheltered upbringing and was always careful to screen herself properly from the sight of men. My father was more worldly due to his experience in palace society. From him I knew that women of the highest nobility were much freer about such things than the genteel non-noble families who strove so hard to emulate them. Eventually my father calmed her by saying that the farmers should be thought of as no different from the oxen we hitched to our carriages in the city.

—You would not be embarrassed to be ogled by an ox, now, would you? he cajoled.

I thought it only natural that these peasants would be curious about us. Even though they often took on the job of carrying travelers over the Salty Mountain pass, they mostly saw officials. They couldn't have seen too many ladies from the city. I overheard one of them say that indeed the road was overgrown and difficult. I thought they were more like men than they were like oxen – for better or worse.

Shirinuramu   yukiki ni narasu   Shiozuyama   yo ni furu michi wa   karaki mono to zo
Those who porter across Salty Mountain know well how bitter is the path through life.

On the second day of riding in these terrifying litters I had to share mine with the older of the two boys. They were behaving so badly and crying so piteously that Father split them up, put Jōsen with my stepmother and the baby, and relegated the other one to me. Although I dreaded the prospect, in fact it made the trip somewhat easier. With little Nobumichi clinging to me, I felt much braver and calmer than I had the first day. We pegged the reed blind up so we could see out, and I tried to distract him by pointing out unusual bamboos and the occasional wild boar our caravan startled out of the brush. He held my hand tightly in his chubby fist as

93

we were jounced and jerked along the mountain path. We played a game of thinking up names for the puppy Father promised the children they could have in Echizen. I discovered that five-year-old boys are inordinately amused at names for body functions.

—Let's name the dog Barking Butt, he suggested, shaking with giggles.

Eventually he fell asleep, and, noticing the silence, one of our porters inquired,

—Taking a nap, is he now?

The man's accent was very thick, and it took a moment before I realized what he had asked. When I replied that he had indeed gone to sleep, the man barked something to his partner, and after this I sensed a somewhat gentler rhythm to their gait. Perhaps it was my imagination. It was very difficult to have a conversation with them.

By this time, we were past the steepest slopes and into the rolling foothills of the Hokuriku Road. We would soon reach the town of Itsuhata, where we would be met and escorted to the official guesthouse.

TRAVEL RECORD, DAY SEVEN

The last leg of our journey was over the Tsuruga Road running from the town to the coast, then along the shoreline north with a jog inland to Echizen Town.* I was thrilled at our first glimpse of the ocean. Before seeing it, you could sense the briny smell borne by the breeze. Our salty porters returned to Shiozu, and we loaded up our baggage on to a new set of bearers from Echizen who had come to escort us to Father's new post. Coming from the provincial capital, they were a bit more civilized. The road was level, the weather fair, and the scenery spectacular. I had thought Omi Lake was a tremendous body of water, but now seeing this wild northern sea, it was almost as if I had been reborn into a different world. Even my stepmother had nothing to complain about.

*The modern city of Takefu. It now boasts a Murasaki Shikibu Park, featuring a Heian-style garden and monumental bronze statue of our heroine gazing toward the mountains of Echizen she grew to loathe.

Once again I had a litter to myself. The sea breeze blew through my hair and the blue ocean sparkled in the sunlight. I began to feel much better about the journey. A rack of clouds rippled like a mackerel's back overhead, and I only wished Kerria Rose had been alongside me to enjoy these splendid sights.

THE PILLOW BOOK
Makura no Sōshi

Our official residence in Echizen was a large wooden building modeled on a mansion in Miyako the former governor had admired. While it had an impressive audience chamber to accommodate local delegations Father would have to meet, the living quarters were drafty and not very finely finished. The garden was a mess. To the local farmers and fishermen who entered the courtyard fidgeting with wonder, this haphazard structure was the epitome of imperial splendor. Only after you saw the miserable hovels in which they lived could you understand their awe.

On the other side of town from our official residence stood the Matsubara guesthouse. Since almost the first day we arrived in Echizen, Father had gone over there to see a group of Chinese merchants and sailors who had been shipwrecked off the coast. Three or four men drowned in the accident, although amazingly, nearly seventy had been rescued. I looked forward to accompanying him sometime, for I had never seen a real Chinese person before.

The mountains in Echizen were quite different from the elegantly rounded hills of Miyako. They thrust their low craggy backs out of the plain like a dragon emerging from the sea. Everything about Echizen was rougher and wilder than I was used to, and it was rather frightening in the beginning. When I saw the cliffs of the seacoast for the first time, I became giddy gazing at the sudden steep plunge of stone to roiling surf below. Yet gradually I came to appreciate the fact that, because of the sea breeze, Echizen was not plagued by the sticky summer heat that enveloped Miyako. The ocean wind was also responsible for the abrupt way the weather would change from clear to cloudy to rain to clear again, in the space of a morning.

Donning the heavy veils of my traveling costume, I accompanied Father when he inspected the Nine-Headed Dragon River, as the local people called it. I had come to expect that anything in Echizen would be fierce, but I was not prepared for the majestic power, the broad expanse, of that many-headed dragon of a river. Even in flood the Kamo River back home was tame by comparison. The farmers respected the dragon and showed my father their fields and the rich crops they produced. Carrots and radishes grew unbelievably large and straight in that fine, sandy soil.

Back in our garden, a small iridescent jewel of a bird visited the stream after Father had it cleared. I thought it strange that the country people called such a bright little thing a river locust. Father had seen them in the shallows of the Kamo River back in Miyako.

—Kingfishers, he said. They pass through in autumn, on their way south. Usually they travel in pairs. I'm surprised you never noticed them. The Chinese think of them as lovers, and royal ladies make jewelry from their blue feathers.

By the fall we had more or less settled in, but Father became increasingly gloomy. One day he permitted me to come along to the Matsubara guesthouse. We traveled in the official governor's ox carriage, alighting at the outer gate where a military guard was stationed. Everyone bowed to Father, but it all felt rather unreal to me. As we entered the wide court-yard, a strange, musical babbling met our ears. I was entranced! Of course it was all the refugees speaking their native tongue. I was thrilled to think that Father could understand what they were saying. They put their palms together and raised their forearms in greeting as we passed by. The gesture reminded me of those dignified insects, the mantids, my brother kept.

We were shown to the main reception room and served sweet cakes and a pale and bitter greenish brown infusion from a kind of camellia leaf. The resulting brew had a fragrance not unlike wild sasanqua. Father had tried this when he was at court and told me it was called tea, a Chinese health beverage. Then three Chinese gentlemen joined us. They spoke with my father about the weather, the scenery, and foods of China and Japan. Father introduced me, occasioning many polite and complimentary remarks from the three gentlemen. After about two hours of this we departed.

I was rather surprised that the entire interchange had been in our own language – although the Chinese spoke it rather badly. My father uttered nothing in their tongue, and thus I discovered the reason for his gloom. When he had first tried to speak to them in the poetic diction of the Chinese he had studied all his life, Father found to his chagrin that they did not understand a word he said. Likewise, their songlike speech was completely unintelligible to him. Luckily, since they were merchants, they had managed to learn enough of the language of their customers to be able to communicate basic things, but they were not educated men. They could make sense of the things Father wrote down, as long as they were of a prosaic nature. They praised his calligraphy extravagantly, saying it was much better than they themselves could produce. But they had scratched their heads and smiled nervously when presented with one of his poems.

From their laborious explanation Father learned that not all Chinese is the same. In fact it seems that not all Chinese people can even understand one another. One's style of speaking depends on the region one comes from. Yet they also assured Father that his poems and written Chinese could be easily read by a Chinese person better educated than they.

—I will have a chance to see whether or not that is true, said Father grimly. An official delegation representing the Chinese government will be arriving from Miyako soon to discuss what to do with these refugees. If I can't communicate with them, I might as well drag myself back to the capital in disgrace.

It was now clear to me why Father had been given the Echizen assignment. On that snowy spring day when he was summoned to the palace, he had met with Michinaga himself. The regent laid out the situation: A group of shipwrecked Chinese were being detained in Echizen to await the official envoy from their country. But the Miyako court was becoming suspicious of the numbers of Chinese and Korean merchants ending up blown on to our coasts, as if by accident. What was needed was a trusted person to go spend time with these foreigners and figure out what they were up to. Someone with impeccable credentials was required, someone who could communicate in Chinese. Who better than Tametoki? Thus was my father offered his last chance at public office.

How crafty Michinaga was! He knew my father couldn't possibly refuse to be his spy – not after that poem he had written to the emperor. So here was my poor father, interested more in poetry than politics, entrusted with a mission of secrecy and intrigue. I would have laughed if it hadn't been so painful for him. And now the one thing he prided himself on, his Chinese learning, was called into question. I prayed that the officials in the delegation would be able to understand him, and he them.

The storms of fall came sweeping over Echizen. One day the garden still held its few remaining summer blossoms alongside autumnal chrysanthemums and bush clover just starting to bloom. Then a violent storm blew in from the sea, crushing and tumbling everything together in a wild jumble. Only the plumes of the white pampas grass stood tall, blowing wildly in the wind. Of course we had typhoons in Miyako, too, but they did not seem as wantonly violent as this one. My heart felt strangely unsettled.

Messengers came regularly from the capital, bringing news and gossip and taking back Father's meticulous, if rather contentless, reports. They stayed in our guest quarters, having drunk and eaten the local delicacies Father always ordered prepared for them. I listened from behind screens to their relaxed chatter about politics and love affairs, and was thus ensconced, hearing but unseen, when I noticed that all of a sudden one of them lowered his voice and began whispering to Father something that sounded serious. Father's reactions, too, were brief and muted. I strained to hear what they were talking about.

—Found in the river, I thought I heard.

Concerned queries in Father's voice followed, and then,

—About the same age as Your Honor's daughter, I believe.

Who? Who? It was maddening. I leaned forward, trying to absorb sense from the snatches I could hear. I felt like pushing the screen over. Impatiently I snapped my fan open and shut, hoping Father would notice. He cleared his throat and must have indicated to the messenger that I was sitting in earshot, for the man suddenly became jolly and they called for more saké.

Later, after the messengers had retired, Father came to my room, where he knew I would be waiting anxiously. I had not allowed myself to entertain the various possibilities trying to crowd their way into my mind.

—Who? I burst out as soon as he entered. What happened?

Father spoke quietly.

—Your cousin Ruri . . .

—Yes?

—. . . appears to have thrown herself into the Uji River.

—And?

But I already knew what he would say.

—She was found by some fishermen late the next day.

—But why? I exclaimed, my mind reeling.

—I thought perhaps you might know better than I, said my Father gently.

Ruri. I knew that her parents had finally found a bride-groom willing to accept such an unorthodox bride, and Ruri, from the little I had gleaned, seemed to bow to their wishes. I should have guessed that she would have harbored a secret determination.

—She told her parents she wanted to visit the Uji Shrine before her marriage, said Father. They permitted this gladly because they were relieved. They had expected her to resist the idea of marriage. You knew her better than any of us, Fuji. Did she so hate the idea of wedlock?

I could only shake my head, bewildered. I once thought I knew Ruri, but it was now clear I had no insight into her heart. I realized that she would not have been happy to marry, but I would never have thought her capable of such extraordinary resolve. I imagined Ruri traveling with her two maids and an escort to Uji. She would have waited till all were asleep, and then quietly opened the corner door of their lodging and crept out. Did the wail of the wind and the rumbling waters of the Uji River frighten her or stiffen her resolve? With a shudder I remembered a place where the bank was high and all one would have to do was take a step. And then my mind recoiled. How could she have destroyed herself?

All she had to do was take a step. In the dark her robes must have whipped around her legs and billowed out like a camellia blown off the branch. But a flower would float. Ruri's robes and hair would have dragged her down. And the fishermen would have found the ruined blossom entwined with river weeds, pale and green and sodden. I hated the rush of images that unfolded in my mind as I sat there speechless. Ruri, who was more comfortable out in the elements than sequestered behind screens. Perhaps only someone like Ruri could have chosen those savage roaring waters to carry her away from her misery.

I thought of my own life and knew that I did not have the strength to do what she did. I was a coward who ran away to Echizen rather than face my fate.

Although Ruri and I had ceased to be close, her death left me badly shaken. I thought about her constantly as I gazed at the wild forests on the steep mountain slopes of Echizen, and I could scarcely bear to look at the storm-swollen Dragon River. The novelty of wilderness had worn off, and I keenly missed Miyako.

I began to plot out a Genji story in which he was banished from the capital. I had to decide where he should go, and was considering either Suma or Akashi, the places to which Korechika and his brother had been exiled. Like Korechika, one of Grandmother's heroes, Yukihira, had been sent to the lonely coast of Suma, and I finally chose that. I now understood that you could not appreciate your home fully until you left it. Though I had always been glad to return home after short trips away, that feeling was nothing compared to the joy I anticipated on returning from Echizen.

I received a present from Nobutaka. He was familiar with my love of reading and had sent a copy of a pillow book* he said was causing a stir among readers in the capital. His note said that he thought I might like to be kept abreast of literary trends in the civilized world. I had been reading a great deal in Echizen, but all from my father's Chinese library. When I saw the elegantly bound pillow book, I was suddenly ravenous to read something new in Japanese.

My feelings toward Nobutaka softened a bit. I felt guilty that I had not written him as agreed, knowing that part of the reason I avoided writing was that I regretted striking that bargain in the first place. Through temper tantrums I had gotten my way, and now I was stewing in it. Every night I performed the spell of turning my robes inside out in hopes of having a vision of Kerria Rose, but invariably Ruri's pale wet face would float into my dreams and I would wake with a start.

For several days I was deeply engrossed in reading this pillow book by a court lady named Kiyowara Nagiko, in service to Empress Teishi. To be quite honest, it was little more than a hodgepodge of notes, yet it was just what I craved. The style was simultaneously brazen and intimate, like a chatty confidante whispering the latest palace gossip in your ear. I wondered what sort of person the writer was – apparently her palace nickname was Shōnagon. I kept hoping to find something in her work about the empress's brother Korechika, for I had heard from one of the messengers that he had been discovered sneaking back to the capital to visit his dying mother, only to be ordered to return to his post in exile. There

*The most famous pillow book in Japanese literature is Sei Shōnagon's. The term itself referred to a notebook that one kept near at hand (by one's pillow) to jot down random thoughts.

was not a whiff of this particular scandal in the pillow book, but I was not disappointed to find other gossip about Korechika.

I was reading a scene that must have taken place about four years earlier. Korechika was visiting the emperor and empress, discussing literature until it became so late the serving ladies began falling asleep at their posts. Even the emperor finally dozed off. By this time it was dawn, and Nagiko records that she pointed this out.

—Well, if it's dawn, there's no sense in going to bed, is there? Korechika said, laughing with his sister.

The emperor was beyond hearing their banter at this point. Just then a rooster escaped from somewhere and went squawking noisily outside the corridor. Ichijō awoke with a start, whereupon Korechika recited the words of a Chinese poem: "Lo, the prudent monarch rises from his sleep." Everyone was impressed with his quick wit, reported the pillow book's author.

It was a trivial incident, but it sounded wonderful. Even though my life in the capital never touched the splendid goings-on in the palace, the fact of having lived so close at hand, being able to hear bits and snatches of the lives of those elegant people, was enough to make one feel elevated. Now, stuck in Echizen, I felt myself slowly turning into a rustic clod. This Shōnagon lady went on to write that on the following night, after everyone else had retired, Korechika offered to escort her along the corridors to her room. She described his white court cloak dazzling in the moonlight, and how he touched her sleeve, warning her not to trip. He quoted a line from the Tang poet Jia Dao: "As the traveler journeys by the pale light of the waning moon" – which she found thrilling. Of course who wouldn't be thrilled to be in such a situation with someone like Korechika? I wondered whether he spent the night with her. She didn't say.

I was intrigued, too, by this lady's categories of things. Her lists of birds, of insects, of flowering trees, reminded me of Ruri and the seasonal lists we had put together two summers before. Many of the lists in the pillow book were full of personal opinions on this and that. Although reading

Shōnagon's list of "elegant things" or even "disagreeable things" filled me with longing for Miyako, I got the impression that she herself might be a rather difficult person. Why in the world would she include wild goose eggs in her enumeration of elegant things? She began to strike me as perverse.

In fact the more I read, the more I came to feel that this pillow book was mostly about fashionable matters designed to make the author appear clever. In the beginning, I was quite taken by the intimate style and unusual subjects she took up, but after a while I decided that she was rather conceited. Her pronouncements were littered with Chinese characters that, on closer reading, seemed inserted only to impress. I couldn't see that they particularly enhanced what she was trying to say. This was all the more surprising considering that her father had been an esteemed poet of the Pear Pavilion Group.

And then, I was taken aback to find a paragraph mentioning Nobutaka. As she told it, he had insisted on wearing full-dress court silks while on a pilgrimage, causing all the people he passed to gape in wonder at the unusual sight. This was just before his appointment as governor of Chikuzen. Was she implying his fancy clothing had won him the post?

Such an unflattering portrait made me wonder whether Nobutaka had even bothered to read this pillow book before sending it to me. I began to worry – perhaps he really was a dullard. And yet, I supposed, it was possible that he *had* read it and magnanimously brushed off the insult as not worthy of comment. Or, again, perhaps he was so eager to please me that he sent me his copy before giving himself the opportunity to read it? So either he didn't know that he had been insulted, or he knew but didn't care. I continued to fret – perhaps he found out from someone else after sending me the manuscript and was now mortified. It was very difficult to come to an opinion, and it gave me a headache every time I tried to make up my mind about him.

I came across the draft of a letter I wrote to Kerria Rose around this time. Mostly I complained to her about Nobutaka, but I also sent her this:

My Dear Older Sister,

So what do you think of the *Pillow Book* everyone has been reading? It seems to me that this Sei Shōnagon is dreadfully taken with herself. She thinks it so clever, dropping Chinese characters all over her writings, but if you look at her phrases closely, they don't hold up so well. People like this who go out of their way to be sensitive in every situation, trying so hard to capture any moment of interest, however slight, are bound to look ridiculous and superficial. It seems to me that when you think of yourself as so superior, you are bound to come to a bad end someday. How can the future possibly turn out well for someone like this?

How smugly I predicted her downfall from my rustic perch in Echizen. Not even in my dreams did I imagine I would one day meet Shōnagon after my prophecy had come true.

BRIGHT COUNTRY

Ming-gwok

Disturbing news arrived from the capital early that winter. An envoy came via the neighboring province of Wakasa to tell Father that the notorious Chinese merchant Shu Ninsō had been officially charged with harassing the governor. Shu was well known as the most senior Chinese doing business in our country.* He had been here almost ten years and spoke our

*In the tenth century, trading with China was never a matter of straightforward commerce. From the perspective of the Chinese, who regarded themselves as the center of the civilized universe, any goods brought from foreign states were classed as tribute; any Chinese goods that flowed out were "bestowed" as a favor from a superior to a tributary. This relationship did not sit well with the Japanese, who

language fluently. Father conveyed this news to the refugees at the Matsubara house, who naturally got upset. At the time I wondered if he should have told them. He was supposed to be getting information *from* them, after all, not giving it *to* them. Father said they protested mightily that Shu was being treated unfairly.

Over the years Shu had been the main purveyor of Chinese luxury items to Empress Teishi, among other royal persons. He extended her credit even while her branch of the family was undergoing political difficulties. Certainly her brother Korechika was in no position to pay her obligations. Shu apparently pressed his claims through the governor of Wakasa. It was hardly likely that the imperial court would favor a merchant's case over the sensibilities of the empress, though, and so they charged Shu with harassment in order to deport him without payment. It occurred to me that Michinaga could have resolved the issue by paying Teishi's bills, but he did not lift a finger. Then it struck me that perhaps he secretly enjoyed the awkward position the empress was in. After all, she was not *his* daughter.

As the weather grew colder that first winter in Echizen, my spirits drooped more each day. Sitting alone in my room, I was dreaming of home, paging through my almanac of ceremonies in the capital, when I noticed that it was the beginning of the fortnight called First Snows. From my room I could see Mount Hinodake, where the snow was already

stopped sending embassies to China in the year 873. At the same time, they still craved Chinese porcelains, damasks, paintings, books, and scriptures. A few daring Chinese merchants were willing to pursue this market, at great risk to themselves, for the considerable profits they could amass. Such merchants might count on being blown off course and would "happen" to land on the shores of Japan, the Island Kingdom. Before government officials could even get to their ship and survey the contents, many items would already have been siphoned off by local traders. This unofficial trade had been tolerated for decades, but by this time the court was becoming suspicious of the growing number of landings by Chinese and Korean vessels. Not without reason, they feared invasion by their powerful western neighbors.

piled depressingly high.

Each season in Echizen was extreme. In summer the clouds would suddenly pile up and release a deluge of rain, falling so hard it was as if the land had in a blink become the sea; the autumn typhoons were vehement; and now the winter promised to be deep and cold.

Koko ni kaku Hino no sugimura uzumu yuki Oshio no matsu ni kyou ya magaeru
As I sit here and write, the cedars on Mount Hino are already buried in snow; today they remind me of the pines of Oshio.

Fishermen brought pale green, half-dried squid and long-legged red crabs to the house. The tender white crab meat was unlike anything I had ever tasted. How I wished I could have shared it with Kerria Rose. I couldn't help but think about the banquets, dances, and festivals that cluster at the end of the year in the capital. Back home, when the first snow fell, everyone enjoyed watching it swirl and frost the red berries of the nandina. We piled charcoal into the hibachi and toasted rice cakes. I shivered when I recalled how cozy it was. In Echizen the cold descended so quickly that it seemed we were already in the dead of winter when in fact it had just begun. The children were cooped up inside much of the time, and their noise grated on my nerves. It hardly mattered whether it was playful whooping or unhappy whining, especially when I was trying to write about Genji. I preferred to spend my days dreaming of Miyako and the Shining Prince rather than focus on my gloomy surroundings.

Day after day the snow sifted down from the skies, quietly piling up until everything man-made was buried under huge white mounds. It was not beautiful; it was a dreadful nuisance. Some men came to clear paths so we could get out of the house. The children ran outside and, scooping the snow into a little hill, scrambled up it.

—Come on, they shouted. Come out and see!

Nobunori joined them but I was not tempted. I wrote,

Furusato ni   kaeru yamaji no   sore naraba   kokoro ya yuku to   yuki mo mitemashi
If it were Kaeruyama mountain road on the journey home,
    then my heart would rejoice to see the snow.

But it wasn't. I was thoroughly sick of snow and of Echizen. I wished desperately to go back to Miyako, but, of course, it was quite impossible to go anywhere until the snows melted. My Chinese calendar description of this period of time was *Walling Ourselves Up, Winter Deepens*. It described exactly how I felt – walled up. Perhaps the weather in China was more like that of Echizen than like Miyako. I used to feel that Chinese descriptions of winter were exaggerated, but now I understood.

Finally, one bright snowy day we received an announcement that the Chinese embassy had arrived. They had landed on the coast of Wakasa with difficulty in this cold weather and then traveled inland to Echizen Town. They were staying at a villa near their compatriots in the Matsubara guesthouse. An elegantly worded Chinese poem of greeting was addressed to the Honorable Governor of Echizen from the delegation leader, a man named Shū Seishō. At least that was how I read his name looking over Father's shoulder. Father corrected me to say it the Chinese way – Jyo Shichang.

Trepidation tempering his excitement, Father put on his official robes to go welcome them. Here would be an educated Chinese official, the sort of person the merchants said would be able to appreciate his poems. I fervently hoped it was true. I was in a nervous state all day until Father came home jubilant. Master Jyo was indeed a scholar who appeared delighted by Father's Chinese poem of welcome. Further-more, when this gentleman spontaneously composed one in response, Father happily exclaimed that it was just like a scene in the classics. I could tell he was immensely relieved. He told me he had invited Master Jyo and his four companions to our house as a gesture of hospitality.

Along with three officials whose names I didn't quite catch, Master Jyo was traveling with his son, a slender young man

107

who looked to be about my age. Observing protocol, I had to remained behind screens as they talked. I gathered that they had been living in Japan for the past five years, most of the time in Miyako in the practically deserted grand embassy halls on Suzaku Avenue. The son, whose name was Meikoku (or Ming-gwok, as I later learned to say it in Chinese), spoke excellent Japanese and seemed very cultured. While our fathers toasted each other with cups of saké, discussing parallel imagery in the poetic form called the *fu*, I made bold to speak to the young man Ming-gwok, and so, hesitantly at first, we began a conversation about places in the capital.

After a while he asked me why I had to sit behind the screen so he couldn't see my face, and I hardly knew what to say. No one had ever asked me such a thing.

—Chinese women don't use screens, then? I asked.

—No, they don't, said Ming-gwok. It seems rather silly.

Again, I was taken aback and felt my face get hot. What should I do? I would be mortified to embarrass Father in front of his guests, but here was this polite Chinese man saying I was behaving in a silly fashion. I tried to discover whether Father had been following our little exchange, but it seemed he was completely engrossed in his conversation with Master Jyo. Hesitantly I pushed the screen partly to one side and found myself looking into clear curious eyes over which hovered a pair of beautiful moth eyebrows that would have been the envy of any woman.

Looking over the top edge of my fan, I noticed he had a straight, rather high-bridged nose and a nice mouth. He was smiling almost conspiratorially. Perhaps his face was a little too slender to be considered really handsome, but it was an intriguing face. He was wearing a dark blue silk robe lined in gray squirrel fur, cut more narrowly than Japanese dress, as were his white silk trousers. The sleeves were not as wide as ours, either. Like his father, he wore a close-fitting neat black scholar's cap with tails that looked like swallows' wings.

Our fathers didn't notice us. There I sat, my face most intimately exposed, while Ming-gwok simply took it for granted. I continued to hold my fan in front of my nose, but as we talked I began to forget that he was a man and a stranger, and several times even lowered my fan in amazement at things he said. Ming-gwok was astonishingly knowledgeable about our country and about Miyako. And he didn't behave at all like a Japanese man would have under the circumstances. When he mentioned the pines of Oshio, southwest of Miyako near the Ohara Shrine, I nearly swooned with surprise, and I showed him the poem I had written just the other day, recalling that very scene. Not only had Ming-gwok been there, he even knew it was the family shrine for the Fujiwara clan. Then, to my surprise, he dashed off the following response to my poem:

Oshioyama   matsuba no uwaba ni   kyou ya sa wa   mine no usuyuki   hana to miyuramu
If today on Oshio Mountain snow were to dust the pine
*   needles, I would say the frosting on the peaks would*
*   seem like blossoms.*

I was astounded – not only at the speed with which he composed it but at his sensitivity in picking up my images. I had to remind myself that Ming-gwok was not Japanese. Despite the fact that we Japanese apply great effort to the study of Chinese literature, it had never occurred to me that a Chinese would bother to learn our forms of expression. He brushed off my exclamations with a charming shrug, saying that my poem reminded him of a line from Fan Yun's "Song of Parting":

Long ago, when I left, the snow was like flowers
Now, when I return, the flowers are like snow.

Only later did it strike me that he had also perfectly illustrated the parallel poetic structure our fathers had been discussing! I began to think perhaps the winter in Echizen wouldn't be quite so bleak, after all.

Every other day Father made a trip to the Chinese villa, or else they came to ours. I did not raise any discussion about accompanying him – I simply got ready and waited in the carriage as if there were no question but that I go, too. Father

109

had found a soulmate in Master Jyo. They happily spent hours drinking and composing couplets in Chinese. Father enthused about his exquisite manners and compared him to a famous Han-dynasty philosopher. He even wrote things like that in his reports back to the capital. I doubted whether he was learning much that would be of use to Michinaga, but he was certainly living out the dream of his scholar-poet ideal. I went along with him in order to spend time with Ming-gwok.

By now it was very cold in Echizen. In my Chinese calendar we entered the phase called *The Tiger Begins to Roam*. Ming-gwok had actually seen a real tiger! I had imagined such a beast to be like a large fierce dog, but he said tigers were much more graceful than any dog.

—Imagine a cat as large as a dragon, and you will have an idea of a tiger, he said. When the weather gets very cold, their prey becomes scarce, so tigers have to roam farther and farther in search of food.

He knew so much about so many things. There are no tigers in Japan, of course.

One day I had taken my thirteen-string koto out and set up its bridges in a Chinese tuning. I intended to practice longer, but my fingers became so stiff that I left the instrument out while I went to warm my hands at the hibachi. Just then, Ming-gwok arrived with his father and their retainers. He spied the koto sitting out and asked me to play something. It was really too embarrassing. Not only was I out of practice, but the notion of playing for an audience of Chinese connoisseurs was incapacitating. I demurred, falling back on the excuse that my fingers were frozen. There was an awkward silence and then Ming-gwok asked if he might try the instrument. I was only too glad to relinquish my place and I handed him a set of bamboo finger picks.

Ming-gwok ran his fingers across the strings.

—A familiar mode, he remarked. Let's see whether you know this piece.

He proceeded to play a composition in the modality in which I had set the bridges. The tune was familiar yet different.

110

—That was "Harusugi," said my father when he had finished. "Remembrance of Springs Past," but you have added embellishments I have never heard before. Well done, young man!

He was beaming delightedly. Master Jyo, however, did not smile.

—That's enough, he said gruffly to his son.

Ming-gwok said nothing and meekly removed the picks from his fingers. Father appeared slightly bewildered at this stern display.

—My son has spent too much time playing frivolous songs, explained Master Jyo. Better he should have practiced the *gu ghim* and learned its subtleties.

My father was intrigued, for the seven-string *gu ghim*, or *kinnokoto* as we call it, was his own musical love.

—And Master Jyo, he inquired, do you play the venerable *gu ghim*?

Master Jyo admitted that he had indeed devoted some time to this instrument, although he claimed to be but an amateur. Father then had his manservant fetch his own seven-string koto from his room. He carefully unwrapped its silk bindings and placed it before Master Jyo.

—Please favor us with a tune, he begged.

And so Master Jyo played. The room was totally silent except for the singing, whispering, plaintive notes that emerged from the seven strings under Master Jyo's skillful fingers. When the last note died away, Father sighed.

—Might I ask you for some pointers on vibrato? he ventured. I have never heard such depth, such a range, as you have just demonstrated.

Master Jyo graciously complied. Later I wrote down all I remembered of what he said, for the lecture he proceeded to give was quite detailed.

—I shall discuss the type of vibrato known as *ngim*, he began. There are more than ten varieties of *ngim*, but these are the most useful. First, the finger of the left hand moves quickly up and down over the note.

He demonstrated.

—This is known as "a cold cicada bemoans the coming of

111

autumn." The cicada's sad, rocking drone should be imitated. Then there is the "long *ngim*," a drawn-out vibrato that recalls the cry of a dove announcing rain. The "thread *ngim*" is a thin vibrato. It should make the listener think of confidential whispering. The "playful *ngim*" is a swinging sort of vibrato evoking the image of fallen blossoms floating down the stream.

Master Jyo played a short passage to demonstrate each of these sounds. I could see my father trying frantically to absorb everything he said.

—Then, of course, most subtle is the "settled *ngim*," where one hardly moves the finger at all. Some handbooks say that the finger remains still but the timbre should be influenced by the pulsing of the blood in the fingertip as it presses the string down on the board a little more fully and heavily than usual.

He played a note and continued to listen intently, even when its echoes had become completely inaudible – to me at least. Father knitted his brows earnestly, sucking in his breath.

Master Jyo finally raised his finger from the board of the instrument.

—And the Daoists say, he remarked, the greatest music has the most tenuous notes.

As the days went by, I came to feel quite comfortable around Ming-gwok. He was taller than most Japanese men, and slender, and because his clothing did not stick out as much as our robes, he seemed more lithe and graceful. His father, Master Jyo, was serious and punctilious, except when drinking, but even then he always wore his scholar's hat. Ming-gwok didn't like to wear his unless he had to. When they came to our house, Ming-gwok slipped away to visit me as soon as he had made his formal greetings to my father. The first thing he did was remove his cap. He told me that the earliest explorers from China who had visited the land of Wa wrote about the primitive state of Japanese life, remarking that the men of our country were so barbaric they did not wear caps at all.

—That's one barbarian custom I like, he said, smoothing his hair.

Oddly enough, I learned many things about Japan from Ming-gwok. I hadn't even realized that in ancient times our country had been ruled by a queen.

Ming-gwok's family was from Jianzhou in the northern part of China. He said that when his father was sent on a mission to the land of Wa, his family despaired at the thought of his spending so much time in a barbarian place. I realized with shock that they felt about going to Miyako the same way my stepmother felt about going to Echizen! Of course, Ming-gwok hastened to add when he saw the surprise on my face, Japan has changed a lot since the first Chinese explorers came. It was now a very civilized place, with much to interest a person, even a Chinese. Since he came here he had come to realize that, although most Chinese would probably never believe him.

It did shake up one's sense of things to think that the city one had always regarded as the center of civilization was someone else's hinterland. If Miyako was but a periphery to the Chinese, imagine what they would have thought of Echizen! Suddenly I found myself burning with embarrassment. But Ming-gwok did not seem to scorn my company. On the contrary, although the situation was exceptional, it seemed he sought my company as much as I sought his.

THE SNOW, THE MOON

Setsu getsu

Ming-gwok and I fell into an easy routine of visits, and I now began to appreciate Echizen. Back in Miyako I would never have been able to converse freely with a man without setting up curtains and screens in order to keep up appearances. Even the snow didn't bother me so much now. One day there was such a great snowstorm that I assumed the Chinese would not come, even though Father had been planning a get-together. I was scuffing about the house glumly when I heard the children shout that visitors had arrived.

I rushed to the verandah to see the group of five Chinese and two servants, all wearing high deerskin boots, stomping though the deep snow. Ming-gwok's cheeks were bright pink from the cold, and his breath came out of his mouth in little frozen puffs. The children, bundled in mounds of padded clothing, tumbled out the gate to meet them in the courtyard. And then, instead of coming directly in, Ming-gwok reached down with both hands and scooped up a little ball of snow. He packed some more on to it and, without warning, tossed it at Nobumichi. The child was so surprised he just stood there, mouth hanging open. Ming-gwok made another ball of snow and handed it to him, then quickly made one more and lobbed it at the dog who was running about barking excitedly. Nobumichi threw the snowball at his little brother and then made his own. Although the Chinese usually intimidated him, even Nobunori came out and joined the snow battle.

Watching them, I felt a pang of regret that I could not join in. At one point little Jōsen tripped and fell into a snowdrift. Ming-gwok was first to his side, setting him upright like a stuffed doll, quieting his howls. Finally he picked him up and carried him, snot streaming from both nostrils, over to the verandah to the arms of a waiting housemaid. I was standing behind a wooden storm door, which I had moved ajar a few inches in order to see out. Ming-gwok caught my eye and smiled.

—Why don't you come out? he said soundlessly, moving his lips.

I covered my mouth with my sleeve, laughing. Then I wondered if he was serious. Could a Chinese woman have played openly in the snow? Somehow I doubted it.

Laughing and shouting, they finally moved into the foyer and shook off their snowy boots and overcoats. Jōsen kept calling the dog Snowball, a name that then stuck – never mind that the dog was brown. Even Father was affected by the ruddy good humor of it all, standing on the side with Master Jyo. Of course neither of them threw a snowball.

The Chinese had brought a treat. Calling for hot water, Master Jyo proposed to show my father the new style of tea-drinking that was gaining vogue in China. In Echizen we had become quite accustomed to drinking tea, a habit adopted from our Chinese friends. From Ming-gwok I learned that the best vessel from which to drink the infusion was a porcelain cup glazed the colour of a thrush's egg.

—The blue of the cup makes the green of the tea look more inviting, he explained. A white cup makes the tea look pinkish and muddy.

That day, however, they had brought an altogether different kind of tea. Instead of the dried brick of roasted tea leaves which we drank boiled in salted water, this tea was a glowing green fine powder, spooned into a dark brown ceramic bowl. Hot water was added without salt, and the brew then whipped with a whisk of split bamboo. The resulting mix was quite potent. Even the color was intoxicating – especially in winter when there was nothing fresh and green outdoors. To see that verdant bowlful was a reminder that spring would eventually return. Since each season felt more intense in Echizen, I could only look forward in wonder to the unfolding of spring.

In the afternoon it snowed again, so we invited the Chinese to spend the night rather than attempt to tramp back through the deepening drifts. My stepmother pulled out every bit of clothing we had brought from home, laying it all out in the reception room. She was pleased at the way the Chinese admired her trousseau silks.

—You see, she pointed out to my father, wasn't it a good idea to have brought these things along, after all? What kind of an impression would we have made on these gentlemen if we didn't have proper bedding to offer?

With good humor, my father praised her farsightedness and sent her off, gratified, to put the children to bed.

Now that we had been in Echizen for a while, my stepmother had taken firm charge of the household. Loosed from her mother's meddling, she had learned to make

115

decisions on her own, and it was not long before she discovered the satisfaction of exercising her will. The heretofore mouthless gardenia turned into a nag.

Perhaps it was the effect of the luxuriously green tea, but I had trouble falling asleep that night, even though we all retired quite late. The moon had also risen late, a few days past full, and the snow had stopped falling. It was a bright windless night. I was conscious of the large room packed with our sleeping guests – no, I must admit, I was keenly aware that Ming-gwok was sleeping in my house, so close by. I got up and pushed open the storm door to look at the moon. To my surprise, Ming-gwok was sitting there on the verandah.

—Why don't you come out? he repeated his invitation from earlier in the day.

—Would a Chinese girl do that? I asked.

—If I asked her to, he lied.

—Well then, I said, knowing full well that he was joking, I will.

—Wait, he said. Take these things and put them on. You'll find it will be a lot easier.

He pushed a bundle through the door I had unlatched. I had the distinct feeling that he had been waiting for me. Ducking back into my room, I unwrapped the carrying cloth and found a set of Chinese padded trousers, fur-lined jacket, and leather boots. I tied my long hair back with a cord and tucked it into the trousers, which, in the Chinese style, only reached my ankles instead of trailing like our trousers. It felt strange for my feet to be uncovered. I tried on the boots. They were very large so I took them off and put on a pair of my brother's cloth boots first, then pulled the Chinese ones over them. This was better – now they would stay on my feet. Finally I tried on the jacket over my white underrobe. Its sleeves bunched up under the close-fitting arms, and the hems stuck out below.

—Come on!

Ming-gwok had moved right up to my door.

—Be quiet! I whispered.

Unfastening the jacket, I took off the robe and put his jacket back on over my naked skin. The fur was soft, but it

116

felt very strange to be so narrowly attired. I was not used to having my arms encased.

—I'm coming, I whispered back, and pushed the door open enough to squeeze out on to the verandah.

—Here, one more thing.

Ming-gwok was wearing a hat lined with fur. He pulled a similar one out of his jacket and put it on my head.

—It's cold here in barbarian country, he said.

He took my hand and we stepped noiselessly to the end of the balustrade. At the edge, Ming-gwok jumped off into the snow, and since I was holding his hand, I jumped, too. I must have jumped into a pile of snow at some point when I was small, because it was not a totally unfamiliar feeling, but I was not as graceful as Ming-gwok, and landed in a heap. Snickering not unkindly, he pulled me to my feet and brushed off the snow. I was gasping and laughing at the novelty of – well, the whole thing.

We began walking toward a bamboo grove on a hill behind the house on the side facing away from town. The tall bamboos were thickly garbed in snow and cast deep shadows in the moonlight. Every so often one would let slip its robe of snow to fall to the ground with a thump, startling in the soft white silence. I grasped Ming-gwok's hand more tightly, and we walked on without speaking for a while.

I was reminded of an autumn night long ago when Chifuru and I stayed up under a bright late moon. I never thought I would feel about a man the way I felt about Chifuru (or Ruri, or Kerria Rose, for that matter). I had been enthralled by Korechika, but he was so far removed from my world that he might as well be an apparition. Genji was more real to me than Korechika, but, of course, he was my own fiction. Ming-gwok was a real person – and yet he wasn't, in a way. He was such a complete outsider that I hardly knew how to compose my feelings toward him. Strangely, though, I was totally at ease in his presence. To be able to be silent with someone is, I think, the ultimate test of a karmic connection.

—You know, Ming-gwok said, his voice rippling through the silence, I have come to find black teeth attractive, though at first they seemed very creepy to me.

—Don't Chinese ladies stain their teeth? I asked.

—Never, he replied. They pluck their eyebrows and draw ones that look like moth antennae higher on their foreheads, just as you Japanese do, but black teeth – never.

—You don't think it's barbaric, then? I asked him.

—Not any more, he said, lightly touching my cheek.

We walked on in a world of shadows. Every bit of color had been buried in the deep whiteness that reflected innumerable shades of gray behind the glistening pools of moonlight. Ming-gwok said the bright moon reminded him of a Chinese tale. As we wandered, he told it to me, and, as I remember, the story went like this:

Once there was a man named Wang Tziyu who lived a hermit's life, away from the mundane cares of society. He took great joy in viewing the spring blossoms and the autumn moon. Being deeply sensitive to the beauty of things, he was struck one winter evening by the pure moonlight shining down after a heavy snow. The sight so stirred his heart he wished he could share the experience with a friend. So he took his boat and began poling down the river to visit Dai Andao.

Well, it was a very long way, so by the time Wang arrived at his friend's cottage, dawn was breaking. The mood was now entirely different from what had inspired him to set out in the first place. Just as he reached his friend's gate, Wang turned around and went home, without even a word of greeting to Dai.

—That's very strange, I said. Why did he do that?

—That's what all the people asked Wang, said Ming-gwok, crunching the snow with his boots.

—Wang told them a poem, which I don't remember the exact wording of, but in effect it went: "I had set my mind and hurried off to view the moon with a friend. Though we did not meet face-to-face, why should the pleasure be less?"

—This, dear Fuji, shows how vastly refined and sensitive this person Wang was. Personally I prefer meeting you face-to-face to view the moon with, but then, I am not such a sensitive person.

Ming-gwok took my cold hands and pressed them to his chest under his fur-lined jacket. He buried his nose in the hair that had blown free at the edge of my cap. I teased him that he was indeed insensitive if he could endure my icy hands against his warm skin, but he shook his head and I felt his warm breath on my neck.

We found a bank of snow that had drifted into a soft hill.

—Watch, said Ming-gwok.

He stood facing me and spread his arms. Then he fell backward into the drift.

—What are you doing? I said.

—Try it, he answered from the snow. The quiet is amazingly loud.

I thought maybe this was some Chinese winter custom, and I followed his example. Holding my arms out – so strange not to have wide sleeves hanging from them – I allowed myself to fall backward. The tips of our outstretched fingers just touched. The snow held me like a child's doll in a pose. It was very still, and indeed, the sense of silence was almost physical. An owl hooted. Another bamboo let fall its burden of snow. The soft sounds only emphasized the deep quiet. Words seemed unnecessary.

Eventually we got cold, and Ming-gwok helped me up. We made out way back to the house, taking care to stay in the shadows as much as possible. Dawn had not quite broken, and the pale yellow moon now hung low in the western sky. When we reached the edge of the verandah, Ming-gwok boosted me, then pulled himself up. We crept along to the spot outside the reception room where the guests were sleeping, and he quietly let himself back in. I continued to the door outside my room and was about to do the same when I heard my father cough. I did see his storm door move slightly? I ducked into my room, my heart fluttering.

Quickly I peeled off the wet Chinese clothing and hid it. My skin was hot but my hair retained the cold from outside. At one point my cap had fallen off and Ming-gwok took my loose hair into his slender white fingers and buried his face in it. He said someday he would send me some of the Chinese perfumed oil his mother used. I lay down under my pile of padded robes, but left my cold hair outside the quilts, spread in tangled disarray. My dreams were tumbled in disarray as well.

Kurokami no   chisuji no kami no   midaregami   katsu omoimidare   omoimidaruru
A thousand strands of black hair, tangled hair – like them
  my thoughts, tangling and entangled.

Ming-gwok was like no one I'd ever met. There we were walking by ourselves in the moonlight, in the snow, in Echizen. If I were to write such a scene in Genji, people would dismiss it as unbelievable. I remembered I had once gotten into a terrible argument with Ruri about not introducing impossible things into Genji. Now I had come to see that reality could be more unreal than anything one could dream up in fiction.

THE EAST WIND MELTS THE ICE

Higashikaze

Spring came. The first seasonal of the new year was *The East Wind Melts the Ice*, followed by *Larvae Twitch in Their Cocoons*. It was still cold in Echizen, but one could smell the change of season in the air. We were kept unusually busy with the new year rituals, because, as the emperor's representative, Father had responsibility for maintaining the decorum of civilization in the province. In a rare moment of leisure he told me that he had written to Nobutaka, and I blanched. I didn't dare ask what he had written, for I was almost certain that he saw me sneaking home that snowy night, although he never mentioned it. Actually the only thing he inquired was whether I had started corresponding with Nobutaka myself.

Feeling guilty about my promise to do so, yet unmoved to write anything like a love poem, I copied some Genji stories and sent those to Nobutaka along with a letter of thanks for his gift of that Shōnagon woman's pillow book. I still avoided writing anything more personal, and I requested him not to show my stories to anyone else.

Soon thereafter, I received a letter from Nobutaka saying that he wanted to come meet the Chinese in the New Year. "I want to tell them," he started pointedly, "that everything melts in the spring." Then I was quite sure that Father had said something in his letter. Could Nobutaka seriously be threatening to come to Echizen? After much fretting, I composed this poem and sent it to him:

Haru naredo   Shirane no mi yuki   iya tsumori   tokubeki hodo no   itsu to naki kana
It may be spring but snow is till mounded thick on Mount Shirane – not likely to melt away anytime soon.

Usually I showed my poems to Father, but since this one was rather rude, I sent it on my own. Knowing it was not in Father's nature to force me into anything, I took liberties. After all, if Nobutaka didn't like my poem, he could always terminate things. I persuaded myself that I was keeping my part of the bargain by writing at all.

By the time of the spring equinox in the second month, I was intoxicated with the beauty of this magnificent season. Even the renowned *sakura* of Yoshino back home could not compare to the mountains full of blooming wild cherries with their sweet fragrance. The people of Echizen called them birch cherries. As I continued to write about the various women Genji took up with, I often thought of them in terms of flowering plants, for it had always seemed to me that plants have personalities just as people do. I saved the idea of the birch cherry. Later, when I imagined the character Murasaki, the child whom Genji discovered and then concealed to raise as his perfect woman, I put a birch cherry in her garden.

But generally that spring I let Genji languish. It was hard to concentrate on creating adventures for him when my own life itself had become a fantasy out of an imaginary romance. Father turned a blind eye when Ming-gwok and I slipped away for hours alone in the fragrant hills. This was not Miyako, so we did not need to worry about gossips. We seldom saw anyone, except once or twice a woodcutter who immediately ran away, probably thinking he had seen a pair of ghosts. We had a favorite place, a small clump of wild cherry trees near a stream. The blossoms were so thick that we were hidden entirely as soon as we lay down on the mossy ground.

We collected images to fashion into poems. Ming-gwok told me the story of the Chinese poet Li He, who went riding off on his donkey with a tattered brocade bag slung over his back. When he found an inspiration, he immediately wrote it down and threw it into his sack. Then, when he got home, Li He emptied out his bag of treasures – like a bag of fragrant mushrooms, said Ming-gwok – and worked them into poems.

Waking life was like a dream. Only when I was alone at night did guilty voices assail my conscience. I was a most unfilial daughter. My father had arranged a very advantageous match for me, and what did I do but wriggle out of it. I had agreed to begin a relationship with Nobutaka by corresponding, yet I avoided even that, writing just enough to barely fulfill the terms of my promise. The idea that the daughter of a person of my father's position would be intimately involved with a foreigner was so astonishing that I'm quite sure no one ever considered it. In any case, I could only abandon myself to the force of the karmic connection pulling me toward Ming-gwok, for no matter how short a time. We were keenly conscious as we gazed up at the cherry petals, already beginning to let go one by one, that this dreamworld was brief.

The wild beauty of the countryside inspired me to unearth a sketch book I had hardly touched since arriving in Echizen. Mostly I liked to draw flowers and plants, although I did try to depict some of the odd peasant dwellings we saw on our journey to Echizen. I drew only in private because I was embarrassed by my lack of skill.

Ming-gwok surprised me at my desk one day. I was engrossed in sketching a cherry blossom and didn't hear the group of Chinese arrive. I had no idea how long he had been watching me and was mortified. I tried to shuffle my drawings out of sight, but he sat down beside me and quietly pulled my sleeve aside.

—Please let me see, he asked. You never told me you drew things.

—My chicken scratchings hardly deserve the term, I said lightly, for he seemed so serious. I scribble, that's all. People have always criticized my drawings, so I don't let anyone see.

—But you write so well, how can they not be good? Ming-gwok persisted.

I had showed him my Genji stories and he seemed to find them interesting.

—I had painting lessons when I was a child in China, he continued. And my father is actually something of an artist. I'll show you his sketches sometime. He has been keeping a journal on this trip to help him make his report to the emperor after we return home.

Neither of us had ever mentioned leaving Echizen before this. I suppose because it was inevitable, there was no need to speak of it. Still, it gave me a frisson to think that the time was coming, probably soon, when I would never see Ming-gwok again.

—What are you thinking about, Fuji? Will you lend me your brush or not?

I guess I hadn't heard his offer to show me how he would draw a cherry blossom. Shaking off my sudden glum chill, I handed Ming-gwok the brush and a clean sheet of paper.

He examined the brush.

—This is all right for writing, he stated. But don't you have anything a little fatter for drawing?

I pulled out my box of brushes and showed him everything I had. He picked out two others, saying that they would do, although next time he would bring some proper ones, and when he got back to China, he would send me some really fine ones. Then he examined the wild birch cherry I had brought in and placed in a vase on my writing table.

—These are quite different from the cherries in Miyako, he remarked.

—Yes, they have a fragrance, I said.

—But also more petals per flower, and the buds are a different shape.

He concentrated for another minute, then began to draw. I was astonished at what he produced.

—Those really are wild cherry blossoms, I said admiringly. Ming-gwok put down the brush.

—It's a question of drawing what you see, not what you think you see, he said.

I laughed.

—Does that mean you couldn't paint anything imaginary? I asked him.

—Not at all, he replied. I can see with my eyes closed, too.

To demonstrate, he sketched a picture of a tale he told me one snowy night in winter, the one about the hermit Wang poling his boat down the river toward his friend Dai's house. I was speechless. With a few skillful strokes he captured the posture, the essence, of man, boat, and river – and the river wasn't even sketched!

—You are the king of drawing, I told him in all seriousness. He snorted.

—There are some tricks, he said. Of course when you practice, it becomes easier. You can draw these things, too. I can show you what my teacher showed me.

I reminded him that I was notorious in my family for being good at words, bad at pictures. He dismissed that as nonsense.

—Being good at words means you can handle a brush. That's the main thing. If I can be frank, Fuji – and please don't take this personally – the things your countrymen praise in the way of painting seem rather clumsy to Chinese eyes.

He was primarily referring to the paintings in illustrated story scrolls, I think.

—Granted the colors can be rather nice, if you like that kind of decoration, and the composition has its charm, but Japanese drawing itself – if that is the standard people criticize you for not attaining, all the better! You should be aspiring to a different standard.

In China, I came to understand, the most noble genre of

painting is the landscape. Painters practice drawing all manner of things like trees, rocks, clouds, flowers, and buildings, but none of that makes a difference if you can't compose them all into a scene. Composition is what distinguishes a great painter.

Ming-gwok's father was an amateur landscape painter. Along with collecting rocks, painting was his great passion. Ming-gwok did not share his interest in stones but had absorbed his love of painting. He had been drawing since childhood. Someday, he said, he would attempt landscapes, but he was not ready yet. He still needed more practice at the elements.

Hesitantly I asked whether he would teach me, and he agreed.

I suggested grass orchids, something I felt confident of, but Ming-gwok waved his hand in contempt.

—Boring. Five-year-olds do grass orchids.

He decided to begin my lesson with drawing the dog. So we went out into the courtyard and he called for Snowball.

—Notice the way he walks toward us, lifting his head expecting a treat, said Ming-gwok. Remember that.

Then he picked up a stick.

—See how he crouches and waits.

Ming-gwok tossed the stick and Snowball ran joyfully after it. He brought it back and barked for Ming-gwok to throw it again.

—See how his tail lifts when he's excited.

I was surprised at the things I had never been aware of before in the simple actions of a dog. Finally Snowball got tired and went to lie down in a patch of sunlight. I saw how his head rested on his paws and his tail curled around his hindquarters. Such an expressive thing, a dog's tail. I had never noticed it before.

We went back to my room for brushes and paper. Ming-gwok drew Snowball in the various poses we had observed. I copied his drawings. As we worked, Ming-gwok asked me if I had ever heard the Chinese story about two girls and a spotted dog.

—Remind me to tell you when we're finished, he said.

Just then Nobunori came clumping noisily down the hallway.

—They've hatched! he called out loudly. My mantises have hatched!

He was carrying one of his insect cages, and it was spilling over with tiny, fresh-green preying mantis hatchlings. My stepmother had ordered him to take the cage outside before they all escaped in the house. Back in Miyako she had been too shy even to look at her stepson. Ming-gwok asked Nobunori whether he might see some of his insects, and, flattered, my brother led him off to his room.

I continued to practice drawing until Ming-gwok came back some time later with various cages holding a grasshopper, a beetle, and an adult mantis. He took a sheet of paper and began to draw. After making me copy his sketches, he gave the original portraits to my brother when he returned the caged insects. Nobunori was thrilled. After this, he ceased making backhanded comments about the Chinese, Ming-gwok in particular, as he used to do in order to annoy me.

We rinsed our brushes and put our drawings away. The warm spring air was making us drowsy. I lay my head on Ming-gwok's lap and reminded him that he was going to tell me a Chinese tale about a spotted dog. I hardly knew what to make of the strange story he proceeded to relate.

TALES OF CHINA

Kara Monogatari

—Once upon a time, he began, there lived in the capital a couple who had an only daughter. They moved to a small village so as to bring her up untainted by corrupt influences. When the girl came of age, her parents arranged for her to be married. But so carefully had they raised her, exposed to nothing so much as a strong breeze, that the maiden was repelled at the very thought of marriage.

—Did she threaten to cut her hair and put on nun's robes? I asked.

—Oh, you know this story? inquired Ming-gwok.

—No, just guessing, I said.

For a moment it occurred to me that this tale might be one of Ming-gwok's jokes. I had told him about the scene with my father when I threatened to take vows unless he let me come to Echizen.

—Yes, she claimed she would renounce the world, and then she ran away. She took along one companion – her best friend, the daughter of her nursemaid, who was a beautiful girl like her mistress. The two of them journeyed deep into the mountains where they each built a reed hut and lived happily with only one another for company.

Again, I wondered whether Ming-gwok was making something up to tease me. I had told him many things I had never revealed to anyone before – such as my deep feelings for Chifuru and other women, and my terrible experience with the lieutenant of the archery. Yet it wasn't his nature to be cruel, so I kept quiet and let him continue.

—Stop squirming, said Ming-gwok. Get comfortable and I'll go on.

—Sorry.

—Then one day the girl's parents made their way through the forest and finally found their dwellings. The girl shed tears of bitter guilt on seeing them, yet she was still not moved to return no matter how they tried to convince her. Finally they gave up and left the girls to themselves.

—Sometimes parents really don't have a clue when it comes to understanding their children, remarked Ming-gwok, interrupting his own story. They are at a complete loss as to how to deal with them.

I was lucky to have a father like mine, but I realized this was rather unusual. I sensed that Ming-gwok did not agree with his father on many things, and that tension was growing between them.

—My great-grandfather wrote a famous poem on that subject, I said, quoting:

127

Hito no oya no   kokoro no yami ni   aranedomo   ko wo omou michi ni   madoinuru kana

*A parent's heart does not seek the darkness, yet will it lose
its way in thinking about his child.*

—That's Kanesuke's poem, said Ming-gwok in surprise.
It's from the second imperial poetry collection – your great-
grandfather?

We were both amazed: he, that Kanesuke was my ancestor;
I, that he recognized the poem. But by then I should have
ceased being surprised at Ming-gwok's knowledge of our
literature.

—You must understand, he continued. That's a sentiment
that could hardly even be expressed in Chinese.

—What do you mean?

—Oh, the very idea that a parent might not be able to
understand his child – or perhaps I should say, the idea that a
child might have his own reasons for doing what he does. In
our country the parent is always correct, and there is no
possibility of the child defying parental wishes. Of course
there are stories where such things happen, but always with
dire results. It upsets the order of heaven, you see.

—But we Japanese also believe that a child ought to obey
his parent's wishes, I protested.

—So why aren't you back in Miyako, married to
Nobutaka? Ming-gwok asked.

I sat up abruptly.

—Why are you asking me that? I said reproachfully. It will
happen soon enough.

Ming-gwok extended his hand.

—Sorry, I shouldn't have said that. I had an argument with
my father last night, and I guess it's still bothering me.

—An argument?

—Yes. We have to return to China next month.

—Oh. I see.

Ming-gwok was silent for a moment. I felt he was
struggling whether to say something else but finally decided
against it.

—Come back here, he said instead, pretending to scold.

He took hold of my hair and gently pulled.

—I'll tell you the rest of the story. I haven't even gotten to the dog. So one day a dog came around to where the girls were living . . .

—What kind of dog?

—A handsome dog. It settled in front of the nursemaid's daughter's reed hut, and since she was rather bored, she fed it and showed it affection. One day while holding the dog on her lap, she allowed it to lick her breasts, and she found her feelings toward the animal growing more involved and difficult to control.

—Ming-gwok, are you making this up?

—I swear I'm not, he protested.

—Pretty soon, there was not a barrier left between them, if you know what I mean. The girl recognized that this affection was excessive and rather unsavory, but she couldn't help herself. She told herself it must be due to some previous deep karmic connection.

—Ming-gwok!

—Hey, I'm teaching you the Chinese classics.* Don't interrupt the teacher.

I had experienced Ming-gwok's odd sense of humor many times by now, but still sometimes I wondered. He continued with a perfectly straight face.

—Since the girl went often to her friend's hut, she became curious about the scratch marks on her companion's shoulders. They were clearly visible through her thin summer robes. She pressed her friend to tell her what caused them, but the girl was too embarrassed to reveal her relationship with the dog.

—Finally, unable to avoid the incessant questioning, the maid's daughter told her mistress to come visit her hut if she wanted to see the source of the marks. And then, even though she knew she was being observed, she still got into bed with the dog. When she saw them together, far from being repelled, the other girl felt a pang of loneliness, and so she summoned

*The story Ming-gwok told Murasaki is indeed strange, but he did not make it up. It can be found in a collection known as *Tales from China (Kara Monogatari)* that appeared in Japan in the twelfth century.

the dog to come to her hut as well. She found him to be a loving animal indeed.

—That's disgusting. Is that the end?

—No. There's a moral.

—Is this what comes of not following your parents' wishes? I asked. Being reduced to utter depravity?

—That would be the Chinese moral, yes.

—I would say it was the parents' fault originally for shielding the girl so completely that she was unprepared for normal life, I said.

Ming-gowk then recited the following:

Asamashi ya nado kedamono ni uchitokuru   sa koso mukashi no chigiri nari tomo
Is it so outrageous to make love with an animal? Even if that love must spring from karmic vows of former lives?

—Even though humans attempt to shun improper liaisons, when they result from such strong bonds of karma, how can they be avoided?

Ming-gwok made this statement in the manner of a priest intoning a moral tale.

—Don't you want to know the dog's name? he asked, switching to his own voice.

—I'm afraid to ask, I answered.

—Well, it was Snowball! replied Ming-gwok gleefully.

—Oh, you liar! I exclaimed.

—No, really, it was, he asserted. That's why I was reminded of this story.

—You are a strange one, I remarked.

I had no reason to think Ming-gwok would lie to me. His experience was so much broader than mine, there was nothing for it but to accept his word. True, he occasionally played on my gullibility, telling an outrageous story with a straight face, but he would always burst out laughing at my astonished expression and admit when he was joking.

Things I had always believed to be natural facts were not necessarily so, I was coming to see. Ming-gwok told me about his mother and sisters left behind in China while his father

130

carried out his mission abroad. His mother was beautiful, he said, but even more than her beauty his father valued her competence in family matters: overseeing the cooking, weaving, and most of all, caring for her parents-in-law.

—The very idea that a man would move into his wife's family's home, as you do in Japan, is horrifying to proper Chinese, Ming-gwok told me.

According to his father, "Wives take care of the practical things so that husbands may study." Yet Master Jyo, for all that he may have appreciated his wife's practicality, shared the common Chinese predilection for pubescent girls, according to Ming-gwok. Ming-gwok himself had been too young when they left China to have experienced the excursions to the Green Houses where dancers compressed their feet into tiny shoes curled up like new moons, but when he came of age, he father had regaled him with tales of the pleasures to be had in such places.

—One day, when I turned fifteen, my father gave me a book that explained various things about men and women, he said. The male is predominantly yang, the female, yin; but they need one another to achieve proper balance. It becomes rather a battle, you see, each trying to take from the other without giving up one's own essence. That is why men like young girls. They are not so strong – a woman's yin force is not fully developed until she reaches about twenty.

He looked at me.

—That doesn't seem quite fair, does it? Much better to spar with a partner who starts out with a full set of yin.

—Hmmm, I murmured, blushing at his frank discussion of something Japanese women think about in flowery euphemism, and certainly never discuss directly with men.

—Yes, ideally a man should have as many partners as possible, Ming-gwok continued. This is a well-known technique for increasing longevity. The man should be able to bring the woman to the point where her yin overflows with excitement, yet he himself holds his essence back so that it is reabsorbed and nourishes the brain.

—Very interesting, I said.

—Oh, I suppose so, replied Ming-gwok matter-of-factly,

but that is not the most interesting thing about men and women. Frankly your Genji stories do more to capture the mysterious bonds that ensnare the sexes than my Daoist technical manuals do.

I looked directly at him and my eyes filled with tears.

Not long after Ming-gwok told me the strange tale about Snowball, Father informed me that the Chinese had to leave Echizen right away. He appeared grim. To me, it felt as though my insides had been scooped away, leaving a hollow shell like those ghostly yellow husks left behind on tree trunks by departed cicadas.

—I fear the Council of State is preparing to declare war on China, Father said quietly. If Master Jyo is still here when that happens, I shall be obliged to arrest him.

The ignominy of taking his friend into custody offended my father's very nature. Yet if he warned the Chinese of the court's impending plans, he would be a traitor. I was aghast at the position he suddenly found himself in.

—I have sent Master Jyo a poem about the glory of returning to one's home village after the rigors of a military campaign, Father continued. I trust that he will understand.

Sure enough, a poem came in reply, and also a letter saying that the delegation would begin immediate preparation for departure.

Father arranged a picnic outing as a farewell party for the Chinese.* Everyone from Master Jyo's delegation, several of the shipwrecked merchants, our family, and two other Echizen officials and their families were included. My step-mother supervised the preparation of three dozen lacquered boxes of food.

We brought along our writing supplies. Father and Master

*It would have broken Tametoki's heart had he ever seen the report that Jyo Shichang made to the Chinese court upon his return. A section, forever preserved in volume 491 of the official *History of the Sung*, mentions Jyo's exchange of poetry with an unnamed Japanese official (circumstantially quite likely to have been Tametoki), whose efforts Jyo dismissed as 'shallow, ornate, and without interest."

Jyo were planning to compose lengthy farewell elegies of a formal nature. Ming-gwok and I were going to go off and draw. As a farewell present, Ming-gwok gave me a celadon brush rest in the shape of five mountains and a deep purple stone ink palette that his teacher had given him when he left China. He said he hoped I would think of him when I wrote about Genji.

—And I love that color, deep murasaki, he said.

EXILE

Nagashi

Once again I was alone, with only Genji to share my anguish. Even before coming to Echizen I had toyed with the idea of writing a story of Genji in exile. I had been musing on poor Korechika's fate at the time – dismayed when Michinaga ordered him away to the Suma coast. I had vaguely thought I might use Genji's affair with the Lady of the Night of the Hazy Moon to tie those stories together. Now, with Ming-gwok gone, I buried myself in Genji's troubles.

I reread my earlier drafts. My description of the palace machinations leading up to Genji's exile rang true. At the time I wrote that part, we had all been so caught up in the events surrounding the deaths, scandals, accusations, and curses that, after listening to Father's reports, I felt I could portray how palace intrigue might play itself out. Describing Genji's sad farewells to all of the ladies he had loved in the capital was not difficult, either. Once I had gotten Genji to Suma, however, I began to drift. From this point, I was dissatisfied with what I had written. I had no idea what I was talking about before I came to Echizen. Genji in exile was nothing but a shadow of what I had read in Bai Juyi – some sort of Chinese notion of poetic retreat. Back then I didn't know what exile felt like. It is always a mistake to write about something you don't know.

The worst aspect of exile is to be marooned in a place where no one can share your insights. Now that the Chinese had gone, there was nothing to brighten the weary days. Rusticity was no longer charming, it was wretched. When messengers came from Miyako to confer with Father, I took to detaining them shamelessly, pumping them for news of the most ordinary goings-on back in the city. Did they know the big weeping cherry by the river at Nijō Avenue? How was its bloom that spring? I hung on the words of dullards I would have squirmed to dismiss had I been forced to listen to them back home. Then I realized – this must be how Genji feels.

Now when I wrote of his despair in Suma, I understood.

On our arrival in Echizen, Father had ordered the residence completely renovated, plantings set out, a deep garden stream dug. He was enthusiastic about the quaint thatched structures, insisting that all the fences be maintained in their original style. The novelty *was* rather charming at first. I often thought that house would have made a pleasant retreat if it had been but a half day's trip from the capital. Now in its second season, the garden was beginning to take shape, but the more it took root, the more depressed I got. I didn't want to take root in Echizen.

A daily stream of local people came to work on Father's projects, bring provisions, or sometimes just gawk. Their habits were bizarre. One day our cook set out food for the gardeners when I happened to be looking out at the flowering trees. Although I felt I should avert my eyes, I was fascinated by the spectacle as they ingested their food. First, they picked up the bowls of rice and lifted them to their faces. When they put them down a moment later, the bowls were empty. They proceeded to do the same thing to the dishes of vegetables and condiments. It was very peculiar. I hardly knew whether such an activity should be called eating.

I thought it was probably not a good idea for the children to be exposed to this kind of thing.

One night a sudden wind sprang up, followed by a storm of demonic strength. The air crashed with thunder all night, and the raindrops battered the doors like an army sent by the dragon king of the sea. Plagued by nightmares of ships pitching in mountainous waves, I didn't sleep at all. I had kept an oil lamp by my bedside ever since Ming-gwok told me about the poet Wang Liqi's advice to do this in case you woke in the middle of the night:

—Get right up if you awake, said the poet. Inspiration must be seized precisely when your spirit is clear and vigorous.

I did light the lamp, but my spirit was hardly vigorous. And drafts blowing through the walls extinguished the flame before I could write anything.

In the fourth month a messenger I had never seen before appeared at the house. He had a packet for me alone. Father was suspicious. Thus far he had refrained from commenting on my sparse correspondence with Nobutaka. He had never said anything about Ming-gwok. With no need to speak, Father and I understood that I would eventually marry Nobutaka, and also that whatever had occurred in Echizen was merely a dream – real at the time but ultimately without substance. Father, too, had been moody since the Chinese left.

Unlike the official messengers from the capital, this private courier did not tarry long, refusing our offer of lodging. He accepted some food and water and then departed, claiming another delivery in the town. In the later afternoon Father called me to his study. The slender package lay unopened on the low table that served as his writing desk.

—You understand, Fuji, he said gently. They were strangers in a strange land.

I nodded, suddenly feeling guilty. I hung my head and my hair fell across my face, hiding my tears. Father was the only one who could even begin to understand, yet precisely because he was my father I could not confide in him. A wave of remorse washed over me at how selfish and unfilial I had been. Were I to judge my actions dispassionately, the enormity of my sins was staggering. Yet, even as I floundered in remorse it occurred to me that Father did understand. He could never say so, but somehow his silence and lack of reproach in the face of so much he could reproach me for spoke for itself.

Dusk was gathering, and we could hear the sharp voice of an early summer cuckoo calling from the woods. The sound brought back poignant memories.

—The Kamo Festival will be taking place in a few days, said Father. Perhaps it was a mistake, after all, to drag you to this uncivilized place. I didn't like the thought of being parted from you, Fuji, but now I'm afraid I acted selfishly.

My sniffling got louder.

Father cleared his throat.

—Perhaps we should think about arranging your trip home this year? he suggested. You don't need to decide right away, he added as I gulped back a sob.

So many reasons for tears. My head was in a daze. Guilt, sorrow, loneliness, and apprehension at the thought of marriage, mixed with joy at the thought of seeing the capital again. I covered my face with the thin silk of my white sleeve and sobbed. All this time Father sat there wordlessly, and I had the feeling he was using my tears to mourn his own loss of his great friendship with Master Jyo.

As we sat there, the shadows grew long, and eventually the room became dark. Hearing our voices, the servant had not dared enter to light the oil lamps. I could not see Father's face, nor he mine. At least the shadows helped to preserve my shredded dignity. As a thin new moon rose smoothly in the sky, I stumbled as I rose to go. Father spoke.

—Don't forget your letter, he said.

Back in my room, I lit the lantern and examined the packet. The outer wrapping was coarse tan bark-paper, and it was addressed from a place called Tsunokami. I unfolded this rough envelope and found a piece of smooth sturdy mulberry-bark paper with the following poem inscribed in Ming-gwok's distinctive hand:

Naniwagata   muretaru tori no   morotomo ni   tachiiru mono to   omowamashikaba
If only I could once again hope to be with you, just as the birds all flock together on the beaches of Naniwa.

He had written it en route; how long ago? I wondered. Was he still in Japan, or even now embarked on the dangerous sea journey back to his country? I wept, recalling the thunder-storm that had caused me a sleepless night. It was just as well it was impossible for me to answer. What could I have said?

A CLEAR DAY IN RAINY SEASON

Satsukibare

Mock orange came into bloom on the hillsides of Echizen just as it did in the capital. I thought in particular of a stretch along the route to the Kamo Shrine that was bordered in mock orange shrubs. Though the flowers are not particularly shapely, there is something pleasing about the way they cluster whitely against the dark green of the leaves, and the combination of those two colors, deep green and white, seems so cool at the beginning of hot weather. Perhaps my eye had become jaded from the glorious Echizen spring. For some reason the plant did not appear as interesting in the country-side. I could not even be sure it was the same flower until I gathered a branch to smell and check whether it had the hollow stem of the *u no hana*.

When the mock orange bloomed, I knew the long rains would soon be upon us. During this season my mother used to slip into depression, and I feared the same tendency in myself. Even in Miyako the incessant rain, *shi-to shi-to shi-to*, day after day, became dreary. It occurred to me to wonder whether my Chinese calendar mentioned long rains. When I checked, the closest thing was the last fortnight of spring, called Grain Rain – implying that the Chinese probably planted their rice during this season just as we do. But I no longer took for granted the commonly received notions about China. Ming-gwok said that where he came from, they didn't grow rice at all; they grew wheat and millet and barley. He liked rice, but was otherwise quite scathing about the food in our country. When presented with a bowl of delicately simmered vegetables, he once joked,

—This would be an excellent dish . . . for my horse.

Grain Rain encompassed three seasonals: a five-day period called *Floating Weeds Appear*, followed by *Doves Spread Their Wings*, and then by *The Phoenix Descends into the Mulberry*. Every aspect of the Chinese calendar reminded me of Ming-gwok. I thought of how he liked the image of the phoenix and clouds. He once gave me a piece of brocade with that pattern, and afterward I always associated it with him.

I continued to look for examples of Chinese rain. Summer, starting in the fourth month, was full of damp images. First came a five-day seasonal called *Peepers Sing*; then five days as *Earthworms Come Out*; then *Cucumber Flourishes*. Frogs, earthworms, and cucumbers all had a moist nature, but long, depressing rains apparently were not a feature of Chinese weather. Their Great Rains didn't sweep through until the very end of summer. If only Ming-gwok were still here, I sighed. I could have asked him whether the Chinese suffered from ennui the way we Japanese do.

It was early summer, yet the skies in Echizen were still sunny. Did I dare hope the rains of Echizen would be less dreary than those in Miyako? I could smell smoke faintly in the air. I thought it came from the fishermen's fires as they burned seaweed for salt, but Father said it was smoldering brushwood from huts in the mountains behind the house. It was a faintly acrid but not unpleasant smell. I made a note to myself to try adding a hint of bitterness to the sweet fumes of my incense blends. It might make them more interesting.

The rains did come, of course, pounding the fallen mock orange blossoms into the muddy ground just as they did in Miyako. It was much worse in Echizen. How could I have imagined it would not be? Back home I could have played music with friends, or spent an afternoon at a temple with Kerria Rose, or just have written a poem to someone, knowing that I could plan on an answer the next day, not weeks later.

When I was little, I watched my mother lay out her light silk dresses for summer and prepare the pots of starch for stiffening the hems. We did this when the rains began. Mother's family paid close attention to the fashionable colors and provided her with an immense wardrobe every season. Her winter robes were layer upon layer of soft beaten silk, lined and padded with silk floss. She took great satisfaction in devising her own blends of incense to perfume them.

At the change of season, Mother put away the lined dresses and began sewing her unlined summer silks. Unlike the soft warm winter layers, these light robes were starched stiff so as to stand away from the skin. Mother's summer robes were smooth and cool to touch, and she liked to have fresh ones every year. In the fall she always gave away her used summer clothing to the maidservants. Of course it was too extravagant to obtain new lined robes every winter.

—Lined robes are different, Mother told me. One wants them soft, and they get softer the more they are worn. Also, since they're not starched, the fabric doesn't weaken so quickly. You become fond of your winter robes. It's like greeting an old friend when you see a particular favourite come out of storage in the fall.

Mother also taught me that the lined robes should be done in the more classic color combinations so one didn't tire of them. Yet, for the same reason, the unlined summer robes were more exciting. One year, I think I must have been about seven years old, Mother had a set of five robes made up in a combination she said was called *Flowering Iris*. The top robe was deep blue-green. It was worn over a layer of pale green, another of white, one of dark pink, and finally, one of light pink. The undergown for this ensemble was white. I was allowed to help starch and pinch the hems back. I thought it was the most beautiful set of colors I'd ever seen and begged Mother to give it to me at the end of summer. I don't think I ever actually wore it because by the time I was old enough, it had been tattered by years of playing dress-up.

Why did those interminable rains evoke such melancholy when in fact the memories they brought back were fond? It must be the recalling that is sad, I decided. The person, the situation, have vanished. I could not imagine going to the trouble of starching my dresses in Echizen. The rains induced such tedium, sometimes I hardly felt like bothering to get dressed at all. There were days when I stayed in my room all day, wrapped in an old Chinese jacket Ming-gwok had left behind.

Occasionally a bright clear day broke the sodden stretch of the fifth month. On one such day the family went into Echizen Town to attend a poetry contest beginning with a competition for the longest roots of the *ayame* plant. As the official representative of the emperor, Father had been invited to judge. I found this provincial aping of the culture of Miyako too depressing. I winced just looking at those grinning rustics with their self-satisfied airs, so convinced were they of being at the height of fashion. I decided it would be better to stay home by myself. My stepmother, on the contrary, liked occasions where she could preside as the grand lady from Miyako. No one actually saw her behind her screened enclosure, but she went to great pains – even sending home for fabrics – to create a gorgeous effect, trailing her hems to provide the locals with glimpses of her elegance peeking out from beneath the blinds.

A few days later we experienced another of those bright clearings. From a distance I heard a faint sound of singing with flutes and drums and a strange soft rhythmic clattering. The children clamored to investigate, and since I was bored I decided to accompany them. A pair of local servants offered to guide us to the paddies where the farmers had begun the ceremonial setting-out of the rice seedlings. About two dozen young girls dressed in white and wearing broad straw hats were knee-deep in the watery fields. They appeared to be dancing, but extraordinarily slowly, as they thrust the bright green rice plants into the muck. Their movements were governed by a monotonous melody coming from an orchestra of men playing shrill flutes, hand drums, large drums, bells, and strings of wooden clackers.

Our manservant pointed out that one of the rice-planting maidens was Kazu, a local girl who worked as a maid in our house. She was the daughter of the village headman. I thought perhaps she might be the one Nobunori had been fooling around with, although I had rarely seen her and couldn't really say that I recognized her among the other village girls. The young women were oddly graceful as they plodded through their dance in the mud. I was reminded of the snowy egrets wading in the shallows of the Kamo River back home.

I was becoming less self-conscious when I went out to view the countryside, although I was still glad of a traveling costume with a curtained hat. I felt more comfortable observing local ceremonies knowing I couldn't be seen. Yet this time I hardly needed worry. Even as we drew close to the fields, no one glanced at us. The farmers were deeply engrossed, paying no more attention to us than they did to the iridescent black-winged dragonflies that darted above the paddies.

Our garrulous guide was simply bursting with information. For a few minutes he sang along with the orchestra in the field. He had often played the drum for rice-planting in years past, he said, and that was his son out there now – the fine fellow gleaming with sweat, playing the *taiko* drum – trained him himself, he did, finally letting him take his spot just this year because he was strong and it really takes a lot out of a man to stand there in this heat and humidity pounding that drum, yes indeed. He droned on like a cicada.

Despite his language grating on my ears, I learned that the farmers believe the music attracts the gods, who journey from near and far in order to reside in the fields during the fifth month, when rice is planted.

I remember thinking how unusual that was. In religious ceremonies in Miyako, the gods were always summoned in the dark hours of the morning, never broad noon. But soon our servant said the same thing, that rice-planting was the only time the gods were invoked during daylight.

—Gives you a chill, don't it? He shivered to emphasize his words. You can feel them in the paddies. So many gods, you can't take a step without saying a prayer. Everyone is afeared and nobody goes out much this month – except, of course, to tend the fields.

Suddenly a thought struck me. In Miyako, too, we had the Taboos of the Fifth Month. Men and women are forbidden

141

congress of any kind, and even the emperor and empress take up separate dwellings during this period. Everyone says that the fact that men and women are isolated makes the tedium of the rainy season even worse. Thinking how to phrase my question delicately, I turned to the old farmer and asked,

—During rice-planting, do the girls and boys of the village, well, avoid one another?

—Of course! he spluttered. You don't think we're animals here, do you? This is sacred time. The gods don't like that kind of stuff going on when they're visiting. The idea!

He looked at me strangely and moved away to banter with the children. I was afraid I had insulted him, yet it was a relief to watch the ceremonies for a while without the barrage of comment. There were rice paddies in Miyako, but I had never observed them being worked. I knew so little about rice, that grain we ate every day without bothering to think where it comes from. From this time on I was always aware that it emerges from god-infused mud.

Something else occurred to me. It seemed unlikely that the farmers would have copied the custom of avoiding members of the opposite sex. Could it be coincidence that they seemed to be observing the Fifth Month Taboos? I had been irritated at the way they adopted the game of comparing roots, but now I began to wonder who was copying whom. In Miyako we observed taboos when it was convenient, avoiding the subject when it wasn't. Sensitive to gossip, city people hesitate to go contrary to custom, but in Miyako I certainly never felt that I was tiptoeing through a field awash with gods.

The farmers in Echizen felt that they were. The ancient *Chronicles of Japan* name our country *Mizuho no Kuni*, the Land of Fresh Rice Ears. Could it be that even the royal court followed customs that originated in the sacred mud of the rice paddies?

We had been away exactly one year.

Kerria Rose had written to me every month of that year. She was my faithful link to events in the capital, and I was guiltily aware that I had never written a thing to her about Minggwok. Instead, I unburdened my misgivings about Nobutaka,

142

and she wrote back in such sincere commiseration that I felt more guilty still. I may have come to Echizen to escape Nobutaka, but had it not been for that, I never would have met Ming-gwok. And there were times I thought it would have been better, after all, if I had never met Ming-gwok. Yet that was like saying it would be better not to look at cherry blossoms because you feel sad when they fall.

Ever alert to gossip, Kerria Rose wrote of whispers that Nobutaka had been chasing after the daughter of the governor of Omi. Soon thereafter, I received a letter from Nobutaka declaring, "My love for you is undivided!"

What was I to think?

He must have known that I would eventually hear the rumors, so he went on insisting on his faithful devotion in a rather tiresome way. Finally I became annoyed. I sent him this poem:

Mizuumi ni   tomo yobu chidori   koto naraba   yaso no minato ni   koe taenaseso
The plover cries to its mate on [Omi] lake; so if that's how it is, nothing's stopping you from calling at many ports.

I wondered whether a man could be involved with several women at the same time without creating rancor among them. I had never met the governor of Omi's daughter, yet when I read Kerria Rose's letter, I found myself hating the woman. This was all the more odd given that I didn't love Nobutaka. What would it take for a man to be able to handle a number of relationships with finesse? It was something to think about. Nobutaka didn't seem to be able to manage it, but I was sure Genji could.

From a man's point of view, jealousy is a woman's most egregious fault. From a woman's standpoint, a roving man is the worst. It is astonishing that men and women get along at all, when you think about it.

I managed to pull myself through the rainy season by keeping busy with Genji. I remembered an occasion with Ming-gwok that gave me an idea to rework the scene where Genji took leave of Murasaki. We had been talking about Chinese art.

Although we spoke of painting, underlying our words was a painful awareness of what we could not discuss. Since the idea of our togetherness had always been officially ignored, it was difficult to talk about parting.

My face was turned away from him, but I could see Ming-gwok's reflection in the polished bronze mirror on its wooden stand in the corner of the room.

—If only I could keep your reflection here in this mirror after you have gone, I said lightly.

Ming-gwok moved closer to the mirror stand to smooth his hair.

—I've lost weight, he said. Look how thin my face has gotten. Maybe I *will* become just a reflection myself.

He glanced at me.

—Why don't I do that? I'll stay behind in your mirror, and when you gaze at it you can see me.

And, of course, after that I did think of Ming-gwok whenever I looked in my mirror and was seized with melancholy every time I brushed on powder.

Even having Genji, I had to make a great effort to keep myself from succumbing to despair. When the monsoons ended, I no longer had the excuse of dreary weather for my depression, but I seldom ventured out. The hot sun beat down on the farmers' fields, and the glaring greenness was almost painful. I preferred to skulk inside, deep in the shadows of the house. The stream Father had dug in the garden was my only companion that summer; thinking of diversions for Genji, my only escape. I came to depend exclusively on him to lift my mood.

I decided to have Genji paint landscapes of his surroundings on Suma. He created a diary of his exile in pictures. Since Ming-gwok was no longer there to coach me, I was disinclined to draw, but having Genji do so gave me a reason to get my brushes out again. As he sketched the mountains and coastline, Genji came to see them in a new way. He looked beyond the conventional renditions of mountain and sea, returning again and again to paint different aspects of the scenery. His skill was incomparable. On his eventual return to

Miyako, people would weep at the powerful emotions his paintings evoked.

The smell of burning seaweed hung in the air. I found it queer when we first came, but eventually became accustomed to its sharp odor and thought it not at all unpleasant. In order for Genji to be able to sketch a fisherwoman gathering salt, I volunteered to accompany the children on an excursion to the shore. Watching the tough-skinned women tend their fires, I thought of the phrase "piling up grief like firewood." The line suggested a poem for Genji to send back to the capital.

In the meantime, I sent one of my sketches of a fisherwoman with a pile of firewood at her feet to Nobutaka with the following:

Yomo no umi ni [shio yaku ama] no kokoro kara yaku to wa kakaru [nageki o ya tsumu]
By the wide ocean, roasting salt, the fisherwoman's heart burns as she piles up her grief like firewood.

The picture of the "fisherwoman roasting salt" stood in for that phrase, and the sketch of the pile of kindling was meant to recall the line about "piling up firewood/grief."

I wondered if he would figure it out.

Eventually I came to a dead end with Genji in Suma. I was fed up with his depression and loneliness. I knew I had to think of a way to pull him out of it. At this point I got depressed all over again reading of Genji's miasma, and I was sure that anyone else reading it would be ready to put it down in boredom at this point, too. I needed someone to engage his attention. Looking at Genji from a different character's perspective might help, I thought.

I had been playing my koto again to try to improve my mood, and Father had even joined me a few times. He used to play rather well himself, although he gave up around the time my skill began to surpass his. What a poignant and awkward moment that was. For a brief period he continued offering suggestions, and I continued to listen until we both realized that teacher and pupil had been reversed. He had begun his

145

study of this thirteen-stringed instrument rather late in life, so although he learned quickly, he forgot quickly, too. It just goes to show that things like music really must be absorbed when one is young. If you have mastered a certain amount of technique as a child, you can always brush it up later in life, even if you've not played for years. If Father stayed with the seven-string *kinnokoto* he had always played, no one could match him – especially now that he had absorbed a few lessons from Master Jyo.

In any case, we enjoyed playing some simple compositions together, and it gave me an idea for my new characters.

I recalled the people to whom I had been close over the years, concluding that relationships are usually composed of one who is anchored and one who floats. Although generally women are the anchored ones, I have experienced both. I had been writing from Genji's floating perspective for some time, so I decided to change.

The Akashi coast lies near Suma. There I installed an eccentric Buddhist lay priest with his wife and daughter. It may have seemed odd, on the face of it, for such a character to actually dwell by choice in a place of exile like Akashi, but people do retreat from the capital for valid reasons. I thought of him as a cultured and educated man, wealthy from inherited lands but disillusioned with court politics. While wishing to withdraw from society and its entanglements by living in Akashi, at the same time he wanted worldly success for his daughter and raised her as carefully as any Miyako-bred lady.

Ruri would have said that was completely contradictory, but by this time I knew that that's how people are.

As I played my koto one night when the full moon rose over the mountain behind our house, I imagined I was a young woman like the daughter in Akashi, playing exquisite melodies doomed to fall on the rough ears of farmers and fishermen. She dreams of a romantic figure who would appear one day, like a miracle dropped from the moon, who could truly appreciate her. A miracle, yes, but not impossible. I needed to devise a way for Genji to discover this lady, to be the answer to her prayers.

Genji's strength was that he was a man of action who wasn't always poking and probing his own mind. At one time in my life, I regarded this as a virtue. Genji had a certain purity of heart because he was equally sincere to each woman he loved in all his numerous affairs. I have never been able to say whether it was because Genji changed, or because I changed, that this very characteristic came to be his greatest weakness.

Unhappy in Suma, Genji performed a purification ceremony – like the one I myself had done back when I was plotting to escape to Echizen. But hidden guilty feelings will manifest themselves sooner or later. Thinking only of how unfairly he had been treated in the capital by jealous political rivals, Genji tried to coax pity from the gods. He thought he was purifying himself by ritually transferring his most trivial and mundane sins to a paper figure to be set adrift on the wide plain of the sea. How satisfying to feel one's impurities brushed off and washed away! I remember standing on the bank of the Kamo River, feeling absolved of my petty sins. How we delude ourselves! Genji buries any thought of the deeper sin he committed by pursuing his father's new wife.

Nature rebels. The wind suddenly picks up, the sky darkens, and the smooth ocean surface heaves up in terrifying waves.

Genji's entourage retreated in terror at the sudden, bizarre storm. In principle, I didn't like to rely on the supernatural to move my story along, but sometimes that seemed the most plausible course. As the baneful weather continued, the ghost of the dead emperor, Genji's father, came to him in a dream, telling Genji to leave Suma by boat. So, the following dawn, there it was, a small boat on the Suma shore. The spirit had also visited the Akashi priest in a dream, instructing him to prepare a boat and send it to Suma as soon as the waves died down. Recognizing this omen from his own dream, Genji complied. Thus was he brought to Akashi.

Then, strangely, as I was writing about the Akashi Lady awaiting her miracle, she began to whisper her own thoughts to me. Her personality turned out to be rather different from my original idea. It became clear that she was not thrilled, after all, to find Genji at her doorstep. She was embarrassed by her father's efforts to lure him as a suitor, convinced she would suffer in comparison to Genji's other ladies back in the capital. Certain that she could never be anything to him but a rustic dalliance, her pride rebelled. She would rather throw herself into the sea than be used and discarded by a man like Genji.

I was rather surprised at what a stubborn figure she turned out to be. It was as if she knew what I had in store for her, and resisted that fate. I resolved that Genji would not leave her in Akashi. This lady would somehow get to Miyako and come into her own.

I was absorbed in my writing again. The season of Greater Heat began in the eighth month. I happened to look at my Chinese calendar to find *Rotted Weeds Metamorphose into Fireflies* as the first five-day seasonal. With a start, I remembered Ruri. What would she have thought of the way Genji's adventures were unfolding? I sent everything I wrote to Kerria Rose, who loved all of it uncritically. Actually the person whose opinion I would have most liked to hear was Ming-gwok. The Chinese idea about the genesis of fireflies reminded me that each season contained one of these truly odd metamorphoses. In spring moles became quails; in summer the rotted grasses turned into fireflies; autumn had sparrows diving into the water becoming clams; and in winter the pheasants did the same to become monster mollusks.

Ming-gwok wasn't able to tell me much about such things. He said this calendar is very ancient and that even Chinese scholars don't always know what all the units mean. He had never thought much about it himself until I asked.

—Isn't that strange? he had remarked. Sometimes it takes an outsider to point out the interest in things that have become overly familiar.

He became intrigued, and we drew a mandala of the year, filling in all the seasonal units, to see if that might reveal order and correspondences. We did not come up with much besides a confirmation of what we already knew. The great majority of phrases concerned the activities of insects, animals, frogs, fish, birds, and plants. The action of water, of natural phenomena, and metaphysical states made up the rest. Human activities figured not at all.

It had been very humid. After a short summer downpour in the early evening, the outer edges of the garden glimmered with the lights of fireflies. I was again struck by the different way Chinese and Japanese view these things. The Chinese regarded fireflies as born from fallen vegetation which rots in the humid heat, yet there was no emotion in that observation.

There in the Echizen countryside people had the notion that fireflies are the souls of dead babies and young children. Not resigned to settling in the underworld so soon, these tiny phosphorescent spirits cluster at the edges of marshy fields, at the edges of human society. The village children chased and captured them, but, claiming there was something slightly pitiful and creepy about the insects, the adults refused to let the children bring them into the houses.

I received another letter from Nobutaka. He had splashed drops of vermilion here and there on the paper and written, "Look here, the color of my tears."

Perhaps he had a sense of humor, after all. I decided to push him a bit with this poem:

Kurenai no   namida zo itodo   utomaruru   utsuru kokoro no   iro ni miyureba
Blood-red tears are even more hateful – crimson, the quick-to-fade color of inconstant love.

He was, after all, already married.

I had to admit that Father's garden, which I had resented earlier in the year, was splendid in the early days of fall. One cool evening I climbed the hill behind our house, from where I could catch a glimpse of the sea. I imagined I heard the voice of fishermen chanting as they pulled their nets in from their boats. As the sound grew louder, I realized that it was coming from a wedge of wild geese winging its way in the direction of the capital. I suddenly yearned to follow them.

149

Hatsukari wa   koishiki hito no   tsura nare ya   tabi no sora tobu   koe no kanashiki

First wild geese, companions of one I hold dear; their mournful cries traverse the sky.

I decided I would go back to Miyako. I told Father of my decision, and he said he would instruct the next official messenger to bring a suitable entourage to escort me home.

HEART PIERCING AUTUMN

Kokorozukushi no aki

Winds of autumn, saddest season of all, scattered the remaining leaves from the trees. With listless days and restless nights, the end of my stay in Echizen drew near. Lying awake, I heard the cry of the little night owl as chill moonlight poured through bare branches in an ancient image of autumnal sadness.

We took the route that went over Kaeruyama.* How often I had made this trip in my imagination. The sights of travel inspired a stream of poems, but I culled them and at the end of each day wrote down only one. The paths were full of huge spiderwebs. In one place, ten or twenty of the creatures had spun their nets together into arachnid palaces with attached pavilions, each one littered with the bundles of provisions its occupant had prepared. At the time, spiders did not seem like a suitable topic for poetry, but their image lived quietly in my mind for many years.

At a place called Yobisaka, where our voices echoed across the pass, the stony road grew steep, and the porters found it difficult to carry the litter I was riding in. I could sense the poles digging into their shoulders, and at every misstep I was afraid we would all plunge down a deep ravine. Suddenly a

*Literally, "Going Home Mountain."

horde of chattering monkeys descended from the trees.

It seemed they were calling to us,

—Hey, you travelers!

And I felt like calling back,

—Hey, you monkeys!

Watching their droll play and swaggering confidence, I quite forgot my fear.

Mashi mo nao   ochikatabito no   koe kawase   ware koshiwaburu   Tago no Yobisaka
Let's call to each other, the monkeys and the travelers, here where the Yobisaka Pass at Tago is so difficult to cross.

We boarded a boat to sail back down the length of Omi Lake to Otsu. This time we hugged the eastern shore, and the trip was not as bad as I had feared. From the lake I could see the white snow capping Mount Ibuki.

—Not so impressive, not after the snow I've seen in Echizen, I thought.

Na ni takaki   koshi no shirayama   yukinarete   Ibuki no take wo   nani to koso mine
Since getting used to the north's famously snowy ranges, Ibuki's peak does not seem like much.

Leaving Echizen farther behind each day, I was haunted by what Ming-gwok must have felt as he made this same journey. We sailed past Iso in the early evening, and I heard the eerie cries of cranes calling on the beach. Of course there was no way to reach him, but if there were, I would have sent this:

Isogakure   onaji kokoro ni   tazu zo naku   na ga omoiizuru   hito ya tare zo mo
In the cove at Iso the crane cries as I cry; who can it be she yearns for?

I realized that when we finally reached Miyako, I would be stepping into a new life and would have to stop thinking about Ming-gwok. This journey was the last time I could freely caress my memories. I imagined a small lacquered box inlaid with silver and gold in a pattern of curling waves, inset with

151

silver cranes. Into this imaginary box I placed all my memories of Ming-gwok and secretly tucked it away in my heart.

I asked to stop at Ishiyama for one night because it was already dark when we disembarked at Otsu. It didn't feel right to push ahead only to arrive in the capital in the dead of night. Besides, I wanted to have a service said for Auntie there at the temple to which she had often retreated in times of distress. I stayed up the rest of the night fingering my sutra beads, listening to the monks' chanting.

At dawn the yawning priests departed for their quarters, and I wandered over to a deserted area next to the sutra-storage building. Pilgrims were already up and about. An old stupa had fallen on its side and people were walking over it as if it were just another piece of stone.

Kokoro ate ni   ana katajikena   koke museru   hotoke no mikao   sotoba mienedo
I would guess that stone to be the revered face of the Buddha; yet covered pitifully in moss, it hardly seems a sacred stupa.

Late that day we arrived at Grandmother's house, and I was home in Miyako.

I had to reaccustom myself to the rhythm of city life. When we were first in Echizen, I was impatient with how laggardly people were. The pace of life in the country was maddeningly slow. Then, imperceptibly, I must have slowed down myself, for now I found that the quick tempo of life in the capital tired me out.

Father's house was unoccupied except for a caretaker. I wouldn't have wanted to stay there by myself in any case. Grandmother's house, where I had spent much of my child-hood, felt more like home. That old mansion would eventually be mine, but I hadn't yet decided whether or not I would live there.* It would depend on how things went with Nobutaka.

*For the Heian nobility, houses were usually inherited by daughters. Sons were expected to support themselves through their stipends from the court.

My cousin had been running the house for years, taking care of things for Grandmother. I suspected she might have had mixed feelings about welcoming me home, so I assured her that if I stayed, I would wish her family to continue living there as well. I knew myself well enough to realize that if I were alone for too long my solitary tendencies were likely to take over in a most unhealthy way.

My cousin's children were unfailingly well behaved and a delight to have around, yet, amazingly enough, I missed my noisy half brothers.

The first thing I did upon my return to Miyako was to write a storm of letters to renew various acquaintances. Imagine my surprise when several friends wrote back to say they had already seen some of my Genji writing. I was shocked. My stories seemed to have flown off like a flock of unruly sparrows. Kerria Rose swore that she had not shown her copies to anyone, and I had no reason to doubt her. The only possible conclusion was that Nobutaka had shown his around – as I had expressly requested him not to do. I was outraged. What a fool I was to have thought I could trust that man!

I sent him a message by word of mouth, to the effect that I would have nothing further to do with him unless he returned all my manuscripts. When my messenger got back, he said that Nobutaka seemed surprised at the curt request but said he would return everything if that's what I desired.

Betrayed and bitter, I hardly felt like writing but composed the following:

Tojitarishi   ue no usurahi   tokenagara   sa wa taene to ya   yama no shitamizu
Long frozen, the icy surface was about to melt, then you say "don't bother" to the mountain stream?

Why did he think I came back to Miyako? I had no choice but to go through with this marriage. I was twenty-five years old, and no one else would have me. Father was far away, and in any case, I had made my pledge to Nobutaka long ago. I had fleeting regrets that I hadn't become a nun, after all. But then, I told myself sternly, it was foolish to imagine the

153

outcome of choices not made. Resigned, I sent the poem to Nobutaka. I did not have the luxury of ceasing correspondence.

Apparently Nobutaka was drunk when my poem arrived at his house, and he began complaining to his friends about his prickly fiancée with her icy metaphors. Egged on by his companions, he answered my poem thus:

Kochikaze ni   tokuru bakari wo   soko miyuru   ishima no mizu wa   taeba taenamu
Since it only melted when the east wind blew, it must have been shallow indeed – if the water flowing through the rocks should cease, then let it!

"I shall say no more," he added.

It was more than a little embarrassing to discover later that our exchange of poems had been observed that evening by all of Nobutaka's cronies, including Kintō and other famous poets. Had I realized this at the time, I might not have been so forthright. Recklessly I responded:

Iitaeba   sa koso wa taeme   nani ka sono   Mihara no ike wo   tsutsumi shi mo semu
You say "no more," so let it be so. Why should I cringe before Lake Mihara's angry waves?

Little did I know that Nobutaka's friends, who had watched him fire off his drunken response, were curiously awaiting my reaction. I gathered that it caused a good deal of merriment at his expense when it came. Despite it all, they seemed to think that I would be a good match for Nobutaka, and they encouraged him to be conciliatory. In the dead of night this poem arrived:

Takekaranu   hitokazu nami wa   wakikaeri   Mihara no ike ni   tatedo kai nashi
I am not stalwart, and the puny waves of anger that rose on Lake Mihara have come to nothing.

This established a truce of sorts between us. Our wary courtship continued in small steps through the spring, summer, and fall of that year.

154

I fretted about Nobutaka, but my heart was more concerned about Kerria Rose. Of course I had rushed to meet her soon after my return to Miyako, but later I felt she put off meeting a second time. She was very tender at first, but then, after our embraces, she said something was different, and she accused me of loving another woman in Echizen. She suspected as much, she said, because she sensed great gaps in my letters, as if I were avoiding mentioning something important.

She was perceptive – although, of course, the empty space she felt was due to Ming-gwok, not a lady friend. I protested that I had no women friends in Echizen, and this was true enough. She seemed mollified at the time. I knew the whole truth would have caused her far more pain than what she imagined.

We met several more times, but I, too, began to feel that our intimacy had become strained. Although I had vowed not to open the imaginary box in which I had encased my memories of Ming-gwok, the immediacy of an intimate situation unlocked a torrent of remembrance and I was overcome. She was right, of course. I had changed. My memories of Ming-gwok did not reside only in my head.

Kerria Rose regarded men as beasts, and she had been my main source of sympathy concerning Nobutaka. She did not believe it possible to enjoy the same sort of passion with a man that two women can freely express, and before I went to Echizen I would have agreed with her. When I came back to Miyako, I knew different, but I could never have conveyed that to her. She would have felt doubly betrayed.

And yet, my feelings for her had not changed. It was distressing that something like this should come between us right then, when there was so little time left before my marriage. I sent her this poem:

Wasururu wa   ukiyo no tsune to   omou ni mo   mi wo yaru kata no   naki zo wabinuru
To be forgotten is not unusual in these sad times – what is depressing is the lack of consolation.

I continued to live at my grandmother's house, but it felt

unreal. The surroundings of my early childhood were all around me, unchanged. I had the uncanny feeling that I might go into a room and find my mother sitting at her mirror. I ought to have been able to run to her and tell her about the strangest dreams I had about traveling to far Echizen, about meeting Chinese people, about falling love.

—You must love things with all your soul, my mother had once said, and leave the rest to your karma.

—Remember this, she would say as she drew my attention to one or another thing she found engaging. She might point to the edge of a deep green, yellow-spotted *tsuwabuki* leaf, which had been artistically chewed by some insect, or a pea-green vireo perched momentarily on the garden plum tree, cocking its head this way and that whistling *hō-ho-ke-kyō* before flying off. She cultivated an extraordinary consciousness of the tangible beauties in her world, almost as if collecting them in her memory before they perished. Of course they did not perish – she did. Yet in retrospect, I suppose from her I had absorbed the ability to endure my own losses.

In any case, my fantasy about living in my childhood soon dissolved. It was unavoidable. Nobutaka had been occupied with rehearsals for his performance in the Kamo Festival, but as soon as the festivities were over, he announced his intention to visit us in person.

My cousin and I suddenly realized how shabby Grandmother's house looked and flew into a whirl to make the old place presentable. In fact we used the excuse of Nobutaka'a impending visit to redo all the blinds and hangings in the main hall and get fresh green mats for the sitting area. A redecorating was long overdue. Grandmother was notorious for hating to spend money, and as her eyesight worsened, she didn't notice the frayed edges and the faded colors of things. Probably she saw them only in her mind's eye anyway. In her memory they would always have the vibrant hues of her wedding silks.

Grandmother had toppled over one day during the time I was in Echizen, and my cousin said that for weeks she couldn't move one side of her body. She eventually recovered some ability to move but had not been the same since then. She called us by names of people she knew when she was young, people long since dead. She called me by my mother's name. Yet, as long as Grandmother was still nominally in charge, my cousin had been hesitant to spend money on the house. Of course I authorized all the necessary repairs and refurbishments.

This put my cousin in very good spirits. She set about calling carpenters and selecting patterns for the bindings of the mats. She planned to dye the hangings for the curtain stands herself, and we discussed what color compositions to try. I was very fond of the combination of purple and green – either a deep violet combined with pale green, or dark green with lavender. My cousin agreed to these colors and chose the latter set. Her good humor was catching, and I found myself enjoying all these domestic preparations – until I remembered what inspired them, and got nervous again.

The day for Nobutaka's visit arrived. The house looked fine. I had gone past being resigned and was even a little impatient to get the meeting over with. We waited and waited. As it grew dark, my cousin lit lamps.

—What could have happened? she murmured and fretted.

Finally she sent one of our more discreet scullery maids over to the kitchen at Nobutaka's mansion to see what she could find out. The maid returned to report that Master Nobutaka had gotten delayed by an unexpected visitor and was now too far gone in his cups to go out himself. In fact, just after our maid returned, a messenger came from the mansion to say that the master would visit the day after next instead. The man was the sort of self-important, officious servant I detest. He seemed to expect us to give him a letter to take back.

I had been hearing rumors that Nobutaka's wife was unhappy with this situation, and so naturally I thought that his failure to appear was due to her detaining him out of jealousy. If only she knew how much I sympathized! I had composed a poem while I was waiting, and gave this to the manservant:

Taga sato mo   toi mo ya kuru to   hototogisu   kokoro no kagiri   machi zo wabinishi
He will come to each village in turn, the hototogisu, *so I*
    waited patiently.

Secretly I was thinking primarily of the irresponsible nature
of the *hototogisu* bird, but the poem seemed to prod
Nobutaka to feel a little guilty. His reply, arriving the next
day, was uncharacteristically passionate:

Kejikakute   tare mo kokoro wa   mienikemu   kotoba hedatenu   chigiri to mogana
To become close, one must see into the other's heart; if only
    I could pledge my love by deeds instead of words.

I interpreted this as a declaration that Nobutaka wished to
consummate our union.

My cousin thought it would help calm my nerves if I had a bit
of saké before Nobutaka arrived, so although I didn't usually
drink (it was frowned on in Father's house, and I remembered
well his strict warnings about it), I took a few cups. Nobutaka
arrived long after it had gotten dark. Since he had sent that
rather explicit poem about pledging his love with action, I
expected that this would be the night he claimed marital
rights. Perhaps it was boldness inspired by the saké, but I
decided there was no point in being coy at my age.

His face was rather red, so I assumed Nobutaka, too, had
tippled before he left his house. When he sat close by my
curtains, I could indeed smell that he had. All the better, I
thought. He would be less likely to notice my own breath.
Bodly I invited him to draw aside the blind and join me
behind the curtain. We spoke of this and that. He asked if I
had heard from my father recently, and finally, after several
awkward pauses, I threw myself into his arms. He seemed
surprised.

After a bit of fumbling and excuses that he was more
fatigued than he realized, he bade me good night and said he
would visit again soon.

I did not sleep the rest of the night. As soon as it was light, I

158

wrote this poem, although, upon reflection, decided not to send it:

Hedateji to   naraishi hodo ni   natsugoromo   usuki kokoro wo   mazu shirarenuru
You say let us be close; but when I approached, I found your love to be as thin as a summer gown.

No one would ever accuse Nobutaka of not being punctilious. Before breakfast his morning-after poem was promptly delivered:

Uchishinobi   nagekiakaseba   shinonome no   hogaraka ni dani   yume wo minu kana
The remains of the night passed in anguished sighs, and when dawn reddened the eastern sky, I had not even glimpsed a dream of you.

It was not bad. Nor was it particularly good. I felt indifferent. I did not send the poem about love as thin as a summer gown, but instead this rather conventional response to the images he had used:

Shinonome no   sora kiriwatari   itsu shika to   aki no keshiki ni   yo wa narikeri
The pink clouds of dawn are obscured by mist, and all it takes is a moment for the season to change to fall.

Perhaps it was unfair to imply that he was already tired of me, but I felt I was playing a game that I already knew the outcome of. In any case, it was almost the seventh month, the beginning of fall.*

As the holiday Tanabata approached, the stars twinkled like fireflies in the field of heaven. I wondered why stars are not used more in poems. In the heavens the sun is the goddess Amaterasu, our ancestress, while the moon has gathered all of our poetic impulses. The stars are practically ignored. A long time ago I heard a story that stars are the remains of a tribe of evil deities banished by the sun goddess.

*The word *aki* means both "autumn" and "to tire of."

How Ming-gwok laughed when I told him that. He said the Chinese emperor had an entire bureau of learned men devoted to studying the stars. They had mapped the heavens and identified the star seats of numerous celestial beings. I was humbled and somewhat embarrassed. We Japanese have no idea of these things. The only stars we pay any attention to are the herd boy and the weaver maiden, who come together this one night of the year on Tanabata, the seventh day of the seventh month. Even this festival was learned from the Chinese long ago when the capital of our country was still in the Asuka plains.

I saw a magpie sitting on the garden wall, remembering how they are all supposed to fly up to heaven this day to create a bridge spanning the silver river of stars separating the lovers. When little boys see one of these birds loitering around the fields or riverbank, they are encouraged to throw stones at it to remind the bird of its duty in heaven. I imagined my brother had taken the children to the fields in Echizen to throw stones at magpies again. But maybe not – the year before, he had to explain what they were doing to an angry farmer who caught them at the edge of his rice field. The country people had never heard of this Tanabata festival. My father felt obliged to invite a delegation of farmers to the courtyard of the house and explain the story.

Little girls much prefer to fold paper dolls and tie colored threads to branches of bamboo. I spent the day with my cousin's little girls, helping them inscribe their wishes and hopes on the dolls, and later we sent them down the river, bearing their prayers to the gods. All the children dashed outside first thing in the morning to chant for good weather. If it rained this day, the magpies would be too wet and tired to form a good bridge, and the herd boy and weaver girl would miss their once-a-year tryst.

The adults regarded all of these activities as charming, but the main interest for the older children was in the evening. It has long been the custom for unmarried men and women to meet unchaperoned on the wide stone banks of the Kamo River on this night. I must have been about eighteen the one time I ventured out with some of my girlfriends. Our purpose

160

was secretly to tail my brother, Nobunori, to see what he did when he met a girl – but unfortunately he gave us the slip right away. We wandered about for a while, and whenever we ourselves were approached by a young man, we giggled and refused to leave our group. Then one girl – I forget her name now – recognized a young man she had previously seen on horseback at some ceremony and left with him. Losing one of our party put a damper on our spirits, and the rest of us returned home shortly after, as I recall.

My cousin asked me if was planning to stroll the riverbank this evening. I assumed she was joking. The weather had been fine, and early in the afternoon this poem arrived from Nobutaka:

Oukata ni   omoeba yuyushi   ama no kawa   kyou no ouse wa   urayamarekeri
To cross the River of Heaven is a serious affair, yet today I
*   am envious of their tryst.*

He implied that it was easier for the stars to meet than it was for us. So I sent this reply:

Ama no kawa   ouse wa yoso no   kumoi nite   taenu chigirishi   yoyo ni asezu wa
The meeting of the stars is a heavenly affair; above the
*   clouds their eternal pledge endures through the ages.*

Not like our human entanglements on earth, is what I was thinking, although the way it was worded, he could interpret the image as a comparison rather than a contrast if he so chose.

Predictably he read the poem as encouraging, and as he was passing in front of my house on his way to the palace, he sent in a note: "I would like to see you now, just as you are."
To which I replied:

Naozari no   tayori ni towamu   hitogoto ni   uchitokete shi mo   mieji to zo omou
I hardly think I would show myself at every casual request
*   that comes to my door.*

He certainly was one to take liberties.

THE EXORCISM

Oni no kage

An invitation arrived to a *sumai* exhibition to be held at a private mansion the day before the start of the official wrestling matches.* Since Nobutaka had made a point of asking me specifically, I felt I could not refuse. He had visited again, during the day, in order to discuss some economic matters. Our meeting was cordial enough, though quite perfunctory. Normally he would have had these discussions with my father. I gathered that he had made some arrangements so I would not have to live in close quarters with his established family. I suggested that I might continue to live in my grandmother's house, and he made a vague response that I interpreted as his not dismissing the idea out of hand. He seemed a little pale, and I wondered if he was feeling all right.

I was acutely sensitive to the feelings of his other women – perhaps overly so. I knew that Nobutaka's first wife had a long history of expressing her jealousy and unhappiness with the other wives, concubines, and affairs. She had even, rumor went, once dumped a censer of ashes over Nobutaka's head in a fit of rage when he was courting one of the women he later married. I should have realized that as a grandmother in her fifties, Nobutaka's first wife was not now likely to be raising a fuss about another woman. I didn't understand this until later, but in fact all the other wives had long since made peace with one another and resigned themselves to Nobutaka's philandering ways.

Because each woman was supported in her own stylish house with a comfortable allowance, no one raised a fuss. On the contrary, the established wives seemed to take it for granted that a new marriage was a good tonic for a middle-aged gentleman. The only thing that puzzled them was my own advanced age. They would have expected a compliant young beauty of a bride in her teens – not an old maid of

Sumai was basically the same sport as the modern *sumo*.

162

twenty-five with a reputation as a bookworm.

I was conscious of time passing and looked back over my calendar of the seasons. The year begins with the rising mists of spring, followed by all of the spring things so celebrated in poetry. Summer comes along almost as an afterthought. Then the year divides. Autumn should begin with the sound of the wind, a coolness in the breeze. Then there is another burst of poetic topics taking up autumnal themes. Winter is but an afterthought to autumn.

My Chinese calendar agreed. The first phase of autumn is *The Cool Wind Arrives*. Yet that year we seemed to be stuck in a never-ending summer. It was so dreadfully hot many people fell ill, and there were fears that the plague would erupt again. The miasma did not even spare the emperor and his revered mother, the dowager empress, who both took sick. Everyone was afraid of being next, and the *sumai* match was not well attended.

I myself went, but wondered whose mansion I was taken to. It was in the southern quarter of the city, past Sixth Avenue, in an area I was not terribly familiar with. The house had been built recently, but its design was so well conceived and its garden so perfectly constructed, it felt as if it had naturally grown there. I saw the poet Kintō, my father's old friend, and inquired of him.

He hesitated before answering, and then what he said in a low voice shocked me.

—This is the house Nobutaka has been secretly constructing for his new bride, whispered Kintō. I emphasize "secretly," although I am not sure it isn't time she knew how much he cares for her.

I could barely pay attention to the strapping wrestlers after what Kintō said. First, I was mortified to think that this great scholar and poet was familiar with anything that had passed between Nobutaka and myself. But then, selfish creature that I am, my eyes began to drink in the magnificent garden. I could not for a moment believe that it had been built for me. The lustrous zelkova wood of the balcony I was leaning on – my house!

I allowed myself to peek at the furnishings inside – the lacquered shelves, the finely woven and edged mats, the paulownia wood chests! Everything had been done in the most up-to-date and elegant fashion. The verandahs, polished by peach pits, shone like mirrors. I was overwhelmed. Nobutaka had done this.

Nobutaka. With shame I realized that I noticed only then that he was not in the audience.

I received a message that Nobutaka was very ill. No one seemed to know whether his symptoms were the precursor to the pox or whether they indicated possession by an evil spirit. All I was able to glean was that he was experiencing a great pressure in his chest and that it was difficult for him to breathe.

I decided I had to visit him even though he was convalescing at his main house. There was an awkward moment when I arrived, but a woman about my age, whom I recognized as his daughter, was very gracious. She led me to the main reception room, where a number of priests had been chanting for Nobutaka's recovery. They were now waiting for a famous exorcist who had been summoned several days ago but, because of his busy schedule, was not able to visit until now.

I had come at an inopportune time, but the daughter urged me to stay and sit with other friends and family members who had gathered for the exorcism.* She mistakenly assumed that I was among those invited. It would have been even more rude

*Illness was often interpreted as the result of the body being infested by an angry spirit. To cure a person thus afflicted, it was necessary to obtain the services of a Buddhist specialist called a *genza*, who would chant powerful spells to exorcise the ghost. By this means he would transfer the spirit to the body of a medium, try to make it identify itself, and convince it to abandon its host. A spirit might be that of a deceased person who died holding a grievance, or it was even possible for a "living spirit" (*ikisudama*) to fly from the body of a live person to torment another. Muraskai writes of both kinds in the *Tale of Genji*. She treated the spirits almost as if they were emotions so powerful they could not be pent up in the minds and bodies that generated them.

to decline, however, so I stayed. Nobutaka himself lay on a curtained dais behind a four-foot-high screen. We could not see him.

The lattice windows of the south and east sides of the room were fully opened to catch a faint breeze from the spacious courtyard beyond, which was shadowed by massive pine trees. I had barely had a chance to take in the splendour of Nobutaka's main house when a ripple of murmuring among the guests indicated that the exorcist had arrived. I turned my head to see a grave young man being escorted into the room. I had expected a grizzled cleric, but here was a handsome priest who looked to be in his thirties. He was led to a hassock placed in front of the curtained dais. There he knelt and bowed while an assistant immediately began laying out his religious implements. The priest took up a clove-scented fan and began to recite the Magic Incantation of the Thousand Hands.

As some point a young girl of about twelve crept into the room. She crawled up to the dais and settled in front of a smaller screen next to the priest, ready to accept the transfer of the evil spirit afflicting Nobutaka. I had witnessed similar scenes many times when my older sister was alive. Takako had been particularly prone to illness caused by wandering spirits. In her case, the priests were always old, the mediums always dirty-faced children. I had never witnessed an exorcism as elegant as this.

In fact, as I thought back, this was the first time I had ever seen these services performed for a man. I think it is relatively rare for spirits to possess men unless they are under immense political pressure or otherwise in an uncommonly fragile state. For some reason, women tend to be more susceptible to these unwelcome infestations. Of course I immediately wondered whether my unsympathetic treatment of Nobutaka was partly to blame, and I wished I had chosen some other time to visit.

The medium was a handsome girl, plump and clear-faced. She was wearing a pale orange, stiff unlined gown and long eggshell-colored trousers more suitable to an older woman than a young girl – although they looked surprisingly attractive on her. The assistant handed her a polished wooden wand as the priest began to intone the sacred mystic syllables. The girl shut her eyes tightly and began to tremble and sway, her body reacting to the sharp staccato bursts of the priest's mantra. Soon she fell into a trance and slumped to the floor, the most awful groans and wails escaping her lips. We in the audience flinched, despite the fact that we knew the moans were coming from the possessing spirit, not the girl herself.

Still, I thought, she would no doubt have been embarrassed to find herself exposed like this in front of so many people. Others must have noticed, too, for someone edged over to her curtain and tried to straighten the girl's disarrayed clothing.

By this time it was the middle of the afternoon. The priest had drawn the spirit out in a climax of screams for mercy. We expected him to dismiss the creature with orders to stay away, but instead the priest prolonged its agony by insisting it identify itself. The spirit refused, or perhaps was unable, so finally the priest let it go. We were all in awe of his authority. Best of all, the patient appeared to obtain relief right away. One of Nobutaka's attendants who had been with him on the curtained dais now stepped out and announced that his master was now breathing easily and his fever had broken.

Members of the family expressed their deep gratitude to the exorcist, who was gathering up his things. They pressed him to stay while they performed an offering, but the young priest had more patients waiting and politely declined their entreaties. I found his dignity most impressive.

Once the drama of the exorcism had faded, my feelings of being a stranger in the bosom of Nobutaka's family bubbled up again. I noticed that the lady who had bade me stay was gazing at me during the ceremony. I could hardly request to speak to Nobutaka under these circumstances and decided I would return home and write to him instead. People were paying their respects, so I joined a larger group just leaving the house, and as I murmured my hopes for Nobutaka's continued recovery, his daughter asked me directly,

—Are you the one who writes the Genji stories?

Needless to say, I was taken aback. Did she see me as the person who was upsetting the order of her house? A competitor for her father's affections, a rival to her mother's position? All these thoughts rushed to my mind, and I felt myself turning bright red.

—I like your stories very much, she said simply before I could muster a reply.

Then she turned and fled back into the house.

THE THAW

Tokemizu

The wind shifted, and it was not simply that the oppressive heat suddenly dissipated. I sensed a deeper change. The air felt heavy, and clouds gathered. We heard the wind even before we felt its sudden chill. Fat drops of rain started down and were soon driven violently sideways. Everyone rushed to close shutters which for weeks had been open their widest to catch any breath of breeze. I had to rummage in my closet to find a padded robe – when just that morning it had been so stifling I could hardly bear the weight of an unlined silk gown on my skin.

Autumn was arrogant that year. I had always considered autumn's nature to be darkly yin, compared to spring's clear masculine character, but a bright yang fierceness pervaded that fall.

Nobutaka moved into the new house on Sixth Avenue as a way to elude the ghost that continued to plague him even after the exorcism. The priests were baffled, and finally the doctor of divination suggested the change of residence as a way to shake the thing. Nobutaka sent a message inviting me to visit him there.

I wondered if his problem had something to do with the fact that this was the time of year when spirits tended to roam. Souls wander during the seventh month, especially around the time of the full moon. Could it be that they feel the pull of the feast of ancestral spirits when they are invited back to the homes of the living? Since they are celebrated, remembered, and assuaged, why wouldn't they be eager for the solace and attention? But the reason could be opposite, as well. Perhaps the ancestor ceremony occurs when it does because the spirits are restless then, so we celebrate them in order to appease them. After all, even the spirit of a loved one would become horrid if it lingered on.

In any case, spirits or no, the time had come to make amends with Nobutaka, and I prepared to visit the mansion on Sixth Avenue a second time. Knowing what I did from Kintō, I paid much closer attention to the building upon arriving. I noticed first of all that the wall surrounding the mansion was unusual – elegant, but in a playful kind of way. Circular pieces of ceramic tile had been inset along the upper edge of the wall with a scalloped pattern of connected half-rounds running beneath them. From the street the tops of the maple trees in the garden could be seen, the tips of the leaves just beginning to turn color. Once inside the main gate, I stepped out of my plain carriage, which was then pulled next to Nobutaka's grand one in the carriage house. I was escorted through the inner gate into the garden.

I was confident that at least I remembered the garden, but it was all changed. This day it overflowed with chrysanthemums of every size and shape. I was certain they had not been there the month before. Tall, spidery yellow blooms trailed delicate petals from plants by the edge of the pond; mounds of little white wild chrysanthemums with yellow eyes rambled through the young mulberry trees. I knew that the flowers of these could be dried and made into an infusion to cure headaches. Clumps of maroon, of bronze, of gold, of yellow, clustered in containers along the verandahs and walkways. The effect was intoxicating. I simply had to explore some of the nooks in this garden before I went in the house.

Still, I was mindful that I was trying to be conciliatory, and vowed to limit my wandering. Lifting my head toward the main building, I noticed that the blinds were rolled up. Peering closer, I was startled to see Nobutaka sitting just inside the verandah watching me. He didn't appear sick at all.

—Take your time, he called. The chrysanthemums are nice this time of year, don't you agree?

This caught me off guard, and I quickly lowered my face. An ornamented comb fell out of my hair onto the ground. This was not going the way I expected.

—Here, let me show you something.

Nobutaka rose and stepped to the edge of the railing. He jumped down to the ground, surprisingly graceful for someone his age. A servant rushed up immediately with a pair of wooden clogs.

Nobutaka thrust his feet into them without even looking down. I fumbled for my fan to cover my face. It was odd. In Echizen I had become accustomed to going about with the trappings of screens, blinds, and fans for modesty, but in Miyako the idea of a man's gazing at me in broad daylight felt quite indecent. Nobutaka had caught me by surprise. Even in my confusion I could tell he was amused. I had come with my heart prepared to feel sorry for him, but my sympathy gave way to wary regard.

Nobutaka waited a moment while I found my fan, then strode off toward the bridge connecting the front garden to the little island in the middle of the pond. I followed, clinging to the railing in order not to slip on the steeply pitched arch of the bridge.

The island had been planted with the Seven Autumn Shrubs, composed so carefully it reminded me of a giant tray arrangement. A stand of pampas grass waved its silvery plumes above a bush of deep pink pea-flowered lespedeza; some scattered low dianthus revealed feathered white blooms (they were the wild kind from the mountains rather than the pink ones people usually cultivate in their gardens); a grouping of violet-blue bellflowers, their puffy buds charmingly unopened, was bordered by a bamboo support for a kuzu vine and some lavender mistflowers, while the delicate greenish-yellow umbels of the maidenflower trembled in the light breeze. It was like a tableau from a painted screen. I had a sudden impression that there ought to be a poem inscribed somewhere on this scene. Suddenly a pair of mandarin ducks swam out from behind the fishing pavilion at the edge of the pond.

—Now, there's a good omen, said Nobutaka.

I blushed behind my fan. It was if he had choreographed the birds. He gestured toward the mulberry grove.

—In a few years, when they're mature, we'll start silk-worms on them, he said. Our own little silk farm. The people at the main house are envious. When they heard about the mulberries, they clamored for a share of silkworms, too.

I wished he hadn't brought up the main house, but I had resolved that since there was nothing I could do about the feelings of his other ladies, I would stop fretting. I would invite them to graze their silkworms on these trees.

I could tell Nobutaka was just about bursting with pride in this garden. As well he might, for it was lovely. I wondered if he knew that I now knew it was intended for me.

—Shall we step over to the pavilion? he asked, offering his hand to steady my footing on the slope of the bridge.

—The garden is exquisite, I said.

—Just wait till you see it in the spring, he exulted, proceeding to point out plans for transforming the island into a spring tableau.

I assumed this was his way of indicating that he expected I would be living here by then.

—I look forward to it, I replied.

And this was how I accepted.

We walked to the edge of the garden by the gate where I had come in, stepping up to the corridor leading out to the fishing pavilion. The servant who had been following us lined up our garden clogs neatly on a flat stone placed there for that purpose. On the polished wooden floor of the corridor I let down my long trousers which had been tucked up outside, and tried to reset my comb as it slipped again.

Built up on pillars directly over the waters of the pond and completely open-sided, the pavilion was furnished with portable mats divided by a low screen. Nobutaka had brought out some paintings and scrolls which people had recently given him as presents during his convalescence.

—Here's an interesting one, he said, unwrapping the faded

bindings on an old ash-colored wooden box.

He lifted out a hand scroll and unrolled it in front of me. Someone had drawn the grotesque form of a woman possessed. Directly behind her stood a young priest striving to tie down an evil spirit – apparently the man's former wife, demonically transformed by jealousy. The husband sat chanting a sutra in an effort to exorcise the spirit.

Nobutaka asked what I thought of it.

My reaction shaped itself in the form of a poem, so I requested some paper and a brush. I wrote:

Naki hito ni   kagoto wa kakete   wazurau mo   ono ga kokoro no   oni ni ya wa aranu
He acts as if the dead one were the cause, but is it not more likely he is wracked by internal devils?

Maple leaves rustled in the breeze and the mandarin ducks dipped in and out of the water, shaking the drops from their wings when they surfaced. Nobutaka read my poem and gazed at the scene.

—You do insist on testing me, he remarked.

Then he took the brush and wrote:

Kotowari ya   kimi ga kokoro no   yami nareba   oni no kage to wa   shiruku miyuramu
I beg to differ. It's your heart immersed in the dark that so clearly knows the shape of devils.

I read his words, recognizing their truth with a sudden shock. My resistance to Nobutaka lay less in any fault of his than it did in my own stubbornness. Feeling stung, I didn't notice that he seemed to be waiting for me to say something. He broke the awkward silence himself.

—You're quite right, actually. He smiled. I'm sure the devils we don't confront within ourselves are that ones that cause the most problems.

Then he said, carefully,

—Do you think your Shining Genji would like this garden?

I realized then that my opinion mattered to Nobutaka, and I wondered why it had taken me so long to appreciate that. His sensibilities were very different from mine, it was true. He

171

was much lighter, unencumbered by the melancholy shadows that gathered around me. But perhaps this was not a bad thing.

Would Genji like this garden? Clearly Nobutaka had been thinking about Genji when he designed it. How interesting.

I turned to him and said,

—Someday Genji will build his own house at an address very like Sixth Avenue. And he will make gardens for each season, I added. Perhaps you could help me design them?

Nobutaka blinked. I think he was rather pleased to have been asked.

Later that evening, after I had returned to Grandmother's house, this poem arrived.

Nobutaka used the images from my poems earlier in the year to rather nice effect:

Mine samumi   iwama koureru   tanimizu no   yukusue shimo zo   fukaku naruramu
The waters of the valley stream, once frozen in the mountain peaks, from here on out will flow deep and strong.

I moved into the Sixth Avenue house shortly after the Feast of Double Yang on the ninth day of the ninth month. Our marriage ceremony was simplicity itself: three lacquered cups of saké, each sipped thrice. Given the circumstances and our ages as bride and groom, an elaborate banquet for the families would hardly have been appropriate. Nobutaka did send the obligatory matrimonial rice cakes to my grandmother's house, and a few days later arranged a poetry party for his friends. Many poems were composed (all lost now), much saké was drunk.

THE NORTHERN PERSONAGE

Kita no kata

People often remarked how unusual the house on Sixth Avenue was – more garden than building. The main hall was as one would expect: a large central room surrounded by eaves chambers opening on to the surrounding verandah. I did not use many interior screens and blinds, for I liked the feel of the large open room rather than breaking up the space. Two covered corridors led off the east and west sides of the main building, again as one would expect, but in this case the pavilions attached to them were tiny. The eastern wing was my study and writing room, the western one was Nobutaka's private chamber, although being a man who disliked solitude, he seldom used it.

I preferred to keep the main building open and free of clutter, while the space where I worked on Genji was cramped and filled with all sorts of little objects I had collected about me over the years.

—They inspire me in various way, I remember telling a friend who asked about the little boxes, lacquered objects, dried flowers, and twigs of unusual shape that were scattered around. Clinging to a shelf was the brittle golden husk of a cicada I had plucked from under the eaves earlier in the fall. To gaze at the intricacies of its crenellated body, its rent back where it slipped out as if shedding a Chinese jacket, made me wonder at the fragile tenacity of living things. No one came in that room unless expressly invited. Even Nobutaka stayed out.

The entire property was surrounded by a simple fence of rammed earth: a modest wall, although with a rather unusual design. Sections of this fence were all that eventually survived the fire. The main entrance gate on the west side was of cypress wood, unpainted, with dark bronze fixtures. It opened onto a raked pebble yard. Carriages were parked in a shed to the right. On foot, a person would walk across the pebbles and through the inner gate, formed by a gap in two covered walkways: the one on the right led to the fishing pavilion at

173

the west end of the garden lake; the walkway on the left led to the western wing of the house.

Guests were supposed to walk a meandering path through the garden to reach the main staircase, but they seldom did. Most visitors entered through the west wing. Since Nobutaka was unconcerned with maintaining a private room there, his annex for all practical purposes served as the entrance to the house.

The garden itself took up three-quarters of the estate. On the far side, by the south wall, stood a grove of mulberry trees on a small man-made hill. Mulberries would grow fast, so these had been planted as saplings. Some of the larger pines, on the other hand, had been laboriously dug up from the mountains and transplanted full size. About half of those managed to survive the trauma of uprooting the replanting (not a bad rate, I was told). Those pines were the biggest expense of all the garden plantings.

In front of the hill of mulberries was a pond with a small island in the middle, accessible by a rounded bridge on the side facing the house, and a path of raised rocks on the side facing the mulberries. Stepping across these stones made an adventure for a small child, for it was easy to trip into the shallow water. Children were not allowed to cross the path-bridge without a nursemaid holding their hand. If they complained, the servants would tell them it was a floating dream bridge and if they didn't behave, it would melt and they would drown. Such nonsense to put in children's ears, yet it was effective. In summer I picked bouquets of wild carnations, and in the fall I particularly liked the puffed blue buds of the bell-flowers.

The fishing pavilion was my favorite place of all. This was an open-sided structure extending over the west end of the pond. Perhaps the Chinese who invented this building actually used it as a platform for catching fish. We fished with our eyes only. In the summer it was cooler than the house, although if the weather was very hot, the water turned green and smelled of algae. Turtles basked on stones and carp rose lazily up to your hand. You could sit out there in any season – even winter, if you took a charcoal brazier out with you.

Sitting on the steps of the south side of the main building, cherry trees to my right, camellias to my left, I looked past a clump of plums and a large willow at the edge of the lake until my gaze was lost in the mulberry grove that from there seemed far distant from the house. Since the trees screened the back fence, they created the illusion of an endless vista. Nobutaka had fashioned the stream to resemble the tracks left by a crawling dragon. Stones were placed where the course narrowed and the intensified flow of water would have overflowed the bank; then where the stream widened again into a calmer flow, he had spread white sand in a gentle shore.

Nobutaka spared no expense in furnishing the eastern wing of the house to my liking. Luckily for him, my tastes were simple. I had a set of soft foldable reed mats edged in striped silk that I layered four deep to sleep on. My cushions were dyed dark yellow, and the curtains also yellow, with a pattern of mottled blue spots. When I wrote, I found the color blue helped focus my mind, while yellow gave me inspiration. I had three curtain screens made of unlacquered zelkova wood, with sets of hangings to change through the seasons. In early winter I put up the oyster-shell-pale ones, which deepened to russet at the bottom, accented by dark purple streamers.

I had brought my writing table from storage in our old house. It was a bit worn, but a fine old piece that was once owned by my ancestor Kanesuke. I didn't like a room where everything was brand-new and unused. It was much more comfortable to mix the elegant new furnishings with familiar pieces. The dragon-track stream reached out from the garden pond, flowing directly beneath my room. When the weather turned chilly I kept the shutters closed, looking forward to spring when I would take them off altogether and open the room completely to the garden.

I spent most of my time in the cozy eastern wing, reading or gazing out at the pond and the garden stones. When Nobutaka visited, I withdrew to the northern room, furnished with a grand platform dais bed of black lacquer hung with curtains. To prevent illness, Nobutaka had hung a rhinoceros horn at one end and, to repel evil spirits, mirrors at the other.

He was quite scrupulous about arranging things like this for his health. Given his history of illness, I could understand the precautions.

Sometimes I reflected on this shift in my life. Now that the marriage I had dreaded for so long had taken place, I felt strangely happy and at peace in beautiful and congenial surroundings. I had every means at hand to continue writing, and an understanding husband who made few demands. He had just been appointed governor of Yamashiro, so he could well afford the upkeep of the elaborate gardens.

It was true we were an improbable match. Nobutaka was as gregarious as I was solitary. He sought out crowds and gaiety; I sought quiet. He was always getting into awkward situations because he was flamboyant but, to be honest, not terribly clever. Still, he was good-humored and generous, and people liked him. Gradually the strong currents of misunderstanding that had arisen from our different natures ebbed away and were replaced by a certain harmony. Although he occasionally surprised me with a decent poem, on the whole Nobutaka's literary skill was pedestrian. He was the first to acknowledge this. Yet he appreciated Genji. I came to understand that he showed my stories around because he was proud of them. It had never occurred to him that I had seriously meant he should keep the manuscript under cover.

In hindsight, perhaps my own motives were mixed. After he sent that pillow book to Echizen, I had felt pricked to prove that even though I was living in the hinterlands I could write something just as interesting as the likes of Sei Shōnagon.

When Nobutaka was away, which was most of the time, I often slept on the same platform dais in the eastern wing where I spent my days. I usually awoke just before dawn and lay quietly, listening to the small crackling, creaking sounds the house made as the sun warmed it. I preferred to write in the early morning when my mind was unclouded by the various household decisions and social obligations I would have to deal with later in the day. The maids knew not to disturb me until after breakfast. Only then did I leave Genji's world, have some rice gruel and fruit, and attend to messages and letters and directions to the servants according to Nobutaka's plans for the day.

Nobutaka continued to be preoccupied with his health. He obtained a copy of Dr. Tamba's treatise on Chinese medical science which he showed me one day. According to that book, one of the most important secrets to long life is to have frequent sex, preferably with as many partners as possible – although a man must be careful not to let any of his precious liquid escape or all benefit will be lost. Ming-gwok had said something similar, but, of course, I pretended to be ignorant of these Chinese theories. Nobutaka asked my help in following the prescriptions, so I did my best to oblige.

Whenever his presence was not required for the ceremonies of the new year at court, Nobutaka came to the Sixth Avenue house to practice Chinese longevity techniques. It never failed to amuse me that while it took my women no less than half an hour to dress me properly, with the pull of one sash, everything came undone in an instant. For a while I was rather sore from this unaccustomed attention, but there came a day when I found myself looking forward to his visits. I blushed when I considered what they must be thinking at the main house!

Genji writing was going well. I had developed deeper insights into this character, especially his relations with women. At one point I had struggled with the question of how Genji would manage to keep jealousy from poisoning his many liaisons. It used to be impossible for me to imagine that his women wouldn't hate one another, but now I was beginning to see how women's emotions accommodate. It helps a great deal if they live separately, of course. How lucky I was.

For the new year greeting I made my first visit to the main house since the previous summer's exorcism. Nobutaka asked me to send over a batch of the gruel I had prepared for him according to our family's special recipe, the one using dried persimmons and chestnuts. I had been so caught up in my new life as a married woman in Miyako that I had not been thinking much about my family in Echizen, but while supervising the preparation of the gruel, I was overcome with nostalgia. In his unaccustomed role of father-in-law, Father had written many letters to Nobutaka. He found the relationship gratifying and a bit humorous, since the two men were almost the same age.

I packed the gruel mixture into some fine antique lacquered boxes that I remembered were stowed away at Father's house. One of our old family servants had been caretaking the place, and he obliged me by fetching them out of storage. Fitted with their lids and wrapped with pristine paper strings, the boxes made an elegant present. I had them sent to the main house for a few days before I visited.

I had to smile, recalling the apprehension I felt approaching the main house the previous summer. Now I was a different person. The ladies of the household were quite complimentary about the boxes and food, and Nobutaka's second-eldest daughter, who had spoken to me before about Genji, seemed delighted with the fresh copies of several new stories I slipped to her as I left.

As I thought about it, all Nobutaka's other women were in fact perfectly polite and friendly in summer as well. My reactions of dread and embarrassment at the time were caused entirely by my own frame of mind. In reality, nothing had changed except me myself.

Nobutaka was often called to the palace on various matters. One day he came to me directly from his business there, full of praise for the magnificent plum trees blooming in the palace front courtyard – a deep red one on the left, white on the right. Their blossoms were beginning to scatter, he said, and in the bright spring sunlight the swirling petals were marvelous to behold. He was anxious to plant a set of plums just like them in our own garden at Sixth Avenue. Father was quite partial to plum trees as well, but he liked a really ancient tree that almost seemed dead, with bluish patches of lichen here and there on the trunk. Then, from one fresh twig growing out of a grizzled branch, a few fat buds appeared. That is the sort of plum a scholar appreciates.

Nobutaka was in an excellent mood and quite vigorous.

We practiced several positions from Dr. Tamba's manual, but finally Nobutaka lost control and all our efforts were wasted. He didn't seem too concerned, though, saying that we could always try again. His goal was, in the Chinese phrase, "to make the Yellow River flow backward"; that is, to cause the male essential fluid to reabsorb upward in the body so as to nourish the brain. Again, according to the book, the best way to increase the strength of the yang was to maintain the excitement of the yin – at which Nobutaka had become quite adept.

We received a most interesting letter from Father. He had just seen one of the emissaries making his rounds from the eastern provinces back to the capital. While traveling on the wide plain of Suruga he observed the sacred mountain called Fuji sending up plumes of smoke. People told him the mountain had been making ominous noises and they were afraid. Then, in the middle of the night, from his lodging some distance away, he was awakened by a terrific explosion. Without thinking, he ran outside and was just in time to see plumes of fire shooting out of the mountain peak and running down the sides. Around him villagers were shouting and crying, although they appeared to be in no actual danger from the fierce activity of the mountain across the plain. The air was sulfurous and unpleasant as the emissary gathered his baggage and set off. Even by dawn the sky refused to lighten, and the entire day of traveling was clouded by the mountain's smoke.

—One imagines a soul's journey through hell would look like this, he told Father. Indeed, his description of the flames and smoke and frightened people darting wild-eyed from the houses could have come directly from one of Genshin's paintings of hell.

Around the beginning of summer I began to feel rather unwell. Instead of rising early, I remained curled up behind my curtains until the sun was well up. Slowly I dressed, feeling a little unsteady, and crawled out to sit on the verandah to breathe the fresh morning air of the garden. Nobutaka noticed my lassitude and sent for his physician to prescribe a treatment. In the meantime, I could see that among the cherry trees well into their bloom there were one or two that reminded me strongly of the birch cherries of Echizen. I made a note to myself to ask Nobutaka about them. I tried putting a graceful cherry branch into a vase, but the petals fell almost immediately, so I replaced it with some straight knobby peach branches full of buds just beginning to open.

Orite miba   chika masari seyo   momo no hana   omoiguma naki   sakura oshimaji
Now that you are plucked, peach blossoms, look your best; you needn't be jealous of the heartless cherry.

Nobutaka came back from conferring with his physician and noticed the vase of flowers I had arranged. I told him the problem I had had with the cherry blossoms and showed him my poem. He responded:

Momo to iu   na mo aru mono wo   toki no ma ni   chiru sakura ni mo   omoiotosaji
With the splendid name Momo, the peach ought not feel inferior to the quick-to-scatter cherry.

We agreed that cherry blossoms were overrated. There are so many other lovely flowering trees that poets seldom write about. The Chinese have a high regard for delicate white pear flowers as well as the robust peach. Why must we always sing the praises of plum and cherry alone? When the petals scatter, and both pear and cherry are swaying in the evening breeze, it is quite impossible to tell them apart in any case.

Hana to iwabe   izure ka nioi   nashi to mimu   chirikau iro no   koto naranaku ni
Neither the cherry, loveliest of flowers, nor lowly pear has much scent; neither is there a difference in the way they fall.

After his consultation with Nobutaka, the physician came to see me. I was feeling even more lethargic than usual and spoke to him from inside my curtained dais in the east wing. He requested me to hold my arm out so he could feel my pulse. He asked whether perchance I had recently dreamed of cats, and then gently pushing my arm back through the curtains, he cleared his throat and said,

—From what your husband has told me, madam, and from the looks of it, I humbly suggest the diagnosis of pregnancy.

I felt so weak since the onset of my condition that I was barely able to lift my writing brush. Nobutaka was worried and busied the physician with concocting various remedies, yet I could not keep anything down.

—It's very strange, he remarked. None of the other wives experienced anything like this.

His concern was touching.

A bit of queasiness was to be expected, I understood, but my own reaction seemed excessive. I could not abide certain smells – anything the least bit oily made me retch. Sucking on a sour pickled apricot sometimes helped a little.

Also, I began to be afflicted with terrible headaches, unlike anything I had ever felt. I didn't see how I could survive if they kept up. The doctor believed the problem to be an evil sprit, so Nobutaka engaged priests to chant for me. Their efforts did some good, and I doubled my own prayers to Kannon, Bodhisattva of Mercy.

Just around this time the imperial palace burned, and my husband was kept busy helping with the relocation to a temporary residence. No one of importance was injured, but many beautiful things were destroyed. Nobutaka sent inquires as to my condition every day.

Despite the usual oppressive summer heat, I started to feel slightly better. I was even planning to wash my hair on the seventh, since that was an auspicious day, and I didn't know when I'd be able to manage the task again. After that had been accomplished, Nobutaka presented me with the maternity sash.

During those days of my pregnancy I was often overcome with a sense of unreality. I had difficulty enough thinking of myself as a married woman, let alone a mother. My own body became a stranger in my unsettled, dreamlike state. Could it be that by the end of the year, if all went well, there would be a baby in the house? I could imagine it, but there was another terrifying outcome that was equally possible. From the time the pregnancy sash was tied I would be in a state of defilement, and if I should die before the child was born, my soul would be lost. I ceased writing anything of Genji and instead devoted all my meager energy to copying the Lotus Sutra.

The main house expressed concern. Nobutaka's second-eldest daughter wrote often, enclosing samples of incense blends she had prepared. My sense of smell had developed in an extraordinary way. Although I continued to have an aversion to the odors of food, I was able to discern the ingredients of perfumes with heightened perception.

I moved back to Grandmother's house for the last several months of my confinement. I didn't like to leave my garden, but it was a relief not to have to manage a household. I was told that the chrysanthemums at Sixth Avenue were even more spectacular that year, and I missed seeing them. My husband had the servants wrap the partially open blooms with silk floss one night, and although he had to be at court all day for the festivities of the ninth, he made sure the floss was gathered in a covered ceramic dish and brought over to me late in the morning. Such an amount! I rubbed not only my face but my entire body with the beneficial dew. As I ran my hand over my swollen belly, the child within stirred energetically. I felt certain it was a boy.

The sweet flag and artemisia sachet balls were taken down throughout Grandmother's house and replaced with fresh pomanders of chrysanthemum and rue. I inhaled the bracing, faintly bitter scent of chrysanthemum. People say it increases longevity, but whether it did or not, its fragrance was certainly restorative.

Besides the usual ceremonies and dances, so much was going on at the temporary palace during the eleventh month that my husband was seldom able to visit me. Michinaga's twelve-year-old daughter, Shōshi, was presented as a consort to Emperor Ichijō on the first of the month. Over the past year I had asked Nobutaka so many questions about life at court that he had gradually become more observant. When he came by after Shōshi's presentation, he was bursting with details of the ceremony, knowing that I would be anxious to hear his account.

Young Shōshi herself was quite a beauty, he said. Only twelve, she comported herself with a maturity far beyond her years. Her glossy hair, trailing five or six inches beyond her height, elicited much comment. The ladies-in-waiting of Shōshi's retinue were dressed in magnificent brocade jackets of the forbidden colors,* along with stiff silk trains with wave-and-shell patterns stenciled in silver. For a girl to be chosen as an attendant, it was not enough that her father hold high rank, or that she be good-tempered – only the most polished and socially graceful were accepted. Ah, how enviable to be chosen as a member of this young lady's coterie.

He described a fabulous set of folding screens decorated with paintings and poems by exalted people. He mentioned in particular a picture of a blooming wisteria with a poem by Kintō. He couldn't read the whole thing from where he stood, but it was something about a purple cloud. Nothing was haphazard or left to chance for Shōshi's presentation. Michinaga himself seems to have supervised every detail. As I listened to my husband's account of the numbers and layers of robes everyone wore, I was struck by the opulence of the clothing compared to what Grandmother had told me of earlier times. It was hard to believe that ladies in the old days went about dressed in so few layers, with such meager padding. Nowadays women are always prone to ailments caused by cold weather. To ward off chills, they pile on such mounds of clothing they are in danger of looking like cocoons. It is the fashion, I suppose. Probably even an empress of yore only wore a fraction of what modern people would consider adequate.

Emperor Ichijō must have been twenty years old. His other

---

*Forbidden colors (*kinjiki*) referred to various shades of red and purple, but also to certain patterned weaves of silk that could be worn only by women of third rank and higher.

wives were all older than he. According to my husband, the emperor behaved much better at this ceremony than he had when Empress Teishi was first presented. Well, naturally – the emperor was ten years old then, and Teishi fourteen. Girls mature faster than boys in any case, so the discrepancy in their ages must have seemed even greater than it was. Yet they appeared to have gotten along well, and despite all the problems with her family, Teishi seemed to have a hold on Ichijō's affections still. She was the only one of his wives who had managed to produce a child, and she was due to give birth to another.

I suppose this was the reason Michinaga was anxious to have his own daughter make her court appearance as soon as possible. His position as regent would not be secure until he had an imperial grandson. From what my husband said, every item of Shōshi's furnishings was splendid beyond compare. Every object made of wood was covered with gold lacquer and mother-of-pearl. And while the robes of her attendants were fabulous, anything Shōshi herself wore, no matter how briefly, was so exquisitely dyed and perfumed that one should like to preserve it forever as a masterpiece. Michinaga presented his daughter to Ichijō as a radiant jewel in an opulent setting. It occurred to me that Empress Teishi must be miserable. I wondered if Sei Shōnagon was still with her, still writing entries into her pillow book.

As the year drew to a close, I became restless and strangely energetic, preoccupied with sewing and putting things in order. I thought perhaps it was because at year's end everyone always feels like clearing up unfinished business, but my cousin laughed and assured me that this was a sign that the time for giving birth was drawing near. I had grown accustomed to living with my unwieldy body, having almost forgotten what it was like to sleep through the night without being kicked from within. It sometimes seemed as if pregnancy would go on forever, although I knew, of course, that it couldn't. Either I would die or there would be a child. I was grateful to my cousin, who so constantly reassured me, but I was also afraid.

184

Early in the morning on the seventh of the month my labor started, and by midafternoon a girl child was safely delivered. In contrast to the long unpleasantness of the pregnancy, the birth itself was painful but swift. Empress Teishi gave birth to a prince the very same day.

Nobutaka supervised the offerings of thanks, but he was able to come visit me and his new daughter only once before he left as imperial messenger to the Usa Shrine. It was a prestigious appointment, but he would be gone for two months.

After giving birth, I didn't feel at all frail and was tempted to breast-feed the infant myself. The doctor, however, frowned on the idea. He said a woman's essential energy was weakened from the experience of pregnancy and birth, and nursing would deplete it further. He prescribed a wet nurse for the baby, cheese for me. I wrote to Nobutaka about naming the child, and he agreed to the name Katako, suggested by my father. The Chinese graph *kata* – upright, chaste, and strong – is more often used in boys' names, but that didn't bother me, and Nobutaka had no objection. We planned the official naming ceremony for a time after he returned from his duties at the Usa Shrine.

Staying at my grandmother's house, I was coddled like an infant myself. My cousin cheerfully took on the burden of caring for me and the baby just as if she were my own mother. For once, I was happy to let all responsibilities slip and to lie all day under the quilts with little Koko. I found I could not possibly call the tiny creature who clung to me "Katako." I knew she would grow into the name.

The house was full of decorations for the new year. Nobutaka had a supply of huge mirror-smooth rice cakes sent over. Then the main house sent a bunch of hare wands made of camellia wood to hang on the pillars.* Their paper streamers were done in fanciful modern color combinations

*Hare wands were sticks of trees or shrubs thought to have evil-dispelling, yang qualities, which were then decorated with paper streamers and sent on the first day of the hare – the hare being regarded as an animal of yang nature. In Heian times as well as now, rice cakes round as mirrors were displayed at the beginning of the new year.

rather than the classic red, yellow, green, white, and black. Missing my garden, I told myself it was not at its best in that season. We would all be back there, in any case, by the time the cherries came into bloom.

On the fifteenth I volunteered to prepare the full-moon gruel again. Our recipe had gotten quite a reputation. My cousin, her husband and children, and all the servants pitched in. We made great quantities to give out to all the relatives as well as to the people at Nobutaka's main house. They had been very solicitous of me and the baby since Nobutaka himself had been away, and I wanted to show my gratitude.

My cousin had five children, so it was always lively at Grandmother's house. I rather enjoyed it. Masako, the youngest, a charming child of four, was fascinated by her new little cousin. She often slipped into my room to chat and play with the baby. I tried to imagine Katako at her age. There were several peeled elderwood stirring sticks left from cooking the gruel, so, of course, the children ran about the house, sneaking up on one another and the adults, too, to whack them with a stick. Because she was the youngest, Masako would get switched by all the others but could never catch them back. Tearfully she retreated to my room late in the day.

—Auntie Fuji, I can't get anyone at all, she sobbed.

I smoothed her hair and told her that luck came to the ones who got whacked, not the wielders of the stick.

—It means you will have lots of boy babies, I said, and she brightened.

Then, pretending to return to the fray, she turned suddenly and tapped my leg with her stick.

—That's for your next one, she sang, and dashed away.

I had to smile. I was beginning to think it would be nice to have lots of children.

Nobutaka returned to the capital in the second month, but I did not see him for several days because he was so busy with official duties at the temporary palace and various things needing his attention at the main house. I planned to move back to Sixth Avenue with the baby that month. I preferred

186

him to meet us there, where the surroundings were quieter than at my cousin's boisterous household.

I had heard that Michinaga's daughter Shōshi was leaving the palace in order to prepare for a ceremonial new entrance as empress. This was odd, and I was eager to find out from my husband what was going on. Teishi was empress, after all, and furthermore had just given birth to a prince. Even the regent couldn't simply depose the empress – especially when everyone knew how fond the emperor was of her.

Something else puzzled me. While it seemed he was undermining Empress Teishi, Michinaga pardoned her brother Korechika at the same time, allowing him to return to the capital. I found my thoughts dwelling on this man Michinaga. Even though he had maneuvered my father into becoming his spy, our family was greatly in his debt for the Echizen posting. His way, apparently, was never to press his will without bestowing a favor at the same time.

Nobutaka's official carriage took us back to the Sixth Avenue house. The morning was balmy, and blossoming plums sent petals scattering on each puff of spring breeze. I could hardly wait to see my garden again.

I liked to sit with the baby wrapped up at my side, out in the pavilion off the western wing of the house. The wisteria buds, grown fat, would soon burst out in magnificent purple waves. I was working on a story of Genji back in Miyako. An occasion arose for him to pull out the sketches he painted in exile, and in retrospect, from the vantage of his comfortable existence back at court, Suma would seem poignant.

I had been hearing more rumors about goings-on above the clouds* and was simply dying of curiosity for details. Nobutaka was finally able to spend a bit of time with me after being on call for most of the second month. According to him, Empress Teishi had been staying in the imperial quarters ever since Shōshi had returned to her mother's house. The emperor

*"Above the clouds" (*kumo no ue*) was another metaphor for the imperial palace.

spent all his time with Teishi and her children, the five-year-old princess and the baby prince born the same day as our own Katako. I could understand the emperor's feelings. Even those who dwell above the clouds are subject to the emotions that bind parent and child.

—If only you could have seen the magnificent brocades Shōshi was wearing before she left the palace, remarked Nobutaka as we were looking at some picture scrolls out on the pavilion.

Knowing how I loved textiles, he now made a special effort to observe them more closely while he was on duty. Nobutaka's rank gave him the privilege of entering the emperor's private residence within the palace grounds. From him I could get a much better idea of palace life than I had ever gleaned from my father. Father had hovered on the fringes of the ninefold enclosure, but he was never anything like an intimate there.

—You would have been fascinated, my husband continued. Her mantle was Chinese damask – and it was the real stuff, imported I'm sure. I've never seen our local weavers able to match this. It was a plum-red color, and the figure was double-flowered plums. I wasn't close enough to see how the work was done, but it looked as if the designs in the warp and weft diverged in opposite directions. It was an eye-catcher, I'll tell you that. It's simply mind-boggling what Michinaga must be spending to create his daughter's ongoing displays!

—And how does the emperor feel about all this? I asked.

—It's very interesting, my husband declared. Ichijō is captivated by novelty, like anyone, but he is a gentle man who loves beautiful things of all sorts. Naturally he is drawn to Shōshi because she is young and attractive. Also, her father has stocked her apartments with fabulous treasures. He is always assured of finding something novel to interest him when he visits. There is no reason for him not to show preference to Shōshi – yet Teishi has been with him a long time. She is the mother of his two children. In some ways, I think he feels more at ease with her.

—And what about the rumor that Shōshi is going to be made empress? I asked him.

188

Nobutaka smiled vaguely and rubbed his chin. Then he said that he would tell me what had been decided, even though it hadn't been officially announced yet, if I promised not to say a word to anyone.

—Whom would I tell? I asked, picking up the infant, who had begun to cry in her basket.

I now had more sympathy for women like my stepmother, whom I used to scorn for being so easily distracted. A mother's ears are unnaturally sharp, and her own child's least whimper can obscure the most interesting conversation.

—Yes, Shōshi will receive the imperial title at the end of the month, my husband confided.

—What about Empress Teishi?

—Teishi will also be promoted.

—How can an empress be promoted? I asked.

—Shōshi will take Teishi's previous title, and Teishi will be given a new one, said Nobutaka with a slight smile.

—But there's no precedent for that, I protested. It doesn't make any sense.

—On the contrary, my husband corrected me. There may be no precedent, but it makes a great deal of sense.

On a moment's reflection, of course he was right. From Michinaga's point of view it made all the sense in the world. So we were to have two empresses – one with children but poor karma; the other with riches and excellent connections, and youth.

My husband had never spent any time actually holding his other children when they were infants. Now they were all grown, and perhaps because it occurred to him that he might not have many more at his age, he clumsily attempted to pick up the baby and soothe her when she fussed. I felt sure with Katako he would be more like an indulgent grandfather than a strict father.

I was sent a lovely picture scroll by an old friend of Father's. I showed it to Nobutaka one night when he stayed late. One painting in particular moved me. It depicted some women who had opened up a side door and were sitting at the edge of their room looking out at a blossoming pear tree. The others had fallen asleep, but an old woman, resting her chin in her hand, was gazing raptly at the scene. I could easily imagine it as I looked over at our own blooming pear tree, and I composed the following, based on the viewpoint of the old woman:

Haru no yo no   yami no madoi ni   iro naranu   kokoro ni hana no   ka wo zo shimetsuru
Lost in the dark spring night, color and passion gone, one's heart yet steeps in the fragrant bloom.

We had not made love since I had given birth, but that didn't bother me. I urged Nobutaka to choose a painting he liked and turn out a poem on it. He picked a picture but then insisted that I compose the poem for him because he was tired, and besides I was much more skillful than he in such matters. He continued to flatter me so much that I finally gave in.

In another section of the scroll was a scene of an oxcart. The same group of figures was viewing the autumn foliage at Sagano. One of the older serving women reached to break off a branch of purple, pea-flowered *hagi*. Since Nobutaka liked puns, I concocted this:

Saoshika no   shika narawaseru   hagi nare ya   tachiyoru kara ni   onore orefusa
The hagi loves the deer, and thus, dear, bends as you approach.

It was a little silly, but he thought it clever.

Summer began. How pleasant the sun felt early in the morning. When I went out onto the verandah, the cat was sure to be there already, having found the best place to stretch out and bask in the warm rays. Nobutaka chided me for being so fond of cats, but after he told me about the way cats were treated at the palace, even he had to admit I was not as cat-crazy as the emperor and empress. Late last summer when one of the palace cats had a litter of kittens, the emperor summoned both ministers of state to attend a birth ceremony. The kittens were then assigned a palace lady as personal nurse. Empress Teishi took one of the pretty spotted ones into

190

her own entourage and called it Lady Miyaubu. She even bestowed a lacquered cap of noble rank on the creature.

Miyaubu had quite an adventure last month, according to the story Nobutaka heard from Tadakata, the imperial chamberlain. Apparently the kitty's nurse was annoyed that the cat would not come in from the verandah when she called it. (Ignorant woman. Everyone knows cats hate to be ordered about.) So instead of coaxing it, this ridiculous lady summoned one of the dogs to come give the cat a scare. The dog, Okinamaro, rushed in barking, and the terrified Miyaubu dashed behind a screen into the imperial dining room. The emperor himself happened to be sitting there, and he picked up the frightened cat, cradling it in his arms.

The emperor was quite angry with the dog. He called his chamberlain to punish Okinamaro and banish him from the palace, and then he dismissed the lady who had been in charge of the cat. It served the woman right, I dare say, for she showed a great lack of sense. Tadakata felt the whole thing was silly, since the dog was just acting according to its nature, but he was obliged to follow the emperor's orders. He and Sanefusa took the poor dog outside the gates and flogged it almost to death.

—The emperor is somewhat frustrated these days, my husband remarked after relating this story. There is not a great deal of influence he can bring to bear on matters outside of imperial ceremonies. Michinaga advises him on every move. Perhaps it's not surprising he takes his feelings out on the animals. And, oh yes, I almost forgot to tell you. There is a rumor that Empress Teishi may be pregnant again. She left the palace right after that incident with the cat.

Young Shōshi was due to be crowned empress in the fourth month. Involved in refurbishing the imperial apartments, Nobutaka had been telling us about the preparations. Since I had never seen the imperial quarters, I queried him endlessly about the details. Everything was splendid and new, he reported. Shōshi's curtained platform was black lacquer with mother-of-pearl inlay on the sides. The corner pillars supporting the ceiling were of the same design, also inlaid. The tatami mats on the platform were edged in damask, and the curtains between the pillars were of the most delicately dyed silk bombycine with long brocade streamers.

An imperial dining bench of rosewood with mother-of-pearl inlay sat nearby. It consisted of two sections put together and covered with mats edged in black and white damask. The armrest was matching rosewood and there was also a round silk cushion to lean against. The food trays were probably lacquer with inlay, my husband supposed, but he hadn't actually seen them. I remarked that I would be quite self-conscious if I had to climb onto a special piece of furniture to eat my meal in splendid isolation, as these imperial persons did. Nobutaka said the young empress seemed born to the role. Even at thirteen she carried herself impressively.

The imperial apartment also had a large white ceramic figure of a Korean dog on one side of the entrance to the curtained platform and a yellow lion on the other. The dog's mouth was closed, the lion's open.

—They are there to keep the curtains from blowing in a breeze, Nobutaka told me. And they help keep evil spirits away as well.

Whatever their function, the fact was that only royalty had such fabulous creatures at their bedsides. My husband said that Shōshi's younger ladies-in-waiting were quite fascinated and amazed by all these imperial accoutrements being assembled for their mistress.

Sometimes I envied my husband for the wonderful scenes he was privileged to see when on palace duty. He was quite blasé about things I would have given my best inkstick to get a glimpse of. I knew it was extremely unlikely that I would ever see the inside of the imperial quarters, though, and I had to content myself with secondhand descriptions. Nobutaka laughed and told me I would absolutely hate palace life, given all the veiled bickering and maneuvering that goes on in the women's quarters.

—Now that Shōshi has become empress, he said, all her ladies-in-waiting have to conform strictly to the rules when it comes to the fabric for their cloaks. Before her ascension, everyone could wear forbidden colors and weaves in order to make a splendid showing, but now only those with rank can wear them. The others have to content themselves with unfigured silks, and they are in a snit. They complain that the palace servants disdain them because they are not turned out as fashionably as their betters.

—When the emperor visits Shōshi in her new apartments, he complains that he used to think of her as a playmate he could relax with, but now she has become so formal and proper he is afraid she will scold him for being frivolous.

—Perhaps the emperor said it as a joke, my husband remarked, for the ladies laugh behind their fans at his reproaches. But I imagine there is a nugget of truth in his discomfort.

The rains of the fifth month came, but I didn't mind them so much. My attention was absorbed in keeping the baby dry and unchafed during the day. I was happy just to gaze out at the beautiful pond in my garden. I could see large patches of green water between dense clumps of iris and water oats, and the whole garden seemed to shimmer in shades of green. I liked the fact that our pond had not been overtended. Left to itself, some parts were rather wild and grown over. At night the green spaces of water glowed in the pale moonlight.

Summer passed quickly. In the seventh month the wrestling matches were arranged with particular care because the crown prince had decided to attend. Nobutaka asked me if I would like to go, but I declined. The heat was frightful.

I heard that Chifuru's family had returned to the capital. We had not corresponded for some time, and I immediately wrote to them. I was shocked when they replied that Chifuru had died at the beginning of summer. Why had no one told me? I thought about how we had written to each other when she was far away in Tsukushi and I was at the opposite end of the empire in Echizen. An exchange of letters could take weeks, yet the thread connecting us remained strong. Then she had one child, and another. I had been miffed when she didn't write as often as I wished, not understanding how motherhood absorbed one's energy.

At the time Chifuru left for the western wilderness, I felt her absence as strongly as if she had died. Yet my letters could follow her, like clouds chasing the moon. Now her journey west continued, through the clouds, on to Amida's paradise, where my letters could not follow, except in smoke. I burned our old correspondence along with incense in her memory. To her family, I sent this poem:

Izukata no   kumoji to kikaba   tazunemashi   tsura hanarekemu   kari ga yukue wo
I yearn to ask what path it followed through the clouds –
the wild goose that flew off, leaving the flock.

The wind bent the reeds at the edge of the pond, and dew collected on the leaves of arching sprays of purple bush clover. Autumn always induces melancholy, and that year was no different. Were I to compare myself to a fruit, it would have to be a persimmon that has begun to soften and lose its astringency. I had been thinking about Genji's plan to bring together the women he had loved over the years. The problem all along was how to reconcile a woman's need for constancy with a man's desire for novelty. I kept thinking how a man abhors a jealous woman, and women fear fickle men, yet it is precisely these tendencies in one gender that provoke those reactions in the other.

Genji would have to quell the breezes of ill will that usually spoil the relations between men and women. Back in Miyako I had Genji build himself a palatial compound where the different women of his life, like the seasons, would dwell in harmony. It was an interesting challenge to arrange the various pavilions and gardens to match the personalities of their inhabitants. Originally I had thought of Genji as the center of this universe of women. Later, as the extended mansion took shape in my mind, I realized that the ladies themselves were of far more interest to me. Hearing of Chifuru's death had brought me up short. Had she ever been happy? It bothered me that I didn't know but could only imagine. I think she probably was. If not, she would have written. Contentment is its own reward; unhappiness pushes one to write. I gave Murasaki the southeast pavilion, the one with the spring garden full of birch cherries and wisteria.

Absorbed as I was in Genji, I still followed the news from the palace with fascination. Empress Teishi was suffering a difficult pregnancy. Nobutaka said that her family had tried to get reputable priests to come to the residence to chant the sutras, but all the famous clerics were chary of involvement lest they fall into bad odor with Michinaga. They sent unreliable substitutes who fell asleep during perfunctory readings. Teishi's brother Korechika had practically become a monk himself, so exclusively did he devote himself to her well-being. How unlike the swaggeringly handsome courtier he was before his exile – he now practiced abstinence and conducted himself with monkish seriousness. He only hope for the future was that his sister survive and the baby prince someday attain the throne, a possibility that seemed to fade before his eyes.

My husband was quite pleased to have been asked to perform a dance in a music pageant at court in the tenth month. He conducted extra rehearsals at the Sixth Avenue mansion rather than at the main house, and I could see that he really was an uncommonly fine dancer. The reconstruction of the palace was finally complete, and the emperor was to move back in time for the Gosechi Dances* in the eleventh month. Once again Nobutaka would be busy with the relocation. My husband had no official part in those performances, but he dearly loved to hang around the rehearsals – partly, I was sure, to eye the pretty dancers.

I noticed that the moss in the garden looked particularly beautiful in winter. One could appreciate its deep glowing green without the distraction of other flowering plants. Even though everyone thinks of moss as a characteristically

*These dances were part of the courtly entertainment for the Great Thanksgiving Service held in the eleventh month. Each group of dancers was sponsored by a royal person, and infinite pains were taken to present one's protégée in an elegant fashion.

summer thing, I made a note to myself to put moss in Genji's winter garden.

My husband said Empress Teishi herself was to sponsor a set of dancers for the Gosechi Festival. A group of her attendants, including Sei Shōnagon, was visiting the palace. I gathered that the lady who wrote the pillow book was renowned for her repartee. Nobutaka joined a small crowd of nobles that hung around the Shōnagon to gossip and reminisce about the old days when Michitaka was regent. My husband said she was not his type at all, but her wit and self-assurance left the younger women tongue-tied.

The emperor summoned Teishi's ladies numerous times to hear about her condition and how she spent her days. He was worried, anyone could see, but there was little he could do. He tried to get his mother, the dowager empress Senshi, to intercede and make things easier for Teishi. Senshi was the only one who held any sway over her brother Michinaga.

Teishi's baby was due in a month, and I couldn't shake a sense of foreboding. I wondered why I was moved to such an extent by her plight. It was quite possible that everything might turn out fine for her. Perhaps my sympathetic misgiving arose from the fact that she, like I, lay close to Michinaga's powerful shadow and would be affected by it no matter what. Unlike the empress, I myself was an insignificant blade of grass, but even the grass would be trampled if it happened to be underfoot.

Our little Katako celebrated the beginning of her second year. She was a plump and rosy child, with four teeth already. In the spring of the new year I knew I should pay special attention to the tooth-hardening foods and herbs. How one's perspective changes when one has a child to look out for. Every snivel sends a mother to distraction, afraid that if great care is not exercised, the cough will develop into an illness in the chest. I could hardly have borne it if something were to happen to this child.

We were so close to the end of the year the calendar rollers were visible. There would always be something about the year's drawing to a close that pricked me with misgivings.

Never again would I think that a year's misfortune was done before the year was completely out. It was strange that this feeling persisted even after a year of such quiet contentment.

Just to be safe, even though these were not abstinence days for me, I fixed willow-wood taboo tags to my dress and stayed inside. Nevertheless, Nobutaka visited right before the close of the year and insisted on coming in. He had just come from the palace, and I could tell immediately from his somber face that something dreadful had happened.

Two nights before, Empress Teishi had been seized by the pangs of labor, and after a relatively easy time, a girl child was born. Although her attendants were disappointed that it wasn't a prince, at least the empress had survived the ordeal, and the only remaining worry was the afterbirth. The priests set to chanting furiously, and Korechika rushed to send out payments to all the major temples to commission prayers. Yet the afterbirth did not come. By dawn the empress lay still. An imperial messenger was dispatched to inform the emperor of her death.

The court plunged into mourning, and all the official new year festivities were canceled. My husband made the expected round of visits to keep up his connections, but the gloom emanating from the palace put a damper on everything. The poor emperor secluded himself in his own quarters, refusing to come out ever since the snowy day of Teishi's burial. They had found poems the empress had scribbled on scraps of paper and hung on the curtain streamers during her last days. She had been morbidly aware of her impending death, writing that "though her body not be transformed into clouds or smoke," she hoped the emperor would think of her as he gazed at dew on the grass. Ichijō interpreted this to mean she did not wish to be cremated. How very depressed she must have been. It's hard to imagine how she could have survived given the inauspicious shroud of poems she wove for herself. She even denied her family the pitiful consolation of glimpsing a wisp of smoke suspended over the funeral plain.

Nobutaka reported to the palace every day. The atmosphere there was strained, he told me. The emperor finally invited Shōshi to visit his imperial quarters to cheer him up, but she avoided the summons, preferring to remain in her own suite. The emperor was not inclined to visit her there. I found this rather shocking but could see that it must have been rather awkward for her.

Dowager Empress Senshi took the motherless newborn princess under her wing.

Spring went by under a cloud of gray mourning. In the third month the peach blossoms were so vibrant I brought them indoors and decided to set out all of Katako's dolls at the house. I pulled my own childhood dolls from storage, and Nobutaka brought over a number of new ones, including prince and princess dolls he had commissioned from the same famous dollmaker who made the ones the royal children played with at the palace. Katako was still too young to handle them, but she reached out for the colorful fabrics and beautiful shapes. We put them on stands in the main room.

Late in the day I was roused out of my study by the baby's cries and loud shouts from the nurse. The cat had gotten in and was investigating the offerings placed before the dolls. When she jumped on one of the stands, it had flipped over, sending the dolls tumbling and frightening Katako, who began to wail. I hurried in and, seeing what had happened, picked up the dolls and straightened the little bowls and dishes. The child watched from her nurse's lap, calming as she saw things set aright. I thought then that she was a sensitive child. I could imagine that some babies would have laughed and clapped their hands at the excitement.

The weather was unseasonably warm. I had all the lattices of the house drawn open completely to the garden. Sturdy branches of flowering peach were arranged in huge Chinese vases in the main hall near the dolls, and smaller vases of cherry blossoms set out near the entry. I waited for my husband, who had promised to come by to see the dolls. It grew dark, and I had the maids light the oil lamps in the hall. The effect of the flickering light on the brocade of the doll's robes was even more beautiful than it had been in daylight, and I anticipated Nobutaka's pleasure when he saw the elegant display. He had thrown himself completely into the building of this house and garden and came here whenever he could.

It grew very late, and the lantern candles guttered down. I had fallen asleep and woken with a start in the dark room. Nobutaka had not come. I called a sleepy servant to close up the shutters, and went back to the northern chamber where the baby was sleeping with her nurse. When it got light, I sent a messenger to the main house to see what had happened to hold him up. The petals of the cherry blossoms I had arranged in the entry had already started to drop, so I swept them away.

Around noon the messenger came back accompanied by Nobutaka's chief manservant.

—I regret to inform you, madam, he announced in a tight voice, Master Nobutaka was taken ill yesterday evening, and his soul departed at dawn. You may come join the other wives in an attempt to summon it back.

My shock was so great I couldn't respond. The steward bowed and said gently,

—There is need for haste.

I nodded and called for my traveling robes, but he raised his hand and told me a carriage was ready and I should just come as I was.

We arrived at the main house in time to see the doctor of divination who was acting as Returner climb to the roof, carrying one of Nobutaka's robes. Standing on the ridge facing north, he called out in the direction of darkness and ghosts,

—Fujiwara Nobutaka! Return!

And again, the same long, drawn-out call. And yet a third time. Each time he beckoned with the robe, trying to induce the spirit back from its northward journey into darkness. After the third call, the Returner folded the garment and threw it down in front of the house. One of Nobutaka's sons carefully scooped it up and, placing it in a metal receptacle, carried it into the house to where the body was resting. We followed.

If the Returner had been successful, the soul would have been snared in the robe and then, when the robe was spread out over Nobutaka, it would have returned to the body. I joined the wives and children and we waited. By evening it was clear that my husband's spirit was not coming back. Before us lay the empty husk.

My father was granted permission to shorten his stay in Echizen, and he and the family came back to Miyako early that summer.

AN INK-BLACK HAZE

Sumizome ni kasumu sora

For the year following my husband's death I put on black mourning. I ceased writing altogether. Not only was Genji banished from my thoughts, I did not even note entries in my diary. I don't think I even set down a poem during that entire time. Steeped in remorse, when I took up my brush it was only to copy out the Lotus Sutra. One day, looking for more paper, I seized upon my journal and used the reverse sides of those sheets to continue my devotions.* This was the only way I could think of to begin to atone for my years of recalcitrance and selfishness.

My father and the family returned to Miyako and stayed with me in the house on Sixth Avenue until the end of summer. With my father, stepmother, and three children in the northern wing, and Nobunori in the western annex, we

---

*Centuries later, a legend sprang up that Murasaki had been inspired to write her *Tale of Genji* while gazing at the full moon at Ishiyama Temple. It was said that in the haste of her inspiration she began scribbling on the backs of scrolls of sutras. Such sacrilege (were it true) also fed into the medieval notion that Murasaki was suffering in hell for the sin of writing fiction.

It was more likely in fact for people to copy religious works on the back sides of letters or secular texts that the other way around.

were always bumping into one another – yet their noisy energy made life bearable and provided me a thread connecting to society. Had it not been for them and my young daughter, I would probably have renounced the world altogether. In the fall Father took his family back to his official residence, although he continued to visit me and Katako almost every day. I did not go out myself.

He was having difficulty with readjusting to life in the city. I teased him he was like Bai Juyi returning to Luoyang after three years in charge of a province. All the poet cared about was two exotic garden rocks and the pet crane he had brought back with him. But Father bested me by quoting from another of the same poet's works called "Newly Planted Bamboo":

> Having charge of a town suited me not;
> I shut my gates as autumn grasses grew.
> How could I suit my love of nature?
> I planted over a hundred stalks of bamboo.

Perhaps this gave him the idea. When he wasn't composing poems in Chinese, he began planning a garden.

—Well, why not a hundred stalks of bamboo? he decided.

He drew on his love of Chinese poetry to fuel his newfound interest in gardening. So I said to him,

—Why not some exotic rocks and a pet crane, too?

When Dowager Empress Senshi was given a magnificent celebration for her fortieth birthday that autumn, Father attended and presented a poem. He told me all about the festivities, but I no longer heard the inside gossip about the emperor and empress that my husband used to relate. I only knew what everyone else knew. When the newly rebuilt imperial palace also burned down, I thought of how Nobutaka would have been right in the thick of things; and when soon thereafter Senshi herself sickened, I missed the detailed daily accounts of her condition. She died at the end of the year. There was no one left who had anything like her kind of influence over Michinaga. People muttered that the devastating fires and royal deaths were signs of the decay of

201

the age of Buddha's Law and that we should continue to expect even worse in the years to come.

One of my friends was known as Lady Saishō after entering Shōshi's service. This lady sent me a poem one hazy evening in spring not long after the empress dowager had passed away. The official mourning period for my husband had not yet ended, and I was still steeped in gloom. Shaishō had written:

Kumo no ue mo   mono omou haru wa   sumizome ni   kasumu sora sae   aware naru kana
**Spring brings mourning even above the clouds, and the sky
is dark with an ink-black haze of sadness.**

Her poem jolted me out of self-pity. I was not the only one in black, after all. I began to emerge from my cocoon of mourning as I searched for words to reply to Saishō's poem:

Nani ka kono   hodo naki sode wo   nurasuramu   kasumi no koromo   nabete kiru yo ni
**How can it be that I still cry into my insignificant sleeve
when the whole world is garbed in deepest mourning?**

During that time I went out only to attend memorial rites for my husband at the main house. At the end of one year the entire family and an extensive group of Nobutaka's friends gathered for the annual memorial. I noticed his second-eldest daughter at the service, looking fragile in her heavy mourning, wearing a gown of the deepest black. Nobutaka's grown-up children, all in black, stood out in the field of gray robes like the shadows of plovers on an overcast riverbank. She told me she had found a sheaf of jottings in a hand resembling that of her father, and wondered whether I would like to see them. Undoubtedly among them would be poems from the various affairs that had so put me off before our marriage, but I said I would be grateful for a glimpse. I was touched that she should have given them to me rather than someone else. I could imagine it was just a painful for her to read them. I sent her this poem:

Yuugiri ni   mishimagakureshi   oshi no ka no   ato wo miru miru   madowaruru kana

The mandarin duck has disappeared in the evening mist, and the young one can only gaze, lost, at traces left behind.

I couldn't help but notice that in the year since my husband died the family had neglected the gardens and even let the everyday maintenance of the great house slip. The cherries were blooming in abundance, but the buildings were looking a little dilapidated. Soon after I returned home, a beautiful branch of cherry blossoms arrived with the accompanying poem from Nobutaka's daughter:

Chiru hana wo   nagekishi hito wa   ko no moto no   sabishiki koto ya   kanete shiririkemu

When he lamented the scattering blossoms, he already knew the sorrow that would remain with his children beneath the tree.

Although my husband had not been particularly moody, every so often he was seized by a sudden melancholy and talked of the boundless sadness of life. Even his drinking companions had rarely seen this side of Nobutaka.

When the period of mourning officially ended, Father urged me to take off my iron-gray robes and change to brighter colors. He said I was a stubborn creature and that my emotions, once set, were as slow to turn as a ceremonial oxcart. He reminded me how I had resisted Nobutaka for years before our marriage.

—And now, I suppose, you will insist on mourning him equally long, he scolded. The other wives have all changed back to colors, so it will look strange if you are the only one to persist in grays. These things are not simply a matter of one's own feelings. You must be sensitive to what others think.

Of course he was right. Sunk in my own misery, I never considered how it would appear to the people at the main house for me to continue to wear mourning after they had changed – as if their feelings were shallow in comparison to mine. So even though my heart remained dark, I changed my garb as society expected. As with so many things, I was realizing, it was necessary to cloak one's inner feelings.

I put together a set of robes in shades of yellow, white, and greens, a combination my mother had often worn in early summer. She said it was called *Flowering Calamondin*, explaining that wearing a deep yellow robe next to a white one reminds us how we often see both golden fruit and white blossom together on that citrus tree. When little Katako saw me that morning, she clapped her hands and lisped,

—Pretty dress, Mama!

Of course she must have grown tired of seeing me in gray for so long.

The days passed uneventfully. Though no longer in mourning, I seldom went out. The plague continued to rage, and it would have been foolhardy to tempt those demons. One day I received a visit from my friend Lady Saishō as she was taking a brief leave of absence from imperial service. It seemed to me she led a glamorous life, and I was envious. She protested.

—It is wearying, she said.

She relished the chance to get away. I couldn't help pressing her for stories of life at court. Since my husband died, I had been completely in the dark.

She told me about the latest scandal concerning the death of Prince Tametaka. He was having an affair with Izumi Shikibu – another of those literary ladies who had gotten themselves a reputation. The prince was notorious for pursuing his amorous adventures without regard to what anyone thought. The streets may have been seething with demons at night and befouled by the corpses of plague victims piled up at the corners, but none of this deterred him from visiting his lover. With such recklessness, his death should not have come as a surprise, but Saishō said his father, the retired emperor, refused to believe it.

—Just keep looking, they say he begged. You're sure to find him somewhere.

About the same time, the crown prince's consort Seishi, who had been quite ill all year, suddenly made a miraculous recovery.

—Finally, said Saishō, there was something positive. But then, just as suddenly, the crown prince's other consort, Genshi, died horribly, blood gushing out her nose and mouth. It makes you wonder, she said darkly, if there wasn't some sort of connection.

—What do you mean? I asked her.

—Well, people are saying it's too much of a coincidence that Seishi, who had been at death's door, suddenly recovered just when Genshi, who hadn't been at all sick, was stricken. It has all the signs of a curse.

I nodded, reminded with a shiver of my husband's comment that I should surely hate palace life with its morbid bickering and deadly rivalries. I began to see why Saishō might be relieved to get away from that atmosphere for a while.

—It is bad-mannered of me to speak ill of the dead, but I've heard strange rumors about Genshi, I said. I know the crown prince found her difficult. My husband mentioned that once when he was a guest at their residence, Genshi rolled up the blinds and stood there with her robes open, exposing her breasts. The crown prince was embarrassed, and the guests all stared at the floor. My husband said they didn't know whether to stay or leave.

Saishō said the story was quite believable and accorded with things she herself had heard. Once when a group of students from the university was composing Chinese poetry at the crown prince's mansion, Genshi began throwing bags of gold dust at them from behind her screen. The students felt they had to pretend enthusiasm and scramble for the bags, but in fact they found it quite undignified. Genshi also made loud comments about their poetry.

We agreed that she was probably not completely right in the head. Saishō lifted her thick hair off the back of her neck and twisted it over her shoulder. It was hot, even with all the doors completely open to the garden.

—And yet Genshi was Korechika's sister, I mused, thinking of the string of misfortunes that had plagued that unlucky man.

—Poor Korechika! responded Saishō. First he loses his

sister the empress, and now Genshi. How can there be any future for him? Michitaka's karma has completely fizzled out. His daughters are dead, and his sons twist in the wind without support. Unless you're connected to Michinaga these days, your prospects are not very bright.

Yes, I thought to myself, it's just as well Michinaga seems to think well of Father. The regent gave him many presents when he returned from Echizen, praising his work with the Chinese.

I asked Saishō what it was like living with Empress Shōshi as a mistress. I had expected her to say that Shōshi was completely spoiled, but she surprised me.

—Her Majesty is quite serious, she said. Perhaps overly so. And punctilious to a fault. There was a lady-in-waiting (I won't mention names, and in any case you don't know her) who was a bit careless and often spoke out of turn. She did this at an important event last year, shocking Her Majesty. The woman was dismissed, and everyone else took it as a warning not to be forward. The incident has had a bit of a damping effect on life, I must say. Of course it is preferable to do nothing rather than embarrass oneself doing something rash or silly on a public occasion. Still, now I feel we are constantly living in fear of taking a false step.

—Perhaps when the empress matures a bit, she won't be so strict, I said. When people get older, they come to understand that everyone has their good points and bad, and all of us make mistakes. She is probably even more severe with herself than with her ladies.

—Ah, that's quite true, said Saishō.

Then I asked my friend something that I had been wondering about for a long time.

—What about the empress's father, Michinaga? Personally, I mean. Does he spend much time in Shōshi's quarters?

Saishō lowered her eyes.

—Constantly, she murmured. One must always be on guard. Fortunately he is easily distracted.

—Oh, I said, guessing from her blushes that Michinaga had more than a roving eye.

—Do you remember Sei Shōnagon, the one who wrote the

pillow book everyone was reading? asked Saishō, changing the subject.

—Yes, I've read parts of it, I said. What has become of her?

—She went into Genshi's service after Teishi died. I wonder what she'll do now? How inconvenient when one's mistresses keep passing away.

I was sitting out on the fishing pavilion hoping to catch a faint breeze. On the table lay a picture scroll open to a section with a painting of a famous place called Shiogama in Mutsu. The "salt flats" of the name of the place made me think of the fires the fishermen make to boil salt from the brine. I was sunk in a melancholy mood, and the image of briny plumes of smoke reminded me of the smoky funeral plain on the day of my husband's cremation. I composed this poem:

Mishi hito no   keburi to narishi   yuube yori   na zo mutsumashiki   shiogam no ura
Since that evening when the one I loved turned into smoke, the name Shiogama Bay always reminds me of him.

I felt very old, as though my life were drawing to a close. After Lady Saishō's visit I realized that never again would I be in a position to follow life at court, even at a remove, and that the likelihood of learning anything new I could apply to Genji was practically nil. My inspiration had run dry.

In the fall I was surprised to receive a visit from Chifuru's brother, who had just returned to Miyako from a posting somewhere far away. He had married a lady I knew slightly, but she had died, leaving him with two children. His story was sad, but even as I listened sympathetically, I began to get the feeling that he was not simply paying a courtesy visit to reminisce about his deceased sister. Ultimately I became convinced that he was casting about for a new wife and mother for his children. I tried to deflect him gently, for I was quite sure I should never marry again.

About a week after this visit, I heard someone knocking at my gate late at night. I made no move to open it, and eventually whoever it was gave up. The next morning this poem arrived:

Yo no tomo ni   araki kaze fuku   nishi no umi mo   isobe ni nami wa   yosezu to ya mishi
Since the beginning of time, rough winds have whipped the western seas, and I have never known the waves not to eventually break upon the shore.

I found such confidence irritating and wrote back:

Kaerite wa   omoishirinu ya   iwakado ni   ukite yorikeru   kishi no adanami
As they retreat, surely the fickle waves understand it is of no use to pound against this rocky shore.

I was fairly sure that after this I would not hear from him again.

A thin snow cloaked the garden in a light robe of white. As I looked out, it struck me that this was precisely the effect one strives for in dressing in summer – a gauzy white gown worn over trousers of a single color. I pointed this out to Katako, but, of course, she was too young to understand such things.

—How can the garden wear a summer dress in winter? she asked, puzzled.

—No, it is we who wear white in summer to remind us of the cool snow, I replied.

But she still seemed confused, and suddenly I saw the world from the point of view of a child, free from the layers and shades of meaning with which we adults are always draping our perceptions.

I was reminded of a night when we were served some wild boar meat which Father had managed to procure. He had developed a taste for deer, boar, and other wild game from our sojourn in Echizen, and since these meats were not so easy to obtain in Miyako, he was delighted when he could get them. Of course we called boar meat "pheasant" and venison "duck" when we ate them, in order to disguise their four-legged origins – but Katako was not fooled. The child could barely tolerate the thought of eating fish or fowl, let alone a four-legged

208

creature. She pushed her plate away and stubbornly refused to eat another bite. She must have been around three years old at the time. Oddly she loved a certain little river fish, but she seemed to have convinced herself it was a kind of floating vegetable.

The new year came, and among the usual salutations that streamed into the house was a letter from Chifuru's brother, apparently still a lonely widower. He inquired whether the change of season meant that perhaps my door was now open. What thick skin that man had! I replied:

Taga sato no   haru no tayori ni   uguisu no   kasumi ni tozuru   yado wo touramu
What village can he be from, this warbler who comes,
chirping of spring, to a house still enfolded in the mist?

I bore him no ill will, and I certainly hoped he would find himself a wife, but really, he was too much.

Father was again without position at court, but he didn't seem to mind. He was always welcome in official circles, basking as he did in Michinaga's good graces, and was regularly summoned to poetry gatherings. In the second month he had been invited to Michinaga's eldest son's coming-of-age ceremony, held at the Biwa Mansion. Michinaga had just bought that lovely old house and property the year before from an elderly widow. In the summer the grove of ancient loquat trees in its garden produced an astonishing quantity of fruit. This I knew firsthand, for we used to visit there when I was a child.

Father came home overawed by the magnificence of the celebration and splendid presents for the participants. The palace minister who conferred the cap of adulthood on the boy was given an entire set of silk robes, two horses, and a falcon. Even spectators like Father were given beautiful commemorative fans as souvenirs.

There was a heavy fall of spring snow that day, and when Father returned from the festivities, I was reminded of that snowy day seven years ago when he came home from his meeting with Michinaga bearing the news that was to change

209

out lives. Back then I could see no farther than the end of my nose in my anxious desire to escape from marriage by fleeing to Echizen, and now to think after all I had been through, here I was back in Miyako, a widow, caring only about my child and my garden.

I took great pains to see that the garden was well maintained. Spring was the season when I was most rewarded. As the plum trees finished announcing spring, they dropped their blossoms in favor of leaves while the cherry and iris came into their prime. I told the gardener to snip off all the remaining double-camellia blooms. They were lovely in winter when their hardy flowers cling to the branch even under a late snow, but by now they were tired and should have had the grace to fall. A double camellia can be completely brown yet hold fast to the bough as if thinking itself still worthy of being admired. I pointed this out to Father, and he laughed, remarking that he once knew an elderly coquette at the palace who was just like one of those camellias.

Father was in a good humor. The younger boys were proving much keener at their studies than Nobunori had ever been, and Father drilled them every day in the classics. And, he said, there might yet be a chance for Nobunori. Father had been probing his court connections to see whether there was a minor position that someone of Nobunori's meager talents could fill. Even to be a scribe would at least give him official standing. He was rather good-looking, and if he just kept his mouth shut, he would not make a bad impression. He had no trouble finding women who thought him charming and, indeed, even fancied himself a poet. If one were to judge by his success in getting into ladies' boudoirs, I suppose his opinion was justified.

Once again the rains came, putting everyone out of sorts. It had been drizzling all day without break when a group of Nobunori's friends came over late one afternoon when I was visiting Father's house. They called for saké and settled down to serious drinking and uninhibited discussion. The young men made no attempt to keep their voices down, so I was privy to much of what they said without making the least attempt to eavesdrop. They had started to tease my brother about his poetic prowess and demanded to see some of his correspondence with various ladies. I heard Nobunori say that maybe he would let them see certain letters, but there were others he would not. Of course this only piqued their curiosity, and someone protested that those were precisely the ones they wanted to look at.

—The letters from women who feel abused, who sit alone all night just waiting for you to appear – those are the letters we should like to see, I heard another say.

I could tell my brother was flattered by the attention and could hear a shuffling of papers as he pulled out mementos of his conquests and passed them around. How mortified those ladies would have been had they seen the delicate sentiments they had committed to paper being bandied about by Nobunori's cronies! I heard the young men trying to guess the identities of the women, and the laughter when someone guessed correctly.

Two of Nobunori's friends had already obtained positions at court, one as guards officer and the other as a scribe in the Bureau of Ceremonial. One could tell by the air of assurance in their voices that they were more sophisticated than the others in the ways of love. As afternoon turned to evening, these two came to dominate the discussion. From my point of view, sitting quietly behind some screens, it was instructive, if infuriating.

The young man who held the position of scribe made as if to sound experienced for his age.

—It's sad but true, I heard him say. The ideal woman is rare, if she even exists at all. You catch a glimpse of someone who appears interesting, and so you start up a correspondence. At first her little notes and poems have your intrigued. You imagine her fine sensibilities and cultivation. But pretty soon it turns out that her pale spidery handwriting, which you thought charming at first, reveals a lack of depth. You realize it was mostly your imagination, after all. They all have pride, and it's not that they don't have genuine skills – but unfortunately they always fall short of your expectations.

My brother had the nerve to agree.

—They are all so coddled, someone else groused. Their parents imagine brilliant futures for them and sprinkle around rumors of their daughters' accomplishments. You hear the gossip and get excited – ah, here at last is someone truly special! But what you find is that the girl has a small talent that she has taken too seriously, while reality is never up to the rumor.

Hearing the group of young men sigh in doleful agreement, I couldn't decide whether to be amused or indignant at their self-serving complaints. Needless to say, none of them were married. It is indeed strange how the notion of ideal qualities, once felt to be all-important, slowly fades after a choice has been made. If you were to actually find a person who in every way matched your ideal, in a short time you would grow bored, I am convinced. The most interesting part of an intimate relationship is how a person comes to appreciate unnoticed qualities in another. I was quite ready to dismiss my brother's friends as all being as callow as he when a rather more thoughtful voice spoke up.

—The most pleasing women come from the middle ranks, he said. (I wondered who was speaking.) Well-born ladies who are beautiful and also happen to have influential backing are beyond the reach of guys like us in any case. We might as well forget them.

—What do you mean by the middle ranks? someone questioned.

—Women with good pedigrees whose families have fallen?

—Or, said another, perhaps those whose backgrounds are humble but have risen through a combination of money and luck?

—No, said the first voice. I mean mainly girls whose families are respectable although not of the highest rank, who have spent time on duty in the provinces. They understand how to comport themselves in decent society and can deal with luxury, but have also learned a more practical bent and don't take everything for granted. I can think of several women who fit this description.

He proceeded to name names, and I could imagine my brother's friends taking mental notes.

—Yes, they are charming and savvy, he continued. When girls like this go into court service, they are the ones upon whom fortune has a way of smiling. I have seen it time and again.

—It really helps, I heard Nobunori say, for a girl to be rich.

—Not necessarily, the guards officer (I think it was) spoke up. One is hardly surprised to find well-brought-up girls who are talented and pretty enough. What I find intriguing is that there are uncommonly good-looking girls whom nobody has ever heard of, going to waste in overgrown cottages.

—You mean commoners? asked someone, the tinge of a sneer in his voice.

—Of course not, replied the officer, irritated. A quick roll with a pretty serving girl can be good fun, but I'm talking about something more interesting – let's say a girl of good but not conspicuous family, who has managed to acquire a genteel manner and some accomplishment in music and calligraphy. She has suffered some form of letdown in the world – perhaps her mother has died, or her father's position has lapsed, or her brother is an ass – but she herself is like a hidden flower among the weeds. Someone like this is all the more interesting because unexpected.

Judging from the thoughtful way the other young men sucked in their breath, I could tell they were intrigued.

—And she is less likely to be jealous or demanding, the speaker added.

—That's the worst, someone stated. I hate it when they're always wanting to know where you've been, who you've seen, why you didn't come earlier.

Nobunori disagreed.

—No, the worst is one who thinks she's so smart she is always littering her poems with Chinese characters and making you feel inadequate. At the first sign of higher learning, that's my cue to bow out.

I shouldn't have been surprised to hear my brother say such a thing, but it was distasteful nevertheless. I was sure I would have a low opinion of any lady who pursued a relationship with him.

—No, the worst is a woman who is exquisitely sensitive,

213

someone else opined. Say it's the ninth and you're tearing your hair because you are required to present a Chinese poem for the occasion. There she is with some sentiments about dew on the chrysanthemum that she expects you to respond to. If it were some other time when you weren't quite so rushed, you might think it sweet, but you find yourself wishing she'd learn to restrain her aesthetic impulses. It becomes tiresome.

Then I heard a drunk-sounding voice cut through the babble of complaints.

—What I like is a woman who is ready to fuck as soon as you rustle her curtains.

This outburst caused much laughter and pounding on the tables. After this, it was nearly impossible to follow what else was said. In general I dislike gatherings where men are drinking and the atmosphere degenerates like this, but that day I found myself feeling nostalgic in the face of the maleness of it all, realizing that for me romance was a thing of the past.

Nothing awakens old memories like the moon. On the fourteenth of the month it came floating majestically out during a break in the long rains. I lay awake deep inside my room where I could look out at the clear night sky without even moving to the verandah. As the lacking-one-night-from-full moon traveled west, my thoughts followed it to where Ming-gwok must now be dwelling. He, too, had undoubtedly married by now, I thought to myself, but as to what his wife, his home, his children might look like, I could not begin to imagine. I had never met a Chinese woman. My mind drifted back to Echizen, where my memories were almost painfully sharp.

By the cries of plovers calling one another as they swooped over the river I knew it was dawn. Now I might sleep, but before I did, I crawled over to my writing table and jotted this down:

Tomo chidori   morogoe ni naku   akebono wa   hitori nezame no   toko mo tanomoshi
Dawn breaks with plovers, like lovers, calling one another; and wakened in bed alone, I take some comfort in the sound.

*

214

Father had mentioned that one of Genshin's disciples, a priest named Jakushō, was leaving for China soon. I was seized with an impulse to try to send a message to Ming-gwok along with him. It was ridiculous, of course, to even dream of burdening a holy pilgrim with something of this nature, but I couldn't stop myself from preparing it anyway. If it was hopeless to send it over the sea, I would burn it and perhaps the smoke would eventually waft into Ming-gwok's dreams.

I copied a line of Chinese from a poem by Bai Juyi:

My thoughts are with you, dear friend, though two thousand leagues away.

Of the many nights I lay awake gazing at the moon, I wrote a Japanese poem:

Miru hodo zo   shibashi nagusamu   meguri awamu   tsuki no miyako wa   haruka naredomo
For that brief time while I gaze upon it I am consoled, though the city where the moon returns is far, far away.

I assumed other eyes would see it, so I left it unsigned. Anyone else would think it from a presumptuous courtier Ming-gwok had met on his sojourn to barbarian lands.

Once I had gotten this far, there was no one but Father I could turn to for advice. When he heard my request, he squinted doubtfully, but at least he asked to see the content. He sighed, for it was something he could have just as easily written to Master Jyo.

—All right, he finally said. I'll do my best. But remember, Jakushō is a monk, and he'll be laden down with things to take to monasteries on his pilgrimage. He'll probably say no.

I was surprised that Father even agreed to try. He decided to address it to Master Jyo.

—But if it ever gets there – which I doubt it will, you understand – your friend will surely recognize your handwriting.

I nodded.

Father smiled and shook his head.

Much to Father's surprise, Jaukshō agreed to take the letter.

KERRIA ROSE UNFADED

Usuki to mo mizu

Just around this time when the skies cleared, Michinaga sponsored a huge poetry gathering. Father prepared three Chinese rhapsodies that he rehearsed endlessly at home, trying to decide which one to present. The party was a grand affair, featuring the most famous poets, composing both Chinese and native verse. Father came home tired but elated. After regaling us with details of the banquet, the other poets, and various tidbits of palace gossip, he whispered that he would like a chance to speak with me alone. We went out to the fishing pavilion later that afternoon just as the hint of a breeze arose to ruffle the water of the pond. Judging from Father's cheerful expression, I was expecting to hear that Michinaga had mentioned another official posting for him. Imagine my surprise when Father said that Michinaga had indeed drawn him aside, but it was to speak to him about my Genji writing!

—You should feel honored, Father insisted. Michinaga is aware of Genji and he has indicated an interest in you. In fact, he seems quite taken with your Shining Prince. This could lead to some splendid possibilities for your future.

I could feel my face reddening. How could Michinaga have seen my tales? It occurred to me that my husband was probably responsible, although he had never said anything to me. But then, after my fierce reaction to his showing my manuscripts around before we were married, he was probably afraid to. The thought of Michinaga reading my work was unnerving.

—What am I to do? I asked.

—Oh, there's nothing firm yet, said Father, brushing away a mosquito that had settled on his temple. Just be calm and we'll see what develops.

He speared a delicate pale orange loquat from a plate and fastidiously nibbled the flesh away from its plump black seeds.

—I suppose, at least, you should keep on with Genji, he said. You are still writing about him, are you not?

216

I shrugged vaguely. In fact I had not written anything for a long time, and only recently had I been inspired to pick up my brush again – but Father could not have known that. Since he had long ago expressed his disapproval of what he called "your frivolous tales," I seldom showed him anything I had written about the Shining Prince. We had a tacit arrangement – he never asked, I never brought it up. Now that Michinaga appeared interested, however, Father seemed to think he'd better not ignore Genji, after all. The pair of wood ducks paddled silently across the open water followed by their five recently hatched ducklings. We watched them disappear into the reeds.

—Perhaps you might let me see what scrapes you've gotten your handsome prince into recently, Father said mildly. Michinaga did say he thought it quite a coincidence that Genji was exiled to Suma just like Korechika.

This remark startled me.

—Many people have been exiled to Suma, I said quickly. Besides, Genji went on his own; he wasn't exactly exiled.

Father just looked at me.

—Yes, of course. I wasn't suggesting anything. It's just that you must realize that your future is greatly dependent on Michinaga – as is mine.

—Yes, I often think about that, I said slowly.

I wondered if I truly had, though. I had certainly brooded about Michinaga and puzzled over what motivated his friendliness toward Father, but it never occurred to me that he would pay the slightest attention to an insignificant creature such as myself. This was unsettling, and I felt more than a trifle exposed. I imagined Father was more nervous than he let on as well. And what did he mean about my "future"? Surely he didn't think someone of my age was a candidate for court service? I had given up that dream long ago. My goals for the future were modest. I had what I needed from my husband's estate and my mother's inheritance, so I did not need to worry about educating my daughter properly and finding her a good match when the time came.

After my husband died I didn't feel like writing, but then I discovered that Genji could give me respite from the dreary brooding that otherwise crept over me like a fog. I sent drafts out and enjoyed the praise from friends and acquaintances who read them. Most of my readers were women. It was hard to imagine that my stories would come under the gaze of Michinaga. I needed time to think about what this might mean. And now I was obliged to show my scribblings to Father as well.

He seemed to be waiting for a response, or at least an indication that I understood I was now to be careful of what I wrote abut Genji.

—Well, I said, trying to imagine something that would cause no controversy, I've been working on a section in which Genji and some of his friends talk about women. You can see that when I'm finished with it.

—That would be excellent, Father beamed. And Michinaga did say that he looked forward to reading more.

—That's wonderful, I said flatly, considering with dismay how it would feel to write knowing that Michinaga was looking over my shoulder.

Father's remarks notwithstanding, I remained strangely drawn to Korechika and his fading fortunes. My friend Saishō told me that Emperor Ichijō was a doting father. His greatest joy was spending time with the royal children, she said. The motherless young prince was attended by his aunt Mikushigedono, who dropped everything to be with the boy when her sister Teishi died. Naturally the emperor came into frequent contact with this lady when he visited his children, and these visits had ripened into an affair that was the talk of the court.

I asked Saishō how the empress felt about this. She said her mistress was not the jealous sort and did not care one way or the other about the emperor's wandering. Even if that was true, I imagined that Michinaga was probably not so blasé. He would not feel secure until a royal grandson appeared in his daughter's womb. Ichijō's involvement with a woman in Korechika's family threatened that. Saishō said that Mikushigedono was the image of the dead empress, so it was no wonder Ichijō was attracted to her. Korechika rejoiced that his last remaining sister had made such a splendid liaison.

The two brothers had taken very different paths since they first crossed Michinaga and were punished. Taka'ie made a practice of calling on Michinaga frequently and even accompanied him falcon hunting. Korechika, on the other hand, kept his distance, exulting in events that clearly needled the regent. It seemed to me that he was tempting fate.

That summer I heard that Kerria Rose had contracted the plague and was very ill. No one expected her to live and her family was waiting for the end when, instead, to everyone's amazement, she recovered. We had not corresponded for a long time, but I felt a strong urge to see her again. I visited and was at first somewhat put off because she received me from behind a formal set of screens. I felt she was still angry and was denying our formal intimacy altogether. Conversation was awkward. Then, as I was thinking there was really no point in staying much longer, I heard a muffled sob from behind the screen. I crawled to the edge and gently angled it slightly so I could see her. She was bent over, with a pale gray robe draped over her head. I reached out my hand to touch her shoulder and she lifted her head abruptly.

Her face! I must have flinched, for she drooped back immediately and began to cry. The pox had scarred her beautiful smooth skin to the texture of badly tanned leather.

—I should have died, she moaned.

She pulled the robe over her head and rocked back and forth on her cushions. I was horrified. I had never stopped to think. The house was very quiet and her low keening seemed to echo endlessly. Without a word, I put my arms around her and held her close, rocking with her in her grief until she finally became still. I slowly stroked her poor dear face with my fingertips, and she let me.

On my way him I detoured past the temple where Kerria Rose and I had first become close many years ago. On the wild slopes behind the garden, bushes of double-petaled kerria rose were in full bloom. I broke off a branch and had one of my runners take it to her house. The next day I received as a reply a single-petaled flower that she had managed to find still blooming somewhere even though its season was mostly over. I was deeply touched and sent her this poem:

Orikara wo   hitoe ni mezuru   hana no iro wa   usuki wo mitsutsu   usuki to mo mizu
There was a season when the color of this single-petaled flower was well loved. Has it faded? Not to me.

I began bringing the child with me when I visited Kerria Rose. At first my friend was embarrassed and stayed behind her screen, but gradually she left the screen more open and covered her face with a fan. Finally she dispensed with the fan, and Katako was so used to her at that point that the sight of her scarred face caused only a momentary flutter.

One day, very calmly, Kerria Rose told me she had decided to become a nun. Her family didn't like the idea, but as she pointed out, since she had never married there was really nothing holding her back. She did not have the ties that made it difficult for most people to disentangle themselves from the world. I said nothing to discourage her, although her father would later come to me hoping to enlist my support in changing her mind. She told me how she had come to her decision.

She said that before her illness she had been very proud of her looks. This surprised me.

—You never struck me as vain, I protested.

—No, she said. I didn't make a think of it with others, but privately it was important to me. I never left my brows unplucked, nor failed to blacken my teeth every four days. You once told me my skin was like a fresh white peach, and I treasured that remark more than all the poems you ever sent.

I had to smile at her honesty.

—And my main interest was in creating beautiful surroundings. My time was occupied with choosing the colors for dyeing my gowns, blending scents for sachets and incense, and practicing calligraphy so I could vary the style of my writing to match the sentiment of the poem. These things seemed to make life beautiful and worth living.

—They do help, I interjected.

—But they are not enough, she replied. You have a child.

220

That is something that makes life worth living. Although I could not abide the thought of marriage, I shall always regret not having a child. Passion I had had enough of. The excitement of falling in love, the stolen moments of intimacy, the pangs of jealousy, and the tears at parting – one doesn't need a man to experience love.

—But when you became ill, I asked, something changed?

Katako was out on the verandah trying to entice sparrows with crumbs. Kerria Rose glanced at the child and sighed.

—Yes. I was in such pain I thought I would surely die. Then I must have been delirious for some time, for I don't remember the days passing. When my fever finally broke and I was not dead, after all, I awoke to find my body transformed. I now had the blotchy pocked skin of some sort of hellish demon. The notion of occupying my days trying to create beauty seemed ludicrous.

She slowly opened and closed the heavy fan she was holding. Her beautiful white hands had been unaffected by the pox.

—I am my parents' sole surviving child. You recall that you and I met at a temple for services for our sisters, who died around the same time. My mother and father gave up long ago trying to convince me to take a husband, and they seem pitifully happy to have a descendant at all, not matter how unsatisfactory a daughter I have been. They could not understand my anguish at being alive.

—Yes, of course, I said. They felt their prayers had been answered when you recovered, and so for you now to say you wish to renounce the world is a cruel blow. I understand their feelings even as I understand yours. I myself have considered pursuing a religious life, although it is not practical for me, especially as my daughter is so young.

There was a sudden outburst of activity outside the verandah as the old gardener who had been helping Katako attract the birds plopped an open-mesh basket down, trapping a pair of sparrows. The child was thrilled and came running in to us begging to keep them as pets.

Everything in Kerria Rose's room and garden reflected her exquisite taste. Her soft silk hangings were dyed in a pattern of floating woodgrain, and the blinds, fully rolled up to frame the garden view, were edged in perfectly matched diamond-pattern Chinese-weave silk. Outside the maple trees were a brocade of rich hues of russet, gold, yellow, and carmine. A scattering of bright leaves floated on the dark water of the pond. The hibachi on the mat between us was carved from a single block of zelkova wood inlaid with a design of quail and grasses in mother-of-pearl. We did not need it for warmth, but the pellet of incense that smoldered in the coals pervaded the room with a complex blend hinting of plum, salt, and moss. Kerria Rose was a master of creating unusual scents.

Yet in a way, the beauty of the surroundings only underscored what she was saying. What could be more evanescent than maple leaves dying in a blaze of scarlet? Silks grow dusty and decayed, and incense is nothing until it perishes in smoke. There are times when a poem may attain immortality, but more often the sentiments we struggle to phrase so artfully become meaningless after the person we have written to is gone. True beauty is ephemeral. One may reach a point in life when this is not enough to sustain a person through the sadness of things.

Still, was it right to cause suffering to others, even when one's deepest desires inevitably led to that result? There were tears in my friend's father's voice as he begged me to keep her from taking the tonsure. Her parents were quite elderly, and I reasoned that she would soon enough have the opportunity to follow her religious inclination. Besides, were she to harbor regrets later, it would make it all the more difficult to achieve the tranquillity she sought. So I counseled her to wait before taking the final steps. I advised her to begin her religious life gradually, passing her time making copies of sutras to clarify and calm her mind.

We had both changed as the years passed, experienced different things, softened our views. Of all the people I had once been close to, so many had passed away that I treasured Kerria Rose all the more now that our friendship was revived. She would be the first to see drafts of my writing, and her comments were always astute and encouraging.

*

That winter I finished two stories that I was writing more or less in tandem. One was about Genji's entanglement with a proud beautiful lady of high rank, the widow of a crown prince; the other, his encounter with a shy flower hidden away in the weeds. After I had written a scene in which Genji and his friends sat around discussing various kinds of women, I felt Genji would be eager to sample a broader field. The first woman was Rokujō, the lady of the Sixth Ward. Slightly older than Genji, she was absolutely impeccable in taste, looks, and artistic skills. Genji spent a long time pursuing her, for she was not one of those silly palace girls who succumbed, over-awed, when he glanced their way. Yet after finally attaining her, he found it hard to maintain his ardor. Jealous and bitter, the Rokujō Lady was convinced the difference in their ages caused him to lose interest.

I gave these stories to Kerria Rose for comment. The fact that she was my most devoted reader strengthened my feeling that she was not really ready to renounce the world. Ever since the previous summer I had been fretting over the public exposure of my stories, and she had helped me overcome my self-consciousness. Her major criticism, which I had been trying to remedy, was that Genji was a little too perfect, and I ought to explore his defects.

—You have always said you are so concerned that your stories be believable, she said. Let's face it, men are basically flawed. Even Genji.

Since I had a model of flaws to look to in my brother, Nobunori, I decided to borrow some of his for my other story.

I had always been curious why men are attracted to weak and pliant women rather than more accomplished ones. My brother's opinion that higher learning in a lady turned his interest off is more common than one would like to think. I created for Genji a love object of precisely the kind my brother and his friends seemed to think would be most alluring. Genji accidentally discovered her when he went to visit his old nursemaid, who was living in a run-down section of the city. A mysterious lady is glimpsed behind the trellises of the house next door. She sends him a poem together with the common but fragrant gourdflower called *yūgao* which is growing rampant under the eaves of her ramshackle house.

Genji visits her – always late at night, always incognito – and she does whatever he desires, submitting to his most lewd demands. She is childlike, yet in sexual matters, experienced. Genji finds the combination irresistible and neglects both his wife and his elegant mistress. He may pause to puzzle why this quiet, fragile girl should have such a powerful hold over him, for she is not extraordinarily beautiful or particularly clever. But, being Genji, he stops short of probing too deeply. He satisfies himself with the ready explanation that such a wild infatuation must be rooted in a bond from a previous life. Rashly he decides to carry the girl away to a deserted mansion in order to pursue his passion without interference. He tells her he will be as faithful as "the patient river of the patient loons."*

I had no doubt that if Genji were to spend a few solid weeks with this lady whom he thought of as the *yūgao* that reveals its face only in the evening, he would become bored. I was struggling with various ideas of how the story might develop when Kerria Rose surprised me by suggesting flatly that Yūgao should die. My friend couldn't stand the sort of woman who bent all her wiles to ensnaring a man. Still less did she like the idea of a woman in helpless thrall to the whims of a selfish philanderer. She felt Yūgao was a complete ninny.

—Genji is beginning to annoy me, she grumbled.

—But you are the one who complained he was too perfect, I pointed out. I protested that her opinions were extreme.

After thinking over her comments, though, I realized that she had pointed the way for me to work out the story. In dying, Yūgao would be enshrined as an ideal in Genji's memory. In all his numerous conquests he would never again meet anyone as compliant. She wouldn't be around long enough for him to get bored with her. But how should she die?

—Have the Rukujō kill her, suggested Kerria Rose coolly.

—What? Have you gone out of your mind? I gasped. The Rokujō Lady is the epitome of elegance, not a murderer! It is

---

*An image of a love that would outlast even a river that never runs dry.

completely out of character for her to even think of such an action.

I was beginning to seriously doubt Kerria Rose's judgment.

—So, she won't think of it, said my friend. What if her spirit leaves her body while she sleeps and does the deed without her even being aware of it? She can be shocked when she finds her hair and clothes permeated with the fumes of burnt poppy, realizing she has been exorcised.

I thought about Kerria Rose's outrageous suggestion for a long time, finally realizing that it was perfect.

I decided to give poor Yūgao an additional identity to tie her into my earlier story. I made her the lost former mistress of Genji's best friend, the Middle Captain. She was the very lady he sighed about losing in their discussion of women one rainy night in spring.

—Put in a child, said Kerria Rose. That will give you an opening for another story later on.

Father just shook his head when I let him read the two tales.

—I guess I'm old-fashioned, he said. I don't understand all the histrionics.

But neither did he think there was anything in the stories contaminated by politics that certain quarters might find objectionable. He appreciated the image of the river of the patient loons that comes from our most ancient native poetry collection. Interestingly he couldn't understand why Genji was so infatuated with the gourdflower girl in the first place.

—That part is just not convincing to me, he complained. Why would a man like Genji neglect a lady of beauty and refinement for this tramp?

I had to smile. Father really was different from ordinary men, and I loved him for it.

MOTTLED BAMBOO

Karatake

New postings and promotions were announced at court in the first month. Nobunori received a position as scribe. He was jubilant; Father was relieved. This gave my brother a foothold of respectability. Now, if he could only manage not to do something outrageous, he ought to progress well enough. We worried because his drinking had become something of a problem. Father admonished him to try to make it through the celebrations of the new year season without getting soused in public.

That spring I received a strange packet from my husband's daughter. She said it had been delivered to the main house by a courier who dealt in Chinese goods for the court. The man grumbled that it was his last delivery and that he had had a devil of a time finding its destination. The packet itself was battered as if it had been in transit for a long while. A faded note attached firmly to the wrapping read "to the wife of Fujiwara Nobutaka, Governor of Yamashiro Province." That had been my husband's posting back before we were married. Presumably it had traveled to Yamashiro and then back to the capital, where the courier at length had located Nobutaka's main house.

My husband's daughter seemed a little embarrassed when she brought it to me.

—We did not know what it was, but were intrigued because we guessed it had come from China. We could not imagine who would send us something from so far away, she told me apologetically. They had opened it.

I didn't know what to say. She pushed the packet toward me.

—We figured it had to be for you, she continued. Please open it and solve this mystery.

I untied the knots they had done back up, and smoothed out the thick, worn tan paper that had been packed around a slender, plain wooden box. I took off the lid. Nestled inside lay a set of fine Chinese painting brushes.

I was quite stunned.

—Was there no note? I asked.

Nobutaka's daughter directed my attention to the underside of the lid. On it was inscribed a poem in a distinctive masculine hand:

Oozora wo   kayou maboroshi   yume ni dani   miekonu tama no   yukue tazuneyo

Wizard who crosses the great skies, seek out the one whom I cannot see, even in my dreams.

—Does this mean anything to you? she asked.

—Yes, I replied slowly. That is, I think that these brushes are meant for me.

—But the part about the wizard, she persisted. What's that about?

—I would imagine it refers to the famous Chinese poem "Everlasting Sorrow," I answered. You know, the part where the emperor sends a magical wizard to look for his dead lady, Yang Gueifei.

—I guess whoever sent these brushes figured it would be a miracle if they ever reached you, Nobutaka's daughter said brightly.

She sat there expectantly, hesitant to pry, but clearly hoping for more of an explanation.

—It has to do with our time in Echizen, I said lamely. Some Chinese people Father got to know.

—Oh, I see, she replied, disappointed.

She had probably hoped for something more romantic.

Casting about for a way to change the subject, I remembered her interest in Genji. My brother and his friends' fascination with mysterious ladies tucked away in unlikely places had continued to inspire me, and I had recently finished another variation on this theme. What if Genji were to follow a promising lead only to find the lady to be something of a joke? This would test my hero's much vaunted sensitivity! I wrote this tale quickly, somewhat as a lark, and had not yet even made a proper copy. I gave it to the girl with the proviso that she return it soon and not show it to anyone else. She was thrilled.

After she left, I sat for quite some time in my study, picking up the brushes one after another, thinking about many things from the past.

Late that spring, my friend Saishō took a leave of absence from court. I invited her to come view the birch cherries in my garden. She had expressed interest in those trees after reading about them in one of my stories. I had snipped off a number of branches (which needed pruning in any case) and carried them into my room. Seeing those blossoms there in a vase brought back such poignant memories that I took out the new brushes Ming-gwok had sent, and tried to paint them. I was struck yet again by how much he had taught me about how to observe things. But I also thought about how Nobutaka had taken the trouble to transport these trees from the north and plant them in this garden to surprise me.

Saishō politely admired the sketches.

—They are so natural, she said, picking one up. However did you learn to paint like that?

It was a brilliantly clear day, and the air was soft and fragrant. We were sitting close to the edge of the verandah overlooking a swath of purple and white irises in bloom. How beautiful she looked. Her self-assurance left me in awe. Saishō asked about my recent Genji writing. Although she had not yet seen the newest stories, she had ready pretty much everything I'd written about Genji thus far. Then she told me that she had shown her copies to three or four other ladies in the empress's apartments.

—They are all women of excellent taste and discretion, she assured me when I expressed uneasiness about promiscuous manuscripts.

—Don't worry. I don't let anyone copy them. Usually a few of us gather in one of our apartments and I read the stories aloud.

She sighed.

—You don't know how tedious life can be in the palace. It seems we're either frantically rushing to get things ready for some event, or else we're sitting around waiting, bored. The rhythm of life in the women's quarters is very jarring. Reading your tales of Genji helps pass the time.

I thanked her for her kind words, at the same time thinking how odd it was that all parents of young ladies, regardless of rank, harbored an ambition to send daughters to court. Of course serving at the palace is prestigious, yet it must be very hard on girls whose personalities, for one reason or another, did not fit. I could understand the allure, but I had come to the conclusion that I much preferred hearing about the scandals than being involved in them. It was lucky for me, after all, that I was not a lady-in-waiting.

The latest was that Michinaga had taken up with one of the new members of his daughter's entourage. Saishō said the strain of putting up with his constant flirtation was unbearable. All the women had to deal with him one way or another. But now that Michinaga had begun to concentrate his attention on one girl, Lady Dainagon, everybody else enjoyed some respite. The situation was made even more awkward because Michinaga's main wife, Rinshi, was very jealous. If she heard that her husband had been favoring a particular woman, she went out of her way to make life difficult for her. In this case, however, Lady Dainagon was her own niece, so Rinshi's reaction would be unpredictable.

The other bit of news was that poor Mikushigedono was pregnant with the emperor's child. Since this affair could never obtain official sanction, there was no question of a formal announcement. She withdrew from the palace to escape gossip but apparently was quite unwell. Korechika, meanwhile, frantically commissioned prayers for her pregnancy and safe delivery.

—It's pathetic, Saishō said. The poor girl is in constant pain. It was easy for the emperor to fall in love with Mikushigedono because the girl reminded him so much of her sister the dead empress.

But she herself did not encourage him. In my opinion Korechika was behind the affair from the start.

Saishō adjusted the layers of her sleeves. Even her casual visiting dress was more elegant than anything I had ever put on in my life.

—Her only wish was to be there to rear her little nephew

and nieces, and now she ends up separated from them, she said, shaking her head. The children who brought her to Ichijō's attention in the first place are now alone again, poor dears.

One day in early summer I heard that, without a word to anyone, Kerria Rose slipped away to a temple in the eastern hills and took the tonsure. Her parents were in shock. Knowing her feelings, I should not have been taken unaware, yet I was stung that she hadn't breathed a hint of her intentions. Would she still write to me? Could she possibly want to read my tales after renouncing the world? Desolate, I plucked a morning glory vine from the garden and sent it to her with this poem:

Kienu ma no   mi wo mo shiru shiru   asagao no   tsuyu to arasou   yo wo nageku kana
I know, I know how quickly they fade, the dew and the morning glory both; yet knowledge doesn't serve to stanch my grief at the world's evanescence.

I thought I had lost not only my closest friend but also my most perceptive reader and critic.

I was more depressed than ever during the rains that year, constantly thinking about how easy it was for everything most precious simply to vanish. Then little Katako fell ill, and I was distraught. My stepmother, who had brought up three and never lost a child herself, tried to convince me it was just a childish fever, but I feared the worst. Could this wan lassitude be the first symptom of plague? I spent the sticky gray days hovering at my daughter's side. The priest suggested arranging some mottled bamboo in a vase to make the prayers for her recovery more effective. As I watched Katako's old nursemaid praying fervently in front of the bamboo, I felt the sad contradictions of a mother's heart:

Wakatake no   oiyuku sue wo   inoru kana   kono yo wo ushi to   itou mono kara
Although I can hardly bear the sadness of this world, here I am praying for the longevity of this little bamboo.

What will become of the child? I agonized. Should she survive, was there anything but misery awaiting her in the future? Yet even if I knew this to be the case, the thought of those plump red cheeks growing sallow, those little hands that grasped mine going limp, was enough to drive me to despair.

After about four days, Katako's fever broke and she recovered, but it took me much longer to shake my sense of dread.

Autumn arrived, bringing the kind of clear, cool days that make one feel the world is too beautiful to last. I was melancholy, yet at the same time restless. If it hadn't been for the child, I might have done something rash. If only we could prevent our hearts from latching onto things, we would not suffer their loss so cruelly. I sorely missed Kerria Rose, at the same time envying her resolve to cast away ties to the world. Feeling guilty, as if pulling at the hems of her skirts like a pathetic child, from time to time I tried sending messages or poems. She did not respond. I sent this poem, but it was returned, unopened:

Kakitaete   hito mo kozue mo   nageki koso   hate wa awade no   mori to narikere
Someone stops writing and leaves me miserable – leaves in a forest of regret.

And then Mikushigedono died. Korechika had taken her into his own house after she left the palace, but all his care made not a bit of difference. His last slender hope destroyed by an unborn child – how bitter for him. Everywhere people were talking about the grim spiral of disappointment afflicting that family. The emperor sequestered himself in his quarters. It seems he really did love Mikushigedono. I'm sure she was no more than seventeen.

231

ABOVE THE CLOUDS

Kumo no ue

Every time Michinaga held a poetry banquet, he invited my father. Even for official ceremonies having nothing to do with Chinese poetry, Father often received preferred seats. During the Kamo Festival that year, for example, Father was invited to join Michinaga's entourage at the special viewing stand set up on First Avenue to watch the procession for the Purification of the Virgin. The regent always had a grandstand erected for this parade, but that year Michinaga's boy had been appointed Kamo messenger, so he took special pains with the festival preparations. It was extraordinary.

Father tried to persuade me to come along. He even said that Michinaga had made a point of mentioning my name, saying he hoped that "she will avail herself of this opportunity to take in the splendor of an occasion that would do even Prince Genji proud." Was I being flattered? I hardly knew what to make of such an invitation, but I was tempted. I had been cooped up for a long while and welcomed a chance to see a bit of the world again. Still, I declined the offer to enter the viewing gallery and took our carriage instead.

Sight-seeing carriages like mine, all decked out for the festival, filled every available space along First Avenue. The congestion was a little frightening. I had made sure to arrive early in order to get a good view of the procession and the main viewing stand opposite, where Father would be. Vehicles continued to arrive all morning until I was completely hemmed in. I could see across the broad avenue to the extended gallery roofed in cypress bark and edged with handsome capped railings. In fact it was so wide I never did catch a glimpse of Father, who, I discovered later, was standing at the far western end. I did see Retired Emperor Kazan parading back and forth in front of the viewing stand in a gorgeous gold-lacquered wickerwork carriage.

Kazan's entourage provided quite a show. Out pranced forty muscular senior pages from his temple, followed by twenty junior pages with plumes of heartvine waving from their chaplets. After them an assortment of costumed courtiers fluttered red fans as they crisscrossed the area in front of the stand. Kazan had clearly put a lot of thought into choreographing his appearance. Prince Atsumichi was also there with his retinue. Gossip flew from carriage to carriage concerning the woman riding in the back of the prince's conveyance. I heard she was none other than his dead brother's erstwhile paramour, Izumi Shikibu. This flagrant spectacle made me curious to see some of her poems – by this time, she had quite a literary reputation. I suspected that people were swayed by her flamboyant personality.

About fifty yards from where my carriage was parked I observed two other carriages embroiled in a fight. The first vehicle, a not-quite-new wickerwork affair with elegant green-shading-to-yellow inner curtains, was already in place when a rather grander carriage belonging to someone of high rank came pushing through the throng, looking for a spot with a good view. The outriders from the first carriage were not about to be shoved aside, and some of the younger ones insulted the grooms of the second carriage. A fierce brawl erupted, resulting in damage to the older carriages as it was swept far back to the rear of the lines. I imagined the ladies inside must have been mortified and enraged. They could no longer see anything from their disadvantaged position, but neither could they leave because of the dense crowd. They had to remain there, fuming, no doubt, until people dispersed.

The sheer number of spectators that year surpassed anything previously seen. Besides every carriage in the city clustering toward First Avenue like ants to syrup, there were a number of scattered viewing stands, gorgeously embellished with beautiful colored sleeves hanging out from behind blinds. I was most fascinated by the people standing in the crowd. Among them were toothless crones, their wispy hair tucked into the backs of their robes, so eager to see that they jostled their wiry bodies against well-born ladies in curtained sedge hats. Even nuns and others who had renounced the world were there, losing their footing and tottering in the crush. I saw extravagantly decorated carriages in which I recognized the self-conscious daughters of provincial governors. Undoubtedly others were similarly appraising my own.

I remember this day also as the first time I caught a glimpse of Michinaga. He was standing in the center of the viewing stand. My vantage point was such that I had an unobstructed view of him, right down to the play of emotions across his face. Father had said Michinaga was a handsome man, but I could never be sure what to make of Father's assessments of a person's physical qualities. He had deemed certain ladies beautiful whom I found to be quite ordinary upon meeting. And I could never trust his judgment as to what makes a man attractive. Still, general consensus held that Michinaga was by far the best of the three brothers. From his gestures I could see that he had a commanding bearing – and yet, when his chubby little son, dressed in the garb of the Kamo messenger, passed in front of the stand, I could almost see tears of parental pride glistening in the regent's eye.

The procession continued for at least two more hours. Young ladies attached to the household staff of various princes, great lords, and noble families passed by in flocks of ten, twenty, or thirty. Some were in matching costume; others, more clever, had coordinated the colors of their robes for a more interesting effect. Perhaps the first five women would be wearing pale lavender, the next group medium violet, and the last ones deep purple. Even during those years it was the fashion to deck oneself out in a fantastic number of robes. Father always told the women of his own household that five robes were quite sufficient even for the most formal occasion, but had any of these young ladies on parade limited herself thus, she would have appeared positively undressed. Ten or twelve robes were the minimum as far as I could tell, and I even saw a woman who I swear had on eighteen. When you pile on that many singlets, however, the sheer bulk of fabric builds to the point where a short woman is simply buried in her clothing. Only the taller girls could carry this style at all gracefully. Fashion is a bizarre mistress.

As the bevies of girls passed by, Michinaga would call down asking where they were from and summon them over for a closer look. They would reply in high, formal voices that they were with the household of prince so-and-so, or such-and-such lord, and Michinaga would admire the attractive ones and dismiss the others with a smile. I was having a good time watching these scenes unfold. My enjoyment was increased by the fact that I could see all without being seen myself.

Early one summer morning after the Kamo Festival I found a cricket on the floor. I showed it to Katako and explained that we were in the five-day seasonal called *Crickets Come into the Walls*, just as the Chinese calendar said. She appeared interested, so, as a game, I began teaching her. To my delight, she was eager to learn writing. I selected some brushes and rubbed a puddle of ink to begin her lessons. How fitting that the next seasonal unit was *The Eagle-Hawk Studies and Learns*. The child must have been about five years old. Guiltily I was relieved that she was clever. What would I have done had she not been intelligent? I suppose I should have loved her in any case, but it was good that she was quick.

Father told me that Michinaga had taken pity on Korechika, who had been idling without official rank of any sort, and had reinstated him as a member of the Council of Nobles.

—Without sisters or daughters, Korechika is powerless, so it is easy for Michinaga to be magnanimous, I pointed out.

—Nevertheless, Father reminded me, it was hardly required of him. He could as easily have chosen to be vindictive.

Father was then, and always remained, an enthusiastic supporter of the regent. Michinaga, for his part, always diplomatically deferred to Father in the matter of Chinese poetry.

For the rest of the summer and fall I helped Katako learn to hold a brush and practice her letters while I wrote about Genji. In the eleventh month Father was invited to Michinaga's fortieth-birthday celebration at the Tsuchimikado, his wife's famously elegant mansion. Father had been there once before, the year my husband died. Then it was Empress Dowager Senshi's fortieth-year fete. Despite the long prayers for health that infuse these events, it was much on everyone's mind that the regent's older sister had died just a few months after that celebration meant to invoke her longevity. Michinaga was determined to banish those associations. The mansion had been completely rethatched and plastered, and the wood polished to a fine soft sheen. Even the emperor and empress attended, occupying the main hall and western wing with their retinues.

People of Father's rank occupied tents set up on the grounds – by far the best spot to enjoy the scenery, he said. On the built-up hills in the garden the autumn foliage had already peaked, but that just highlighted the ivy creeper trailing from the pines on the island. Ivy creeper leaves shimmered in shades of crimson, dark red, deep green, and yellow, reflecting in the lake like Chinese brocade.

Then, reported Father, boats full of musicians came out from behind the island as if emerging from the brocade pattern. The music vibrated in the chill air with a deep resonance most incredibly beautiful. He hoped that someday I would have the opportunity to visit the Tsuchimikado. And then, he ventured to say, I surely would if everything worked out, but he wouldn't explain further.

A few days later it all became clear – quite horribly so. I was so upset with Father I could hardly trust myself to speak. When he had offered his birthday greeting to Michinaga, the regent flattered him by saying it was in Tametoki's power to give him the best present of all. "Why, anything, anything at all, my lord" – I could just hear my father exclaiming. And then Michinaga said he would like the author of the Genji stories to join the empress's retinue and come serve in the palace.

—Your daughter could teach my daughter a lot, said Michinaga, according to Father. And the emperor will be more inclined to visit Shōshi's apartments if there are interesting stories being read.

The honor was so great that there was nothing Tametoki could do but bow and scrape in joyful acquiescence.

—Are you sure Michinaga wasn't drunk when he made this proposal? I asked when Father had finished telling me his wonderful news.

236

I hadn't meant to sound scornful, but it was the only tone that masked my panic.

—Oh, he undoubtedly was drunk, Father responded, but that has nothing to do with the validity of the invitation.

—I need time to think, I said.

—You are expected at the palace by the end of the month, Father mumbled.

—What! I shrieked. That is utterly preposterous – it is impossible – I couldn't possibly – I couldn't – really – how could I?

Something I thought I had wanted all my life, had given up as unrealistic, and further had convinced myself would have been unsuitable, was now suddenly dropped in my lap – not even as a possibility to hope and scheme for, or a likelihood to pray for, but as a real order that had to be responded to within that very month! My mind reeled. I would have to leave my child! My garden! I prayed for more time.

And then, five days later, the imperial residence again burned to the ground. I was awakened by a faint roar of clamoring voices in the distance and a thin smell of smoke in the frigid air. Father and Nobunori ran out, joining a throng of people heading toward the palace, but it was too late even to approach the blazing central buildings. Three ladies-in-waiting lost their lives when one of the roofs collapsed. The emperor and empress were safe, thankfully, and moved to Michinaga's Eastern Third Avenue Mansion. But the emperor was depressed, I head, to the point of considering giving up the throne. He seemed to think the recurring conflagrations were directed at him, indications of divine displeasure.

I felt a pang of guilt myself. I had been praying for something momentous to intervene to prevent my having to leave home, having to leave my child. What did I expect? Surely, though, my power was not such that the palace would burn merely on account of my fears? Perhaps I secretly hoped Michinaga would suddenly change his mind and say,

—Upon reflection, those Genji stories are rather ridiculous – I don't want the person who dreamed them up to have any influence on the empress.

Would that have made me happy? I wondered.

—Yes, a voice inside said. You could stay as you are, not be separated from your child or your family or your beloved garden. Scribbling away, inventing adventures for your handsome hero, you could slowly grow old, scurrying in and out of your study.

Is that what I wanted? Would I rather Michinaga found my writing dull and not worth bothering with, then? I almost had myself believing I would be happier thus.

Of course when I forced myself to think things through, I knew I didn't want that. Although it had been disconcerting at first, I had gotten used to the idea that my stories circulated in the palace and that Michinaga himself read them. At first I feared the exposure would paralyze my writing, but it had not. It made my vision of Genji stronger. Yet I was afraid to go to the palace myself. My husband had convinced me I was terribly unsuited to the glibness and lack of privacy of palace life. Listening to my friend Saishō's complaints, I shuddered at her dark vision of jealousy and spite rampant in the women's quarters. Her anecdotes about Michinaga worried me as well, although, with all the beautiful women subject to his beck and call, I could hardly imagine that Michinaga would be interested in an old widow like me except as the scribe of Genji. But then, what *did* Michinaga want from Genji?

My thoughts were torn this way and that as a violent storm swept my heart. I looked at my child, and I thought I would give up writing rather than leave her. Then I listened to Father's arguments and was turned to accept his point of view. What an unbelievable honor! What an amazing piece of luck! A moldering widow of thirty-three offered a position that any woman in the country would die for. A chance to see for myself the intimacies of the aristocrats my husband used to tell me of. A chance to see with my own eyes the beautiful rooms of the imperial quarters, the dances, the ceremonies I had until now depended on others to describe. I ought to regard it, if nothing else, as a chance to absorb the atmosphere where Genji dwelt. When I thought of it this way, I could hardly refuse.

Not that I could refuse in any case.

I remembered how I had once grieved over my fate when

Father told me I was to marry, and then gradually I recovered. Thinking thus, I wrote:

Kazu naranu   kokoro ni mi wo ba   makasenedo   mi ni shitagau wa   kokoro narikeri
Fate is unmoved by one's pitiful hopes; what changes, bowing to fate, is what one hopes for.

It appeared to be my destiny to enter the court. I decided not to resist. I should have been overjoyed, but instead there I was struggling with my perverse emotions.

Kokoro dani   ikanaru mi ni ka   kanauramu   omoishiredomo   omoishirarezu
Is there a fate that could possibly satisfy me? And as to what I might hope for, I cannot even imagine.

Because of the fire, the usual dances and ceremonies marking the end of the year were canceled. Getting the emperor installed in Michinaga's Eastern Third Avenue Mansion took first priority. Since everything was so unsettled, I was able to postpone my court debut until the very last day of the year. We celebrated Katako's sixth birthday in the middle of a great bustle of preparation.

Messengers arrived with bolts of silk material that we sat for days sewing into gorgeous robes. Some were layered and padded with silk floss, others were unlined. Umé, our old servant, sat with us trying to help, but she would sometimes forget to knot the thread only to find after sewing that the whole seam came apart. Other times she sewed two pieces back to front, and they had to be taken apart and resewn. The younger women became impatient with her. Tempers flared. Everything had to be prepared in such a hurry. The finished robes were carefully packed in paulownia-wood boxes that were then piled up in the main hall.

Katako was caught up in the excitement. She caught my hands as she saw the boxes being readied to take away.

—Who are all these beautiful robes for? she wanted to know.

I realized that she did not yet grasp what was happening.

—They're for your mother, I told her. I'm going to visit Her Highness, the empress.

The child was thrilled. She begged me to take her to see the empress, too.

I put down my needle and stroked her hair.

—I can't take you this time, I said. But you will have your chance, I'm sure.

To dispel her disappointment, I had one of the women sew her a set of robes using leftover pieces of silk from the many bolts that lay about the room. She made a set for my stepmother's daughter as well, and the two little girls played court. The older child insisted on being empress, so Katako pretended to be me coming to visit.

Of course she didn't realize that I would be away for so long.

My departure was like a dream. I had postponed it as long as possible, until the last day of the year. My heart was a heavy weight in my chest as I bade good-bye to my stepmother, brothers, and especially my little daughter. Father accompanied me to the Eastern Third Avenue Mansion where the imperial family was living until Emperor Ichijō's private palace was finished. When Michinaga's father, Kane'ie, owned this house, he had enlarged it, constructing the west wing to be an exact replica of the Hall of Cool Breezes in the palace compound. At the time, people sneered that he was being presumptuous, I recall Auntie telling me. But perhaps he had the foresight to know that his grandson Ichijō, who was born there, would someday return as emperor.

I confess at first it was a bit of a letdown not to be going to the palace itself. I had been there often in my imagination, based on the accounts of my father and husband. We would approach from the eastern side, passing over the moat and through one of the gates in the earthen embankments. Then we would dismount from the carriage to walk the rest of the way past grand buildings and hidden gardens to the palace compound, and then through its gates, threading our way down corridors and over verandahs to the imperial residence in the Hall of Cool Breezes.

Instead, just before noon, Father and I arrived at the mansion – which was grand enough for a private estate to be sure, but there was neither moat nor embankment to cross. We left our carriage at the usual place before proceeding to the building's main hall. A chamberlain from the bureau of the empress's household met us and gave Father instructions about where to have my things delivered. Then he indicated that I was to follow him. No ceremony. Such a momentous event for our family was just hiring another maidservant as far as the imperial household was concerned. I lowered my new fan and glanced at Father. We had already said our farewells. I bowed to him, and he bowed to the official.

—I trust she won't cause you too much trouble, Father said, polite as always, if in a rather old-fashioned way.

In a hurry to wrap up this bit of business, the chamberlain merely grunted in reply. Father pretended not to notice his rudeness.

Thank goodness I would see my friend Saishō soon, I thought. It would be unbelievably awful to walk into this not knowing a soul.

Holding my fan in front of my face, I was taken through hallways leading from the main building to the western wing. The chamberlain exchanged greetings with people we passed but did not introduce me. In fact he said not a word to me the whole time. I had to shake the feeling that I was a naughty child being led away for punishment. We exited the central building over a corridor bridging over to the western addition. Underneath it ran a little stream, babbling quietly despite the cold, the sedges on its banks rimmed in crystal sheets of ice. The interior of the main building had been fairly warm because of all the people busily rushing about on important errands, but the chill air of the outside corridor caused our breath to swirl out in frosty clouds. Then we were in the imperial chambers. When I first saw the inside of this building, I forgot my self-consciousness and was deeply moved. The sacred presence of the emperor and empress was overwhelming.

So often had I asked my husband to describe this part of the real palace that I found myself recognizing the rooms and the painted screens we passed. I had to remind myself that this place was but a replica, yet from what I could tell as I glanced about, everything had been copied right down to the pictures on the sliding doors. (The ladies I later met told me it felt odd to be in a place that seemed so familiar, yet because of its smaller scale, always slightly off.)

We walked under a double set of shingled eaves projecting over the verandah. I recalled my husband saying that they were constructed this way so the emperor could enjoy the sound of the rain striking the shingles. That would be pleasant, I imagined, but because they were so deep, the eaves made the verandah gloomy that winter afternoon. I could barely make out the painting on the partition at the end of the corridor. It helped that I knew what it was supposed to be. My husband had often mentioned this grotesque painting from Chinese legend, showing fishermen with spindly elongated arms and legs fishing from rocky crags off a rough seacoast. Nobutaka had said he found it strange that such a weird painting should be in so prominent a place in the palace.

—It's the sort of thing your father would like, he had remarked.

The chamberlain slid open this partition to enter the northern eaves chambers where women like myself were quartered. The painting on the women's side was more conventional – Japanese fishermen in their boats on the Uji River. I could hear the low murmuring of feminine voices, punctuated by laughter. A petite lady much younger than I came out to meet us. She was elegantly dressed, pale and lovely and a little plump. I was presented to her as the new lady-in-waiting for Her Majesty. She introduced herself as Dainagon, mistress of the wardrobe. Her name caught my ear. I wondered whether this was Rinshi's niece, the same person my friend said was Michinaga's current favorite? In contrast to the indifferent chamberlain, she was most welcoming.

—Your reputation precedes you, she said after the chamberlain left. We are glad you have decided to join us. I hear you are already acquainted with our Lady Saishō, so I have arranged for you to share a room with her. Your boxes will be put there when they arrive.

Doors slid quietly open as we passed down the outer

corridor, and warmed scented air wafted from the tiny rooms as ladies peeked out to steal a look. Lady Dainagon whispered their names and family connections as we walked by, but we didn't stop to speak to anyone. I would be formally introduced later.

—Tonight, all Her Majesty's ladies must attend the *tsuina* ceremony for exorcising the plague demons, said my guide. It will be a little strange since we are not actually at the palace, but it will be performed here in the main courtyard in His Majesty's view, and then the demon-chasers will proceed to the palace grounds* to repeat the rituals. If you've never seen the ceremony before (of course I had not!), I think you'll find it interesting. The leader of the exorcists is going to be good this year. The young man won several wrestling matches last summer. His flesh is awe-inspiring, although, of course, tonight he will be clothed – black robes over red trousers, and the most terrifying four-eyed golden mask. It will make your heart beat faster when he thrusts his spear about and circles his great shield.

Lady Dainagon's enthusiasm was such that my usual reticence momentarily deserted me.

—Your description reminds me of an ancient Chinese ritual mentioned in *The Book of Rites,* I said, trying to be engaging.

The mistress of the wardrobe glanced at me.

—I don't know about that, she said. Our court has performed it for three hundred years. But you may very well be right. I'm told that you are very learned in things Chinese.

I could tell I had spoken out of turn, and I blushed. How was one supposed to converse here? Did I want people to regard me as scholarly? I silently berated myself to be more careful. It was disconcerting to think that everyone had already formed an opinion of me by way of Genji. I wondered what they were thinking.

We arrived at the room I was to share with Saishō, and Lady Dainagon excused herself. Once alone with my friend,

*In the most recent fire, only the imperial living quarters had been destroyed. They were only one part of the palace compound. The large ceremonial hall was unscathed in the fire.

I'm afraid I became rather weepy. The past weeks had been a great strain.

The first few days after my arrival I felt like an imposter. The rituals of imperial life ruled the existence of all the ladies, and the rhythm of our duties felt unnatural. It took me a while to get used to the fact that there are no lavatories in the imperial quarters.* This required a bit of planning and being careful of how much one drank.

During that time I was introduced to everyone and formally presented to Empress Shōshi. The empress was eighteen years old. I remembered my husband telling me how dignified she was even at thirteen when she became empress. He was right – she had a gravity far exceeding her years. Indeed, she seemed a mistress well worth serving. She was gracious enough to compliment my writing and say that she looked forward to hearing more of Genji's adventures. She even indicated that she was particularly fascinated by the Chinese elements and hoped I might go over some Chinese poetry with her sometime. What a surprise! I hardly expected the young empress to be interested in Chinese learning.

I don't know what I would have done without Saishō. She let me know which ladies I could trust and which ones smiled like snakes. Most were not so bad. I became friendly with Kodayū, Genshikibu, Miyagi no Jijū, Gosechi no Ben, Ukon, Kohyōe, Koemon, Muma, and Yasurai, the lady from Ise. Everyone went by a nickname, and mine became Murasaki after several of the ladies agreed she was their favorite character in my tales.

The new year ceremonies had been scaled back because of our temporary quarters, and we had more free time than was usual. Some ladies were granted leave to go home so that those who remained wouldn't be so cramped. There were times when we were under pressure to dress quickly and rush

*Because of notions of ritual purity, such unclean structures as outhouses were not built in the imperial residence chambers. When nature called, servants would bring chamber pots and immediately carry them away again.

to attend Her Majesty, and then there were long stretches with nothing to do except talk to one another. During these great chunks of leisure I came to know a few of the women better. On the whole, the living situation was more congenial than I had expected. Absorbed in the newness of it all, I had neither the time nor inclination to write about Genji.

I had my first glimpse of Emperor Ichijō my first evening when all the ladies followed the empress to watch the demon-chasing ceremony. The garden courtyard was brilliant with torchlight, and there sat the emperor himself, holding a set of rattle drums, twisting them enthusiastically. He was smiling and appeared good-natured. His Majesty was twenty-six. After that first night, I had the privilege of seeing him at close hand as he visited Her Majesty's apartments, and was struck by what a splendid-looking pair they made.

So caught up in my unaccustomed living situation and the excitement of being close to their imperial highnesses, I almost forgot my worries. I had been unprepared to be so deeply moved in the imperial presence. But there came a morning when all my trepidation returned in a rush. As Michinaga was leaving his daughter's apartments, his eyes wandered over the group of bowing ladies, coming to rest on me.

—Ah, Tametoki's daughter! he exclaimed.

I flinched.

—I've been wanting to talk with you.

He told me to meet him at this time the next day in an enclosure called the Demon Room just off the Courtiers' Hall. The room was called that only because one wall was decorated with a painting of a Chinese demon, but it was hard, nevertheless, not to see this as an ill omen. I could fell all the other ladies taking note of Michinaga's summons and was self-conscious for the rest of the day. When we had finished with our duties that evening, I lay wide awake next to Saishō, twisting my sleeve in anxious fingers. What she had told me earlier about Michinaga was not comforting.

She expressed surprise that Michinaga had moved so quickly to invite me to meet with him in private. Usually he waited several months before inspecting a new lady who joined his daughter's entourage. Saishō also said this was something most of the ladies in the empress's employ went through, and I shouldn't feel ashamed. Dealing with Michinaga was just one of the inconvenient facts about palace life one had to accept. Even so, things were better now than they used to be, she said. And, if it were any consolation, after satisfying his initial curiosity, Michinaga usually left one alone. The women referred to this encounter as their initiation. The fact that it looked like I would accomplish mine in record time called for congratulations.

I listened in disbelief to my friend's matter-of-fact-tone. Women who spent their lives at court did indeed become cynical. Unable to sleep, I got up and rummaged around for my inkstone:

Mi no usa wa   kokoro no uchi ni   shitaikite   ima kokonoe zo   omoimidaruru

I became entranced with the court, but now it seems my wretched fate is enfolded in worries.

OUT OF DARKNESS

Kuraki yori

Sympathy from the other ladies-in-waiting was not forthcoming. Indeed, after Saishō's counsel, I realized that what I had felt in their eyes was mainly curiosity and a touch of invidiousness. Had I really been singled out with such undue haste? At my age? Perhaps I was not awful-looking, but I think if I had been a true beauty, I would have known it by then.

We rose early, as it was our shift to attend the empress in the morning. Saishō tried to bolster my courage as the dishes for the morning meal were cleared away and the time came for me to make my way to the Demon Room. She came with me as far as the Courtiers' Hall and snapped her finger and

246

thumb to wish me luck. I slid open the door to the small room and entered.

There was no one there, so I sat down and arranged the hems of my skirts. I fiddled with my fan. I stared at the picture of the Chinese hero pressing his booted foot into the neck of a repulsive-looking demon. I was acutely aware of the fact that there wasn't even a screen to hide behind. After about half an hour I heard loud voices coming down the corridor, and Michinaga himself entered.

—Tametoki's daughter! He smiled. How good of you to join us! And how are you known these days? One of Prince Genji's ladies, I believe?

—They call me Murasaki, I said, clearing my throat.

—Ah, yes. That's what the empress told me. Murasaki. Very good, he said. Your tales have made a big impression, you know.

I thanked him.

—No really! he said, looking at me so intently I blushed behind my fan. Your Genji is quite a fellow. Quite a fellow, indeed.

This compliment coming from the regent was most flattering, but to tell the truth I was a little nonplussed. I'm not sure what I expected, but listening to Michinaga praise Genji was not it. He then asked whether I was familiar with an imperial poetry collection sponsored by Retired Emperor Kazan that had been completed the previous spring.

—The *Collection of Gleanings?* I asked, somewhat mystified. Father had brought one of the first copies home, and I had in fact quickly read through it, although only one or two of the poems had struck me as outstanding. I tried now to remember them.

—Yes, he said. The first imperial anthology to be compiled in over fifty years. Supervised entirely by Kintō. It is meant to be a paragon of literary style, a compendium of the finest expressions of the poetic heart distilled into one volume. Kintō and Kazan are staking their literary immortality on this collection.

—By the way, he added, did you know that Kintō and I are precisely the same age?

247

—Ah, really? I asked, now thoroughly bewildered.

—Yes, right down to the day of our birth. It seems we've been rivals all our lives. As it turns out, fortune has smiled upon my career at court, and Kintō's as a poet. Normally that's a division that works quite well.

—Normally, Your Excellency? I inquired.

—Kintō's reputation is unsurpassed, stated Michinaga. I recognize that along with everyone else. The problem is . . .

He hesitated. At this point I must have lowered my fan from my face in amazement.

—The problem is, I don't always agree with his judgment of what makes a poem distinguished.

My father had the highest respect for Kintō, and the notion that anyone would dare to disagree with his poetic judgment amounted to heresy. But this was Michinaga.

—I will be frank with you, Tametoki's daughter, he said, looking right at me so that I quickly put my fan up again. My era is about to dawn. I can feel it. If my dreams have not been one great illusion, my daughters will bear royal sons.

I was utterly bewildered. Was he concerned with poetry or dynasty? And why would the regent talk to me about either? The whole thing was highly irregular. After a pause, Michinaga asked my opinion of the *Collection of Gleanings*. Tongue-tied, I offered the only poem that had stuck in my mind. As a whole, the poems in the collection were mostly in the old style. Kintō was quite tradition-minded, after all, but I had not even thought twice about that when Father first showed me the collection. What stood out were the few modern ones, in particular a poem by Izumi Shikibu, which I had been a little surprised to see included because of her scandalous reputation.

When I said this, Michinaga became quite excited.

—Yes! Yes! he almost shouted. That's it precisely! I somehow knew you would understand!

His intensity was alarming. For a moment I even thought that he was going to grab me. But, self-absorbed, he continued talking. He said that the crux of his problem with Kintō was their long-standing argument about the literary works that should represent the era – Michinaga's era. Kintō claimed authority from his position as official court poet.

—But I disagreed, Michinaga shouted, startling me again. Just because he's the most emulated poet at court, he takes the position that he best understands poetry. We were drinking and arguing as usual when Kintō finally deigned to ask me what poems I thought were suitable for the new anthology. He had not even bothered to ask my opinion before this. So I said I would choose one, but only on the condition he agree to include it.

And then it dawned on me. This was the poem that stood out. Izumi Shikibu's poem.

—We will be remembered for our poetry, Michinaga went on. I know this as deeply as I know how to oversee this country. This is how we will rule the future – with our literature. We must preserve the right poems, not just the genteel ones that Kintō favors or the clever ones that hinge on tricks. Kintō has forgotten that poetry must have its seeds in the heart.

Michinaga became agitated as he spoke about his rival. Then suddenly his manner softened and turned almost wistful.

—If only I could compose *waka* myself, he said. I can't, you know – absolutely no talent for it.

I felt that perhaps I ought to demur and say something flattering, but he cut me off immediately.

—No, no. It's true. I've accepted that and it doesn't bother me anymore.

—I may not be able to compose them, he continued, but I can tell what makes them good. Yes, I am confident of that, despite the fact that nobody seems to take my judgment seriously. The retired emperor resents me because my brother tricked him into giving up the throne. I am perfectly well aware of the fact that he put Kintō in charge of the poetry project just to gall me. The deluded man thinks an emperor is actually supposed to rule. This is his way of getting revenge, he imagines. Unless I'm very drunk I refuse to compose *waka* myself, so for the same reason, they all assume that I've given up any right to comment. Poetry is theirs, they think – the one corner Michinaga cannot control.

At this point, Michinaga looked directly at me, almost

249

through me, it seemed, as if he were trying to envision something dim and far away.

—They may be right, he continued. If they truly knew how much this concerns me, they would try even harder to thwart me. Kintō and I argue when we drink, but he always thinks I'm joking or just being contrary. I have had to hide my true feelings in order to have any influence at all on the collections.

—"Out of darkness," I whispered.

—Yes, like Izumi's poem. It's the only one in the whole thing that has a soul. When you recognized that, I knew that you would understand. When I first read your stories, I realized that Kintō had failed. The poetry ceased to matter so much.

I couldn't imagine what the regent was getting at, or what I ought to say. I was fascinated by the changing expressions on Michinaga's face. Here indeed was a man capable of anything, I thought. I remembered to raise my fan to my face.

—Genji is the one who will be remembered, he said.

And once again I dropped my fan in surprise.

Dazed by this encounter, all I could do was bow to the floor as Michinaga stood up and straightened his hat strings. He swept out of the Demon Room. After he was gone, I crept back through the northern corridor to my quarters.

I sat there gazing out into the bleak garden at the trees wrapped in straw for protection against the cold. Patches of snow still lay on the ground. Spring was late that year, and the plums as yet showed little sign of blooming. Saishō startled me from this solitary reverie early in the afternoon when she returned from her duties.

She apologized. Of course she misconstrued the reason for my silence, venturing to ask if it had been too awful. How could I have begun to explain to her the nature of my strange encounter with Michinaga? I fiddled about starting a new piece of charcoal in the hibachi.

—It wasn't like that at all, I finally said. Michinaga never laid a hand on me. Of course I was expecting something like that, but he was quite courteous.

Saishō was dumbfounded.

—Well then, she finally asked, what's the matter?

250

—Michinaga wants to be Genji, I said, attempting a smile. He wants those who read the tales of Genji in the future to know they were inspired by the glorious reign of Michinaga.

—Michinaga as Genji? She was incredulous. The world's most sensitive lover? She made a face. Have you ever seen any of Michinaga's poems? He avoids poetry altogether unless he is drunk. Even then, he has obviously prepared his poems in advance.

—Yes, I replied quietly. He is keenly aware of his faults as a poet. He always compares himself to Kintō, and of course comes up short. You know what was odd? I suddenly recalled. I had this entire conversation with Michinaga without benefit of any screen whatsoever. For some reason I cannot now fathom, I even neglected to cover my face with my fan. It was like being in another world, like Echizen, where normal rules didn't apply.

Saishō tried to hide her reaction, but I know she found this admission of intimacy more shocking than the sexual encounter she had first assumed.

—When I met privately with Michinaga, she said primly, it was dark. At least he never saw my face.

In her opinion I had suffered a familiarity with Michinaga far more invasive than the intimacies the rest of the ladies had had to endure.

That was not the only time Michinaga summoned me. About ten days later he called me to his quarters rather late in the evening when he was already quite drunk. This time he behaved the way he usually did with serving ladies. I was incensed and came back to my room in a huff.

Saishō had the gall to say she was relieved.

—There was something unnatural about the way you were carrying on, she stated. Conversing face-to-face like that.

We ended up quarreling, and I was so upset I went home the next day.

I overhead people whispering that it was indecorous for me to have come home so quickly, but it seemed to me I had been away for an age. I wept tears of joy to see my little daughter and hovered about her in an entirely new way. She enjoyed

251

my full attention. We had lessons in reading and writing every day, and I gave in to her demands to lay "matching shells" for hours on end.

Someone had given us a very nice set of three hundred and sixty polished clamshells painted with matched scenes on the insides. Katako had developed an extremely sharp eye for the subtle natural patterns on the outsides of the half-shells – all so similar yet precisely matched to one and only one other. With glee she chose her match, clicking it snugly into place with the other half she held in her sleeve. Unable to stifle a smirk of satisfaction, she then held them both out to show off the paired scenes painted inside as proof that she had indeed found a pair. She could hardly restrain herself from pointing out which shell to pick as I dithered on my turn, for she knew that every time I missed, her pile would be larger. I was amused to see her practically bite her tongue to keep her knowledge to herself.

Even though I played with her for hours, I was not tranquil, and I could tell that Katako was starting to realize I had not come home for good. At some point I would have to return to the palace.

Kuraki yori   kuraki michi ni zo   irinubeki   haruka ni terase   yama no ha no tsuki
Out of darkness, yet shall I follow a path of greater darkness; from the mountain crest, far-off moon, give me light.

Izumi's poem kept echoing in my head. Out of darkness, I, too, felt I had entered onto a path of even greater darkness, yet I could see no moon at all. What was I to do? I knew I couldn't stay home long, and Father was already annoyed with me for coming back so soon. Were I to tell him about my conversations with Michinaga, he would have been shocked. I don't know what would have bothered him more – the idea that the regent treated me like any other serving lady available to his whim, or that he secretly despised Kintō's notions of poetry. Either way, my father would have been disappointed.

My mind was in utter confusion. Furthermore, I was afraid I had estranged myself from the very people at the palace who had been kindest to me. How wretched I was! It seemed my only happiness lay in spending time with my child, doing lessons with her, listening to her prattle.

I lay awake at night thinking about things Michinaga had said. I believed he had the will to do whatever he decided. After observing him from afar over the years, when I actually saw him in front of me, he was more like a force of nature than a man. To be in Michinaga's presence was like being caught in an earthquake or watching the rising of the waters of the Kamo River in the rainy season. One was simply overcome.

Michinaga was extraordinary in ways I could only have imagined. I marveled at his influence in inserting Izumi's remarkable poem into Kazan and Kintō's collection. To think that he and Kintō had such different ideas about poetry! I had known Kintō all my life, for he was a close friend and loyal supporter of my father. It would never have occurred to me to question his taste as poetic arbiter. Yet I had to admit that Michinaga was right. If one looked at Kintō's work with a clear eye, it was suitable for illustrating scenes on painted screens, but hardly touched the heart.

Out of growing curiosity in light of Michinaga's words, I borrowed Father's copy of the *Collection of Gleanings* to reread. Most of the writers represented were official poets trying to be artful. Kintō had worked hard to link his selection to the classic collection, the *Kokinshū*, which preserved the best poetry of its era in order to reflect the glory of Emperor Daigo's reign. Following this precedent, Kintō and Kazan had similar aspirations for their *Gleanings,* yet putting these two works side by side, it was hard not to feel that most of Kintō's gleanings were but echoes of the past.

There were exceptions, of course. Father particularly liked the entries by Yoshitada, notable for their quaint subject matter like "cobwebs" and "wormwood." He even liked to think he had some influence on Kintō's choosing them. Some people denounced Yoshitada as a madman, and the poet himself had been ostracized from court gatherings. Was Kintō really so daring to include them, though? Looked at another way, these poems were interesting more for their eccentricity than any lasting beauty or depth.

I pulled my well-worn copy of *Wake Old and New* from the shelf and reread Ki no Tsurayuki's introduction to the old collection. Our family took great pride that my great-grandfather Kanesuke had been a close friend of Tsurayuki's and had influenced his selections. As I read the first sentence of the old work, I began to realize more clearly the difference between the two collections. Tsurayuki had written: "Japanese poetry has its seeds in the human heart, whence it flourishes into leaves of words. Rooted in this world we experience many things, and by the words of our poems express them."

I recalled, as well, Father's most ancient texts on Chinese poetics, which insist the origin of the poetic impulse must lie in nature rather than purposeful art. "Insect carving" was how one scholar derided the overly crafted work of his contemporaries.

I pondered Michinaga's words:

—This is how we will rule the future – with our literature. Kintō has forgotten that poetry must have its seeds in the heart.

At the time, I couldn't even begin to think about what the regent had subsequently said: that the poetry ceased to matter so much because now there was Genji.

PENT-UP WATERS

Odae no mizu

The thought of returning to the palace filled me with dread, yet every day I received messages from people at court. "How are you feeling?" they would ask. Or, "Will you be back in time for cherry blossoms?" Not too long after I fled back home, Michinaga sponsored a horse race at his wife's mansion. Someone wrote me that he had invited Retired Emperor Kazan as guest of honor. It was exactly the sort of thing Kazan loved, and again I marveled at Michinaga's cleverness. Flattery is a fine way to win over a person harboring a grudge.

For someone who had taken Buddhist vows, Kazan took unseemly delight in horse races. Surely Michinaga was not unaware that the spectacle of monks whooping at the victory of their team put Kazan in a rather absurd light. He presented the former emperor with many gifts, including a rare, eggshell-colored horse, before personally escorting him home. Thus Michinaga got the cachet of an imperial personage showing up at his private party, while Kazan was so happy with his presents that his old animosities began to melt. Michinaga had the satisfaction of pleasing that vain old man while at the same time making him look faintly ridiculous.

I also heard that Kazan was planning a cockfight at his residence to which all the royal young men and sons of important persons were invited. To my surprise, my brother, Nobunori, managed to wangle an invitation. Teams were appointed. Each side fanned out over the countryside looking for fierce birds, quarreling when both claimed to have spotted a good fighting cock first. Kazan was quite fond of one of his sons, the Fifth Prince, but cared little for the Sixth. The two princes were put on opposing teams. Kazan tried to set up the Left Team with the best cocks for the Fifth Prince. On the day of the fight, however, the birds of the Right won match after match. My brother reported that Kazan flew into a rage, to the concealed amusement of many, spoiling the carefree effect of the event he had taken such pains to prepare.

Nobunori told me the details of the cockfight when he came home from Kazan's mansion, intoxicated by the fury of the birds, the stylish company, and a liberal amount of saké. As brother and sister we had never been close, but this time Nobu lingered outside my curtains, as if trying to figure out how to say what was on his mind.

—Don't you miss being at court? he finally asked. Isn't it boring for you to hang around the house when you could be there?

I was not about to reveal to him the reason I left the imperial quarters, but for once, my brother had noticed my mood. Yes, it was a bit of a letdown to be away from the life of the palace, despite its unpleasantness. Almost despite myself I found my thoughts returning to the ninefold enclosure. Nobunori had also slowly deduced that things were much better for him with a sister in palace service. He realized I was his entrée to races, cockfights, and drinking parties to which he would never otherwise have been invited.

Soon after this, I received a note from Lady Miya no Ben, inquiring when I was planning to come back. She wrote:

Uki koto wo   omoimidarete   aoyagi no   ito hisashiku mo   narinikeru kana
Distressed by that unhappy thing, it seems you have been gone as long as the tangled weeping willow branches.

I spent a long time composing my answer, using her image of the willow:

Tsurezure to   nagame furu hi wa   aoyagi no   itodo uki yo ni   midarete zo furu
The days drag by tediously as the rain falls, my thoughts as tangled in melancholy as the weeping willow branches.

Perhaps it was an exaggeration, but only a little. I really had begun to miss palace life.

At the height of the cherries' bloom Father was invited to a flower-viewing party at Michinaga's house, the temporary palace. He reported that preparations for moving the emperor and empress to the Ichijō Palace were almost complete, so the move would probably take place in a month.

—The quarters will be much more spacious, he admonished me. You will no longer have the excuse of crowding to stay away from your duties. You know, many people came up to me asking when you would return. There was one lady who said something about hoping you weren't still angry with her. She chattered on and on so that half the time I didn't know what she was talking about, but I caught the general idea. You had some sort of unpleasant experience there, there I can tell.

—No, I'm not even going to ask you about it. Father waved his arm to forestall my excuses. It doesn't matter. The point is, whatever happened has not damaged anyone's opinion of you, and you are missed. He lowered his voice to an urgent whisper. Even Michinaga took me aside and said that now that the imperial couple was moving, he hoped you would be persuaded to return to his daughter's service. Michinaga himself noticed that you had left, Fuji!

Father's earnestness made me smile. Had he known what Michinaga had said about Genji, he would have been astounded.

But I could see it was time to go back. Somehow I had to make amends with Saishō. To see if she would forget our quarrel, I wrote her the following poem:

Tojitarishi   iwama no kouri   uchitokeba   odae no mizu mo   kage mieji ya wa
Frozen behind rocks, if only the ice would melt, the pent-up water might reflect my face once more.

It was the same metaphor I had used when Nobutaka was courting. No matter. When two people are uneasy with one another, I can think of no better image than ice, which, at least, can melt. If Saishō replied, I would return, unobtrusively, along with other court women who were planning to go back into service after the move to the Ichijō Palace.

I did not wait long. The next day a charming young boy came to the house bearing a branch of mountain cherry in such effulgent bloom that it left a trail of petals in his wake. Attached to the branch was this poem from Saishō:

Miyamabe no   hana fukimagau   tanikaze ni   musubishi mizu mo   tokezarame ya wa
When the breeze swirls up from the valley to scatter the blossoms on the mountainside, you may be sure the frozen waters will melt.

The minx.

257

I smiled in spite of myself at her sly reference.* The blossoms were certainly scattering.

I returned to my position in the new quarters of the refurbished Ichijō Palace in the first month of summer along with a number of other ladies who had been on extended leave. Summer is a dangerous time. I never allowed my daughter to go outside the house in summe for fear of the demons of pestilence lurking in the muggy vapors of the capital. When I left at this hazardous time of year, Katako was inconsolable. She seemed convinced she would never see me again. I tried to reassure her, but she clung all the harder. No doubt she had overheard people talking about the rampant pox as a sign of the End of the Age of Buddha's Law. Not a few people actually expected the world to end in conflagration and chaos. I had a feeling Katako had been listening to someone reading Genshin's graphic descriptions of hell – that would surely have contributed to her terror at my leaving. I shuddered to think what sort of horrible images must have been conjured up in the mind of an impressionable six-year-old.

This priest, Genshin, seemed to be everywhere, preaching the way to salvation. The world is so corrupt, he insisted, we cannot possibly be saved by our own efforts. From rotten fruit can we expect anything but maggots and flies? Our only hope is to pray for rebirth in Amida Buddha's Pure Land. From there, only there, can souls proceed to enlightenment.

My cousin and her family had started listening to the old priest in earnest. Undoubtedly this is where Katako heard his sermons repeated. I later found out that even Kerria Rose had become one of Genshin's adherents.

Back at the palace, life was far from pleasant. I could hardly believe the rumors some of the women were spreading about

*The verbs *musubu* and *tokeru* describing "frozen" versus "melted" water in the poem also carry the meanings of "tied" versus "unbound." Since clothing was held together by cords, the poem could also mean "surely you will be undressed again."

me. I was very careful not to push myself forward in any way, yet some ladies were complaining that I should be more circumspect and not give myself airs. Did they think I enjoyed Michinaga's summons at odd hours? Did they imagine that I had a choice? My husband knew me very well when he said palace life would not suit me. I suppose I was not consummately diplomatic, yet it was galling to be faulted for airs I most definitely did not feel.

Warinashi ya   hito koso hito to   iwazarame   mizukara mi wo ya   omoisutsubeki
Unbelievable! They won't recognize me as a peer, but do
they expect me to simply give up and slink away?

I had no one with whom I could share my deep uneasiness and the feeling that I did not belong. My father would not have understood, and Saishō and a few other friends could only advise me to let the ill will roll off my back as they did.

—They're just jealous, Saishō said of the women who grumbled every time I was called to Michinaga's rooms.

—Enjoy it.

She felt that another's envy proved one's superiority.

It was wrong of me to continue to write to Kerria Rose, distracting her from her religious devotions, but I thought I should go mad if I lost all connections outside the palace and started to believe that this was the only world that mattered. I was surrounded by people who believed nothing other.

One afternoon as I was feeling morose, Saishō startled me by asking whether living in the palace had helped me write about Genji. This brought me up short. When I first heard about my appointment, my writing had been uppermost in my mind. And, as I had imagined, it was useful to be able to describe certain details of palace life from experience. But, on the whole, I had become disillusioned at how sordid life could be in the royal enclosure. Genji's world was probably unrealistically dignified. Meanwhile, Michinaga constantly tugged my sleeve, demanding more stories that could be read in the empress's chambers in hopes of attracting the emperor to spend more time there. I began to feel that Michinaga thought of Genji as bait. All this made it hard to concentrate.

But, just as I was thinking palace life was so wretched I couldn't stand it, someone would come up and say something wonderfully kind. I realized I had also made friends in a short time, and it was really only a small group of tweezer-tongued harpies that felt obliged to put every newcomer through their gossip mill. Sequestered in my room, I was avoiding contact with anyone when, for the holiday of the fifth day of the fifth month, Lady Koshōshō sent me a pomander with this poem:

Shinobitsuru   ne zo arawaruru   ayamegusa   iwanu ni kuchite   yaminubekereba
Lest they be smothered, we dig the sweet flag roots hidden in the pond; lest they be smothered, our voices must emerge to speak out for you.

I was moved by her thoughtfulness and resolved not to be undone by a few unfair slights. I sent the following poem in response:

Kyou wa kaku   hikikeru mono wo   ayamegusa   waga migakure ni   nurewataritsuru
Hidden away, damp with grateful tears, I and the root have today both been drawn out by you.

The empress paid compliments to my stories. I began to understand that the animosity of certain ladies was directly due to jealousy of the favor she showed me rather than anything her father had done. One rainy day in the sixth month Michinaga came by Shōshi's rooms and noticed that Her Majesty had the Genji tale with her. After the usual comments, he took up a square of paper that had some plums arranged on it and wrote the following:

Sukimono to   na ni shi tatereba   miru hito no   orade suguru wa   araji to zo omou
It has a reputation as a sour fruit, but anyone who sees this plum would surely not pass it by.

So, I thought, he is perfectly capable of turning out something clever, after all. I laughed along with everyone else at his

260

poem, but got the shock of my life when he proceeded to hand it to me. The other ladies tittered and I felt hot blood rushing to my face. I had to reply, though, or risk ridicule. Luckily I was good at this sort of thing, and a response jumped to mind spontaneously. I took the brush and wrote:

Hito ni mada   orareru mono wo   tare ka kono   sukimono zo to wa   kuchinarashikemu
How can anyone be so sure of the sourness of a plum that has never touched his lips?

Nervously I passed my reply to Saishō to recite for me. She did so, and when she paused slightly before the last line, the sound of the falling rain made me aware of how quiet everyone had become. Then she finished, and laughter rippled through the room. Even the empress brought her sleeve to her mouth and said,

—She has you there, Father.

Michinaga, too, was smiling. Clearly he enjoyed this kind of thing.

Saishō beamed at me, as much as if to say, "See, it's not so bad when you let yourself go." And for once, I didn't immediately assume that the laughter was directed at me. It dawned on me that perhaps I might have a place in this world, after all.

LADY OF THE PILLOW BOOK

Sei Shōnagon

There were usually about thirty ladies attending the empress in her private section of the Ichijō Palace. Quarters were cramped; solitude nonexistent. Often it happened that a number of women all had their unclean period of the month come upon them at the same time. They took their leave together, so those left behind had to scramble to perform twice as many duties as usual. And then on days that were auspicious for washing one's hair, of course everyone wanted to have hers done. With two or three women in a household this was not such a chore, but with thirty women the sheer mass of dirty black hair was overwhelming. I'm sorry to say our maidservants could never wash their hair on lucky days because they had to attend ours.

I hated going through this ordeal in winter. Hair took forever to dry, and I ended up chilled for the rest of the day with that cold sodden mass on my back. But it was pleasant during hot weather, especially on the seventh day of the seventh month. Children prayed for clear skies on this day for the magpies to make their bridge in heaven to Tanabata. We prayed it wouldn't rain so that our hair would dry.

For the first Tanabata I spent at the palace I rose early with rest of the women planning to have our maids help us perform this chore. The empress, too, was having her hair washed, ensconced deep in her rooms with only a few of her more familiar ladies-in-waiting attending her. The rest of us were lolling about in the heat, informally dressed, combing our own hair out to dry. Summer had ended, but the day was so hot we were still wearing our sheer white singlets over long trousers. I have never cared for this style. The problem is that a person's navel and nipples are visible under the fabric, and it is a rare woman whose navel is not unattractive.

I noticed that a cluster of ladies had gathered at one corner of the verandah in front of the east wing, and made my way over to the group to see what had caught their attention. Standing in the garden was a woman I had never seen before. She was small and thin with rather sharp features. Her dress was faded, and her long hair, slightly waxy and half gray, was tied back off her face. She held herself very erect, in the way that short people sometimes do, and was talking in a most animated fashion. Several of the ladies appeared to know her. Lady Koshōshō came up behind me and I asked who it was.

—That's Sei Shōnagon, she nudged me. You know, the one who served the other empress and wrote the pillow book several years ago. I'm sure you must have seen it – it was the talk of the court.

—Really! I whispered back. Whose service is she in now?

—No one's, said Koshōshō. After her second mistress died, it seems there was no place for her. She was so deeply connected with Empress Teishi and Korechika that anyone wishing to stay in Michinaga's graces avoided her. It's a pity. She lives by herself, and people say she's become rather unhinged.

I glanced at the small vivacious woman holding the entire group in thrall as she talked, and I hesitated. I tried to imagine how I would feel if I had fallen to her unfortunate state. Would I have had the nerve to come around visiting my rival's court? Unlikely. I would have long since crept off quietly to a convent, no doubt.

I remembered reading snatches of the Shōnagon's pillow book while living in Echizen. Starved for civilization as I was at the time, I drank up everything that evoked the society of Miyako. She was skillful at capturing the essence of palace life, making it all appear so graceful and interesting. But after a while I started to think of her as pretentious. I looked in vain for some sense of the pain Empress Teishi must have been suffering in her awkward position, but Shōnagon never touched on anything but the charming. She also rubbed me the wrong way with her gossipy snippets and how, in every incident, she always came out as the clever one. I had gotten over the insulting things she had written about my husband.

But as I looked at her, standing there so composed despite being completely fallen in the world, it was hard not to feel an odd admiration. She had left court five years before, and clearly her clothing dated from that time, slightly soiled and faded. A faintly unwashed smell emanated from her direction, but she appeared unconcerned. Koshōshō and I edged closer to the knot of ladies on the verandah.

Immediately Sei Shōnagon glanced our way and said,

—Who's this? I'm so out of things these days, I don't know anyone anymore.

Lady Dainagon responded.

—This is Tametoki's daughter. She joined us earlier this year.

Shōnagon cackled.

—Ah yes, the erstwhile Governor Nobutaka's wife, is it not? Author of the Genji stories? I'm so pleased to make your acquaintance. Tell me, how are you known in the women's quarters here? Let me guess – Fujitsubo, perhaps? Prince Genji's forbidden lady?

Her directness was a little startling. I had never met someone so instantly straightforward.

—She's called Murasaki, interposed Miya no Ben.

—Of course! Murasaki! exclaimed the irrepressible Shōnagon. She nodded thoughtfully. Yes, I can see that. Murasaki is the one we'd all like to be. Lucky you.

She squinted in the sunlight.

—Well, Murasaki, I hope we can have a chat sometime. I admire your stories. I do. You are very smart – much smarter than I was. I'll be around for a few more days before I leave on a pilgrimage. You can find me at Korechika's mansion before then.

So Sei Shōnagon was familiar with Genji. I should not have been surprised. I knew that anything one writes will simply drift away like duckweed. One can never know where it will end up. Every woman around me regarded Shōnagon with a mixture of fascination and pity, for were things to take a different turn, her fate could belong to any of us. Yet there was a certain freedom that attended her loss of status. She could stay at Korechika's, for she had nothing more to lose. What did she care what Michinaga thought? I suddenly wanted to ask her about writing while at court. I had always wondered whether she found time to write while in service, or whether she did it all when she was on leave. Also, something about her pillow book had puzzled me since I first read it.

I hadn't the courage to go to Korechika's house myself, but I thought of a way to meet her before she set out on her pilgrimage.

I arranged to leave the palace to attend the annual memorial service for my mother. To meet Shōnagon, I simply left a day earlier, sending her a message that I would be at our family temple if she could spare the time to visit me. I asked my ladies to watch for her while I was at prayers. She arrived, unattended, late in the afternoon. When I came back to the small room the head priest had reserved for me, I found her there fanning herself in the waning heat of the day.

—Ah, the sound of temple bells and conch shells, she said. So satisfying. When you hear those, you really feel you're on a retreat.

With some people one never gets beyond the pleasantries, and with others you feel that unspoken things are understood. This does not necessarily mean that you are alike. In many ways we were oil and water, but I felt a connection to Sei Shōnagon.

It is well known that at age thirty-six a woman is vulnerable. She is open to evil influences and must take special precautions to preserve her physical and spiritual balance during this year. I learned that precisely four years ago, when Shōnagon was at this hazardous age, her mistress Genshi suddenly died. Shōnagon's life was plunged into uncertainty. Perhaps if she had been younger – or older – she would have managed to recover her position, but given her exposed state, she told me, she simply let go. Too weary to try to maneuver another appointment at the time, she was most surprised to find that after she had let everything go, her energy and joy in life came back.

Did she miss life at court? Yes, but then she had her memories to muse upon. Better than most did she know the vagaries of courtly appointments, the sorrows as well as the joys in the imperial enclosure.

—It could never be as good as it once was, she declared.

In answer to my indelicate question about why nothing of Empress Teishi's travails could be seen in her writing, she sighed and looked out toward the mountains.

—I had not intended my random notes to be gathered together, she finally said. They are, as you are aware, simple observations upon everyday things. But then one day I came into possession of a hoard of paper, and the temptation was too great. Korechika had brought the empress a bundle of notebooks, and since there was no immediate need for them to be used for official records, she gave them to me.

—Use these to gather your jottings into a pillow book, she told me.

265

—Who could resist all that pristine paper? I found that once I started scribbling I couldn't stop. I don't know how you go about writing your Genji's adventures, Shōnagon said. But I imagine you must reach a point where the story possesses you and you simply have to put it down on paper.

I smiled. She well understood that particular itch.

—And then, said Shōnagon, my empress's karma plunged. In her final days, when she was pregnant and most unwell, Teishi called me to her side. She told me the only thing that gave her comfort was gazing at my descriptions of the poetry outings we used to take, the games we played, the lists of things we enjoyed. It was so beautiful then, she lamented – when my father was regent.

—I resolved that my pillow book would remain a tribute to Empress Teishi's world. It would not be marred by the difficulties that your horrid Michinaga (begging your pardon) visited upon her. I deliberately left it unorganized, a collection of random jottings. If I had tried to arrange it chronologically, things left unsaid would have been too obvious. Can you believe I used to be criticized for being too friendly with Michinaga?

—You have followed a different path with your Genji, she continued. I can see why Michinaga has snatched you up for his daughter's crew, you know. I suspect he wants to keep an eye on you. When I read your stories of Genji's exile, I couldn't help but think of my dear mistress's brother Korechika. It brought tears to my eyes thinking of him on those wild beaches, missing his loved ones in the capital.

Shōnagon helped herself to a bowl of rice dumplings and beans covered with vine syrup.

—You will excuse me, I hope, she said. Food is one of those luxuries I used to take for granted.

She had not yet eaten that day.

—When it's not around, I don't think about it. But when I sit down and there is something on the table, I suddenly become quite famished. Anyway, with you, it feels like old times, she said between mouthfuls. My perspective has refashioned my memories. Isn't it strange – I have come to the conclusion that all those hours we palace women spent

266

lounging about in our rooms, talking and snacking, complaining of boredom – in retrospect, those are the times I feel most nostalgia for.

She glanced at me and laughed.

—Of course I'd still have to say that the very best part was all the different men we had a chance to flirt with. I never met one like your Prince Genji, though – more's the pity!

—Not even Korechika? I ventured. Since reading her pillow book, I had always wondered whether they were intimately involved.

Shōnagon smiled.

—He was a dear boy, yes. So good-looking and so clever. I suppose he was the closest thing to Genji I ever encountered. But he lacked Genji's delicacy, especially where women were concerned.

She licked the last drop of syrup from her chopsticks and placed them reverently on top of the bowl.

—Men can be hateful, as you know.

It occurred to me as I listened to Shōnagon that her writing had exactly the same spontaneous quality as her speech. She continued in her matter-of-fact way:

—Without the right sensibility, stupid little things can simply ruin a beautiful encounter, she said. For example, dawn arrives – and a man immediately jumps up and starts looking around for his fan and papers. He seems most concerned that the strings of his hat are properly tied, and so you lie there feeling completely forgotten, tossed aside. Don't you hate that? I'm sure Genji would never take leave of a lady that way. Genji knows that a lady appreciates a bit of reluctance to leave in the morning. I just love the way he dawdles until it has become quite light, and the lady herself feels obliged to push him out to protect her reputation.

I found myself smiling at Shōnagon's lack of inhibition. She could make the most insignificant thing interesting merely by her way of relating it. I could just imagine her at court. For her, everything would be a drama in which she was on display. In her telling, quite ordinary events became tales in which she was a character. Even in her fallen state, Shōnagon was like a butterfly flitting from one topic to the next, while I felt myself to be the caterpillar hiding in the shadows, digesting experiences slowly in order to turn them into something else. She suddenly broke off.

—I can tell you think I am despicable, she said quietly, misinterpreting my smile.

I was taken aback.

—I do not, I assured her. It's just that your freedom is dizzying to someone like me.

—It's true I am no longer bound, she stated, carefully arranging her chopsticks in front of the small empty bowl. I understand your circumstances fully, and perhaps someday you will understand mine. There was a time when the etiquette of court society was of paramount importance to me, and I would scorn those who blundered for any reason. I have now reaped full measure of scorn myself in return for my pride in those days.

—I'll tell you something, she said, touching my sleeve with a skinny finger. Once an old nun came around the chapel where my mistress was performing devotions. Like a dog she was, skulking about waiting to snatch the offerings of rice and fruit that had been set out. How we ladies made fun of her! Not a one of us ever considered the pitifulness of her hunger. Did I ever imagine then that I would tumble to her state?

I felt chastened. This was not the same woman who had written the blithely arch pillow book. After she left, it occurred to me that I had never asked her if she were still writing.

THE MAIDENFLOWER IN BLOOM

Ominaeshi sakari

Fall was almost done when suddenly the empress decided to visit her mother's house to enjoy the beautiful autumn foliage for which the Tsuchimikado Mansion was famous. She chose a group of ladies to accompany her, myself among them. At last I would have a chance to see this place my father had so often spoke of. Several other ladies felt they ought to have been included but weren't. I gathered that they were making snide and invidious remarks about me. The simple fact that the empress appeared to enjoy my company had set off a frenzy of jealousy. Earlier in the year I was devastated when people thought ill of me through no fault of my own, but by now I was resigned to the impossibility of pleasing everyone. Some people would feel slighted no matter what happened. Their fixation upon me as the cause of their grievance was due mainly to the fact that I was new.

As the days grew cooler, the autumn colors intensified. I gazed out on the garden with awe. It was every bit as beautiful as Father had described. Michinaga was rather more circumspect here than he was at the palace. Perhaps because this was his wife's house, he refrained from summoning Shōshi's ladies with his usual abandon.

Recently the empress had become enthusiastic about blending incense. Of course she knew a great deal about creating scents already, but someone must have told her about my own interest in perfumes. Our common ancestor Fuyutsugu had assisted Prince Kaya in developing the six classics of incense, and Shōshi thought that I might have secret knowledge of some of the old blend. There was no use pretending to be modest. Following my great-grandfather and father, I had indeed inherited variations on recipes for all six categories of scent and was eager to re-create them for Her Majesty's pleasure. She provided me with assistants and access to every ingredient I needed. It was good to have help for my version of the *Blackness* blend in particular, for the paste required pounding three thousand times with a pestle.

That winter, at her mother's urging, the empress decided to hold a competition to compare various incense blends. Rinshi was an accomplished perfumer and would be contributing her own scents to the contest. I guessed that Rinshi herself possessed private recipes dating back to Emperor Ninmyō's era, for I had heard that she held secret formulae passed down through generations of women – recipes that were not to be

269

revealed to men. I was curious to hear these fragrances* and at the same time felt put on my mettle to demonstrate my own.

Rinshi was suspicious of women her husband favored in any way. The fact that Michinaga summoned me to talk about Genji had not escaped her attention. I was wary of engaging in any sort of competition with her, but since the empress had personally requested this contest, there was nothing to do but try my best.

We were busy for the next ten days at the Tsuchimikado getting everything ready. After each blend had been properly mixed, it was stored in a ceramic jar and sealed over with oiled paper. We buried the jars in the earth to the depth of a lily bulb. It was good to bury them near running war, and we had no trouble finding suitable places by the many streams of the Tsuchimikado gardens. The ingredients would have ripened sufficiently by the beginning of the eleventh month, just in time for the contest.

Of the six categories of scent codified by Fuyutsugu, I prepared samples of three: a *Plum Blossom* scent for spring, a *Royal Steward* for autumn, and *Blackness* for the winter.

This is the recipe I used for the *Plum Blossom* blend:

agalwood	408 grams†	sandalwood	30 grams
seashell	168 grams	musk	12 grams
cloves	120 grams	amber	12 grams
		spikenard	12 grams

First combine the agalwood and cloves and pound in an iron mortar. Add the seashell and sandalwood and mix thoroughly. Add the amber and spikenard, and continue to bray well. Finally add the musk. Mix in the pulp scraped from 20 ripe plum fruits and enough honey to make a good consistency. Pound 500 times.

*Both Chinese and Japanese use the verb "listen" (Jap. *kiku*) to describe the olfactory sensation of registering the scent of incense.
†Translated to modern measurements. Agalwood (or aloeswood) is a tropical hardwood so dense it sinks in water, hence its Japanese name *jinkō*, "sinking fragrance."

*When everything has been blended, roll the mixture
into balls the size of a thrush egg and place in old
ceramic containers (it is best that they not be new).
Cover and bury in the earth for a little more than a
month. When the incense is ready, remove it and use at
once. It begins to lose its flavor as soon as it is exposed
to air.*

And this was my *Blackness* blend:

agalwood	204 grams	frankincense	48 grams
cloves	96 grams	sandalwood	12 grams
seashell	96 grams	musk	12 grams
		amber	12 grams

*Mix all ingredients except the seashell in mortar and
add honey. Pound 3,000 times. Warm the seashell and
add to mixture. Coat with honey. The incense should be
yellowish black. Take care that it is not too dark. Form
into large balls and bury in ceramic jars. This blend
may take extra time to cure depending on the weather.*

I was just a little uneasy about leaving my scents there after
we had gone back to the palace. How could I ever have said
this to the empress? It's not that I didn't trust her mother, but
it would have been ridiculously easy for one of Rinshi's
overeager serving ladies to fiddle with our jars. I decided to
send a set of samples of each blend back to my house and have
Father bury them in my own garden, just in case.

My room, while we were staying at the Tsuchimikado, was
located at the top of the corridor. It was most attractive, and
I had a lovely view of the garden when the blinds were open.
One morning I rose early and opened the shutter to find a light
autumn mist hovering and the dew sparkling on the grasses. I
was thinking how tranquil it was when suddenly I heard a
familiar voice ordering servants to clear the stream of some
twigs that had obstructed its flow. As I watched, Michinaga
came striding from behind the bridge. He headed for a large

clump of maidenflowers growing at its southern edge. I saw him thrust his hand in to pick a single stalk, then turn and walk back toward the building. I was hoping he hadn't seen me, but no such luck – he tossed the delicate yellow-green umbels over the curtain stand, right into my room.

—Don't give it back without a poem! he said.

While Michinaga was perfectly garbed even at this early hour, I had risen to look at the garden without bothering to do my toilette. Embarrassed to be caught so disheveled, I inched back out of sight to fetch out my paper and inkstone. Tongues would be wagging by noon, I just knew.

But the immediate problem was how to respond. Michinaga had thrown me a plain, simple maidenflower, hardly a showy bloom – but then neither was I. The thought gave me an idea, and I wrote:

Ominaeshi   sakari no iro wo   miru kara ni   tsuyu no wakikeru   mi koso shirarure
When I behold the color of this blooming maidenflower, I know deep down the dew plays favorites.

—Pretty sharp for so early in the morning, he remarked after I passed the poem to him over the curtain stand.

I could see he was smiling as he asked for my brush. There was just enough ink remaining in it for him to write a reply on the same piece of paper. He composed it with a quickness that surprised me:

Shiratsuyu wa   wakite mo okaji   ominaeshi   kokoro kara ni ya   iro no somuramu
The glistening dew does not pick and choose – it is the maidenflower that takes on whatever color its heart desires.*

---

*In this exchange, Murasaki is the maidenflower, Michinaga the dew. The word *iro* (color) also can mean sexual allure – this is especially likely in a poem exchanged between a man and a woman. Murasaki is saying that the dew plays favorites by settling on the rather plain maidenflower. Michinaga responds teasingly that this maidenflower is at liberty to "dye itself whatever color its heart desires," i.e. make love to whomever she chooses.

272

The last phrase, "takes on color," was charmingly pale, since the ink was almost gone. Michinaga did not linger for a reaction, and I sat there long after he left, as if in a dream, holding the piece of paper. This little exchange was really not bad. It occurred to me to wonder whether Michinaga was trying to imitate Genji.

The empress returned to the palace on the first of the tenth month, the first day of winter. Since my monthly pollution was upon me, I requested leave to go home for a few days. By this time my daughter was not as frantic as she had been earlier in the year. She had gotten accustomed to the fact that though I frequently had to go away, my absences were not forever, and I did at length return. Father had carefully buried my jars of incense in the garden as I had instructed. He was excited at the prospect of the upcoming competition. Word of it had gotten around, and it seemed likely there would be numerous spectators. I was pinning my hopes on my *Blackness* blend.

I resumed my duties at the palace and helped in the preparations. The eleventh month was an excellent time to hold an incense competition. The chill air was still and held the burning scents as if caught in syrup. Under such conditions, one's nose was not likely to be led astray.

My blends received high marks, to my relief. I realized that even if Rinshi had disturbed my jars, there was nothing I could have done. It would have been impossible to substitute the spare set from home without making a bad impression. I found out later that Michinaga had ordered one of his personal attendants to keep an eye on my jars just to prevent any mishap. This was most thoughtful of him, but it also occurred to me that if Rinshi had realized my scents were being protected thus, she would have been quite furious.

What sort of karma would put me in such a situation at my age?

In any case, the competition was a huge success. My *Plum Blossom* blend was deemed modern and bright with a hint of tartness. I was especially pleased because I had tried something slightly different and hoped it would be a little less sweet than the usual renditions. I had probably been influenced by my friend Kerria Rose's odd blends. The *Royal Steward* scent was also pronounced superior: "intimate without being pushy," the judges said. And then my *Blackness* won the highest acclaim, as I had hardly dare hope. "Tranquil and elegant, most enviably so" was the opinion.

Rinshi's secret *Blackness* blend was excellent, I thought. Although I take pride in my own *Blackness,* I can truly say I would not have minded losing to her version. Perhaps it would even have been better if I had lost. The glow of my victory was short-lived, whereas the animosity it aroused lingered like a trace of smoke.

Some of the other ladies suggested that I put an incense competition into a Genji story in which the various characters would compete with blends that reflected their own tastes. It was an interesting idea. I had been looking for inspiration to get back to writing. Michinaga was always asking what I had done lately. He was aware that Ichijō was sure to visit Shōshi's apartments if he knew that a new episode of Genji was available.

The emperor had liked Genji's interlude with the Akashi Lady during his self-imposed exile in Suma, so I had Genji bring this lady, along with the baby daughter she bore, back to the capital. Murasaki burned with worried jealousy when Genji crept off to spend days fixing up an old mansion for the lady, and she lay awake at night when Genji didn't come home.

Michinaga approved. Yet I was finding it difficult to write while living in the women's quarters at the palace. Constant interruptions caused me to lose my thread of thought. At the same time, it was not much easier at home, where I was always being diverted by my child. How could I refuse her when I was away so much of the time? So when I really wanted to get some writing done, especially when starting a new story, I had to hole up in a secluded place for a while. Michinaga simply could not understand my need for solitude.

We were coming up on the last month of the year, and I had

not been summoned privately by Michinaga since before the incense competition. I was beginning to wonder if I had displeased him in some way. Perhaps he neglected me at Rinshi's behest. After my fragrances won acclaim, I acquired a certain presence at court. I noticed that I was treated with a deference previously lacking. Prominence of this sort made me uncomfortable, though – I always preferred being the observer rather than the observed.

It was not prudent to have been so forward with my incense. Yet what could I have done? The blends were my heritage, and I was obliged to re-create them to my utmost ability. Sometimes I felt that my karma was at war with itself. Why did I have the ability to do things that invited fame while at the same time recoiling inwardly at the attention that ensued? Did I perversely crave it, after all?

I still enjoyed writing most when I was alone and Genji's world became my world. When I emerged from a day of writing, it was hard to adjust to the realities and demands of everyday life. Genji now had to meet numerous expectations. And I myself? I realized that I had been expecting something more after that early morning encounter with Michinaga in the garden at the Tsuchimikado. I had been thrilled, but in the end was forced to conclude it had been merely a morning's diversion to him. In trying to act like my Shining Prince, he had me quite taken in.

I had been at court for a year. It was time to leave.

GRASS UNDER SNOW

Yuki no shita kusa

With the dawn of a new year I felt the urge to write. I could always tell when I was ready to write again, for I became irritable. After participating in the new year observances in a most perfunctory way, I retreated to my late auntie's country estate in the mountains. It was wild and desolate at that time of year, but it suited my mood. I felt a strange kind of peace in being away from society. Thus isolated, I was startled to find a messenger from the palace knocking at my gate on the tenth of the month. Was it impossible to find a place where I would not be pestered? Claiming ritual seclusion, I had one of my attendants receive the message. She came back to my room bearing a letter, saying that the messenger insisted on waiting for a reply.

—He's covered in ice and mud, madam, said the girl.

Had I been in Miyako, I would have sent him away regardless, but being so far removed from the city, I took pity and told the maidservant to give him food and hot water.

As soon as she left the room I opened the envelope of thick Chinese paper redolent of expensive musk. It contained only a request for a poem about spring. There was no signature. It would have been very unlike my mistress, the empress, to send such an order, so I had to assume it had come from Michinaga.

After being ignored for months, I wondered if this was his way of inquiring about my feelings. He wanted a poem about spring? I sent the following:

Miyoshino wa   haru no keshiki ni   kasumedomo   musubohoretaru   yuki no shita kusa
Even Mount Yoshino, famous for its snowy peak, is now enfolded in a spring mist; only here does the depressing snow still bury the matted grass.

I copied it out in watery ink on pale earth-colored paper, so that its effect was disagreeably wan. At this point I really did not care if I never went back to the palace. I looked forward to returning to my own Sixth Avenue house in a few days.

Yet after the messenger had gone, Auntie's house seemed even more forlorn. I knew my servants were grumbling about being dragged up there in this season. They were unhappy to be missing the new year festivities in Miyako. I tried to return to my writing desk, but the scent of Michinaga's letter permeated the room, making it difficult to concentrate.

After two more days I relented, and returned to Father's

house, where I was when promotions were announced on the thirteenth. We were surprised to hear that my brother, Nobunori, had been raised from a lowly scribe to the position of sixth secretary in the Ministry of War. I had expected him to idle for a while as a scribe before progressing. Then it occurred to me that my brother's promotion was actually a token from Michinaga. As soon as the idea struck it seemed so obvious that I blushed. I'm sure other people noticed as well. Even Father raised his eyebrows when the announcements were made. Probably the only person who thought he was advanced on his merits was my brother himself.

There are those, I suppose, who would think a promotion to be a more significant present than a poem.

Still I was not ready to return to service. Being away from the palace allowed me to concentrate. There is nothing so frustrating as being absorbed in the events of a tale and having some distraction from the everyday world impinge at a crucial moment. I was trying to finish several stories involving a new character in Genji's life. My feelings toward Genji had slowly changed since I began writing under Michinaga's shadow. I may have deluded myself into thinking that Michinaga was becoming a little more like Genji, but in fact what had happened was that Genji had become more like Michinaga.

The Shining Prince had brought all his ladies together into one place, providing each with her own pavilion and gardens. I had been thinking fondly of Nobutaka's love of gardening as I built this ideal villa on paper. Genji was the butterfly, visiting each of his flowers in turn. Just as Genji's Rokujō-in Mansion was all arranged, Saishō said to me that Genji was beginning to remind her more of a garden spider than a butterfly.

—There he sits in the middle of his web, she observed. His ladies enwrapped in each of its corners.

I laughed a little uncomfortably. I had to agree that Genji was becoming slightly repulsive, and figured I had better do something to shake his smug web.

Genji was too satisfied with his own virtue in taking care of all the ladies he had ever been involved with – especially the ones who were queer in some way, like the fusty Safflower-

Nosed Princess. How good he was, he told himself, to provide for a creature like that, whom anyone else would have shaken off long ago. Because of my own obsessions, Genji had become a caricature. His lovers filled the wings and pavilions of two houses like an assortment of rare and curious objects.

So I invented a beautiful young girl and named her Ruri. She was the daughter of Yūgao, the lady of the evening face whom Genji loved so madly and briefly in his youth. It was good I followed Kerria Rose's suggestion to weave into Yūgao's story a thread about a child. Now I was ready to pick up that thread. In a way, this Ruri, too, became another of those hidden-away ladies. I said she had been living in a southern province with her nurse's family. With this loyal nursemaid's help, she fled back to Miyako to escape marriage to a brash provincial lord.

I now knew enough about what the palace ladies liked to read to put this in to please them. As much as they might pine for someone as delicate in sensibility as Genji, I had discovered that they got a thrill out of imagining a powerfully built, vigorous male who knows what he wants. All the better if the heroine escapes in the end.

Through the workings of karma, I had two servants discover one another; the daughter's nurse meets the mother's old attendant, and these women bring Ruri into Genji's web. I was pleased with the way this story completed a circle begun many years before. I wanted my readers to contemplate how Genji had changed.

Genji represented Ruri to society as his long-lost daughter, even though he knew full well she wasn't his. As he plotted the process of showing her off to potential suitors in the parental role of matchmaker, he found his own feelings becoming aroused. Long ago, Genji had been a passionate youth swept away in inexplicable ardor for Yūgao; now here was Genji, the suave and lecherous middle-aged minister, trying to seduce Ruri.

Writing Ruri's story got me interested in Genji again. I had named this character after my long-dead friend because I had borrowed a scene she once described to me. I made Genji contrive to show off his new ward's beauty to a potential suitor by releasing a cloud of fireflies into her room – as my cousin had once done when her sister was being courted. Unaware of this association, my readers later convinced me to give this character a more poetic name, so I chose "Tamakazura," an image of bewitchingly beautiful jeweled black hair.

As I was writing, I found it surprisingly enjoyable to thwart Genji's amorous impulses.

In the chill mornings at home I straightened the bedding that Katako had kicked off during the night. I covered her up to her shoulders and lay cupped around her warmth for a few minutes before getting up. The child seemed to have a radiant internal heart. When I shared bedclothes with Saishō in our tiny room at the palace, we buried ourselves under a mound of robes like a pair of moles tucked underground. I adored being with my daughter but had to admit I was starting to miss my friends in the palace. I had grown accustomed to the feeling of importance that naturally arises when one lives in close proximity to Her Majesty. Despite my strained relationship with her mother, and my most peculiar involvement with her father, the empress always acted with courtesy and friendliness toward me. Father could sense that I felt guilty about neglecting my duties and did his best to needle my conscience. Eventually I gave in to his urgings and returned to the palace.

I brought a branch of the red blossoming plum from my garden to present to the empress, along with this poem:

Mumoregi no   shita ni yatsururu   mume no hana   ka wo dani chirase   kumo no ue made
**You plum blossoms have managed to bloom even under the
    obscure bogwood, so scatter your scent now even above
    the clouds.***

I had been back at my station at the palace for but two nights when a summons came from Michinaga. We had had

*Murasaki makes the contrast between her own humble house (under the bogwood – a metaphor for living in obscurity) and the empress living above the clouds, a conventional image for the palace. The plum blossoms bridge this gap with their scent.

no contact since I sent my sour spring poem about the matted grass beneath the snow, and I did not know what to expect.

It was quite late when I made my way through dark corridors to the chambers he had indicated. I had taken a long time plucking my eyebrows and powdering my face, and was wearing a new set of padded robes in a combination of shades of pink, green, and white called *Beneath the Snow* – a new year's gift from Her Majesty. Over these I had tied my stiffly pleated train with a pattern of vines stamped in silver. I also decided to wear my formal Chinese jacket.

I could hear the low sound of men talking as I got close to Michinaga's rooms, so I slowed my steps and then waited for one watch until I heard people leave. Finally I approached and was admitted by a steward who moved a curtain stand aside to make room for me to pass. I sat next to the tented dais where I could hear Michinaga moving about, and arranged the layered edges of my skirt behind the screen: first the green of my underrobe, spreading widest, then three shades of pink done so skillfully they shimmered like petals in the lamplight, and then the top two layers of white, lying lightly, like a coat of snow. Suddenly the curtains parted and Michinaga stepped out somewhat unsteadily, humming to himself. He seemed surprised to see me sitting there. Perhaps he had forgotten he had summoned me.

—Why so formal? he remarked, glancing at my dress and posture.

I bowed low to the floor and expressed a ceremonial greeting for the new year. Even though it was already the second month, this was the first time I had seen him since the year began.

—Yes, yes, another year. He acknowledged my bow. If only it were simply a matter of another year.

He sighed. Puzzled, I straightened up.

—Death, he said dolefully.

—I beg your pardon?

—Forty-two, he repeated. This is the beginning of my forty-second year.* I feel that my goal is almost within my grasp, if

*The word forty-two (*shini*) sounds like the word for death; thus this year in a man's life was considered ill-omened and dangerous.

280

I can only make it through this dangerous year. I have dreamed of an imperial grandson who I sense will be born soon. I must survive to nurture that tender shoot.

I noticed his hair was thinning and the skin under his eyes looked almost purple in the shadow-licked light of the oil lamp. This was not the intensely confident Michinaga I was used to. But then his manner lightened and he said, rather as an aside,

—I haven't seen any ladies, by the way, since the year began.

Was this offered as an explanation for why he hadn't summoned me, either? I wondered.

Michinaga told me he had begun preparations for a pilgrimage to the Sacred Peak of Kinbusen to worship Zaō Gongen.

This explained it. To approach that powerful deity, it was necessary to attain a state of ritual purity. For a period of one hundred days he would abstain from meat, from women (hard for him), from saké (harder still), and any sort of defilement. If pleased, the god would bestow protection from illness and calamity, and ensure long life and flourishing descendants.

—Look here, Michinaga said, sweeping aside the curtain in front of the dais.

I could see an austerely furnished space with a low writing table and a shelf for books. Michinaga pointed to a stack of papers.

—Mantras, he said. All copied by me in just the past five days.

It was an impressive pile. How typical of Michinaga. He always went after whatever he wanted with single-minded concentration. My immediate reaction was that Zaō Gongen had better get ready – never before had there been a supplicant for his blessings like he would encounter in Michinaga.

The regent beckoned me inside the curtain, and knowing that he was pledged to maintain a state of purity, I followed, thinking he wanted to show me his calligraphy. Then I noticed a tray of drinking cups in the corner. Michinaga noted my surprise and smiled.

—My friends this evening convinced me that it would be better to give up my purification efforts for the time being and start the ritual seclusion in the fifth month instead. That way, I'll be headed on my pilgrimage just when the foliage at the Sacred Mountain is at its best.

—Oh, I said, rather flustered. So you're not required to abstain from drinking or anything until then?

—I'm afraid not, he said airily. And so I'm curious to find out what lies "beneath the snow."

—About that poem, I began—

—Not the poem, he interrupted, plucking at my sleeves.

And I realized that he had made a pun on the name of the colors of my costume. Michinaga might not be Genji, but I had to admit he was crafty. I figured that Rinshi didn't yet know about his change in plans and still believed her husband to be in a state of abstinence. That, perhaps, explained his exuberance. And, I suppose, the fact that he had abstained from women since the beginning of the year.

GATHERING CHERRY BLOSSOMS

Sakuragari

By now I had grown accustomed to the rhythms of palace life. Even something as awe-inspiring as attendance on the empress became mundane with familiarity. The more I got to know the other palace women, the more I realized that each had her good points and bad, just like anybody else. Only from the outside did this world appear so impeccable. Yet, I must admit, there are still moments that stand out in my memory as almost impossibly splendid.

One sunny day – it must have been in the third month – as I was walking in the garden with a young woman named Kodayū, we heard a commotion near the front of the palace. When we investigated, it turned out that a messenger had just arrived from the old capital of Nara, bearing a magnificent branch of double-blossomed cherries. Michinaga stood there gazing with cheerful satisfaction on the colorful scene. He saw us and beckoned.

—One of you take these cherries to Her Majesty, he commanded.

I let Kodayū have the honor. She composed the following poem to go with the flowers:

Inishie no   Nara no miyako no   yaezakura   kyou kokonoe ni   nioinuru kana
The double-petaled cherries of ancient Nara today display their blooms in the ninefold enclosure.

Since we were on an official errand, we went round the proper way and were announced into Empress Shōshi's presence. She was delighted with the cherry blossoms and asked me to compose the reply, which I did.

Kokonoe ni   niou wo mireba   sakuragari   kasanete kitaru   haru no sakari ka
We follow the scent of double cherries in the ninefold enclosure, and discover the peak of spring has come again.

The empress was twenty years old, her beauty in as full flower as the thickly petaled deep pink cherry blossoms. There was but one thing lacking in this perfect tableau – why did Shōshi not become pregnant?

More and more I was the one Her Majesty asked to supply a poem when the situation demanded. I can't say they were all good, but sometimes it was more important that they be quick. For example, on the day of the Kamo Festival we all gathered around the empress's young brother Yorimune, who had been chosen as imperial messenger for the occasion. Her Majesty decided that we should present him with a chaplet of mountain cherries, and, as usual, asked me to supply the poem. I couldn't think of anything particularly brilliant, but what I came up with I wrote directly onto the leaves of the garland:

Kamiyo ni wa   ari mo ya shikemu   yamazakura   kyou no kazashi ni   oreru tameshi wa
Was it thus in the age of the gods? We weave mountain cherries into a chaplet on this day.

The effect was novel, and no one seemed to care that the poem itself was simple.

Michinaga began his austerities in the fifth month. An aura of seriousness settled upon the court as people couldn't help feeling it would be bad form to have fun while the regent was abstaining. The monsoon rains put a further damper on life. Lady Dainagon, the mistress of the wardrobe, became deeply depressed. I was not one of her close confidantes at the time, but she clearly suffered from something more than the usual melancholy of the rainy season. She was distracted and made odd mistakes when requisitioning rolls of silk. Directing a group of ladies who were pinching hems with starch, she might suddenly burst into tears and flee to her room. Gossip fluttered up like moths out of an old wardrobe. Dainagon used to be Michinaga's favorite, but it seemed he had not summoned her for quite some time. The situation had always been awkward because Rinshi was her aunt. Some people assumed this fact protected her from Rinshi's wrath, but others thought it exposed her even more. I imagine that the intolerable degree of stress had finally sent her over the edge.

One morning Lady Dainagon lay in her room unable to rise. When this was reported to the empress, Her Majesty became alarmed and called physicians and priests in to assess the case. After whispered consultation, they diagnosed an evil spirit and ordered an exorcism. I joined the group of women requested to attend.

At the onset of her malady, Lady Dainagon had been removed from the palace back to her home, so the rest of us made our way in two carriages to her family's mansion, where the operation was to take place. By the calendar this was not an auspicious day for an outing, and the weather, too, was rainy and forbidding. With four ladies to a carriage, I thought we would expire from humidity – especially when the sun

284

broke through the clouds, turning the puddles on the road to steam.

By the time we arrived at Lady Dainagon's house, the rain had stopped. Raindrops spangled the swaying leaves of the willows along the canal by the gate. Sparrows darting among the branches shook the glittering drops loose as they chattered. I barely had time to notice the gardens, for we were escorted directly inside to the central room. There the patient was lying on a dais surrounded by screens, enveloped in the smoke of burning poppy seed. The exorcist, an elderly cleric experienced in these matters, was already in place with his assistant. He began a low chanting as soon as we all were seated. His aide, the medium who would harbor the spirit and give it voice, was a thin young woman with a rather wide mouth. Her fingers were splayed tensely on the knees of her russet trousers, and her eyes were closed. She swayed slightly, seeming to absorb the words of the incantation. We did not have to wait long for the spirit to manifest itself.

In response to the deep tones of the priest's mantra, Lady Dainagon herself began to twist and moan in a way most foreign to her usual gentle dignified manner. She sat up abruptly and began jabbing the air with her fingers. Her eyes were unfocused, and she muttered incomprehensible things in a gravelly voice. The priest chanted louder, rubbing his beads energetically in her direction, perspiration gleaming on his forehead. Even the collars of his robes were becoming damp. The medium continued to sway but the evil spirit remained stubbornly attached to Lady Dainagon. They continued their efforts for what seemed like a very long time while we sat there, wringing our hands in sympathy at our friend's distress. Kodayū whispered that she hoped the spirit would be transferred soon.

Then the medium let out an eerie high-pitched wail that caused us all to jump. My flesh crawled at the unearthly sound she produced. But Lady Dainagon's own thrashing calmed as soon as the medium began to flail and shout in that uncanny voice. At this sign of success the priest redoubled his efforts to draw the spirit away from Lady Dainagon and into the girl. Now the medium rose from the floor and, rolling her head this way and that, began to stalk around the room, still uttering inhuman wails.

The priest demanded the spirit identify itself. In response the medium pulled her eyelids back with her fingers, and her wide mouth stretched into a snarl. The spirit's resistance was gruesome, and we shrank back, hardly able to watch. After more pacing and crying, the girl finally stood still, facing the priest, and slowly slid one side of her robe off her shoulder. She stood there, hair in a wild tangle, torso half exposed, shuddering. Finally the spirit spoke in a low, breathy voice. We strained to listen, but not all of us heard the same thing.

I thought I heard it say the title "Lady of the Bedchamber," which could have been any number of ladies, alive or passed away. Others head different names, but we could agree that the spirit was female and that it had once been a lady of some rank in the palace. What was its grievance? the exorcist wanted to know. The medium slowly swung her head back and forth and muttered something that sounded to me like "burning heart." The priest now changed his tone and exhorted the spirit to relinquish its unholy hold on the world of the living and seek Buddha's peace. At this point Lady Dainagon herself was quite unconscious, and the thin girl had fallen back to the floor, her flailing limbs gradually calming to a twitch. The spirit finally released its hold.

On our way back to the palace, I couldn't help dwelling on the breathless sobs of that unhappy spirit. It was terrifying to behold the tenacious power of attachment to things of this world. I prayed for Dainagon's recovery, of course, but also for the release of that poor spirit, whoever it was. How terrible to bear a grudge that reached beyond the grave like sticky gray filaments ensnaring the soul in unending misery. How wise Kerria Rose was to have renounced it all!

The priest seemed well satisfied with his afternoon's work. Dainagon's prognosis was good, he announced. He expected a full recovery. He never inquired about the reason for her vulnerability to the possession in the first place. Her companions did not speak of it, either. I guess it was obvious to all of us.

*

During the sixth month Michinaga stepped up his regime of purification in earnest. For the first half of the month he sponsored a full exposition of the thirty chapters of the Lotus Sutra trilogy. I expected I would not see him until he returned from his pilgrimage in the fall, but he summoned me occasionally, although never alone. He always asked if I had written anything new, and when he read something, he was quick to offer comment. To be honest, it was starting to make me uncomfortable. I simply could not shake the feeling that he was only interested in Genji and how Genji could further his ends. I suppose this was flattering, but – dare I even admit it? – it was disheartening as well. I never sank so low that a wandering spirit could seize my mind and body, but I was not invulnerable.

When a woman allows herself to be swayed by a man's blandishments, and grants intimacies, even once, it is difficult to pretend later than it doesn't matter. I could not forget the times Michinaga told me I was unlike all the others. I knew he couldn't possibly have talked with any of them as he did with me. He was no Genji, that was certain, but I had at least felt that, in his own way, he cared for me.

But I wondered if a man like Michinaga could ever really understand any woman. So utterly direct and accustomed to getting his way, how could he imagine the lives of those waiting upon his favor? Luckily for her, his wife was equally straight-forward. Rinshi had no compunction to mask her jealousy. No secret devils for her – they sprang out armed with sharp words at the first suspicion. Rinshi was not a lady I would ever expect to see possessed by spirits, for she had no hidden recesses in which one might take hold. But this was not the way with most of us. More often than not, a woman's feelings are forced away from their roots into strange contortions. I myself had no right to claim Michinaga's favor, and I flinched from revealing to myself how much my life hung upon our meetings. I lived for them and dreaded them at the same time.

Like Genji, Michinaga was self-absorbed and didn't even notice. When Genji's women were possessed by evil spirits and spoke their rages, Genji thought they had succumbed to a woman's worst failing – jealousy. Michinaga and Genji both

287

thought of themselves as objects of women's envy. Neither considered the fact that women really have no other way of escaping the afflictions brought upon them by men unless they die or become nuns. But my other readers understood. When my characters spoke with the voices of demons or wandering spirits, any woman who had lived at court knew the demons spoke what the ladies themselves dared not say.

I was not alone in my perverse and contradictory desires. In the seventh month I was sitting with Lady Koshōshō in her room late at night after we had washed our hair. The doors were open to the garden, and we could hear from outside the walls the noisy meandering of young people on their way to and from the riverbank, celebrating Tanabata. The moonlight cast quivering shadows over the clumps of pampas grass, and from somewhere came the eerie rapping sound of the moorhen. Since the moorhen is a nightbird, if you're half asleep it makes you think at first you've heard someone tapping at your door. Koshōshō had been one of Michinaga's favorites for years, having entered the palace a virgin at seventeen. No other man had dared approach her since he staked his claim. Of course this meant that most of the time she slept alone.

—Did you hear the moorhen? she asked.

I stopped combing my hair and listened.

Tap tap tap.

It sounded close. Perhaps the bird had been disturbed by the revelers down by the riverbank.

Koshōshō took our her brush and wrote:

Ama no to no   tsuki no kayoiji   sasanedomo   ikanaru kata ni   tataku kuina zo

The door of heaven is never locked to the moon's wandering; but from what direction comes the rap of the moorhen?

She was not likely to hear a lover's discreet tapping at her door that night, nor, for that matter, was I. The moonlight was so eerily beautiful I found myself thinking of Genji. How lovely Koshōshō was when I looked at her with Genji's eyes. Her hair was still slightly damp, smelling faintly of the fragrant agalwood comb she had been pulling through it all afternoon. Like a curtain, it hung straight behind the pale profile of her face, the moonlight throwing glints on its iridescent sheen. I moved next to her, and our hands touched when she gave me the writing brush. Koshōshō rubbed the inkstick on the stone for me, and when the puddle of ink was so black it swallowed the moonlight, I wrote:

Maki no to mo   sasade yasurau   tsukikage ni   nani wo akazu to   tataku kuina zo
My wooden door – shall I unlock it, too? The moonlight makes me dither as the moorhen insistently taps.

I discovered that loneliness was much easier to bear when shared.

THE MOORHEN

Tataku kuina

Quiet descended like a heavy curtain in the eighth month after Michinaga finally left on his pilgrimage. So many important people accompanied him that the palace seemed deserted. I was actually relieved to be spared the agony of awaiting summons, the pain whether I was called or not called. It was much easier to write with Michinaga away. I didn't have to worry about his snatching unfinished manuscripts to comment on the progress of a story. In this lull of his absence, one thing became clear – I could not try to please Michinaga with what I wrote about Genji, yet at the same time it was equally impossible for me to actively evade him. Genji had his own karma. I could not deny that Michinaga had slowly influenced Genji's character, but it was not because of anything he directly suggested. Genji had changed on his own. If he had become a bit overbearing, well, that's what happened when one moved up in the world.

That fall I turned my attention to other characters. I was so utterly involved with my fictions that I could barely concentrate on my palace duties. The empress indulged me, and when Michinaga returned, she permitted me to go home for the remainder of the year. My excuse was that I needed solitude to write, although in fact it was the thought of seeing Michinaga again that unnerved me, despite my resolve.

All winter I worked on Genji. By this time it was mildly annoying that people identified me with the character of Murasaki merely because I had taken on that nickname. I began to think that what I most wanted her to do was free herself from the cares of the world by taking the tonsure. Michinaga frowned on this, and so I wrote of Murasaki longing to take vows, while Genji would not permit it.

When I became fatigued writing about Genji and Murasaki, I wrote notes to my father. He was always interested in the people I worked with, so I started describing the various ladies I had come to know at the palace. I was rather shocked when I happened upon a bundle of those letters he had stuck in a book of Chinese poems. Did I even realize in my smug depictions at the time how very like them I had become? For example, I wrote:

Of the ladies in the empress's service, there are some whom you would find quite attractive, and others you wouldn't care for at all.

Lady Dainagon is someone you would like very much, I'm sure. She is quite petite, pale, and lovely. She is almost plump, you might say, and always impeccably dressed. Her hair, which she keeps neatly trimmed, is about a finger's length longer than her height. She went through a difficult period but seems to be recovered. She is thoughtful and her features reflect a fine intelligence. In my opinion she cannot be matched for elegance. Even when she was ill, her manner was charming and graceful. I am very fond of her.

Lady Senji is also rather small, but she is quite slim. Her hair falls just beyond the hems of her robes, and not a strand is ever out of place. She is so exquisitely refined that she quite puts me to shame. As soon as she enters the room, everyone immediately feels on guard. She is quite the epitome of the noble lady. I dare say you would find her a pain.

You know my dear friend Saishō, so I won't bother to tell you about her, but there is another lady with the title Saishō as well, the daughter of Kitano of Third Rank. This lady has a plump and compact figure and looks to be very sharp. When you first meet her, she seems a bit extravagant, but she improves greatly on further acquaintance. When she is talking with you, an engaging smile hovers at the corners of her mouth, and she turns out to be quite lovable and gentle – although I would never say she is perfect.

Lady Koshōshō is very dear, although I worry about her because she is so naïve. She looks as elegant and graceful as the weeping willow in spring, with her slender figure and charming manner – but she is vulnerable to the smallest affront or rumor and simply wilts in dismay at the slightest criticism. I feel quite protective toward her.

Miya no Naishi is also very attractive. She has a rather long torso, so that when she is seated, she has a most imposing and stylish air about her. Her beauty is not solely due to one particular feature, but there is something fresh about her that is appealing. Her hair is as deeply black as the seeds of the leopard lily, and the contrast with her pale skin is striking. Everything about her – the shape of her head, her hair, her forehead – gives an impression of openness and candor. Her manner is never forced, and even if she sometimes talks a bit too much, it would be a much nicer place around here if more people were like her.

Her younger sister is another matter. She is much too plump. Her features are delicate and her hair is glossy as a wet crow's feather, but it cannot be that long, for she wears swatches and extensions to court. Her eyes are pretty and her forehead nicely shaped, though, and she has a charming laugh.

Of the younger women, Kodayū and Genshikibu are the most popular. Kodayū is petite and very stylish. Her hair is her glory. It used to be even thicker than it is now, more than two handspans longer than her height. Recently it has thinned out a bit, sad to say. Her features bespeak a strong character, and she is refreshingly free from airs. She has real poetic ability. Genshikibu is taller and slim. She is of an ideal height to make a good impression in any sort of public procession, for she can wear numerous layers of clothing without looking awkward. Her features are fine and her upbringing is exactly what one would hope for in a girl of good family.

Kohyōe no Jō is considered attractive, but she is rather conventional in my opinion.

You can be sure that all these ladies-in-waiting have been involved with senior courtiers at one time or another, but they have managed to do so with the utmost discretion. By taking precautions even in private they have managed to keep their affairs secret. This is no mean feat around her, I can tell you.

I have mostly described these ladies to you in terms of their looks, but as to their characters – ah, that's a different matter. People are not consistent, you know. Everyone has her idiosyncrasies, and while no one can be considered totally bad, neither is anyone always attractive, restrained, intelligent, tasteful, and trustworthy at all times. It is difficult to know whom to praise.

I am afraid if I continue to write to you about the various people I spend my days with, you will think of me as a terrible gossip. From now on I shall refrain from mentioning anyone who is less than perfect. Thus I will have to tell you about my fictional characters and not my real companions.

Thus did I babble on to Father about my colleagues, no doubt feeling myself to be quite neutral and objective the whole time.

Back at the palace in the new year, I heard whispered speculation that the empress might be pregnant, although it was too soon to tell for sure. I had noticed that she was sleeping rather more than usual and feeling unwell in the mornings. It seemed that Michinaga's pilgrimage to the Sacred Peak was having its intended effect. Shōshi's nurse-maid, of course, wanted to tell him right away, but we all held her back, saying it was better to wait and be sure. Everyone knew what a fuss Michinaga would make at the news.

By the third month the empress's pregnancy was official. As one would expect, Michinaga's joy reached the heavens, and he ordered prayers at all the important temples. The force of his will was just extraordinary. Anyone who happened to be in the way of his rising sun would be blown away like the morning mist. Korechika, for example, had become a creature of the shadows, and all those connected with him were touched by darkness. His dead sister Teishi's son was, at this point, still first in line to become crown prince, but that was likely to change if Empress Shōshi should give birth to a boy. And with Michinaga's luck, how could it be otherwise? Poor little Princess Bishi, whose birth caused the empress's death, had to be removed from the palace because of illness.* The child was only nine – a year older than my Katako. Whenever I saw her at the palace, she reminded me so strongly of my daughter that my heart ached. Here she was now lying in a coma in her uncle's house.

On the fourteen day of that month, my father was appointed imperial secretary, fifth rank, senior lower grade, and minor controller of the Left because of his outstanding knowledge of Chinese. He was elated at the promotion and looked forward to garnering even more invitations to poetry parties because of his rise in status.

Just after the beginning of the summer, the empress returned to her mother's house for the period of her maternity confinement. Again I was included in the small group of ladies she requested to accompany her. By this time I was totally callous to the barbed remarks of those left behind. Our procession as we left the palace for the Tsuchimikado Mansion was otherworldly in its splendor. The throngs of people who watched in wonder as we passed by must have considered it a vision of celestial beings briefly traversing the earth. Sometimes I found it hard to believe I was actually part of this spectacle myself.

I occupied a different room this time, on the corridor bridging the main building and the eastern wing. Lady Saishō

*In addition to the elimination of body wastes, impure functions like menstruation, childbirth, illness, and death had to be removed from palace precincts.

was assigned the unit next to it. The garden stream ran directly under the verandah on my side. When we discovered this arrangement, we decided to take down the screens between the two tiny rooms and make one larger one to share. I loved the whispering sound of the water, especially when I first lay down. The soft murmuring banished troublesome thoughts.

Three alters had been erected in various rooms throughout the mansion for conducting religious services on Shōshi's behalf. The eastern wing had been turned into the main chapel. I could see the candles burning continuously, day and night. Michinaga was likely to be there at any hour, directing his own prayers toward the Sacred Peak, beseeching Zaō Gongen to let his daughter safely deliver a son.

Michinaga was so preoccupied with his prayers that he neglected the usual pomp of the Kamo Festival that year. Rather, he began an Exposition of the Thirty Books of the Lotus Sutra earlier than usual. It turned out that the first chapter of the Fifth Book fell precisely on the fifth day of the fifth month, almost too coincidentally. A magnificent procession of monks and courtiers came to the mansion offering gifts attached to gold and silver branches. Because of the overlap of fifth month, fifth day, and fifth chapter, many people had devised their branches in the shape of sweet flag irises. The offerings are supposed to commemorate the actions of the young Buddha gathering firewood and water for his holy teacher Asita, but my mind perversely kept on transforming this image into a picture of the Buddha himself humbly serving Michinaga. I'm quite sure he planned it to work out this way, and I became irritated when people went on about the miraculous coincidence. Did they think Michinaga couldn't count? We were all supposed to compose poems, so I first wrote rather bluntly:

Tae nari ya   kyou wa satsuki no   itsuka to te   itsutsu no maki no   aeru minori mo
*How miraculously fitting – that today, the fifth day of the
    fifth month, the fifth scroll should be read.*

But by evening my annoyance had faded as I gazed down at

294

the lake in the garden. Its waters were clear to the bottom, even clearer than in daylight, reflecting the light of flares and ceremonial torches. I found that when I concentrated on the words of the Lotus Sutra, all the vanity of life fell away.

Though I had much on my mind, to grow calm I had only to think of Kerria Rose and her life of contemplation. Strangely I found myself fighting back tears.

—Why not take delight in the events of the day? I scolded myself.

Smelling the fresh scent of the bunches of sweet flag leaves that had been hung in our rooms, I wrote:

Kagaribi no   kage mo sawaganu   ikemizu ni   ikuchiyo sumamu   nori no hikari zo
The steady flares reflected in the unrippled lake shine with
*   the clear light of Buddha's eternal law.*

Several of us were waiting on the verandah getting ready to attend evening functions. Lady Dainagon, who was sitting just opposite me, seemed distressed. She was still young and attractive, but occasionally had relapses from her spirit infection. She had always had an extraordinarily pale complexion, but she had gotten thinner recently and seemed very vulnerable. She looked at my poem and sighed deeply. Then she took up the brush and wrote something on her paper. She left it on the table and, pleading a headache, retired to her room. I hesitated, then with Kodayū looking over my shoulder, picked it up. This is what she had written:

Sumeru ike no   soko made terasu   kagaribi no   mabayuki made mo   uki waga mi kana
The brilliant flares illuminating the depths of the clear lake
*   harshly reveal my own depression.*

Kodayū shook her head. Except for one or two malicious souls who delighted in seeing the fall of those once favored, the rest of us were worried about Lady Dainagon. Her hair, once luxuriant and beautifully trimmed, had become dull and wispy.

It is not surprising that the sight of wretched things should make us feel depressed, but I found it more common that a glimpse of something beautiful often had exactly the same result. I could understand Dainagon's reaction, even if some of the other women criticized her poem as excessive.

The ceremonies lasted throughout the night. By daybreak most people had retired, but I was still quite awake. The clouds were just turning pink when I slipped out onto the bridge and, leaning against the balustrade, gazed at the stream flowing out from under the house. Though there was neither mist as in spring nor haze as in autumn, the sky was no less beautiful for their lack. I seized with a sudden desire to show it to someone, so I knocked on the corner shutters of Lady Koshōshō's room. Sleepily she obliged me and crawled out onto the verandah. As we both sat there looking over the garden, I wrote:

Kage mite mo   uki waga namida   ochisoite   kagotogamashiki   taki no oto kana
I look for my reflection yet see only my melancholy tears in the stream, and the sound of the nattering waterfall.

And she took up her own brush and dipped it into the ink on my stone. She wrote:

Hitori ite   namidagumikeru   mizu no omo ni   ukisowaruramu   kage ya izure zo.
Are you alone in damming a flood of tears? Is there not anther reflection floating there on the face of the water?

We talked quietly until it became quite light, and then we went inside to her room. Koshōshō was certainly one of the empress's most elegant ladies, as graceful as a weeping willow. Yet in public she was so shy and diffident she was incapable of making even the most trivial decision by herself. She had been in service much longer than I but remained as naive and innocent as a newcomer. If some unscrupulous person put out a rumor about her, she took it quite to heart and was devastated. She was so vulnerable it made me want to weep. I could not help thinking she was even less suited to palace life than I was.

Koshōshō had been involved with Michinaga longer than anyone else there, and naturally had to bear Rinshi's coldness throughout. Although it seemed she was always just on the point of expiring, she managed to endure. It was comforting to think that I was not alone in "damming a flood of tears."

A long and firm sweet flag corm from yesterday's festivities was lying on the table. Pale yellow with a pinkish tinge on the swelling knobs, the root seemed to burst with vigor.

—That came from His Excellency, said Koshōshō. She picked up the suggestively shaped object and turned it over in her slender hands. Then she set it down and took out her inkstone. She wrote out the following poem and, wrapping up the root, handed them both to me:

Nabete yo no   uki ni nakaruru   ayamegusa   kyou made kakaru   ne zo ikaga miru
In this world of ours, floating away, have you ever seen a
    sweet flag root such as this?
(In this world of ours, weeping sadly, have you ever heard
    a sound such as this?)

I was touched that she should confide in me, and when I got back to my room, I spent a good while thinking of a reply that would address her double images. I finally came up with this and sent it back to her:

Nanigoto to   ayame wa wakade   kyou mo nao   tamoto ni amaru   ne koso taesene
No matter what, the sweet flag is undivided; today my
    sleeve overflows – with such a root, with such a sad
    sound.

On the seventh of that month Kodayū came rushing into my room to tell me that my brother had arrived as an official messenger from the palace. Entrusted with a letter from the emperor to Shōshi, he had delivered it to the empress's steward and was at this very moment sitting in the first bay of the southern gallery of the main building with a group of four or five noblemen whom he knew from cockfights they had attended together. They were pressing cups of saké on him and recounting old times. I became alarmed at this bit of news.

There was nothing I could do, and it happened just as I

feared. By the time the empress's ladies had prepared her reply to be taken back to the palace, my brother was befuddled with drink. He was given the return letter and some gifts which he unsteadily took in his hand as he sat there in a daze. Not even bowing, he nodded his head once. Just once! Then he struggled to his feet and staggered down to the garden, where he attempted to bow, dropped one of the gifts, picked it up, and tottered off. I can just imagine how they snickered on the balcony, watching him go. How hateful it was!

Gossip about his disgraceful performance percolated through the mansion. Lady Koshōshō even asked me,

—Is the sixth secretary at the Ministry of War who was here this afternoon really your brother?

I wish I could have denied it.

Finally, in the sixth month, the Thirty Expositions ended and were relieved from the serious religious atmosphere we had breathed for over a month. Everyone was feeling more relaxed when suddenly Princess Bishi fell desperately ill. At one point it seemed she had been cured. The famous priest Monkyō had enlisted the miraculous healing powers of some buddha to snatch the little princess from the brink of death. But now her illness returned and in a few days claimed the child's life. We did not attend the funeral, fearing inauspicious influence on our mistress. All I could think of was my own child, Katako.

Everyone went about her duties slowly, feeling lethargic from the heat and from sadness. There was not much going on, so we sat torpidly around blocks of ice that had been brought from storage, cooling our faces with slivers the younger women chipped off. Then, on the twelfth day of the sixth month, we were suddenly instructed to make ready to go back to the palace immediately. A mad rush of preparation ensued, without any of us knowing the reason. The empress, who should have been resting, did not complain, but I felt sorry for her nonetheless. We were all speculating whether Michinaga had gone mad, although we should have known better, of course. There was always a good reason for anything Michinaga did.

It soon became clear. Michinaga publicly announced that he felt the emperor was becoming too lonely with Shōshi away for such an extended period, and he thought it only right that she come back to be with her husband for a while until the progress of the pregnancy made it imprudent to stay longer. Ichijō was forced to acknowledge his father-in-law's kindness, although from what I could see he seemed none too happy. Then we found out about the girl. It seemed the emperor had become attached to his junior consort, Akimitsu's daughter, whom he wished to promote to the third rank.

To think that I once puzzled over who was responsible for the decision to award Father the Echizen posting! That there was a time when I naively thought the emperor had even a modicum of influence over decisions of state!

It was impossible to tell what Shōshi thought of being pulled about like this. She always accepted her father's will with perfect acquiescence. I had been spending some time privately with her, since during the discomfort of her pregnancy she asked me to teach her Chinese. We carefully arranged times when the other women were not around and read from the two books of Bai Juyi's New Ballads. Amateur that I am, I suggested that the empress engage a real scholar like my father, but she insisted that she only felt comfortable studying with me.

Earlier in my palace career I had been mercilessly taunted about my Chinese learning. There was a woman called Saemon no Naishi who took a dislike to me from the start. I began to hear all sorts of malicious rumors about myself that I discovered were traceable to her. Once, when the emperor had been listening to someone read aloud from my Genji tales, he apparently remarked.

—This author must have read the *Chronicles of Japan*. She sounds very learned indeed!

Saemon no Naishi heard this and began spreading rumors among the senior courtiers that I was flaunting my knowledge of Chinese. She gave me the nickname "Our Lady of the Chronicles"! How mortified I was at the time. To think that someone such as I, who hesitated to reveal my learning even in front of my women at home, would think of doing so at court! Only the support of understanding friends allowed me to get through those terrible times of self-doubt and chagrin.

There followed a period when I avoided writing even the simplest Chinese graph, and I pretended to be unable to read so much as an inscription on a screen. But the empress took me aside and told me not to mind people like Saemon no Naishi. When she asked me to read to her from the collected works of Bai Juyi, though, we chose times when no one was around to overhear. We each had our reasons to keep these sessions secret. Eventually Michinaga found out about his daughter's interest and had some beautiful copies made of various Chinese texts for her. He thought of it as a good way to educate the child in the womb, naturally assuming it was a boy. Thank goodness Saemon no Naishi never found out that Her Majesty had actually asked me to study with her. I would never have heard the end of it.

Who ever would have thought palace life could be such a constant source of irritation?

By the seventh month the empress was getting almost too big to move around easily, yet it was necessary to go back to her mother's house. Our entourage, much less ostentatious this time, left the Ichijō Palace on the morning of the sixteenth just before daybreak to avoid the heat and fuss, arriving at the Tsuchimikado in time for our morning meal. We all returned to the same rooms we had held before. It seemed so familiar, as if we had never left.

The child was due in the ninth month, but ever impatient, Michinaga had been praying that it arrive sooner. Finally someone told him that there is a fixed term in such matters and that what he was seeking could be disastrous. Hastily he abandoned his supplications for an early birth. If he could have, I think Michinaga would have preferred to gestate this child in his own belly. He was in such a nervous state that no one could bear being around him for long.

One night I thought I heard a quiet knocking on my door, but was not about to investigate. I held my breath, not making a sound for the remainder of the night. The next morning a serving girl furtively passed me this when she brought breakfast:

Yomosugara   kuina yori ke ni   naku naku zo   maki no toguchi ni   tatakiwabitsuru
All night long I cried and cried outside your door, louder even than the rapping of the moorhen.

Michinaga really had taken leave of his senses. I would have felt sorry for him if only he weren't so overbearing. I dashed off the following reply and returned it in the care of the same serving girl.

Tada naraji   to bakari tataku   kuina yue   akete wa ika ni   kuyashikaramashi
The moorhen tapped as if it were an urgent matter; but had I opened my door, how I would have regretted it come morning.

Just before dawn on the eleventh of the eighth month, Her Majesty went over to the Hall of Dedication in the southwest corner of the mansion. Her mother accompanied her in the carriage, and the ladies-in-waiting crossed over the lake by boat. I did not go until later and missed most of the ceremonies. Saishō said twenty preachers crowded into the hall, each one feeling obliged to give a little congratulatory sermon in honor of the empress.

—They kept interrupting each other and getting tongue-tied, and it was hard not to laugh, she confided.

The nobles amused themselves painting small white pagodas on the many paper lotus petals that would be distributed later in the ceremony.

When it was over, the senior courtiers rowed the boats out onto the lake, one after the other. Tadanobu, the master of Her Majesty's household, went all the way across and climbed up to the verandah of the hall. I saw him leaning against the railings of the steps going down to the water's edge. Although none too fond of riding on water, I had allowed myself to be enticed onto a boat with some of the younger women, and from this vantage point saw Michinaga arrive and go in. After a few minutes I noticed Tadanobu

301

creeping up the steps in order to try to exchange a few words with Saishō. I guessed he was trying to take advantage of the opportunity while Her Majesty's attention was engaged by her father. It was quite a performance, what with him on the outside and Saishō inside the screens trying not to appear too intimate. Shōshi disapproved of her women behaving flirtatiously, so we had become discreet to the point of prudery.

The moon rose before it was even dark, floating hazily in the autumn night sky. Michinaga's teenage sons were all in one boat singing modern songs. Back in the main building, we could hear their strong young voices wafting over the water. We could see that the elderly minister of the treasury had gotten in with them, but was now sitting meekly in the stern, loath to take part. His sudden shyness was rather amusing, and the women behind the screens laughed among themselves. I recalled a line from Bai Juyi's ballad "The Ocean Wide," which I murmured aloud:

—"And in the boat he seems to feel his age," I quoted.

Tadanobu must have been listening, for he promptly supplied the next line of the ballad. I was a little embarrassed to have been overheard, but rather impressed that he caught the reference.

From the water, the lyrics of the boys' song floated over to us: "and the duckweed on the lake," came the refrain. One of them played the flute, which somehow intensified the slight chill of the evening breeze. Even the most insignificant thing can have its season.

BIRTH OF A PRINCE
Atsuhira

As autumn deepened, the Tsuchimikido could not have looked more beautiful. The trees down by the lake and the grasses by the stream took on intense colors in the late afternoon, each leaf and blade sharply defined in the slanting golden light. With the stirring of a cool breeze, a sonorous tide of prayer arose from all the buildings, mingling with the murmur of the stream.

In the empress's chamber Her Majesty lay languidly listening to the impressive chanting mixed with the gossip of her ladies. She lay on her side, supported by cushions, and though she did not complain, I could see her discomfort, and my heart went out to her. I noticed that when I was in her presence, my usual disenchantment with the world melted away and I wondered how different my life would have been if I had come into Her Majesty's service earlier. Perhaps then I might have felt more at home in these surroundings.

It was the eighth month. As I look over my journal, I can see that I often lay awake at night. I had written: "The night is deeply advanced and even the moon has clouded over, increasing the blackness of the shadows under the trees. As usual I am awake. If I wish to write when I am staying in the women's quarters, I must do so during these quiet hours before dawn."

That morning, however, I was interrupted by arguing voices passing outside my window.

—Here, let's open the shutters!

—Don't be ridiculous. The servants won't be up this early.

—Attendant! Open up!

Then the booming of gongs from the eastern wing broke the stillness, and the Incantation to the Five Mystic Kings began.

I put away my writing things and listened to the rise and fall of the chant as each priest intoned louder than the person before. It was still dark, but I could hear the thundering steps of twenty priests crossing the bridge to the main building, carrying the consecrated objects the empress would soon need. I opened my shutters in hope of catching a glimpse of the magnificently dressed abbot and bishop wending their way over the Chinese bridges in the garden, through the trees, back to their quarters. Every available space at the mansion had been converted to guest rooms, and the priests had been

303

allocated the stable lodge and library. I convinced myself that I could actually see the gold glinting on their robes in the distance. By this time the maids and servants were assembling, and the shapes of trees and flowers emerged from the shadows in the early light of dawn.

All the nobles were expected to pay court, so they had come crowding into the mansion. They would be there until the birth and in the meantime had to be fed and entertained. We didn't get a moment's peace. In the evenings they draped themselves on the verandah of the east wing and on the bridge, playing music, practicing sutras, or singing popular songs. Naturally the saké flowed freely.

Near the end of the month the incense balls we had started blending several days before were ready to be buried so they would be ripe in time for the Chrysanthemum Festival. All of us who had prepared them gathered in Her Majesty's chamber to receive our portions. When I got back to my room, I slid open the door to find Saishō asleep. She lay with her head pillowed on a writing box, her sleeve covering her face. It was an entrancing scene – like something from a storybook. Her robes were maroon lined with blue-green, and purple lined with dark red, and she was using a glossy deep crimson gown as a coverlet. I couldn't stop myself from reaching over and pulling the sleeve away from her beautiful face. She opened her eyes.

—You look just like a fairy princess, I said.

—Are you out of your mind? she grumbled, propping herself up on one elbow. Waking a person like that!

She had tried to sound irritated, but the delicate flush over her features made her look even more charming than usual.

On the day of the Chrysanthemum Festival I was surprised by an early knock on my door. I crawled out of bed to open it and found one of Rinshi's women, Lady Hyōbu, standing there. In her hand was a bundle of silk cloth that had been set outside all night to absorb dew from the chrysanthemum flowers. She presented it to me with a tight little smile.

—Here, she said. Madam Rinshi sends this especially so

304

that you may wipe away old age. She trusts it will be enough.

I'm afraid I didn't have my wits about me at such an early hour, and in any case Hyōbu retreated before I could think of a reply. Suddenly I remembered the last time I had received such a quantity of dew-soaked cloth – it had been when I was pregnant and my husband had sent over a large bowl of silk floss for me to rub over my entire body. It had been an extravagantly loving gesture. Now I sat there speechless, holding the fragrant material, insulting in its bulk, until Saishō called sleepily from under the pile of robes where we had been sleeping.

—Who was that?

I shook off the memory the smell of the damp cloth had awakened.

—Something from Rinshi, I said.

—Something poisonous? Saishō inquired.

—Hmmm. Sort of. I wonder if many other ladies are the recipients of little gifts this morning, or if I have been singled out for special favor.

—She must have spies everywhere, said Saishō, sitting up and drawing the coverlet around her. I'll bet she knew about the "moorhen tapping" at your door last month. What are you going to do?

I pulled out my inkstone and began furiously rubbing the ink-stick in a puddle of water. It did not take long to come up with something.

—I think I should sent it back with a poem, I said, and showed this to Saishō:

Kiku no tsuyu   wakayu bakari ni   sode furete   hana no aruji ni   chiyo wa yuzuramu
> *I have only to brush my sleeve with the chrysanthemum dew to gain a youthful glow; now I return it to its owner to work a miracle.*

—You wouldn't dare! said Saishō, rolling her eyes and laughing. I smiled and rinsed out my brush.

—You're right, I said. It would serve no purpose. It's probably best just to ignore it.

But I knew when I showed it to Saishō that she would relate

305

the incident and my poem to everyone, and that would be my revenge.

That evening I was in attendance on Her Majesty when incense burners were brought out to test the fragrances we had prepared. From their long hems cascading out from under the blinds, I could see that Lady Koshōshō and Lady Dainagon were in their usual places near the verandah. It was a beautiful moonlit night, and we chatted softly about how lovely the garden looked and how the warm weather meant that it was taking an unusually long time for the vines to show their autumn colors. The empress seemed even more restless than usual, and I had a sudden premonition.

I was called away to run an errand, and stopped at my own room when I had finished. Intending only to rest my eyes, I must have fallen asleep, for about midnight I was awakened by a great bustle and noise. Hearing feet passing back and forth, I poked my head into the hallway and stopped a maid-servant who was rushing by.

—Her Majesty's time has come! the girl gasped breath-lessly, and hurried on.

My premonition had been right. I decided to stay out of the way as long as I could. By dawn, now the tenth, Michinaga was standing in the middle of the main building directing everybody. Shōshi's brothers and other nobles of fourth and fifth rank were busy hanging up curtains and bringing in mats and stacks of coiled rush cushions. An all-white dais had been set up next to the empress's usual one, and she was in the process of moving into it when I arrived at the main hall. People were milling about, trying not to jostle the priests intoning an endless stream of loud chanting to keep evil spirits away. Besides the clerics who had been there for the past few months, a call had gone out to every temple in the capital to send over any priest with a reputation as an exorcist – and so even more of them came crowding in. It seemed all the buddhas in the universe were flying down to this house in response to the urgent summons.

Ladies from the palace began to gather in the eastern gallery. The women assigned as mediums sat on the west side of the white dais, each one isolated by a wall of screens with a curtain. In front of each of these cubicles an attending exorcist prayed raucously. To the south of the white birth chamber sat bishops and archbishops in rows, their voices hoarse from loud praying. Their wails were loud enough to summon the most terrifying guardian deities. Then there must have been forty or more people crammed into the narrow space between the sliding screens behind the north side of the dais. The crush was stupefying. I slipped back to my room for a while.

Not long thereafter, there was a heavy knock on the pillar. I raised the lattice to find Michinaga's personal steward looking harried and impatient.

—His Excellency wants to know why you are not in attendance, the man said brusquely. He told me to fetch you immediately.

I was embarrassed and flustered. In the press and confusion I never thought my absence would be noticed.

—I'm just redoing my makeup, I said as an excuse. I will be along in a few moments.

Before I could close the lattice, the steward put his hand on the frame and said he would wait. I understood from his manner that I was not to dawdle. I didn't really need to powder my face, but made some noise with my cosmetic box before taking several deep breaths and stepping out into the hall. To my surprise we walked briskly past the main building clear over to the western wing. There, removed from the booming noise and jostling crowds surrounding Shōshi, sat Michinaga facing a small private shrine. He seemed to be absorbed in prayer and looked quite gaunt and serious. It was obvious he hadn't slept.

Michinaga turned as the steward quietly announced me before slipping discreetly away. He looked at me piercingly before speaking.

—I need you, said Michinaga slowly.

I waited.

—I need you to record this, he continued. This will be my most glorious moment, and I want a full record of it.

—Of course there are others taking notes, too, he

continued, but I especially want you to write down everything you observe – the good, the bad, whatever happens, just keep a record. I'm depending on you.

I nodded, feeling abashed.

—That's all, he said, and turned back to his shrine.

Though he wasn't looking, I bowed and crept out of the room. If I had had any remaining doubts about the nature of Michinaga's feelings for me, they were answered by this brief exchange. As far as he was concerned, I was nothing more than his scribe, his voice for posterity. I had agreed that I would keep his record for him, but now I began to think coldly about what that meant.

Back in the main building even more people were arriving. It was still early, and undoubtedly some of them had just gotten the news of the empress's condition and rushed over from their homes, but by now there was really no place to put them. I wormed my way back into the northern gallery where the ladies were squeezed in so tightly many had lost the hems of their trains and parts of their sleeves. It was an appalling crush, but there was nothing to do but join it.

All day long Empress Shōshi suffered from labor pains, but there was no progress in the birth. One after another, evil spirits were driven into the mediums, each exorcist bellowing louder than the next. At one point the entire lot of them shrieked incantations in unison. The cacophony was unimaginable. By late afternoon a carriageful of older ladies with midwifery experience arrived from the palace. They crept in and out of the curtains of the white dais but were able to accomplish nothing. You could see them biting their lower lips and hiding their tears. In the back gallery several ladies felt faint and had to be carried out. Others were moaning and swaying, having fallen into trances from the high level of emotion.

The noise and confusion continued into the night. Everyone was very tired, but no one dared leave. Every so often someone would throw handfuls of rice to distract evil spirits, and the grains fell down the necks of our gowns. The ladies who had been with Her Majesty a long time were naturally distraught at the way events were unfolding, and even though

308

I had not been in her service nearly as long as they had, I knew that I was experiencing an event of momentous significance.

Dawn approached. By now it was the eleventh. Michinaga panicked at his daughter's unnaturally long labor. Since there seemed to be no end to the number of evil spirits the exorcists were ferreting out, someone suggested the empress be moved to a different location, even if only within the mansion. Never one to simply let things take their course, Michinaga concurred. At dawn two sets of screens were removed on the north side, and Shōshi was moved into the back gallery. It was not possible to hang blinds there, so she was surrounded by a series of overlapping curtains. The older ladies stayed at her side, but Michinaga, now worried that Her Majesty was being affected by the great crowds, ordered the younger ladies to move over to the south and east corridors. Lady Saishō was one of the few asked to remain inside the curtain, along with the empress's mother and her brother the bishop of Ninnaji Temple.

I was with the ladies just below the two platforms when a group of women, including the nurses of Michinaga's other daughters, came pushing their way in front of the curtains that hung as a divider behind us. This meant that people could now barely pass along the narrow corridor in back, and those who did manage to squeeze through could hardly tell whom they were jostling. To make things worse, whenever they felt like it, the men would look over the curtains at us. I was not surprised at such behavior by Michinaga's sons, but even the usually circumspect Tadanobu, master of Her Majesty's household, and the adviser of the Left, Tsunefusa, seemed to lose all sense of propriety and were stealing peeks with the rest. Caught like birds in a crowded cage, we ourselves finally lost all sense of shame. We no longer bothered attempting to hide our faces, our eyes swollen with tears, rice falling on our heads like snow, and our clothes dreadfully crumpled. We must have been a sorry sight. Yet it occurred to me even then that someday, in retrospect, we might remember this scene and think it amusing.

Certainly there was nothing funny about it at the time. By

late morning it seemed the birth was imminent, and the evil spirits howled and wailed. One of the holy teachers was thrown to the ground by the strength of a possessing demon and had to be rescued by loud prayers from a colleague. Lady Saishō was in charge of a number of women under the priest Eikō, and when none of them were able to accept an emerging spirit, there was an absolute uproar.

Suddenly we saw a delegation of priests enter the curtains with the implements used for giving the tonsure, and a wave of despair swept the crowd. Was Her Majesty dying? We could hardly believe it, and some of the ladies completely lost control of themselves, shrieking and wailing. Then into this scene of utter confusion and disarray strode Michinaga. In a loud and steady voice he began to intone the Lotus Sutra. Gradually the hysteria ebbed, and during this brief lull in the turmoil, the child was born.

The birth of a prince! Word rippled through the crowd from the inner sanctuary, through the great hall, out to the corridors, and beyond. Yet the afterbirth had not come, so the air remained tense. Everyone crowded into the huge area stretching from the main room to the southern gallery all the way out to the balustrades, and chanting began anew. Laymen and priests alike threw themselves on the ground in prayer. I was on the other side of the room, but I heard later that the women from the eastern gallery suddenly came face-to-face with a group of senior nobles. In particular, Lady Kochūjō, who was always very particular about her appearance, ran into First Secretary of the Left Yorisada, with whom she had once been involved. Although she had made herself up very carefully that morning, by now her eyes were red with weeping and her powder had rubbed off in patches. She knew she was a dreadful sight and was quite put out to come across a former lover in such a state.

With difficulty I worked my way toward the birth chamber to find Saishō, and when I did I was shocked to see how her face had changed, too. I hate to think how I myself must have looked. It's probably a good thing we were all in such a collective state of fright that no one would later remember how awful anyone else looked!

Saishō told me that the afterbirth had finally been expelled and the empress was now resting. She was gently lowered to her cushions to lie down after being supported upright by the older women for this extraordinary amount of time. Mother and child were both alive. I thought back to how easy my own experience had been in contrast. Although the pregnancy itself had been dreadful, Katako's birth was mercifully quick.

It was high noon when the announcement was made, yet everyone felt that the morning sun had just risen in a cloudless sky. That Shōshi had survived was reason enough to celebrate, but that the child was a boy made everyone ecstatic. Ladies who yesterday had wilted and this morning been sunk in a misty autumnal sadness now revived and excused themselves to go freshen up in their rooms. Only the older women stayed behind to attend the mother and baby, which was as it should be. Saishō and I took this opportunity to go back to our quarters as well.

We were both drained, Saishō especially so, yet there was hardly a moment to rest. Already servants were scurrying through the women's apartments bearing enormous bundles of clothing. The formal jackets they brought us had been embroidered and inlaid with mother-of-pearl. Had they been unique, we should have admired them extravagantly, no doubt, but everyone had received similar garments, so we mostly ignored them and got on with doing our makeup and fussing about where our good fans had gotten to.

I finished my toilette first. Waiting for Saishō, I slid the window open just a crack to look across the garden toward the southern corner of the main building. Several high nobles were waiting there, and then I saw Michinaga emerge with a great smile on his face, directing that the stream be cleared of leaves. I recalled the last time when I heard that order, and Michinaga had picked a maidenflower and tossed it over the curtain stand into my room. As I thought back, that was probably the high point of my misunderstanding with Michinaga.

Unbelievably he caught sight of me at the open window and headed in my direction.

—Taking notes? he asked broadly. There's still plenty to

311

come – the bathing ceremony, the presentation of the sword, the celebration of the third day, the fifth day, the seventh day, the ninth day. All of it! I expect a record of it all, you know.

Suddenly I felt exhausted.

FULL OF MOONLIGHT

Hikari sashisou

For ten days following the prince's birth, ceremonies were performed relentlessly, one after the other. I felt somewhat under the weather and ill at ease, but nevertheless kept on writing to the point of deep fatigue. Michinaga had ordered me to take notes, so I did my best, mostly writing at night by candlelight. Since I couldn't possible observe everything, I had to rely on information from Saishō, Koshōshō, and other friends. Saishō had the honor of being in charge of the prince's first bath.

Everything at the mansion had been decorated in white since the birth. It was fascinating to see how the ladies whose rank allowed them the forbidden colors comported themselves during this period when all colors were forbidden. Rivalries were intensified, as if the women took up a challenge to see how well they could demonstrate their superiority by using fabric alone. Those of highest rank had their Chinese jackets made from the same figured silk as their mantles, with decorated cuffs, whereas lower ladies, especially the older ones, kept to plain jackets. They were impressive, yet in the end I was struck by how similar everyone looked. Everyone's fan was tasteful without being showy and all were inscribed with the appropriate sorts of sentiments. Surely each lady thought she was being quite original when she painted her own – thus one could sense the ripple of shock as they looked at one another and realized, in the end, what a set of duplicates they all were.

312

Even so, the scene was awesome in its severe beauty. The embroidery was all in silver, and the seams of our trains were outlined in silver thread stitched so thickly it looked like braid. Silver foil was inlaid into patterns in the ribs of the fans. When everyone was assembled, it was like looking at snow-clad mountains by the light of a clear moon – almost blinding, as if the room had been hung with mirrors.

The ceremonies for the third day were arranged by the members of Her Majesty's household staff. They made a presentation of clothing and bedding for the prince in which everything had been lined or wrapped in matching white cloth of an original design. I can't imagine how they were able to orchestrate the event in such a short time. The fifth-day ceremonies were directed by Michinaga himself. Torch-bearers stood everywhere at attention, like human candle-sticks, illuminating the garden and the grand rooms as bright as daylight. Groups of visitors clustered in the shadows while Michinaga's personal retainers scurried about smiling and bowing, accepting congratulations from all.

Michinaga chose eight of his daughter's youngest and most attractive serving women to be the food bearers that evening. In white gowns with white ribbons in their hair, they stood in a double row passing along a series of silver and white trays. The usual complainers groused at having been left out, and I was not the only one to think that they succeeded in making themselves look completely ridiculous.

At the conclusion of ceremonies, many nobles left their seats and wandered out onto the bridge, where they started to gamble with dice. I noticed Michinaga joined them. It was precisely the sort of behavior that used to bother my father about palace life. I could only thank heaven that my brother was on duty at the Ichijō Palace that evening. Had he been present, I'm sure I would have been embarrassed again. There were poems, too, along with the drinking, and the women I was sitting with became nervous lest the cup get passed around to us and we would have to respond. We were telling ourselves how careful one had to be when composing a poem in the presence of Kintō, not only with the actual words but also the reciting. Several of us prepared poems in advance, just in case. Using the images of a round full moon and round full saké cups, I came up with this:

Mezurashiki   hikari sashisou   sakazuki wa   mochinagara koso   ckiyo wo megurame
Wondrously full of the full moon's light, we hand a cup of saké round and pray for fortune through the ages.

But then it got late, and people either left or fell asleep, and no one bothered to ask us for our poems. It was too bad. I think mine would have done quite nicely.

As the moon rose, the night became even brighter and all sorts of staff people emerged from the shadows. There were servants, hairdressers, maids, and cleaning ladies, many of whom I had never seen before. I glimpsed an odd pair, possibly the women in charge of the keys, who were stiffly gotten up in formal dress with a forest of combs sprouting from their hair. I was oddly remained of how, when night fell in Echizen, a whole different world of creatures came out in the dark. The verandah between the entrance to the back corridor and the bridge became so crowded with people that it was impossible for anyone to pass.

I was privileged to be staying in the chamber with the empress that night and was relieved that she seemed to have recovered from her ordeal. She looked so fulfilled and beautiful in the first flush of young motherhood that we felt like showing her off. There was a priest on night duty, so on an impulse I pushed aside the screen, allowing him a glimpse of the empress.

—Here, cleric, I said. I'm sure you have never seen such a marvelous sight before.

Glancing our way, his jaw fell open. He raised his hands together in our direction, exclaiming.

—Ah! You're too kind, too kind!

It pleased me to think that the image of our empress, her shining hair gathered in a thick black river spilling over her white and silver gowns, would live in that man's memory forever.

The following day we were able to catch our breath between the post-birth celebrations of the fifth and the seventh days. Most of us got up late and spent the afternoon in our rooms sewing new costumes, a problem with so many public ceremonies following one upon the next. We couldn't appear in the same clothes for each, yet there was so little time to prepare. By evening, though, we were able to relax a bit. The weather was perfect, and I was sitting out on the bridge corridor with friends when Michinaga's son, Norimichi, came by with some officers. He tried to entice the younger women out onto a boat in the lake and succeeded in persuading about half the group. The shy ones slipped away and stayed indoors, but I could tell by the way they kept glancing out at the lake that they regretted their timidity. From the bridge I watched the shadowy figures in the garden glowing palely in the moonlight. I was again struck by the contrast between the ladies' black hair and the whiteness of their gowns. It was eerily beautiful, more so than if they had been wearing their usual colors.

Earlier in the evening the moon underwent a partial eclipse. One of the younger ladies noticed it first and pointed to the sky in dismay. It was not a good omen. Of all the nights for the sky to be clear! It would have been much better had there been a bit of cloud cover for the moon's indiscretion. One evening in Echizen when a shadow appeared to bite away at the moon's edge, Master Jyo told us that in his country such things were predictable. Father pressed him to explain. Just as Ming-gwok had once told me, his father said that although he himself was not trained to do the calculations, the Chinese emperor had a bureau devoted to tracking the activities of the heavens. Father remarked on what a marvelous thing it would be to foretell eclipses of the sun and moon.

The other women were agonizing among themselves about the sinister portent when Lady Saishō pointed out to them that it had passed, and the moon had now returned to its full splendor. She asked me to think up a poem to make her point, and so I composed this:

Kumori naku   chitose ni sumeru   mizu no omo ni   yadoreru tsuki no   kage mo nodokeshi
Cloudlessly clear unto eternity, the reflected moon lodges peacefully on the water's surface.

315

—You see, she said, Michinaga's karma is so strong that any inauspicious shadows melt away. Just think about Her Majesty's birthing of the prince. We had thought all was lost when Michinaga himself recited the Lotus Sutra, and the child was born.

Just then, a page came to announce that carriages full of ladies from the palace had pulled up to the northern guard-house. We immediately forgot about the moon in our haste to return to our posts. Then we remembered the ladies still out on the lake, who were just then rounding the pine trees on the island, meandering slowly back to shore. Frantically we waved at them to hurry. When they finally got in, they were quite flustered to find that the palace ladies had arrived, and they scolded us for not letting them know.

—Well, we tried our best, we protested, but evidently you couldn't see us waving from the bridge.

—We thought you were just waving for fun, they said sourly in their rush to change clothes.

It was odd that our group still felt uncomfortable in the presence of the palace women.* You would have thought that by then, especially since Her Majesty had given birth to a son, we would have had more confidence. As we rushed to make ourselves presentable, luckily for us Michinaga came out and sat with the visiting ladies. He was more relaxed than I had seen him in months. Genially he exchanged pleasantries and banter and gave them all presents according to rank. This allowed us to regain our composure before joining the group to welcome them to the mansion. The next day's ceremonies were to be sponsored by the palace, so these women had come early in order to set up their equipment. Mostly they just wanted to know the location of various supplies, whom they could get to carry out their orders, and where they were supposed to sleep that evening. They were as little interested in socializing as we were, and after answering their questions and showing them to their quarters, we, too, retired to our rooms.

*The large retinues of ladies-in-waiting in Shōshi's service were not official palace women. They were entirely supported by Fujiwara private funds.

By the seventh day we were all quite worn out. An imperial messenger presented Her Majesty with a willow-wood box containing a scroll listing all the gifts coming from the palace. I was seated just outside the imperial dais, but Koshōshō was inside and she told me that the empress hadn't even looked at the scroll, but simply handed it to her attendants. Gifts were passed out through the curtains in return. Later, when I came looking for Saishō, I peeped in through the curtains at the empress. She was reclining on cushions and seemed rather listless. I was taken aback at how pale and fragile she looked. A small oil lamp hung inside the curtains, and in its clear light her complexion glowed with a translucent delicacy. She looked so young and, despite her lassitude, beautiful – especially with her mass of black hair tied up and arranged in back – hardly the figure one would expect for a person being celebrated as "Mother of the Land." She smiled wanly when she saw me.

—When shall we ever return to our Chinese studies, do you think? she murmured.

I suddenly felt sorry for her. Whenever I became fatigued with the endless sequence of official celebrations, I reminded myself that it was even more onerous for the young empress who had to endure it all in her weakened condition. I said something meant to be reassuring and slipped back out through the curtains. The partying that evening was, if anything, even noisier than the previous nights. I claimed a headache and managed to get away early. Poor Lady Koma was not so lucky, I heard later.

On the eighth day we all put away the white robes, changing back to colors. The white dais was dismantled, and new curtains with a floating woodgrain pattern put up. While it was a relief to the eye to have color again, the icy white had been beautiful in its own way, too. In white, everything was vividly stark, like those line drawings in which everyone's long black hair seems literally to grow from the paper. The ceremonies of the ninth day were sponsored by the crown prince's household, and the serving women wore gowns of deep crimson under transparent jackets of gauze silk. They looked terribly elegant, and our eyes drank in the rich colors.

317

Knowing that this was the last of the official birth events made it rather special. I would have enjoyed it more, however, if I hadn't felt pressed to observe everything in detail and take notes on it all.

WATERBIRDS

Mizutori

In the middle of the night Koshōshō tapped on my door. Awake, as I often was, I heard the rasp of her silk skirts along the floor and the silence when she stopped, even before the quiet tap of her knock. I let her in. Saishō had gone home, so I was alone. The moon, two days past full, hovered over the western hills, throwing the silver shadows in the garden. Koshōshō lay down next to me and yawned delicately.

—You were smart to leave early, she said. Things got awkward. You know Koma, that new serving lady?

Koma was very attractive. She was also young and inexperienced. Somehow she had gotten caught up in a game between some drunken nobles and, not knowing how to make an artful escape, was unable to extricate herself before things had gone too far.

—There were the usual kinds of stupid things, Koshōshō said. They were talking about Shō, the wet nurse, and then old Toshikata said he needed a wet nurse, too. He kept leering at Koma and wheedling her to give him her breast. "Just a taste!" he whined. Then you-know-who kept trying to put his head on her lap.

Innocence, it seems, is irresistible. I felt sorry for the poor girl who would now begin to weave herself the opaque coat of glib brittleness we all learn to wear.

—The truth is, she could have escaped at several points, said Koshōshō, waving her hand in frustration.

—but she seemed totally bewildered. Finally Michinaga

318

took off one of his own robes and offered it to her as a gift.

—And she took it? I asked.

—She was embarrassed and tried to refuse. I'm not even sure she realized what it would mean to accept. Michinaga kept pressing her, though.

—Giving himself the perfect excuse to visit her room later, I added.

—In the end, she had to take it, said Koshōshō.

—Yes, in the end, I suppose we always have to take it, I sighed.

Finally the ceremonies ended. It was a great relief to be off duty and not feel that I had to remember everything in order to write it down. One still and humid evening I was enjoying a quiet chat with Saishō when Michinaga's oldest boy, Yorimichi, wandered by. He was probably about sixteen, but sophisticated for his age. Seeing us, he pushed a corner of the blinds aside and seated himself right there on the door frame. He had already learned that men can always step right into women's conversations. He proceeded to talk about love in the earnest fashion of the young who have just discovered it.

—Women! he lamented. What difficult creatures they can be!

Saishō thought him charming, but I found him unsettling, as if he were playing at being the hero in a romance. Soon he was off, murmuring something about there being too many maidenflowers in the field.

—Really, she said after he was gone, wasn't that just a perfectly Genji thing to do? She quoted the poem that Yorimichi had alluded to:

Ominaeshi   oukaru nobe ni   yadoriseba   ayanaku ada no   na wo ya tachinamu
Should I tarry longer in this field of maidenflowers, I will
*   surely get a bad name.*

—Indeed, I said. He seems precisely too much like the hero of a romance.

Compared to some of the young men, he was not unlikable, though. His father had told him that a man's career depends in

319

no little part on his wife's family, and encouraged the boy to woo Prince Tomohira's daughter. Michinaga seemed to think that I had influence on the prince because of family connections, and he had been dropping broad hints that I say something in Yorimichi's favor. The prince was an admirer of Genji and had been kind to me in the past, so I was in a difficult position. I knew he had long hoped to send his daughter to court as an imperial bride, so the idea of giving her to Yorimichi would be a disappointment. Still, when the full force of Michinaga's will bore down upon a situation, the result was inevitable. When Prince Tomohira asked for my opinion, I had to advise him that resisting Michinaga was futile, and it would be best to offer his daughter to Yorimichi with good grace.

The season changed.* We gave away our raw silk and unlined gowns to the serving women when they brought out the moth-proofed chests of winter padded and lined robes. Shōshi's convalescence was nearly over, yet she could not return to the palace until all traces of impurity from childbirth had been erased. The emperor was waiting impatiently to see his newborn son, so Michinaga surprised everyone by inviting him to come visit the empress at the Tsuchimikado.

We alternated shifts night and day to attend the empress in her curtained dais where she had been cocooned since the birth. She emerged for the first time on the day we changed our robes. The baby prince stayed mostly with his wet nurse, naturally, whose position was made unusually difficult by Michinaga's persistent interest in the infant. He came without fail every morning and evening to see the baby. It didn't matter that the wet nurse might be asleep, dead to the world, Michinaga marched right in and opened up the curtains. The poor woman might wake with a start to find him rummaging in her breast to fondle the infant. I felt sorry for her. The child was really too young to be handled so.

* According to the official calendar, the most emphatic breaks between seasons occurred on the tenth day of the tenth month, when lined winter robes were brought out, and at the beginning of the fourth month, when everyone changed to unlined summer garments.

As for Michinaga, he had gone completely soft for his imperial heir. There was no greater joy for him than to lift the baby up in his arms as if it were an indescribably precious object. He didn't even mind when the young prince suddenly let loose a little stream and wet his robes.

—Look! he chuckled, holding the baby out. I've been blessed by the little fellow! Could there be better proof that my prayers have been answered?

The wet nurse snatched the baby back with an expression of dismay while Michinaga removed his cloak and hung it up to dry.

With only four days remaining to prepare for the emperor's visit, we were run ragged. Anything even slightly worn was repaired, renewed, or replaced. The verandahs were polished with peach pits. The garden was redone as well. Cartloads of rare chrysanthemums were transplanted – white ones fading to purple or else turning yellow on the underside, or red; bright yellow ones in full splendor; and all manner of shapes and sizes grouped in attractive ways. As I looked out at them through the swirling morning mist, they might have come from a magical Daoist garden with the power to vanquish old age.

Would that it were true! I recall moving through those days in an almost dreamlike state. I wished I could borrow the chrysanthemum dew to regain a more youthful outlook on the world. Everywhere confronted with auspicious and joyful celebration, I suffered the perverse and opposite effect of increasing disillusion. I had, by any measure one cared to apply, reached a pinnacle of undreamed-of success. Not only was I accepted into court service, the empress showed, by numerous small kindnesses, that she favored my company. Readers clamored for my Genji stories, and I had a seemingly endless supply of paper.

Why couldn't I simply accept things as they were and be grateful? I wondered. How I envied people whose diaries were simple and who could find joy in life as it is. Surely there was no reason why I shouldn't take pleasure in the marvelous things I was in a position to see and hear – yet all I felt was weariness.

And then I felt even more wretched for allowing myself to go on like that. So what it I was beginning to harbor doubts about my Shining Prince? My readers were happy. I wished I could take a long stretch of time in order to think about Genji, but I was required to immerse myself in palace ceremony, taking notes for Michinaga. But how ridiculous that I should feel bereft simply because I couldn't spend hours in my world of make-believe! Wasn't the reality of my life interesting enough? This is surely the time to let go of grievances, I told myself sternly. What good does it do to dwell on them? Brooding on a nest of grudges will only hatch more grief.

Lifting my head to look out at the dawning day, I saw a family of waterbirds playing on the lake as if they hadn't a care in the world. Then it struck me that to an outside observer they may look as though they were enjoying life, but in fact they must often suffer, too.

Mizutori wo   mizu no ne to ya   yoso ni mimu   ware mo ukitaru   yo wo sugushitsutsu
How can I view the birds on the water with indifference?
Like them, I float through a sad, uncertain world.

I received a note from Koshōshō, who had been on leave for a few days, and while I was composing my reply, suddenly the sky clouded up darkly and it began to rain. I could hear the messenger complaining, and knowing he was in a hurry, I scribbled a closing – "and the sky, too, seems unsettled." I can't now remember my poem, but I must have written one, for in the evening the same messenger returned with Koshōshō's answering verse written on dark purple, cloud-patterned paper.

Kumo ma naku   nagamuru sora mo   kakikurashi   ika ni shinoburn   shigure naruramu
I gaze at lowering skies darkened by endless clouds and my
heart is overcast, too, raining with tears of longing.

We were very close, and I felt her absence keenly. Even at the time, I couldn't remember what my poem had been about, so I replied using her imagery:

Kotowari no   shigure no sora wa   kumo ma aredo   nagamuru sode zo   kawaku ma mo naki
In this season of rainy skies, the clouds sometimes break,
yet my yearning sleeves have no break in which to dry.

I sent it off, glad that I would see her soon, for the imperial visit was scheduled for the following day, and everyone who had been on leave would return. My father was disappointed not to have received an invitation, but he realized that with the large crowd expected, it was unlikely for anyone of his rank to be included – even if he did have a daughter in service. It was strange – he used to be my eyes and ears of palace life, and now I was his.

Koshōshō returned in the chilly hours before dawn on the morning of the imperial visit, so together we dressed and did our hair. Using a comb and my hand, I smoothed her long black hair, which had become tangled by being tucked under her traveling coats. Her hair was completely straight without a ripple. Every now and then I had started to notice a colorless strand in my own hair. They stood out, these pale ones, their texture somehow thicker than an ordinary black hair. I had taken to plucking them out and wrapping them around a chopstick I kept in my cosmetic box. Koshōshō scolded me that it was a morbid habit.

TEN THOUSAND YEARS, A THOUSAND AUTUMNS

Mannen senjū

We had been told that the imperial procession was due to arrive in the morning, so all the ladies had been up fussing with their makeup since before dawn. Counting on the fact that such affairs never start punctually, Koshōshō and I dawdled, figuring we still had plenty of time to replace our rather uninspired fans with better ones. We were still waiting for the new fans when all of a sudden we heard the sound of drums. There was nothing for it but to make do with what we had and hurry over to the main building in a rather undignified manner. We were not the only ones caught unawares, for a surge of ladies arrived from the east wing right at the same moment. In the west building the empress's younger sister Kenshi and her retinue were already demurely in place. Of course they didn't have much choice but to be circumspect, since the west wing was also occupied by a group of high nobles.

The morning sun glittered on the special boats that had been made for the orchestras. The boat for Chinese music had a dragon-headed prow – dragon as master of the waves; and the one for Korean music had a *geki*-bird, master of the wind, carved in wood and painted with gilt. The fabulous creatures looked almost alive gliding majestically on the waters. The drums we had heard were from the water music struck up to greet the emperor's arrival. His palanquin was carried through the south gate, and when the bearers reached the stairs, they hoisted the heavy litter onto their shoulders, kneeling there beneath it, steadying the entire thing on their backs so that the emperor might emerge directly onto the verandah. Normally, of courser, persons of such low rank would never be permitted on the south stairs, but as they crouched there – in considerable distress, it appeared to me – it occurred to me that we were not so different from them. Even those of us who mixed freely with royalty were just as bound by rank as those pitiful bearers.

—How difficult life is, I murmured, and Koshōshō tugged my sleeve.

—Shush, listen to the music, she whispered.

The music wafting from the two boats was indeed exquisite. I felt the reverberations of the drum to the core of my body, and the high notes of the wind instruments hung in the air like golden veils.

Emperor Ichijō emerged from his vehicle with great dignity and proceeded to the throne that had been set up for him at the eastern end of the gallery. The blinds screening the ladies-in-waiting on our side had been raised to allow the handmaids to step out carrying the imperial sword and jewel that accompany the emperor wherever he goes. My old nemesis Saemon no Naishi, the one who once called me Our Lady of the Chronicles, carried the sacred sword on a pillow, and Ben no Naishi bore the sacred necklace in a casket. Their robes and sashes snaked and trailed about them so that they resembled heavenly dancers or figures in a Chinese painting. Ben no Naishi seemed embarrassed and nervous. I wondered why. Saemon no Naishi had a more beautiful face, at least the part you could see around her fan, but certainly from the fan down, Ben no Naishi was by far the more stylish of the two. She wore a lavender and crimson double-layered gown, and a train of blue-green, deepening in hue towards the hem. Her sash was dyed in green and purple checks. The fact that I felt obliged to record things for Michinaga sharpened my eye to such details.

Inside the blinds I looked around at all the ladies carefully dressed in their finest. Normally you can tell at a glance when someone has been less than painstaking with her appearance, but on this day every lady had done her utmost to present herself in the best possible manner. Those who were of a rank to wear the forbidden fabrics were wearing the usual tea-green or crimson Chinese jackets and silk trains with stenciled designs. Underneath, most had on mantles of glossy silk in maroon with crimson linings – except for Muma, who wore lavender, just to be different. Under their mantles, the layered gowns peeked out like a brocade of autumn leaves in shades of saffron, gamboge, purple lined with dark red, and yellow lined with green.

Like the other, older ladies who were not permitted the fabrics of high rank, I was wearing a dark red Chinese jacket of unpatterned weave with five attached damask cuffs. My robes were plain silk, white lined with maroon. The younger ladies, however, sported cuffs in assorted colors, some of them arranged in a most interesting way – for example, white on the outside over maroon and chartreuse, or white with just one pale green lining and then light pink shading to dark red with one white layer interposed. I also noticed some decorated fans which looked very special.

I have to say that altogether we could have been a scene from a painted scroll. Everyone looked gorgeous. The only difference one could detect was our heads – many of the older ladies had hair that was starting to thin, whereas the younger ones still had luxurious tresses. Even so, there were a few exceptions – sad to say for the girls with sparse hair. The real marvel was Rinshi, who must have been forty years old but still had the same glossy black hair as her daughters. I couldn't help thinking at the time that perhaps spite is a tonic that keeps one young.

Also, hair may not be the best indication of a woman's elegance. It seemed to me that a glance at the part of the face that shows just above a woman's fan was sufficient to tell whether or not she was truly refined. Among the empress's ladies, I'm afraid, only a few would stand out as exceptional.

Five palace women had been assigned to Empress Shōshi. They now emerged from the raised blinds in our corner to serve the imperial repast. Their hair was done up in chignons for the task, and I suppose they resembled angels, too, although not particularly angelic ones. Jijū was wearing a tea-green Chinese jacket of plain weave silk, with white robes lined in pale blue-green, and Chikuzen had on a similar jacket over white robes lined in dark red. Both had silver-stenciled trains. Tachibana no Sanmi was the server, but I could not see her properly because of a pillar that blocked my view. Her hair was rolled up as well, and I think she was wearing a green jacket over yellow robes lined in blue-green.

Isn't it ridiculous how vividly memory clings to the trivial details attached to great moments?

When the time came for the baby prince to be presented to the emperor, Michinaga himself carried the infant and placed him in Ichijō's arms. As he did so, the baby gave a little cry, which was audible to everyone because the great room had gone completely silent. Then Saishō stepped out, holding the imperial sword.* All eyes were upon her. This was the moment everyone had waited for – and how quickly it was over. The wet nurse bustled up to retrieve the child and take

* The gesture showed official imperial recognition of the child.

him back to Rinshi's quarters in the western chamber. Saishō rejoined our group. She sat down looking rather flushed, her fine features heightened by her agitation.

—It was all so formal. I was dreadfully nervous, she confided.

I could not imagine myself going out in front of all those important people in that way, but I suppose one could get used to anything with practice. Saishō was not exactly inexperienced.

We had been living at Rinshi's mansion since the previous summer, so I had not seen the emperor for several months. Knowing his attachment to his children, and watching him hold the baby, I felt sorry for him. When Teishi was empress, he had been forced to wait almost a year before getting a glimpse of his firstborn son, Prince Atsuyasu. The formalities that cloak the imperial personage are so heavy that the emperor's private wishes often do not prevail. I imagined his feelings holding this new child were rather mixed. Hope that his beloved Atsuyasu would ever become crown prince was receding like the tide.

I wished my father could have seen the music and dances that were performed that afternoon. I myself missed the Korean numbers and only managed to see the Chinese ones. During the well-known piece "Ten Thousand Years," the baby started to cry, and the minister of the Right exclaimed, "Listen! He harmonizes perfectly with the music!" At this, Kintō, with some companions, began to intone the words to the Chinese poem "Ten Thousand Years, a Thousand Autumns." If only Father could have been there, I thought – he would have put them all to shame!

This was truly the high point. Even Michinaga was moved to tears, exclaiming,

—After today, I can't imagine how I could have been impressed by previous imperial visits. This surely surpasses them all!

He at least had the good sense to recognize his good fortune.

And then the floating orchestra broke into a lively finale of "Great Joy" as the boats skirted the island and receded. The sound of flutes and drums mingled with the wind in the pines, growing fainter in the distance. The effect was ethereal. The stream, clear and limpid, flowed smoothly down to the lake where the breeze riffled the water. By now it was a little cool. His Majesty was wearing only two underjackets, and Jijū, one of the palace ladies, obviously feeling a chill herself, expressed great concern for him. Sitting slightly apart watching her solicitous clucking, we had to hide our amusement.

Jijū's companion Chikuzen, who was sitting with us, began to recollect past occasions when Dowager Empress Senshi had visited the mansion.

—Ah, such times we had! she sighed, bringing up name after name of people long since passed away. It felt inauspicious to go on about the dead under the current circumstances. Several ladies glanced at one another and moved to the other side of the tented platform in order to avoid responding to Chikuzen's increasingly maudlin reminiscences. She looked as though, given the slightest encouragement, she would begin to cry.

When evening fell, Michinaga proceeded to the western wing to announce promotions. The emperor joined him there and, requesting the list of the eligible, approved one after the other. With this, the official ceremonies of the day ended, and Ichijō was at last able to enter Shōshi's curtained dais and visit his wife. They were together for not even an hour before the palanquin was ready to depart, and the emperor had to take his leave. After he had gone, everyone heaved a great sigh, relaxed, and got very drunk. I stayed up rather late myself, talking with Saishō.

On the day following the imperial visit I overslept and missed the messenger from the palace. He came very early, before the morning mist had even cleared. By the time Saishō and I rose, preparations were already under way for the baby prince's ceremonial haircut, which had been put off until his father had seen him for the first time. We had no special duties in this regard, however, so we spent the day relaxing in our room. Saishō was waiting to hear the assignments for the new prince's household staff, for she had a younger sister whom she hoped would be named as one of the ladies-in-waiting for the prince. Unfortunately she was disappointed.

Because of the crowds of visiting dignitaries, the furnishings in Her Majesty's apartments had been kept rather sparse. Now as life returned to normal, the beautiful lacquered chests and curtain stands were brought back and the rooms made luxurious once again. As soon as it got light in the mornings, Rinshi would come in, fussing and cooing over the baby like any fond grandmother. She was civil to all the empress's women, including me.

One evening the moon was especially bright, and I heard someone moving outside at the end of our corridor. It turned out to be Sanenari, the assistant master of Her Majesty's household. I guessed that he was looking for a lady-in-waiting to convey his thanks to the empress for his recent promotion. Apparently the area around the side door was wet from the baby's bathwater, and when he couldn't find anyone there, he came around to our corridor. Sanenari occasionally sent me poems to which I had replied in the past. For a palace official, he was not a bad sort, but I was not in the mood for things to go further between us.

—Is anyone here? I heard him call.

Then he moved to the middle room where I was sitting, pushing up the top half of the shutters that I had forgotten to lock.

—Anyone in? he called again, but I did not reply.

Right then his superior, Tadanobu, joined him, and I decided that it was too rude of me to stay silent, so I gave some noncommittal response. The two of them seemed delighted to have provoked even that.

—You ignore me, but pay attention when it's the master of the household who calls, said Sanenari ruefully. It's understandable, I suppose, but really too bad. Why the need to stand on formality here?

And with that he started to sing a snatch of folk song: "Today is so special, so special, nothing ever gone before could match today . . ."

It was now the middle of the night and the moonlight poured its brightness over the garden. Although I suspected

329

they had been drinking, I found Sanenari's voice surprisingly attractive.

—Do open up the bottom of the lattice, the two of them insisted, and I was almost tempted. Had it been another time or another place . . . but, come morning, it would be too embarrassing to think that I had let these noblemen behave in such a frivolous fashion. Were I younger, such reckless behavior might be excused and put down to naiveté, but I was not in a position to open myself up to such gossip. So I refused. I half expected they might try a little harder to convince me, but they gave up and wandered away. Just to see his reaction, I sent Sanenari this poem the next morning:

Irukata wa   sayaka narikeru   tsukikage wo   uwa no sora ni mo   machishi yoi kana
The bright moon clearly followed another direction; I spent the night waiting under a blank sky.

His reply came back quickly:

Sashiteyuku   yama no ha mo mina   kakikumori   kokoro mo sora ni   kieshi tsukikage
As the moon came near the mountain, it suddenly clouded over, and so the moon's desire was extinguished.

Thank goodness I had not encouraged him! How many ladies succumb in a moment of sentimental weakness only to find that the insistent bright moonlight is extinguished by the first cloud.

OUR LITTLE MURASAKI
Wagamurasaki

Confirming dozens of details with various friends, I finally managed to make a clean copy of all my notes on the birth events and pass them on to Michinaga. He was in an extraordinarily expansive mood and appeared quite pleased. He gave me a set of elegant writing brushes and a supply of fine paper, mentioning that I ought to get back to writing about Genji once the fiftieth-day post-birth ceremony was over.

I had thought my reporting duties would end after the imperial visit, so his remark caught me off guard.

—Did His Excellency want me to report on the fiftieth day as well? I asked.

Michinaga smiled in a most gratifying way.

—If it's not too much of an imposition, was his answer. After a pause,

—And then, you know, when that is over, perhaps you might continue to write up your observations of the Gosechi Dances at year's end back at the palace. It is very good to have a record of these things.

Meekly I protested that there was an official scribe in charge of making records and that my impressionistic jottings could hardly constitute the sort of think he would want to leave for posterity. I also said some complimentary things about Akazome Emon, one of Rinshi's ladies whom, at that time anyway, I respected as a writer. But Michinaga just smiled again and waved his hand to dismiss my objections.

—Yes, I have plenty of people who can record the time and date and who was where, but they don't convey the flavor of these occasions, he said. When I'm old, I want to be able to savor these moments. The rest of the world will no doubt want to know what things were like during the time when Michinaga was in charge of the realm. Genji is all well and good, but don't you think people will be more interested in the real Michinaga?

I was taken aback and thought to myself how surprised posterity might be to read of the drunken revelry of his banquets, or the lecherous gropings of the high-minded ministers who loudly proclaimed Chinese virtues in verse, or the demon-possessed rantings of abandoned ladies, or the endless hours of malicious gossip.

I must have had a strange look on my face, for Michinaga interrupted my bitter reverie impatiently.

—Well, what do you say? he demanded sharply. It's not much to ask a writer that she write, after all.

—No, Your Excellency, I replied. It's not much to ask.

I thanked him for the paper and brushes and crept back to my room utterly depressed.

The fiftieth-day festivities took place on the first of the eleventh month. I was seated directly behind the empress and, as it turned out, did not have a very good view. Saishō was one of the servers, though, so she again assisted me in filling in some details I missed. The baby prince was served by Lady Dainagon, and she, too, was able to tell me later about his tiny platter, the exquisite little bowls like dolls' toys, and the centerpiece arranged to look like a beach scene with the chopsticks resting on the outstretched wings of two crouching cranes.

The wet nurse, Shō, was granted the forbidden fabrics that evening. She looked so young as she carried the little prince behind the curtains where Rinshi took the child from her, emerging from the chamber on her knees with the baby in her arms. I thought it interesting that Rinshi was dressed so formally in her stenciled train and red jacket. Her dress proclaimed her not merely the proud grandmother of a splendid infant but the devoted bearer of a future emperor. Not every emperor's son was destined to attain the throne, but there could be no doubt with this one. You could virtually see the aura of this baby's splendid karma glimmering in Rinshi's arms.

The empress herself was less formally dressed than her mother, but her choice of colors showed her usual good taste. She had on a five-layered set of chestnut-brown robes with sky-blue linings, and a semiformal coat of maroon lined in crimson.

Soon after Michinaga presented the fifty tiny rice cakes to the prince, the nobles and ministers who were sitting in the gallery moved out onto the bridge and started making a drunken racket. Servants were supposed to distribute presents of fine bentwood boxes full of sweets, so they followed the carousers outside and nervously placed the boxes on the balustrade. As it was winter, the sun had set early, and the firebrands in the garden were too dim to illuminate the contents. The boisterous nobles began yelling for torchbearers to come close so they could inspect their gifts. I would never have said so, but I found it rather crass. Finally Michinaga managed to round up his fractious guests and get everyone seated on the verandah in order of rank. The wine cup was passed, and each guest had to recite something felicitous for the empress.

We women were sitting in the gallery, facing out toward the verandah. The blinds had been rolled back, and we were separated from the rows of unruly noblemen only by overlapping sets of curtain stands. Presently we noticed a jiggling of the curtains near where Koshōshō was sitting, then some fingers poked through, and then the curtain came apart at the seam. It was Akimitsu, the minister of the Right.

—He's much too old to be fooling around like this, muttered Lady Dainagon, but the drunken minister paid no attention to our disapproving remarks. He took our fans instead, and whispered dirty jokes to some of the ladies.

A couple of pillar-spans to the east, Major Captain of the Right Sanesuke began to finger the hem and sleeves of our robes. He was normally such a serious individual that we were surprised, and assumed he must be drunk, too. Thinking he would never recognize them, some of the women made fun of him and even pretended to flirt. Imagine their chagrin when it turned out he was not intoxicated at all, but rather, true to character, had been checking out the lavishness of our clothing in order to criticize the empress's extravagance.

It was odd how someone like that could be so officious and yet so shy. He had an absolute dread of public speaking, so we were all wondering what he would do when the cup came to him. And then there were others who could be utterly soused and yet turn even a little folk tune into the most moving and delightful phrase. We were listening to the congratulatory songs that people came up with and commenting on the progress of the saké cup when Father's old friend Kintō stuck his head inside our curtains.

—Excuse me, he said. Is our little Murasaki here by any chance?

—I don't see the likes of Genji anywhere around, I answered tartly. So it's unlikely that Murasaki would be present.

He appeared nonplussed and withdrew to muffled laughter from the ladies.

The formal celebrations were not even finished, but at this rate I could tell it was going to be a terribly drunken affair for the rest of the evening. When Michinaga called on Sanenari to take the saké cup, he got to his feet, and instead of walking in front of the line of nobles where his father was sitting, he went all the way around to the garden and up the steps. Such an elaborate observance of filial respect made Sanenari's father, who was quite drunk, burst into sentimental tears. Of all the men I had come across at the palace, Sanenari was by far the most sincere. Despite our little exchange about the moon's desire, were it not for him, my view of men at the palace would have been utterly cynical. Over in a corner, the provisional middle counselor was pulling at Lady Hyōbu's robes and warbling atrocious songs. Michinaga egged him on with suggestive remarks.

I glanced over at Saishō, who returned my look. We would attempt to leave as soon as an opportunity arose. We were just on our way when Michinaga's two sons and some other gentlemen noisily invaded the eastern gallery and people's attention turned toward the area where we were headed. Saishō and I quickly hid behind some curtain stands, but Michinaga spotted us, and hurrying over, yanked back the curtain. We were caught.

—A poem for the prince! he cried. Then I'll let you go.

I had thought of one back in the gallery when we were listening to the cup go around, and now, embarrassed as I was, fortunately had the presence of mind to recall it. Saishō, for all her previous sangfroid, was dreadfully cowed by our situation and hid her face in her sleeve. I recited:

Ika ni ikaga   kazoeyarubeki   yachitose no   amari hisashiki   kimi ga miyo oba
On the fiftieth day, how can we yet count the limitless years
*   of our young lord's reign?*

—Well done! exclaimed Michinaga. He repeated my poem twice in a loud voice. Then he chanted this:

Ashitazu no   yowai shi araba   kimi go yo to   chitose no kazu mo   kazoetoriten

Had we the life span of the reed-dwelling crane, only then might we count the thousand years in store for this prince.

Everyone was impressed that a man in his condition could produce such a reply. Michinaga seemed impressed himself.

—Did the empress hear that! he said with pride. One of my better ones, if I do say so. I hope somebody is writing this down.

His attention shifted away from us, and Saishō and I breathed sighs of relief. Michinaga walked unsteadily back toward the central hall. I watched him weave his way, presuming he had help preparing his poem in advance. Clearly he wanted to make a good public showing, but I wondered what had happened to his once passionate interest in the quality of poetry. I thought he probably now had other ideas for establishing his immortality. For the moment he seemed satisfied with the way things had turned out.

Saishō and I watched the spectacle of his self-congratulation for a few more minutes.

—I think I make a very good father for an empress! he proclaimed loudly to no one in particular. And she's no disgrace herself for the daughter of a man like me. Mother must think herself very lucky to have such an excellent husband!

Empress Shōshi listened indulgently to her father go on like this, but Rinshi was not amused. She made as if to leave the room, unable to stand his puffing any longer.

—Ah, Mother will scold me if I don't escort her, you know! exclaimed Michinaga as he saw his wife gather her attendants about her.

He rushed straight past the empress's chamber, mumbling to Shōshi as he did,

—Terribly rude of me, my dear, but then, you do owe it all to your poor father in any case . . .

335

Everyone was laughing, and Saishō and I slipped out unnoticed.

FLOATING SADLY

Ukine seshi

Empress Shōshi decided to have a full version of my tales copied onto beautiful paper and bound into books to take back to the palace as a present for the emperor. She enjoined all her ladies to help in the preparation. We gathered in her apartments first thing in the morning to choose paper of various colors and write letters to calligraphers requesting their services. We enclosed sections of the original tale with each, along with sufficient quantities of the new paper for their copies. As the requests were filled, we were kept busy night and day sorting and binding the work that had been finished. On one of these days Michinaga dropped by his daughter's rooms and was dumbfounded by the scene – our sleeves rolled back, our fingers sticky with paste, paper scattered and piled in every corner, and everyone chattering away.

—Here now! he said gruffly to Shōshi. What in the world are you doing in such cold weather? You're supposed to be recuperating!

He was not so annoyed as he pretended, however, because later he brought some gorgeous Chinese paper, brushes, and an elegant inkstone to contribute to the project.

Late one afternoon, after most of the other ladies had finished for the day, Shōshi beckoned me to her side.

—I want to thank you, she said softly. I can't think of who could possibly deserve this more than you.

She indicated that I was to take the inkstone.

—Your stories have been my only joy during this time of confinement. I would undoubtedly have gone out of my mind with boredom had I not had Genji's adventures to distract me.

336

I accepted the gift humbly, even though when I wrote about Genji, I liked to use the old purple inkstone Ming-gwok had given me long ago. Some of the other women found out that Her Majesty had given me the stone and began complaining loudly that I had wheedled it out of her behind their backs. When Shōshi heard their accusations, she went ahead and made me another present of some excellent colored paper and brushes, right in front of them. They were speechless at the time, but I could imagine how they must have denounced me later in private.

I returned to my room to find Saishō waiting for me. She seemed upset.

—I was just coming back to mend a slight tear in my hem when I saw Michinaga slink out of our rooms and hurry off down the hall. I stepped back when I saw him, and so I don't think he noticed me. What do you suppose he was after?

I had a sudden dark thought, and sure enough, when I checked through my things, my own copy of Genji was missing. While I was on duty in the empress's quarters, Michinaga had sneaked into my room and taken an early draft of the tale that I had brought from home for safe-keeping! It was unbelievable.

I probed around the next day, and it did not take long to find out that Michinaga had given the whole thing to his second daughter, Kenshi. Since my only good copy was in pieces being sent out to calligraphers, I no longer had a full version in my possession. My heart sank as I thought how the unpolished draft that had escaped would hurt my reputation. I was discouraged and decided to go stay at Father's house for a few days.

Each day I was there, the flocks of waterfowl passing through Miyako grew larger. Earlier, from the empress's pavilion, I had noticed more birds than usual, but thought it was because her pond was so inviting. I see that in my journal I was looking forward to snow, thinking how beautiful the palace garden would be under a coat of pure white if it snowed before we went back. Yet somehow, during that period of my life, even when I got what I wished for, I was dissatisfied. As

337

I recall, it did snow while I was at Father's house, but it only depressed me. The effect of all that gorgeous snow on that drab, unkempt garden was wasted. Father's ambitious hundred stalks of bamboo had all died, and he had lost interest in gardening.

I tried rereading parts of my tale, but it seemed flat and specious. How could anyone have enjoyed reading it? I wondered. I sank further into self-loathing and depression. Those with whom I used to discuss things of mutual interest must in fact think me vain and superficial, I felt. Then I was ashamed to have such thoughts about my friends in court service and began to find it difficult to write to them. But who else was there? Friends who were important to me before I went to court probably regarded me as just a snobbish lady-in-waiting who would scorn their letters. I regretted the trivial things I had written to Kerria Rose in her hermitage. Perhaps it was too much to expect that she could understand my true feelings, yet it was disappointing. I did not break with her on purpose, nor with others. Yet there were many who simply ceased to correspond as a matter of course. Others stopped coming to see me, assuming that I no longer had a fixed abode. When I left home to serve the empress, everything conspired to make me feel I had entered a different world entirely.

But coming home only made matters worse. It struck me as sad that the only people I should miss in the slightest were a few of my companions at court for whom I felt affection and could entrust secrets to. I found I particularly missed Lady Dainagon, who would often talk to me in a low voice as we lay awake near the empress when we shared night duty. Did this mean that I had in fact succumbed to palace life? What a depressing thought.

With waterbirds on my mind, and all the poems that have been written about pairs of mandarin ducks, I wrote to Dainagon:

Ukine seshi   mizu no ue nomi   koishikute   kamo no uwage ni   sae zo otoranu
We were like a pair of ducks floating sleepless on the water;
I remember with a yearning that pierces sharper than the
frost on their feathers.

338

Her reply was delivered later the same day:

Uchiharau   tomo naki koro no   nezame ni wa   tsugaishi oshi zo   yoha ni koishiki
A lonely duck awakes and, finding no friend to brush her
wings, recalls with longing the nights they were a pair.

It was written so elegantly that I was struck anew by what
an accomplished woman Dainagon was and how she had
languished. She had suffered no major spirit attacks for a long
while and appeared to have recovered from the worst of her
depression. Perhaps she had accepted her lot in life. I should
do the same, I told myself.

Letters started coming from others, too, telling me how
sorry Her Majesty was that I could not be with her to see the
lovely snowfall. I suppose there were gentle hints that I ought
to think about returning, but still I did not go back.

Then I received the following note from Rinshi: "You
obviously did not mean it when you said you would only be
away for a short time. I presume you are prolonging your
absence on purpose, since I tried to stop you."

I tried to remember my last brief encounter with Rinshi
when I was attempting to find out what had become of my
stolen manuscript. I did mention that I was planning to go
home for a bit, but I'm sure she said nothing to make me
change my mind. By her letter, though, clearly she had told
Shōshi she tried to prevent my leaving, and made it look as if
I were staying away out of spite. Out of my sincere feelings for
the empress, I felt I had no choice but to go back to the
mansion.

How cold it was! Two days after I returned to the
Tsuchimikado, we were all told to get ready to go back to the
palace. We arrived there in the middle of the night, chilled to
the bone from our journey. It was an unpleasant ordeal all
around. First we were ordered to be ready for departure by
early evening, so the entire lot of us assembled in our stiff and
formal travel costumes with our hair carefully arranged,
waiting for the carriages. There must have been thirty of us in
the south gallery, and a dozen more palace ladies waiting in

the eastern wing. The hall was barely illuminated, and it was difficult to make out anyone's features, but whispering and grumbling could be heard from all corners. In particular, people were arguing about who was to ride with whom. As the hours wore on, the complaints increased. Finally the carriages pulled up, and Michinaga came round and testily announced that established rules of seating were to be followed.

—Without exception! he barked to quell the burst of protest that arose.

Lady Senshi shared the empress's palanquin, which headed the procession; Rinshi and the wet nurse carried the baby prince in the brocade-covered litter immediately following; Dainagon and Saishō boarded next a carriage with gold fittings; Koshōshō and Ben no Naishi shared a litter; and then I was stuck with Muma in the next vehicle. She seemed to resent my presence for some reason I could not fathom. Perhaps she was just out of sorts, but still, why should she act so high and mighty? She barely spoke to me the entire way, which I considered most petty of her.

When we arrived, the moon was so bright that it was impossible simply to proceed to our rooms unnoticed. I let Muma go ahead of me, and as I watched her gather her skirts close against the cold, stumbling in the eerie shadows, I realized what a sorry sight we must have presented to anyone watching. It was hard to be dignified when freezing. My room was third from the end in the outer gallery. The first thing I did was to discard my stiff formal coat, which seemed to bring the cold in with it, and change into some thick padded clothing. I had just stretched out to rest when Koshōshō came in to commiserate on what an unpleasant experience it had been. I mentioned Muma's frosty demeanour and she told me not to take it to heart. She said Muma was jealous that the empress had mentioned me so often while I was away.

Again, I felt the contradictions of life at court. For every spiteful character like Muma, there was someone understanding like Koshōshō. Seeing her again made me happy for the first time in days. Here she was consoling me when she had more reason than most to be bitter about her lot in life. I got up and was adding more charcoal to the hibachi when we heard footsteps outside in the hallway. It was already late, and I had hoped to be left in peace that evening, but it seemed people had been waiting for our return. We were hardly in the mood for male visitors, yet here was Sanenari with two companions, shivering with hands tucked inside their sleeves, hailing us from the corridor. We made no move to invite them in, and they did not insist for long. It was too cold.

—We'll come back morrow morning, they called out, teeth chattering. It's bitter cold night!

They left by the back entrance. As they hurried off, I couldn't help thinking about the women who were waiting for them at home. I had no regrets for myself, but here was Koshōshō, by any standards a most attractive woman, denied the possibility of a husband, family, and home of her own. If only her father hadn't retired so early in his career, she would have been in a position to make a splendid match. As it was, she would undoubtedly spend the rest of her days in the empress's coterie and eventually retire to a nunnery. We lay down together under a quilted robe and watched the faint glow of the charcoal embers before falling asleep ourselves.

THE GOSECHI DANCES

Gosechi no mai

Michinaga's other set of sons* started hanging around the women's quarters after we got back. While we were staying at Rinshi's house they had kept their distance, but they were not at all shy at the palace. It was unnerving to have them walking in and out all the time, so I made myself scarce claiming to be busy writing. Clearly the Gosechi Dances made little

---

*These three boys were the sons of Michinaga's second wife, Meishi. They were aged sixteen, fifteen and fourteen.

impression on the boys, for they attached themselves to some of the younger ladies, chattering and joking and in general making nuisances of themselves.

I made a point to scrutinize all four dancers with their attendants enter the palace so I could describe the scene as I had been requested to do, but I planned to go home again right after the dances lest I be inveigled to write about the young prince's hundredth-day ceremonies, too. There were several other ladies quite as capable as I in recording such things, and I was growing weary of this kind of scribbling.

The girls arrived at the palace on the night of the twentieth, proceeding to the main hall under the glare of numerous torches. I felt rather sorry for them having to walk in front of all the senior courtiers like that. They seemed nervous, for which I didn't blame them a bit. They were keenly aware that the emperor himself was watching, as was Michinaga. One group of girls wore gorgeous brocade jackets that glittered brilliantly in the torchlight, but they had layered so many robes underneath that they had difficulty in walking. Sanenari's daughter was a dancer that year, with costumes and ornaments provided by the empress. His party was last in line, and to my mind the most attractive.

The following morning the palace filled with senior nobles coming to pay their respects, and the younger ladies-in-waiting were beside themselves with excitement. I'm sure they were happy to be back in the thick of things after having been away from the palace for several months. All day long they ran about commenting on the dancers and their outfits. Everyone crowded into the main hall to see the special performances for the emperor that evening. The fact that Shōshi attended with the baby prince made the occasion even more splendid, and there was much throwing of rice* and shouting.

After a while all the noise gave me a headache, so I came back to my room to rest for a bit, intending to go back later if I felt better. As I was stirring the coals in the hibachi, two

*As at the time of the prince's birth, throwing rice was a ritual to distract evil spirits away from the baby.

young women, Kohyōe and Kohyōbu, also retreated from the festivities and joined me.

—It's so crowded over there, you can hardly see anything! they complained.

We were talking in low voices when suddenly Michinaga stuck his head in the room.

—What do you think you're doing, all of you, sitting around like this? he charged.

Michinaga looked at me.

—Especially you! he said pointedly. Come along now!

Even though I didn't feel up to it, I went back to the dances at his insistence.

As I watched, it seemed to me the dancers were very tense, and then all of a sudden one of them fainted and had to be helped out. At this point the whole thing had a dreamlike quality. Perhaps I was just tired. When it was over, I overheard the younger nobles gossiping about how attractive the dancers' quarters were, and how they could tell the women apart part from the way they sat and the way they did their hair. It seemed rather crass, as if they were comparing sweet flag roots or something.

On the third day the nervous young attendants danced for the emperor. I was looking forward to seeing them but at the same time apprehensive. They were hardly older than my Katako. When they stepped forward as a group, I was overcome with sympathy even though I was not connected to any one in particular. You knew that each child was dressed to the hilt by a sponsor who was quite convinced that his girl was the best, but for the life of me I could not choose among them. I would have to ask someone who paid more attention to the currents of fashion to make a judgment.

Considering the constant pressure these girls were under, all I could think of was how intimidating the experience must be. Maybe they were of high enough rank and intelligence to deal with the situation, but even so, it seemed a shame to subject them to such sharp rivalry at their tender age. In my old-fashioned way, I couldn't imagine exposing Katako to this kind of thing.

As I watched the courtiers come up to take their fans, one

girl took a notion to toss hers to them. She was tall and slender with stunningly beautiful hair, but nevertheless people were taken aback at her nerve. Maybe it should be chalked up to inexperience. Could I say for certain that my own daughter wouldn't be equally gauche, put in such a situation? Did I ever imagine that I myself would be as brash as I had become?

I began to daydream about what the future held in store for me. What if I decided to become callous about feminine modesty and freely show myself openly as Sei Shōnagon did – heedless of the opinions of the world? This fantasy took over my mind so completely that I lost track of the ceremonies I was supposed to be observing. I shook myself uneasily, thinking how untrustworthy one's own mind can be.

After the dances ended, things were rather quiet for a few days. The young men in particular seemed rather bored. Then it came time for the extra festival of the Kamo Shrine for which Michinaga's second son, Norimichi, had been appointed imperial messenger. Because the festival day happened to be taboo for the palace,* Michinaga and all the young men involved in the ceremony arrived the evening before. There was much commotion and coming and going around the women's quarters all night long.

The next morning a formal gift was delivered to Norimichi. I saw a silver box containing a mirror, an agalwood comb, and a silver hairstick for him to use in dressing his sidelocks. The present was arranged on top of a box lid that looked familiar somehow, and I realized with chagrin that it had come from Sanenari, who had misunderstood a trick we played on someone in his daughter's retinue during the time of the dances. When he found out about our joke, he was quite annoyed. Of course he was right to chide us – it was the kind of situation that brings out our worst tendencies. Even though the prank was not my idea, I never once felt sorry for the woman – so I was just as bad as the others. Nevertheless it left a bad taste, and I went home estranged from Sanenari,

*On these taboo days, figured by soothsayers, movement in or out of the palace grounds was prohibited.

and glum in general. I should have left right after the dances, as I had originally planned.

In retrospect it is embarrassing. I shall try not to flinch, and put it down just as it happened. If I ever reach a point of feeling saintly, I ought to reread it.

There was a lady named Sakyō who had once lived in the palace in the retinue of the emperor's junior consort, Gishi. She had left service – no one remembered exactly why – and gone home some time ago. On this particular occasion she had returned to the palace for the Gosechi Dances as an attendant for Sanenari's daughter, where one of Shōshi's women happened to notice her. I confess I disliked Sakyō because she had once had an affair with my husband that caused him to look foolish. Perhaps that's why I was inclined to go along with the other women who often fabricated such tricks just for spite. Some of the young nobles also got involved.

—Fancy someone like that who used to be so high and mighty, creeping back to the palace like this!

—She probably thinks no one notices.

—Well, we should disillusion her, don't you think?

A flurry of furious activity ensued in Shōshi's apartments. Someone looked through the empress's extensive fan collection and picked out one with a picture of the mountain of longevity painted on it. Everyone agreed that would be perfect. They placed the open fan on the lid of a box, arranged dancers' braided cord pendants around it, and added a curved comb with taboo papers, such as a young girl might wear, tied to the ends.

—Here, here, isn't the comb a bit too straight?

One young noble bent it even more in a daringly trendy fashion. It was the sort of thing a very young dancer might have worn – just in case Sakyō missed the allusion on the fan. They added a roll of incense wrapped in white paper, and Kodayū supplied a poem to accompany the gift.

Oukarishi   toyo no miyabito   sashiwakite   shiruki hikage wo   aware to zo mishi
*Among the courtly throng at the ceremony, your cord
pendants stood out, moving us deeply as we watched.*

345

More and more pleased with how this joke was turning out, we then sought a messenger who would not be recognized to deliver the gift. The girl was instructed to say that it was from a lady currently in the junior consort's service so that Sakyō would think it was from her former mistress. The empress was unaware of our malicious intent, and when she saw what we had concocted, she remarked,

—If you are going to send a present like that, you ought to make it more attractive – add some more fans or something.

We were not swayed.

—No, we replied. It would not serve our purpose to be too elegant. If this were from Your Majesty, there would be no need for secrecy in any case. This is our private affair – pretend you didn't notice.

We waited in great anticipation for the messenger to return, worried lest she be recognized and our trick exposed. The girl came back right away hiding a smile.

—They asked me where I was from, so I said the junior consort, and nobody doubted me. They took it in completely.

Some of the ladies permitted themselves little smiles of satisfaction.

Sanenari was Gishi's younger brother. That was why he had her former palace woman join his daughter's assistants for the dances. When Sakyō later realized the gift could only have come from Shōshi's apartments, she was terribly embarrassed to have been publicly exposed in her reduced status. Perhaps this doesn't seem like such a big thing to people who have never lived in the women's quarters of the palace. There was a dark side to that place. Sometimes it reminded me of one of those monstrously extended spider-webs I had seen in Echizen. I tried not to be associated with one clique or another, but it was so easy to be dragged into a petty vendetta like this simply because you had conceived a dislike for someone. Sanenari was displeased with me and asked why we couldn't simply have ignored that poor woman. He was even more annoyed because, under the impression that a gift had come from the empress, he had arranged for the elaborate return gift.

*

346

Around the middle of the twelfth month I took a leave of absence for a few days. I had to speak to Father about Nobunori. It had come to my attention that he had committed another outrageous gaffe at the palace. My brother was one of the secretaries assigned the job of distributing the gifts of cotton cloth to the priests who conducted the early morning services. I'm sure he was hungover, if not actually still drunk, from carousing the night before. Nobunori and someone else carried the chest of cotton from storage and set it down in the chapel where the priest was standing. Then my brother took the bundles meant for the acolytes out onto the verandah and started handing them out. Instead of dividing them equally, he gave a whole pile to one man! The others started grabbing and immediately all was pandemonium. Everyone who witnessed the scene was shocked.

It did my reputation no good to have my brother's stupid antics continually providing tidbits for gossip.

I had forgotten to tell the servants to remove the bridges from my kotos on rainy days, and so when I thought to take them out of the closet after many months of neglect, I found the strings stretched and unable to hold a tuning. I would have to get them both restrung before they were playable. When I was young, I used to enjoy making music, even though I was no virtuoso, and would keep both the thirteen-stringed and six-stringed koto tuned and at the ready. Sometimes I would take one out at dusk, when the hubbub of the day had quieted down, and imagine myself playing for Genji – and then suddenly become self-conscious lest anyone hear me. How silly of me, and how sad! But it was even more pitiful to see the instruments now leaning against the side of a chest accumulating dust and soot.

The chest itself was crammed full of old poems and tales, and had become a home for countless silverfish. They scuttered about so unpleasantly when the chest was opened that I didn't even feel like looking in there anymore. The bookcase next to it was full of Chinese books that I had carefully collected over the years. When loneliness loomed, I would take one or two out to look at only to become aware of my serving women whispering behind my back,

—What kind of lady is it who reads Chinese books?

—This is why she is always so miserable.

—In the past, proper ladies did not even read sutras,

—Let alone Chinese!

I feel like turning to them and saying,

—Yes, that's what is always said, but I've never heard of anyone living longer simply because of observing such prohibitions!

But what good would that have done? They would only have seen it as further proof that I was abnormal, and so I held my tongue. Besides, what they said was only reasonable. I was fully aware that I was my own source of misery.

Everyone reacts differently. Some are born cheerful, open-minded, and sincere. Others are pessimists, amused by nothing, the kind who turn old letters into sutras, carry out penances, and are always clacking their sutra beads – all of which made me wince. I desperately wished I could be more openhearted. Every day I had to consciously resist turning into the kind of curmudgeonly prig I detested.

I was morbidly aware of prying eyes around me even at home, and so hesitated to do even those things a woman in my position ought to allow herself. And this was the privacy of my home! How much more self-conscious I was at court where there were many occasions when I would wish to say something but always thought better of it.

What was the point, I told myself, of trying to explain to people who would never understand? Frankness just stirred up trouble among women who thought only of themselves, always looking for excuses to carp and complain. It was so rare to find anyone who truly understood, I had learned to keep my thoughts to myself. In fact, if I had never had the experience of knowing such a one, I might have said it was impossible. Most people judge everything by their own narrow standards.

Ironically, many thought I was timid. If forced to sit in company, I usually kept my mouth shut when everyone was gossiping and criticizing – not because I was shy, but because I found it petty. I suppose it was not surprising that people

348

came to consider me aloof and dull. When I first arrived at the palace, I was nervous because I suspected people had already formed an opinion of me. Indeed they had. I found out later that I had a reputation of being pretentious and difficult to approach. They whispered that I was prickly, too fond of my tales, haughty, disdainful, cantankerous, scornful, and prone to versifying. Yet after I had been there a while, I heard them say in amazement,

—But when you actually meet her, she is strangely meek, not at all what you might expect!

Clearly they meant their comments as compliments! Yet what was the point in allowing myself to agonize over other people's opinions? It was impossible for me to change my nature. I did wish I were not so perversely standoffish, though. I was afraid that sometimes I put off those for whom I had genuine respect. My only consolation was that Her Majesty often remarked that she had never thought I was the kind of person she would ever feel relaxed with, but in the end she had grown closer to me than any of the others.

When I thought of the mistakes I had made, I tried to consider how I could teach my daughter what to avoid. She was bright and attractive, and there was no reason why she shouldn't have an excellent chance at a good position in court when she was older. Those who flourish in this world are pleasant, gentle, self-possessed, and keep a low profile even when placed in eminent positions, like Lady Saishō. I was convinced that this kind of personality was the key to success for a woman. Most people will forgive anything of someone who is well meaning and never tries to cause embarrassment to others – no matter how many affairs she might have. It is the women who think too highly of their pedigrees and behave pretentiously who draw attention to themselves. And then, even when they take great care over their smallest moves, people will find fault anyway, criticizing every little thing – even how they sit down or take their leave. And of course women who contradict themselves when they talk or disparage their companions leave themselves open to precisely those critiques from others. I learned all this the hard way.

Gradually I discovered people's idiosyncrasies. Some who

wished you ill would glare openly with malicious intent and spread dreadful rumors about you in a fashion designed to enhance themselves. These were obvious and relatively easy to deal with. But others hid their true feelings and appeared to be quite friendly on the surface. Unfortunately I found this out only after a long while and it came as a painful surprise.

When Katako was about nine years old, I felt it not too early to gently mold her attitudes so that by the time she was ready for court they would be instinctive.

—If you refrain from gossiping, I told her, people will be inclined to give you the benefit of the doubt and show goodwill, even if superficially – but often that is good enough.

Pondering what would make a girl's career a successful one, I sharply realized the extent of my own deficiencies. Understanding that actions have consequences is not enough. It is a delusion to think one can ever foresee all the possible consequences of an action. Better to act with sincere goodwill and trust that karma will make things right in the end. Some people are so good-natured they can even love those who hate them. I myself have always found this quite impossible and am a bit squeamish around such sweetness. Does the Buddha himself, in all his compassion, ever say that it's fine to insult the Three Treasures with impunity?

In the real world it's not reasonable to expect that those to whom ill is done will not reciprocate in kind. Those who go out of their way to hurt others deserve to be ridiculed, and so do people who act thoughtlessly and cause mischief even though they don't mean to. Stupidity and carelessness ought not to be excused. Yet I was at a loss as to what to advise Katako when it happens that, despite the best of intentions, you are misunderstood and reviled. Looking at her innocent trusting face, I could only hope that her personality would not develop these dark crevices, moss-grown with worries.

THE CLOSE OF THE YEAR

Toshi kurete

My diary notes that I returned to the palace on the twenty-ninth of the twelfth month – the next to last day of that eventful year. It had been three years to the day since I first entered the empress's service. What a state I had been in then! Everything about their royal highnesses left me in awe, and I was practically paralyzed with anxiety. I could hardly believe that I had become so jaded with life at court in this time.

I spent most of that day with my daughter and didn't even leave my house until after she had gone to sleep. By the time I arrived at the palace Her Majesty was in seclusion, and in any case it was too late to pay my respects, so I put my things away and lay down in my own quarters.

I was tired but couldn't go to sleep. No matter which way I turned I could hear other ladies talking in the next room.

—What a difference from home, where everybody would be asleep by now!

—Yes, there are footsteps all night long at the palace. It's hard to settle down.

They, too, had just come back from home leave. The first night was the hardest. I missed the quiet warmth of Katako's sleeping body and steady breathing. No lover, man or woman, can ever give the same comforting calm as sleeping with a child. I was morbidly aware of the approach of my thirty-seventh year. As I lay awake, fretting and tossing, a poem arose in my mind, so I reached over for my journal and scribbled it down in the wan glow of the light of a coal:

Toshi kurete   waga yo fukete yuku   kaze no oto ni   kokoro no naka no   susamajiki kana
> The year draws to a close, and my life as well; the fierce sound of the wind chills my heart.

The *tsuina* ceremony to cast out evil spirits was over early. I didn't think much of the young man in charge that year. He was too thin to make a very convincing demon-chaser. I came back to my room to relax, and had just finished blackening

351

my teeth and was putting on light makeup when Ben no Naishi came in. Her lips were like plump flower buds, and her eyes drooped charmingly at the corners. She was as good-natured as her features were soft. We talked for a while, and she got so comfortable she fell asleep. I took out my journal and began to write. I could hear Takumi, the maid, sitting just outside in the corridor trying to teach Ateki how to pinch the hems of a dress she had just made.

All of a sudden I was startled by a crashing noise and wailing coming from the direction of Her Majesty's apartments. I dropped my brush and tried to rouse Ben no Naishi. The screams and wails were louder now. It must be a fire, I thought uneasily, although I couldn't smell smoke.

Takumi stuck her frightened face in the room.

—What can it be? she stammered.

—I don't know, I said, but Her Majesty is in residence tonight. We must go see if she's all right.

I finally managed to shake Ben no Naishi awake, and the three of us made our way over to the empress's rooms, trembling with apprehension. The sounds of scuffling and screaming had ceased, but we could still hear crying. Following the muffled sound, we finally reached a small room where we discovered two ladies, Yugei and Kohyōbu, clinging to one another sobbing with fright. They had no clothes on!

In dismay, we clapped our hands and called for help, but the servants and guards had all gone to bed right after the ceremonies ended. No one was around. Takumi managed to rouse a serving girl from the kitchen.

—Quick! I shouted at her, forgetting my rank in my agitation. Fetch the secretary of the Ministry of War! He should be in the main chamber.

Here was a chance for my brother to redeem himself by coming to the rescue, I realized. We waited for help uneasily, conscious of how the two women had been attacked right in the heart of the imperial chambers. Ben no Naishi and I took off our outer cloaks for them to cover themselves until help came, and listened to their terrified account of being grabbed and stripped by assailants they couldn't even see in the dark corridors.

—It was a devil! sobbed Yugei. I could smell his foul breath!

—They had sharp claws and prickles, added Kohyōbu. It was awful!

They were sure they had been the victims of demons whom the ceremonies earlier in the evening had failed to roust.

Takumi then came hurrying in only to inform me that Nobunori had left earlier with all the others. I bit my lip in frustration. If only once, when I needed him, he could be depended upon! A few minutes later his rival, Sukenari, the secretary of the Bureau of Ceremonial, appeared and calmly took charge. He went around the hall lighting the oil lamps and sent a messenger to the imperial storehouse to fetch robes for the two ladies. By this time, a small crowd had gathered and an envoy arrived from the emperor to inquire about the incident. Some of the women just sat there gazing at one another in a state of shock.

—What a terrible experience! they cried, commiserating with the two victims.

—At least they didn't take your formal gowns for the new year ceremonies, someone said.

That was true, and the ladies seemed to consider that they had escaped an even worse fate. As they recovered their composure, I thought to myself how I should never forget the sight of them naked. Their pale bodies bereft of cover reminded me of nothing so much as newborn mice. It was shocking, yet in retrospect rather funny – although I would never dream of saying so.

Somehow or other, the empress managed to sleep through all this commotion and was quite surprised to hear of it the next day.

The new year was certainly off to a bad start. Even though it was New Year's Day, people could talk of nothing but the incident. Some said they had sensed demons in the palace and were critical of the weak character of the crew in charge of expelling them. Someone else suggested the perpetrators might have been human. It was hard to know which would be worse. The thought of demons lurking in the palace corridors was horrible, but the idea that anyone would attack and rob Her Majesty's ladies was outrageous.

*

Late on the third day of the new year I came home from the palace and was dismayed to find that dust had accumulated in my rooms even in this short period of time. They seemed shabby and dilapidated. Despite the fact that it was the new year and one should only compose auspicious poems, I couldn't restrain myself:

Aratamete   kyou shimo mono wo   kanashiki wa   mi no usa ya mata   sama kawarinuru
Freshly new today is the realization of the sadness of it all.
My depression simply changes its form.

It took a great effort of will to conceal my increasingly morbid turn of mind from my daughter. I brought her fans and combs and picture books from the palace. She was fascinated by everything royal, so I told her about the lavish ceremonies for the imperial children, and Emperor Ichijō's peculiar culinary preferences. The emperor was very fond of cheese and was always sending some over to Shōshi's apartments. Most of us didn't care for it and surreptitiously fed it to the palace dogs, who then farted. Once I brought some home for Katako to taste, and knowing that the emperor favored it, she gravely pronounced it delicious.

I brought home remnants of fabric for her to make into clothing for her dolls. Years later I found the letter I enclosed with a present of fabrics that new year tucked away in a box of old dolls:

My Dear Daughter,

I am very sorry I had to leave before you woke on New Year's Day. When you are a little older I shall bring you with me to the palace as I've promised. In the meantime, since you are so interested in fashion, I have saved you some scraps of the cloth from the gowns Lady Dainagon wore for the first three days of the new year when she was in charge of serving Her Majesty the spiced wine and health foods.

On the first day her dress was a double-layered set of crimson and violet, the Chinese jacket was red, and her train was silver-stenciled stiff silk. The next day she changed to a green jacket, and her gown was of cross-woven crimson and purple damask over a deep red glossed silk dress. Her train was dyed in stripes of various colors, one fading into the next. Her outfit on the third day was a formal jacket of maroon figured silk, her gown white Chinese damask with a purple lining worn over a rich red dress lined in pink.

You may use these bits to make outfits for your dolls. Remember, if the gown is dark, the lining should be a shade paler, and if the gown is light, make the lining darker. For the layered robes underneath, you can choose what you like. Lady Dainagon wore this set: pale green; white with a maroon lining; pale yellow; deep yellow; scarlet with a purple lining; and lavender lined in white. Arranging such everyday color combinations in this way produced quite a striking effect. See what you can do. Get your auntie to help you if you have trouble.

On the procession of the third day, Lady Saishō carried the imperial sword again. She walked between the emperor and His Excellency, Michinaga, who was holding the baby prince. Now her outfit was something special. I can't recall every seeing anything like it. It appeared to have thirty of so layers, but the effect was partly done with attached cuffs and linings – otherwise the bulk would have made her a mountain. Her main gown was crimson, thick figured silk, with five cuffs. Over it, her lavender mantle had a pattern of oak leaves lightly embroidered. The formal jacket was deep red, stitched in slanted squares giving a Chinese effect. Even her silk train had three layers. Underneath, she had on a lined crimson robe with seven additional cuffs sewn to the chemise beneath. Over that were four more robes in shades of red, alternating with three and five layers of attached cuffs. Her hair was done up, so you could see how nicely her collars lay, and she looked quite marvelous. She was just the right height to carry this style, with a full figure, fine features, and a beautiful complexion. She looked splendid and acted quite perfectly as always.

I'm not suggesting you attempt this outfit for your dolls, by the way.

When I thought about whom Katako should emulate, Lady Saishō came first to mind. Never pushing herself forward, Saishō still managed to end up with all the plum posts and not incur jealousy. She rarely spoke ill of others, but neither was she a flatterer. You could always depend on her to do the sensible thing. Her only fault, if indeed it was a fault, was that she rarely came out with a poem. But at least she knew her literary limitations and didn't try to inflict gratuitous compositions on her companions. She was rewarded with loyal friends and lovers. Tadanobu thought the world of her.

As I pondered this question of how to be a success at court, I came to the conclusion that literary ambition was more likely than not to bring a woman to a bad end. Look at Sei Shōnagon.

THE SPIDER

Sasagani

Toward the end of spring, as the cherry blossoms were beginning to scatter in the breeze, the empress woke feeling nauseated. At first we attributed her illness to a bad oyster, but after a week, we were all thinking the same thing – could it be that the empress was not ill, but pregnant again? It was true. It seemed that life had looped back on itself. Shōshi had waited ten years for a child, and then to have two pregnancies, one upon the heels of the other like this, amazed everyone. Michinaga's prayers were almost frighteningly effective. With his luck we presumed this one would be a boy as well. Ichijō's other wives were mortified. Why didn't they conceive? Some of them had been with him for many years, and their fathers were gnashing their teeth.

Michinaga was simply beside himself with delight at his daughter's condition. There was now a precedent for everything, and the ordering of prayers and ritual observances was done exactly as it had been the year before. All was going well until one of Shōshi's ladies discovered a scrap of paper with mysterious writing in the empress's chambers. It seemed that someone was trying to direct a curse against the royal mother and child. We had been hearing unpleasant rumors since the beginning of the year that people in Korechika's camp had been shunting evil spells our way, and here now was the proof. Michinaga was furious and summoned Korechika's chief aide to account.

The man died a few days later. Of chagrin, they say. I wondered that contrition could be so lethal. Korechika himself went into seclusion, but reports of a strange malady leaked out through the servants. Although he consumed great quantities of food, he had become quite thin and was always thirsty, they said. To think I used to admire him and picture him in my mind as I was writing about Genji. It was very sad. I hadn't written about Genji for quite a while.

Early that summer we went back to Rinshi's mansion. Our empress's younger sister Kenshi was utterly smitten with the baby prince, and carried him to her quarters to play with all day long. The nursemaids had nothing to do except change a dirty nappy now and then. This suited them fine – they much preferred one another's company to that of a squalling baby, even if it was a prince. As for me, time lay heavy. I was being pressured to write more adventures for Genji but for some reason found it difficult. Genji's world had come to seem rather pallid.

My critical year was half over, and I felt only the weak satisfaction that thus far I had been allowed to avoid disaster. I attributed my survival to the merciful power of Amida Buddha and the numerous copies of the Lotus Sutra I had made. There were times when I felt such a strong pull to the religious life I fantasized about leaving the world. Then I thought about my daughter. Would I ever be able to do what Kerria Rose had done?

357

We were back in the palace by the seventh month, and it came time for the annual *sumai* tournament. The emperor was supposed to view the wrestling, as I recall, but the weather threatened to be bad. The day before the matches, the men-servants preparing the ring kept looking uneasily over their shoulders up at the sky. They were convinced the games would be called. My erstwhile friend Sanenari was such a keen fan of wrestling he kept insisting it would blow over – as if pronouncing would make it so. I was doubtful.

In fact it rained from early in the day, and so, of course, the matches had to be postponed. What a dismal affair. Dejected, Sanenari dropped by the women's quarters and I passed this to him:

Tazuki naki tabi no sora naru   sumai wo ba   ame mo yo ni tou   hito mo araji na

The sumai *match turned out to be as transient as my own dwelling. Is there anyone who would ask to see it on such a rainy night?*

The rain was pouring down in great sheets, drumming loudly on the eaves. He sat outside my blinds for a while, waiting for it to let up. No one else was around and we talked about inconsequential things. In years gone by we had sometimes stayed up quite late whispering through the blinds. Saishō even teased me about a secret lover. In fact, until our misunderstanding about that woman Sakyō during the Gosechi Dances, I considered Sanenari even better than a lover – he was a friend, probably the only man in my entire experience at court whom I could have called that. He reminded me of how we used to write to one another.

Just before he left he asked to borrow my inkstone and some paper, and made this reply to the poem I had given him earlier:

Idomu hito   amata kikoyuru   momoshiki no   sumai ushi to wa   omoishiru ya wa

There are many contenders for the sumai *games, but it seems rather pointless, doesn't it?*

I read it quickly, appreciating Sanenari's fine calligraphy more than the words. Later, when I looked at it again, I saw another way his poem could be interpreted:

> *Many are involved in struggles at the palace; you cannot imagine how troublesome life is at court.*

He was a sensitive man. I could easily imagine the problems he faced. Indeed, the more perceptive one is, the more difficult life at court inevitably turns out to be.

By that fall I had come to the conclusion that my character Murasaki had outlived her usefulness. I had created such a perfect woman that there was nothing left for her to do but die. The fact that people called me Murasaki was, by this time, quite tiresome. I wanted to get out from under her shadow. It took me a long time to realize that I needed to sacrifice her in order to move on. And it took even longer before I realized the problem lay not in Murasaki, but in Genji.

Murasaki was ideal in every respect – beautiful, compliant, thoughtful, sensible. She never flew into resentful rages or turned a cold shoulder when Genji strayed. Genji himself thought her perfect – the person with whom he hoped to share a lotus petal in paradise.

—So why did he stray from her side at all? he asked himself.

Ah, there were so many reasons, but Murasaki would always be there, to forgive.

She had worked hard to be perfect in Genji's eyes, but now Murasaki began to doubt whether perfection was enough. She was terrified that each indiscretion was a rehearsal for the day when Genji would in fact discard her. All right, it would have been rude of him to refuse the emperor's plea that he marry the Third Princess, but did he have to leave her juvenile letters lying around? It was too late for Murasaki to suddenly start reproaching Genji for his affairs and new marriage. She felt she no longer had a voice at all.

Ever since Genji had taken her in as a child, Murasaki had bent her life to pleasing him. What a good pupil she had been.

Genji nurtured her like an exquisite flower, encouraging her bloom of womanhood, nipping inconvenient emotions like jealousy in the bud. But now, what had begun as a passing shadow over the love she bore Genji settled into a permanent dark crack in her heart, and eventually the crack deepened to the point where a wandering spirit saw an opening and took hold.

Murasaki was on the point of death when my readers protested so much I had to revive her. It was near the end of the ninth month, and I had been working at home. Koshōshō thought it too morbid that I was planning to let Murasaki die, and she sent an anxious note to see if I was all right. To assuage her fears, I depicted Murasaki gradually becoming weaker and longing to devote herself to prayers and meditation. It's true I had much on my mind, but I sent her this poem:

Hanasusuki   hawake no tsuyu ya   nani ni kaku   kareyuku nobe ni   kietomaruramu
Nestled in the plumes of pampas grass, why does the dew not leave the withered plain?

I hoped that she, at least, would understand my need to stay away from the palace for a while.

Sanenari, too, wrote to me several times after our rainy-day meeting, hinting that he wanted to reestablish some sort of relationship. I was still fond of him, but I hesitated. Ultimately I thought it best not to reply. I was too wrapped up in the troubles of my fictional characters to spend time on all-too-real ones. Finally he sent me this incongruous poem:

Ori ori ni   kaku to wa miete   sasagani no   ikani omoeba   tayuru naruramu
She used to spin her web from time to time; so why does the spider now break her thread?

Were it anyone but Sanenari, I would have been offended by the imagery. Instead, I took it up, trusting that he would understand my reticence to cast more threads that were doomed to dissolve. People think that busy spiders foretell the arrival of a lover – it was the last day of autumn and I composed the following as a reply:

Shimogare no   asaji ni magau   sasagani no   ikanaru ori ni   kaku to miyuramu
The spider broods, lost among the bleak frost-nipped reeds,
unable to foresee when she will weave her web again.

I did not intend to cut him off completely, but I suppose he should be forgiven for thinking so.

I had been back at the Tsuchimikado Mansion with the empress for just two days right at the beginning of winter when a messenger, panting and dusted with soot, rushed in at dawn bearing the terrible news that the Ichijō Palace had burned to the ground during the night. We were thankful that due to the empress's pregnancy we had not been staying there. The emperor, too, was safe, although distraught. Yet another fire. He moved to the Biwa Mansion, displacing the crown prince. Despite the trauma, I managed to finish the story I had been working on, including Murasaki's death scene.

For the first time in a long while I felt satisfied that I had written something worthwhile. I was seized with a desire to show it to Kerria Rose, even though, because of her religious status, we had not been in contact for a long time. Impulsively I stayed up all night copying the story and in the morning summoned a messenger to search out her retreat in the eastern hills.

To my amazement, she wrote back several days later. I still have her letter.

My Dear Younger Sister,

I read your story with great interest. In fact, you may be surprised to hear that I have managed to follow Genji's adventures all along, even here in my mountain cottage. It sometimes takes a while for them to reach me, but, as you know, once something is written down it has its own life and can make its own way.

I can see that you have reached a turning-point with your tales. I, for one, am sorry to see Murasaki go, but I agree that it was necessary. She made a most beautiful corpse, by the way. It is not always thus.

I wonder whether you have considered letting go of

361

Genji as well? If not, how is he going to spend his days without Murasaki? Don't let him mope about too long. I have trouble imagining Genji old.

I was dumbstruck on reading my old friend's letter, written as if we had last corresponded but yesterday instead of years ago. I was touched that she had been watching Genji's progress all this time, and heartened that amid all my readers' complaints about Murasaki's death, Kerria Rose alone saw the need for it. Now, for the first time, I began to contemplate moving beyond Genji as well. I became excited about writing again.

On the twenty-sixth day of the eleventh month the empress gave birth to another boy. All went easily this time. I avoided Michinaga lest he ask me to take notes again. As it happened, he was preoccupied with the upcoming marriage of his second daughter, Kenshi, to the crown prince.

It must have been around this time that Michinaga invited Izumi Shikibu to join Her Majesty's salon. He had long been an admirer of her poems, and her scandalous reputation, far from putting him off, probably intrigued him. Empress Shōshi, on the other hand, frowned on seductive behavior on the part of her ladies, so anyone who wanted to be in her favor took care never to act too flighty. (This is not to say that we didn't have flirts among us, it's just that they had to be discreet.) I was a little surprised that Michinaga convinced her to take Izumi at all, but I actually welcomed her arrival, thinking she might invigorate our circle.

THE SMALL PINES IN THE FIELD

Nobe ni komatsu

With the start of a new year I felt more confident. All the empress's senior ladies-in-waiting were expected to accompany the two young princes to the temporary court at the Biwa Mansion. Her Majesty should have attended, but she was unwell. I would have liked to stay with her but was obliged to go to court along with the others.

That year Saishō was in charge of serving the imperial meal. As usual, she was most tastefully dressed and looked quite attractive with her hair done up.* The two maids Takumi and Hyōgo assisted her, but they were so plain in comparison I felt sorry for them, and then Lady Fuya, the woman chosen to serve the herb-seeped new year wine, rubbed everyone up the wrong way by being so overbearing. If one must take on one of these public duties, at least one should appear somewhat reticent.

The Empress's Banquet was scheduled for the second day but had to be canceled because of her illness. Unfortunately the word did not get out in time, so everyone turned up anyway and had to be accommodated. We opened up the eastern gallery for them. Michinaga was his usual expansive self, coming out to welcome people with one-year-old Prince Atsuhira in his arms. He pretended to make the child bow his head and greet the guests. At one point he said to Rinshi,

—Shall I take the little one now? and made as if to put Atsuhira down and pick up his new baby brother.

The one-year-old became jealous and began wailing in protest, so Michinaga had to leave the infant and fuss over the first one to placate him. The guests found it very amusing that royal babies should behave like the infants they were.

After a while Michinaga gave the baby back to the women, and the nobles all went to pay their respects to the emperor, who came out to meet them in the Senior Courtiers' Hall. There was music and wine and Michinaga showed every sign of becoming drunk as usual. Foreseeing trouble, I tried to make myself inconspicuous, but it was no use. Michinaga caught sight of me and cried out in a vexed tone,

—Madam! he reproached me. Why did your father slink off

*The usual way for Heian ladies to wear their hair was loose and flowing. Since they only put it up for ceremony, Murasaki found it striking on these occasions.

363

like that when I asked him to attend the concert? Why is he being difficult?

I had no idea what he was talking about and tried to make light of the situation, but he pressed me further.

—Give me a poem to compensate for your father! he said. It's the first Day of the Rat – that should be inspiration. Come on, let's have one!

Caught like this, I drew a blank. I fiddled with my fan, hoping that Michinaga might get distracted – which did not take long. Actually he didn't appear to be all that drunk. It was remarkable how attractive he could still look, even in such a situation, standing there in the light of the torches.

He went over to take a peek at the children, who were by now both fast asleep. Gazing fondly at them, he said,

—It was a pity to see the empress without children for so long. But now, wherever I turn I see a source of joy.

Michinaga glanced at me and quoted a line from an old imperial poetry collection: "If there were no small pines in the field . . ."

I was impressed. That was better than anything new I could have come up with.

The next day I happened to be with Izumi Shikibu in Lady Nakatsukasa's room in the late afternoon. True to spring, the sky had suddenly misted over, though from her room I could only see a tiny section just above the roof of the opposite corridor – the eaves had been built so close together it was impossible to see a large swatch of sky at once. I mentioned Michinaga's impromptu reference to the small pines. To my surprise, Izumi murmured,

—What did he mean by that, do you suppose?

Lady Nakatsukasa quoted,

Ne no hi suru   nobe ni komatsu no   nakariseba   chiyo no tameshi ni   nani wo hikamashi
On the Day of the Rat, if there were no small pines in the fields, then what could we pick to ensure future generations?

She had convincing command of the classics. I could not have quoted the whole thing without error, perhaps, but was rather

364

shocked at Izumi's ignorance. She did have a talent for extemporaneous composition, but my opinion of her as a poetic genius became more tarnished the more I got to know her.

I went home for a few days to celebrate the new year with my daughter and teach her the recipe for our full-moon gruel. She was a thoughtful and competent child, and I dared to hope that she would have a better time of it in court than her mother had. I could breathe more easily now that my unlucky year had passed. Thanks to merciful Kannon, I was able to lie low and avoid disaster. It occurred to me that perhaps I had been able to come through the year unscathed because I had sacrificed my character Murasaki.

I was supposed to go back to the Biwa Mansion for the baby prince's fiftieth-day celebration, and I managed to arrive just before dawn. Poor Koshōshō didn't get there until several hours later when it was already light. She was rather abashed to be so exposed. We had made our two tiny adjoining rooms into one larger one, which we kept this way even when one of us was away. When we were both at court, there was only a curtain stand between us. Michinaga found this amusing.

—What if it happened that one of you were out? Couldn't the other then become friendly with a stranger who came looking for the first?

It was an outrageous thing to say, but not surprising coming from him. Perhaps men do find ladies so easily interchangeable.

We spent the morning getting dressed in our formal clothes and around noon went to attend Her Majesty. Koshōshō wore a red Chinese jacket over robes of white and lavender figured silk, and the usual stenciled train. My jacket was white with chartreuse-green linings, and my robes were crimson lined with purple, and pale green lined with dark green. My train was stenciled in a most modern fashion. All in all, my outfit was so young and modish I was a little self-conscious.

There were seventeen palace women in attendance on Her Majesty. Of course everyone was dressed in her finest, but there were two serving women who showed a lack of taste in their color combinations. Unfortunately for them they had to pass in full view of all the nobles as they brought in the food, and they were subjected to stares and whispers. Saishō was uncharacteristically critical later, but I felt it wasn't such a terrible gaffe. It was just that their colors were all wintry reds and purples lacking a touch of pastel or green. They should have asked someone's advice, since they knew that they would be in such a public position.

After the ceremony of touching the rice cakes to the baby's lips, all the trays were taken away, and I went to sit with Lady Dainagon and Lady Koshōshō in the narrow space between the empress's curtained platform and the eastern gallery. We watched the rest of the entertainment from there. The great ministers sat on the southern verandah, the senior courtiers in the corridor, and the lesser nobles stood around in the garden. Up in the gallery the ministers played music and sang, Kintō himself keeping time with wooden clappers. Down in the garden young men playing flutes blew an accompaniment. I shut my eyes, concentrating on the music flowing by my ears, and the warmth and combined scents emanating from the robes of my two friends as we huddled there in the chilly air. For a rare moment I ceased to think about Genji.

Then, once again Akimitsu, the minister of the Right, made a fool of himself. During this same ceremony for the first prince the year before, he had pushed his way into the women's area and begun telling smutty jokes. Now, being drunk, he tried to pick up a bowl of food sitting between some ornamental cranes on the emperor's table, then stumbled and tipped the whole tray over. The cranes should not have been touched. Michinaga was quite annoyed. The transcendent combination of sound, smell, and warmth I had momentarily enjoyed was utterly ruptured by an upsurge of scolding and grumbling.

At the end of the evening I saw Michinaga present the emperor with a box containing the famous flute named Hafutatsu. Someone near me whispered that he had received it himself from Retired Emperor Kazan only a few days before. It was a grand gesture, and Ichijō was truly surprised,

I think. To a skilled flautist, there could be no more welcome gift than that famous instrument.

THE VIRGIN PRIESTESS

Sai-in

One day that spring, one of my maids from home brought me a letter written to my brother from a certain Lady Chūjō, who was serving in the household of the Virgin Priestess of the Kamo Shrine. The girl had heard Nobunori bragging about his high-flown correspondence with someone, so when she saw him tuck away a letter, she later borrowed it surreptitiously, knowing I would be interested. I remembered thinking long ago that I would probably dislike any woman who became involved with my brother – yet I was curious. Unfolding the letter, I could see immediately that what Nobu took to be high elegance was nothing but a dreadfully affected style. The woman wrote as if no one in the world could possibly be as sensitive as she. I became indignant as I read her opinion that "in judging poetry, no one can rival our princess. She is the only one who can recognize promising talent."

What an odious snob! I would never criticize the Virgin Priestess, but if this Chūjō woman claimed so much for her circle, how was it that they produced so little in the way of actual poems? They had a reputation for elegance and sophistication, but could they really be so much better than the women I saw around me? The self-satisfaction of the letter rankled all afternoon. I wished I could have shown it to Saishō, but the girl had to return it to its hiding place before it was missed. And of course my friend was above that sort of pettiness. I wondered what Kerria Rose would have thought of the things I allowed myself to get worked up over.

In the fifth month that year, I had an opportunity to visit the

Virgin Priestess's mansion myself. I had not been there for quite some time, and since seeing my brother's letter from the lady in her service, I was curious to refresh my impressions.

Indeed the mansion was a beautiful place, famous for viewing the rising evening moon and gorgeous dawn skies; perfect for listening to the call of the *hototogisu* under the blossoming trees. The Virgin Priestess was clearly a woman of great sensitivity, but I though her ladies, while not exactly unfriendly, certainly kept to themselves. The place had an aura of seclusion and mystery completely unlike the commotion surrounding us in Her Majesty's service, where people were traipsing in and out all the time. In contrast, these ladies had little to distract them and were never in the sort of rush we were always in whenever our mistress prepared to visit the emperor or when Michinaga decided to stay over.

Living in the tranquillity of the Priestess's mansion, you would think her ladies couldn't fail to produce excellent poems. I pictured the stiff and serious nobles who visited us at the palace. If they were to come here, I thought, they would surely be inspired to compose exquisite poems in praise of the moon or the flowers.

I drifted into a reverie, imagining that even an old fossil like myself, were I to join this household, would just naturally absorb the elegance of the place. In my fantasy, no one would gossip about me or give me a bad name – even if I were to do something like encounter a man I didn't know and exchange poems with him. I was also convinced that any of our own young ladies would compare favorably with the women here if only they were allowed to live in such gracious surroundings. People may be born with their characters predisposed, yet I couldn't help but think one's environment made a difference.

Ever since reading my brother's letter from Lady Chūjō, I realized I had been feeling defensive about the empress's household. And now that Izumi Shikibu had joined us, it was even more embarrassing. She had a real genius for composing things spontaneously and making quite ordinary sentiments sound special. Because she was so clever, it made the rest of us look dull as dirt. What was our problem? Why didn't we make a better showing?

I was beginning to think it had something to do with the fact that there were no other consorts important enough to keep Shōshi on her mettle. Except for the Virgin Priestess, there was no one in any of the other households who could really challenge us at all. Without any sense of rivalry to spur us on, the result was that we had become smug. It was really quite disgraceful how self-satisfied and full of themselves the upper-ranking women were. Their complacency did nothing to enhance Her Majesty's reputation.

It seemed to me that Shōshi herself had matured, gradually realizing that she had been a bit too reticent in the past. When she learned that the senior courtiers were bored with her household for its lack of verve, she tried to remedy the situation. She used to be so concerned lest someone commit a breach of etiquette that everyone was afraid to put herself out, with the result that many ladies had become exceedingly timid. Unfortunately, now when she exhorted them to be more open, the habit was too ingrained for them to change easily.

—Women who can handle a conversation in an intriguing way or compose a quick reply to an interesting poem are few and far between.

This is what the men were rumored to be saying. Not that I had ever heard them actually say it in so many words, but I knew what they were thinking.

It bothered me that our group had a reputation as such mud hens, but I either swallowed my complaints or wrote them down in letters which I sent to my father or Kerria Rose. Of course I trusted them both completely, but afraid that, written down, words would stray, I begged them to return these letters right away.

Dear Father,
It may strike you that I am criticizing particular women unfairly. I don't mean to. No one is really that much better or worse than anyone else. It seems if they're good in one respect, they are deficient in something else. Please don't think I'm advocating that the older women

act flippantly just when the younger ones are trying to appear more serious. I guess I'm just wishing they were all more flexible.

I do think, for example, that when one is approached by someone and replies with a quick poem, it is ridiculous to write something that gives offense. (I know I have been guilty of this privately in the past, but certainly not since I came to the palace.) It is really not so difficult to come up with something appropriate, even if one can't be brilliant. Yet some women seem to think it is better to turn one's back silently rather than risk a mistake. At the opposite extreme, one or two are always poking their noses into other people's business. Different situations demand different responses. That concept is simply not grasped around here.

Here is an example. Whenever Tadanobu arrives with a message, the senior women who ought to take charge and go out to greet him don't. Instead, they behave like shy children – holding back, pushing one another forward, trying to make themselves invisible. The result is that sometimes none of them goes out, or if one does, she is tongue-tied. Are they unintelligent?

No.

Are they ugly?

No.

It's just that they feel so self-conscious and embarrassed that they might say something silly, they refuse to say anything at all. Women in other households can't possibly behave in such a manner!

You would expect that when women enter imperial service, even the highest-born ladies will figure out what is required of them and act accordingly. But there have been times when I have gotten so impatient with their dithering that either I myself or some other lesser-ranked lady has had to go out to greet the major counselor. He understandably takes this in bad grace. The nobles who want to communicate with Her Majesty all have secret understandings with particular women of their choice. If that lady should happen to be absent when they come to call, they go away disappointed. Really, it is not surprising that they complain this place is moribund.

I'm sure the women in the Virgin Priestess's household know all this and look down on us because of it. What I find galling is that they then declare that they are "the only ones of note" and everyone else is "simply blind and deaf when it comes to taste."

Well, I have certainly written more than I intended. It is easy to slip into criticism of other people and then, once begun, hard to stop. How much more difficult to keep oneself in check. Anyone but you reading my words would assume I am as bad as Lady Chūjō in despising others. I'm afraid my true character has been revealed. But you knew that about me already. Please return this as soon as you have read it. There may be parts that are hard to make out, and places where I may have left out a word or two, but just try to read it through.

Father worried about me. He sent my letter back with a warning that it was not a good idea to be so frank and open with one's opinions in writing. Of course I was aware of that, but by that time I had already written similar things to Kerria Rose.

My Dear Older Sister,

Despite all my complaints, I am still concerned what people think. I'm sure this means I still retain a strong sense of attachment to this world – for my daughter's sake if nothing else. What can I do about it? Sometimes I long to follow your example and renounce everything, but that is not possible. If I manage to accomplish nothing else in my life, I want to prepare Katako for a successful career at court.

My intention has been to reveal all my thoughts to you, the good and the bad, the public matters and private sorrows, and things I really can't go on discussing in writing. Perhaps I have made a mistake. No matter how objectionable a person it, it might not be such a good idea to reveal all in a letter. Your own life can't possibly be this tedious! Is it not detestable how peevish I have become? You must write to me. Your thoughts are worth more than all my useless prattle.

There is so much more I want to tell you, but I don't have a lot of energy these days. Mind you, if my letters ever fell into the wrong hands, even for a moment, it would be a disaster.

A few days ago I tore up and burned a lot of old letters and papers. I used up a pile of Genji drafts to make paper dollhouses this past spring. Actually, since that time I really haven't had much correspondence to speak of. I feel I shouldn't use new paper to write such rambling letters, so I'm afraid that what you're reading here will look very shabby. Please forgive me, I have my reasons and am not trying to be rude. And in any case, you will send this back, I trust.

As always, Kerria Rose encouraged me to break with these ephemeral yet sticky entanglements. I felt that I was a plum not yet ripe enough to drop from the bough, but that the day would come when I might be able to let go.

That autumn was a melancholy one indeed. I knew I had been too critical of other women in the past, yet there I was, having managed to survive but with nothing of note to show for my pains and nothing to rely on in the future. I pretended not to be the sort of person who would abandon herself to despair on an autumn evening when nostalgia is most poignant. I even allowed myself to sit out on the verandah in the moonlight and think about the past.

—Is this the same moon that once praised my beauty? I said to myself, thinking of a Chinese poem, and then suddenly realized I was doing exactly what I claimed not to. I became uneasy and moved inside, continuing to fret and worry.

Sanenari, with whom I used to enjoy corresponding, had neither written nor visited for a long time. I could hardly blame him, after how I responded during our last exchange. Still, I did think our friendship was such that it could withstand some gaps. Now I heard he was paying court to

Izumi Shikibu, of all people! That she was witty I was the first to admit. She could produce poems at will and always managed to include something novel that caught the eye. Yet when it came to a thorough knowledge of the canon, and the ability to judge the work of others, she left a lot to be desired. I could not think of her as a poet of the highest caliber, but I suppose she must have other charms.

The moonlight on an autumn night is so bright, a poem came to me in spite of myself, and I was very tempted to send it to Sanenari.

Oukata no   aki no aware wo   omoiyare   tsuki ni kokoro wa   akugarenu tomo
Think of me in the forgotten sadness of autumn, even though your heart be captured by the moon.

Upon reflection, though, I did not. Had he replied, I would have been obliged to correspond with him again, all the time wondering whether he found Izumi's poems more fascinating. And if he did not reply, I would know he preferred her.

For a year workmen had been busy rebuilding the Ichijō Palace, which had burned the winter before. Now the repairs were complete and the emperor had returned. It was time for the Gosechi Dances, yet I remained at home. I had become engrossed in another attempt to write Genji's death scene, and I knew if I went to the palace for the dances it would be difficult to pick up the thread of my thought again. Also, I was afraid that rumors were creeping about that I intended to finish him off.

People had been upset enough when Murasaki died. If the empress were to ask me to spare Genji, I would be in a difficult position. I told her I had been having inauspicious dreams and needed to be in seclusion to observe a taboo. That was true enough. I had dreamed that my hair was cut and my forehead bared like a nun's, and also that a viper was slithering within my entrails and gnawing at my liver. Somehow I seemed to think in my dream that the proper cure was for a priest to pour water on my right knee. Although the meaning of such a dream is not obvious. I felt it couldn't possibly be good.

While I was at home, I received a message from Saishō saying she missed me and was very sorry I was not there for the dances. To tell the truth, as fond as I was of Saishō, her affection had begun to cloy. She had grown plumper as the years passed, probably from eating at odd hours. I frequently found her guiltily brushing crumbs from her sleeves. She craved attentive expressions of love as much as she did food, and I was often too distracted to satisfy her.

In reply to her message I wrote:

Mezurashi to   kimi shi omowaba   kite miemu   sureru koromo no   hodo suginu tomo
If you truly think the dances are so wonderful, I will try to come – though it's a bit late for those blue-rubbed robes.

Her response was immediate:

Saraba kimi   yamai no koromo   suginu tomo   koishiki hodo ni   kite mo mienamu
Well, then, though the season for dark blue robes has passed, please come wearing them anyway, for the sake of my love.

The first snow of the season tumbled whitely out of a gray sky. That evening another letter came from Saishō with this poem:

Koiwabite   arifuru hodo no   hatsuyuki wa   kienuru ka to zo   utagawarekeru
I live each day burning with missing you, and now the first snow falls – melting as soon as it touches my longing.

I did not respond immediately, but the next day as I gazed out at the low skies and my garden where the flurries were blowing amidst the dried-up reeds, I wrote this:

Tureba kaku   usa nomi masaru   yo wo shirade   aretaru niwa ni   tsumoru hatsuyuki
Thus is falls, unaware of a world where only sadness piles up – the first snow, drifting in a shabby garden.

Poor Saishō. If I had only had the emotional strength, I should have tried to soothe her, but I had turned completely inward. Why was it so difficult, I wondered, to imagine the death of Genji? I had tossed out three different scenarios.

UJI
Uji

When the appointments of the new year were announced, to my utter shock Father had been give the governorship of Echigo Province. I realized this must have been what Michinaga was after him about – and Father gave no hint that this was brewing! I was astonished that a man in his sixty-seventh year would even be considered for such a remote post, for Echigo was another two days' journey past Echizen. Because of Father's advanced age, my brother, Nobunori, was to accompany him. It was hard to imagine he would be very helpful, but at least, off in Echigo, he wouldn't be an embarrassment. At the palace, people offered congratulations on the prestigious cap to Father's career, and I smiled, hiding my apprehension. Father was hale for an old man, but Echigo was a rugged assignment.

During this time I cleared up a misunderstanding with Her Majesty. She finally admitted that she was afraid there would be no more tales if Genji died. I was relieved, and assured her that was not the case. In fact, I said, with Genji gone I would feel more free to write again.

For a long time I couldn't shake the feeling that I had been merely existing from day to day, dully registering the passage of time by take note of the flowers, the singing birds, the way the sky changed from season to season, the moon, the frost, the snow – but in fact I was quite indifferent. What did any of it mean? Sometimes the thought of continuing on in that miasma was simply unbearable. I tried to lift myself out of that depressed state by taking a pilgrimage to Uji to say a prayer for my cousin Ruri, who had thrown herself into that wild and gloomy river many years ago. The trip through the swampy plains southeast of Miyako had gotten me thinking. As I prayed for Ruri, the image of the ghostly Lady of the Uji Bridge rose up before me, and a torrent of inspiration struck.

I had been slowly going mad trying to release myself from the Shining Prince when Kerria Rose suggested a solution brilliant in its simplicity. I just let go of him. Readers could imagine anything they liked. I left him brooding with premonitions but still able to dazzle the world. The only option I did not permit was for Genji to live on into his dotage. He was gone, that was all.

I had expected to feel at least a little bit sad, for it was as if an old friend or member of the family had died – but strangely enough, all I felt was a rising sense of relief. I was free. Inspired, I wrote all summer, making several excursions through the marshy lowlands to Uji, where I gazed from the bridge down at the fiercely flowing river. Battered little rafts, piled high with brushwood, made their way up and down the shoals, each boatman pursuing his own sad, small livelihood at the uncertain mercy of the waters. I stayed at a rustic villa, listening to the ceaseless cobble and complaint of that murmuring water, watching those odd little boats. Though I counted myself among the privileged who live in jeweled palaces in the capital, in truth I felt my life was not so different from those boatmen who drifted from one uncertainty to the next, with no solid ground beneath their feet. How easily one's moorings shift.

I was beginning to feel more at home in lonely Uji than back at the palace, and would have stayed on, furiously scribbling, but I received a message that the emperor was ill and the empress troubled. She requested me to return.

I found her in a tearful state. A number of malignant spirits seemed to be harassing the emperor, and he was sure things could only get worse. Ichijō felt he simply must abdicate, yet Michinaga refused to hear of it.

—I must step down while my mind is still clear, the emperor told Shōshi, hoping to enlist her aid in convincing her father. But the empress herself could not countenance the idea. All she did was cry.

The oppressive heat that summer was enough to tax the most robust, and the frail emperor suffered cruelly. Finally, in the sixth month, he summoned Michinaga and insisted that he be given the tonsure. This time it was granted. Shōshi was inconsolable. Everyone milled about uneasily, not a single lady daring to take leave under the circumstances.

Emperor Ichijō died on the twenty-second day of the sixth month, and the whole world went into morning. Ichijō had become crown prince at the age of four, ascended the throne at seven, and reigned for twenty-five years – longer than any emperor in memory. How can I describe the sadness? We could not accept that he was gone even as the numerous prayer altars were dismantled and the priests clattered off with all their paraphernalia, leaving behind the dark silent reality of his passing. Shōshi stayed with the body for quite a while, but eventually we coaxed her back to her apartment. In a state of numb shock she acquiesced. All her ladies hovered nearby, although we could not say much to offer comfort. Even poetry must wait for raw grief to lose its edge.

After the funeral the empress moved to the Biwa Mansion. Crown Prince Okisada became emperor and was installed with great ceremony in the original imperial quarters – finally repaired after many years. For me it was too late, and I regretted that I had never had the chance to live in the true palace. Shōshi herself professed to be glad not to have set up residence there, for she found it intimidating, and she was frightened of the large empty buildings reputed to be haunted. Her sister Kenshi was named empress.

As everyone expected, Shōshi's son was designated crown prince over the claims of Ichijō's firstborn son by Teishi. So, though he was only three, little Atsuhira had to leave his mother's house to go live in the palace. Having lost the emperor, my mistress was even more depressed to lose the company of her child. At least she had the boy's younger brother with her.

After the emperor died, women began to leave Shōshi's service, one by one. When she moved to the Biwa Mansion, a number of them simply declined to go. I found their casual betrayals galling, and felt obliged to stay on, even forgoing my usual leaves of absence. There at the Biwa Mansion I continued to work on my stories set in Uji, hoping I might be able to offer the empress some distraction from her glum brooding. Unfortunately for her, the Biwa house held such memories from the past that she was constantly reminded of the former emperor. In my box of papers I found a copy of a poem I wrote to Shōshi around this time:

Arishi yo wa   yume ni minashite   namida sae   tomaranu yado zo   kanashikarikeru

The way things were – it now seems a dream. How sad the house where even tears do not stop.

The poem was highly praised, although it did nothing to cheer Her Majesty. Still she flattered me by placing it in her personal collection.

That fall my brother, Nobunori, died in Echigo, an unfinished poem to Lady Chūjō in his hand, according to Father. I had to leave the Biwa Mansion to go home into mourning. Katako was eleven, old enough to wear gray, and the sight of her solemn little figure in mourning weeds suddenly shocked me into the realization that she would soon be mature. She may not have been physically ready to put on the trousers of womanhood, but her mind was grown-up enough to begin to grasp the things she would need to know to enter upon a career at court. Under my guidance she had been studying poetry since she could handle a brush. I encouraged her to try her skill at every opportunity, even if she showed the results to no one.

—Literary skill will get you noticed, I told her, but it won't make you happy. You had better heed your mother's mistakes and try to be more socially successful.

Katako appeared to listen carefully. Although I feared that much of what I said may have gone over her head at the time, I hoped she might recall my words later when she was at court.

*

The following year, at age twenty-three, Shōshi was designated empress dowager. She found it hard to get used to her new title, and when it came time for the official appointment, she wept, remembering the familiar bustle of the previous year when Ichijō had been alive. All was quite in the Biwa Mansion as everyone crowded around her sister, the new empress, in the palace. I thought if Shōshi could visualize her husband dwelling in Amida's Paradise, her heart might be soothed, so I gave her this poem:

Kumo no ue wo   kumo no yoso nite   omoiyaru   tsuki wa kawarazu   ama no shita ni
You remember life above the clouds even now in your overcast state; yet the moon, unchanged, still illuminates all under heaven.

She thanked me for my thoughts and put this poem, too, in her collection.

—I appreciate your poem, she said softly, but what would really cheer me up is to read about Genji again.

I pulled out one of the stories we had collated years ago, and asked her which story she wished to hear. She often chose Tamakazura, the exotic lost daughter, but this time she requested Murasaki's death.

By the end of the tale, she was weeping again.

—Your Majesty, I ventured, perhaps I could read you something new?

I had been absorbed in fashioning my post-Genji tales and was getting ready to present them to her as a surprise. Prior to that, I had showed them to one of two friends who told me they had become so engrossed they couldn't sleep. Their reaction convinced me that the Uji stories would be well received and perhaps help divert the empress.

Genji's descendants took over the tales. As I tried to put the Shining Prince in perspective, I realized that despite his philandering he never lost his sensitivity to the beauty and pathos of life. Oddly enough, now that he was gone, I could see that there was a certain purity about Genji's lack of cynicism, although I no longer felt this a truthful portrayal of any man.

379

Genji was like the sun. People called him Hikaru, the Shining One. When he expired, the light was extinguished. The way I conceived life after Genji, his descendants inherited none of his radiance, only his lingering sensual fragrance. Kaoru, born to Genji's childish bride the Third Princess, was not in fact Genji's son. The girl was raped practically under Genji's nose, with Kaoru as the result. Living a lie made this young man introspective to the point of paralysis. Genji's grandson, Prince Niou, was the opposite – heedless and spoiled, driven by unbridled emotion. Trying to follow Genji's footsteps in their pursuit of romance, they became entangled in jealousy, resentment, and distrust.

—This Kaoru makes himself so unhappy! exclaimed Shōshi, after listening to me read. Why does he fasten only upon women who are bound to bring him pain? It is annoying to listen to his fruitless adventures. Nothing prevents him from creating a lovely relationship except his own dithering.

The empress through Kaoru a very unsatisfactory character, which was discouraging because I felt Kaoru to be very like myself. Here was a man who, at least unconsciously, understood the dissatisfaction of getting what you think you want.

—And for that matter, she continued, your Prince Niou seems to gorge on whatever or whoever takes his fancy, yet he is never satisfied, either. He is like a hungry ghost – actually the both of them are like hungry ghosts. Kaoru reminds me of one of those creatures whose belly is distended with hunger, but whose mouth is the size of a grain of rice.

The empress had been looking at one of Genshin's hell scrolls showing creatures at various levels of depraved existence, and so perhaps she exaggerated. Her comments were not unreasonable, though. It seemed to me that people do a rather good job of creating levels of hell all by themselves, and this was something worth writing about. I had even come to think that these two handsome but defective heroes were more interesting that the radiant Genji. I arranged for them to pursue the same woman. Caught between them, this lady was like a boat unmoored, tossed about by her own conflicting passions as well as the whims of her lovers. In Ukifune I felt I had created a heroine whose heart I could delve into.

Yet the more she heard, the less enthusiastic Shōshi became. I begged her to withhold judgment until she had seen more, for I felt sure she would be drawn in by Ukifune, but in the end the empress remarked that she found the gloomy scenes at Uji distressing. Kaoru frustrated her and she felt Niou to be irresponsible. She much preferred the glittering Genji and his adventures. Was it not possible for me to bring Genji back somehow?

—Perhaps he could be reincarnated? she suggested hopefully.

She would rather have simply bypassed Genji's descendants and their unsavory passions. When my heroine sought to end her life in despair, the empress was shocked.

—Her behavior is unreasonable, Shōshi admonished me. Have her choose one man or the other and be done with it. The empress thought Ukifune should go with Kaoru and cure him of his melancholy.

—Prince Niou does not interest me, she said. But I would like to see you make an effort to make Kaoru happy. Surely you could bring your floating lady into some sort of accord with him?

—I would have thought, I ventured, that she would rather be done with both of them and escape to a nunnery.

—Well, said Shōshi doubtfully, I suppose you can have her try that, but please don't leave her there. It's too depressing.

And so I continued to fret. It seemed the very thing I felt most compelled to pursue also caused me the most pain. I went through black moods when I felt it was all worth nothing. Yet somehow I was driven to continue writing, no matter what the empress or the other ladies said.

I had exhausted myself trying to capture the nature of the twisted relationships into which men and women fall. Freed by Genji's death, I found so much I wanted to explore that I wrote from morning till dark, allowing nothing to distract me. When I was young, I had been concerned lest Genji succumb to flights of magical fantasy. I wanted him to be wonderful but at the same time believable, and my readers, judging from their response, found him so. In amazement, over twenty years, I watched Genji grow until eventually it seemed I myself was merely a tool of his shining person. Was I writing Genji? Or was Genji just using me?

Looking back, it was appalling that I allowed myself to be so confused. I tried to remind myself of the friends with whom I could discuss my innermost thoughts as well as trifling scribblings. Had I stayed at home a widow, would things not have been worse? At court I even managed to make contact with some of the high and mighty. But, looking back, perhaps I was just deceiving myself with this wretched tale, finding comfort in mere foolish words. Sharply aware of my own insignificance, I took bleak satisfaction only in that I had been able to avoid anything that could be considered shameful or improper. Living as a widow, I would have found it even harder to avoid scandal. In the end I finally came to the realization that fiction ultimately creates its own truth.

Or so I thought. When the empress, even in her gentle way, indicated her displeasure with the turn of my Uji writings, my heart filled with despair. I tried to make a convincing case for the heroine Ukifune to turn away from both men. Everyone else in the tale tried to make her into an object of their own desire, or keepsake in place of someone else – surely this was something the empress ought to have been able to empathize with. Only when left alone to quietly reflect on the scriptures did Ukifune begin to sort out her life.

—But she can't just stay a nun, Shōshi pointed out. Who will want to read about her then?

The empress had a point. But even at her request I could not make myself bring Genji back. Then, imagine my dismay when I found out that Shōshi had secretly asked another court lady, Akazome Emon, to write more stories about Genji. The empress was very taken with the character of Tamakazura and wanted to read more about what happened to her after she escaped Genji's clutches by her abrupt marriage.

To her credit, Akazome Emon was hesitant to undertake writing about Genji himself, but she seemed comfortable enough writing about Tamakazura and her children. I had to pretend I was not bothered, but in fact I was devastated. I stopped writing altogether, leaving Ukifune in the nunnery, and unsure of what would happen. I felt I had abandoned her. Tasting the bitterness of life's dregs to the full, I must have written this poem around that time:

Izuku to mo   mi wo yaru kata no   shirareneba   ushi to mitsutsu mo   nagarauru kana
Which way should I go? Where should I put myself? Not knowing the answer, I continue wearily existing.

I had no one to whom I could send it.

To be brutally honest, I had reached a point where I no longer cared about what others said. My attempts to portray the truth of human entanglements had been misunderstood, ending in utter failure. I thought about my literary ancestors and how they strove to balance language and emotion in their poetry. Words for them were transparent to the truths they expressed. For me, try as I might to achieve their clarity of purpose, words had become nothing but a distortion. The more earnestly I chose them, the falser they became. Long ago the Chinese poet Du Mu struggled with this problem and ultimately decided:

In this world unmoored, except for poems, all words are forced.

I no longer had the energy or the will to try to force them. Like a boat adrift, I had lost my bearings in this world unmoored.

The only thing left was to put my trust in Amida Buddha. Unlike Ruri, I could never throw myself in the Uji River. Instead I immersed myself in reading the holy sutras. Kerria Rose asked why I did not now retreat to the mountains, since I had stopped writing and professed to have lost what remained of my attachment to the trials and drudgery of life. Were I to commit myself and turn my back on the world, I might still suffer moments of uncertainty, and then I surely would be unable to climb to the clouds of glory when the Holy One finally did summon me. Only when Katako was established would I truly be free of worldly attachments. I hoped this moment would come soon, for I was afraid if I got much older my eyesight might weaken to the point where I would be unable to read the sutras.

Kerria Rose urged me repeatedly to follow her, but I continued to put her off. It must have seemed to her that I was merely going through the motions of being a true believer, whereas in fact I thought of little else. Perhaps she couldn't fully understand the qualms of someone with as much to atone for as myself – someone who might very well not even qualify for salvation, despite what the priest Genshin preached. So many things reminded me of my sins I became quite miserable if I allowed myself to dwell on them.

Sometime near the end of the rainy season, the little crown prince took ill and came to stay at the Biwa Mansion with his mother. I recall that he recovered quickly and was running around looking quite healthy – but Shōshi was so anxious to keep him with her a while longer she pretended he was still sick. It fell to me to report on the state of things to the messenger who came from the palace to inquire. I told him that while the crown prince's illness did not appear to be serious, he was not fit to attend palace business as there was still some fever. It was a lie a mother could understand.

At that time a number of people, including Michinaga, were feeling under the weather. My close companion Koshōshō complained of headaches and heaviness in her chest. But she was naturally frail and had always pulled through in the past, so I wasn't terribly worried about her. This time, however, she slipped away suddenly. Before anyone realized her condition was serious, she died.

This cruel reminder of life's uncertainty sealed my decision to withdraw from public life.

That autumn I began making short retreats to a little house I called my Gossamer Hermitage in the hills near Kiyomizu Temple. Katako was still at home, busy hour after hour with lessons. I told her that if she worked hard, I would bring her with me to the Biwa Mansion, where she might join me in service to the dowager empress. The child kept her eyes steadily fixed on this goal as she practiced calligraphy, studied incense blends, learned how to mix dyestuffs, and day by day memorized one more piece of the classical poetry canon. She could not know it at the time, but the harder she worked to be allowed to join me in court service, the more she loosened my ties to it. I felt a little guilty at the deception, but in the long run I thought it would be better for her as well.

By the beginning of the new year I had begun to spend more and more time at my Gossamer Hermitage. The simplicity of a small space suited me. I no longer felt like looking at my Chinese books or playing my thirteen-stringed koto. I brought none of them with me. My inkstone, of course, I could not do without, nor some brushes and paper.

Kerria Rose gave me a kind of koto with only one string, which amused me. The idea of making music from a single string! I suddenly recalled a lady name Koma who had been in Her Majesty's service. She had showed promise, but after an unfortunate experience early in her career, withdrew and spent most of her time at home. She continued to harp upon her misfortune, and after a while everyone began avoiding her. She was like a koto "whose bridges are stuck on a single tuning," as the proverb goes. Yet here I had received a koto with no bridges at all.

Then Kerria Rose played it for me. I was astonished at the range of expression she drew from that single string. She told me the instrument was first made by Yukihira when he was exiled to Suma. On those lonely beaches he took a string from his bow and affixed it to a piece of driftwood, marking the points of the scale on the wood with pebbles and bits of seashell. My instrument, too, had coral pebbles inset in the wave-pattern woodgrain of the light paulownia board. It was an appealingly uncomplicated piece of work and expressed well the simplification of my life, from thirteen strings down to one.

My colleagues got used to the fact that I stayed away for longer and longer stretches of time. Yet most of them thought my behavior very strange.

Kodayū visited on the twentieth day of the first month.

385

Together we lit lamps at Kiyomizu Temple in a service for Shōshi, who was ill. Before we left the temple, she plucked a fragrant magnolia leaf from the altar and wrote this on the back:

Kokorozashi   kimi ni kakaguru   tomoshibi no   onaji hikari ni   au ga ureshisa
*It moves me deeply, meeting you here and together offering
lighted lamps to our empress.*

Unlike some of the others, Kodayū understood my increasingly long retreats. She stayed the night, and in the morning, as we stood together observing the snow lingering on the pine branches, she wrote:

Okuyama no   matsuba ni kouru   yuki yori mo   waga mi yo ni furu   hodo zo kanashiki
*More fragile than that snow frozen to the pine needles in
the deep mountains – my own existence in the world.*

We were bundled into floss-padded layers of clothing, but our noses were red with cold, and she sniffled. We had known one another a long time. Kodayū had also become disillusioned with the intrigues of palace life.

The longer I stayed at my retreat, the more natural it felt. Kerria Rose lived close by and we often went together to Kiyomizu Temple for services. In the second month, with the full brilliance of spring bathing the eastern hills in sunlight, I knew I belonged there. It was time to return home to sort through my papers and try to put things in order. Striving for detachment, I looked at every piece of paper. The letters were most difficult. As I rifled through a pile of correspondence, I came across a very frank letter that Lady Koshōshō had once written to me. I couldn't bear simply to throw it away, so I sent it on to Lady Kaga, who had also been close to her, writing this to accompany it:

Kurenu ma no   mi wo ba omowade   hito no yo no   aware wo shiru zo   katsu wa kanashiki
*My own life is so tenuous I hardly give it a thought, yet to
know the demise of another is piercingly sad.*

It was sobering to think that fragile piece of paper, marked with the thoughts flowing from her hand, was all that was left of someone so dear. I added:

Tare ka yo ni nagaraete mimu kakitomeshi ato wa kiesenu katami naredomo
As life flows on, who ever will read it? This keepsake to her whose memory will never die?

If I allowed myself to linger over all the correspondence I had saved, I would never finish, I scolded myself. But neither could I bring myself to burn it. At the end of the day I packed it all in one large trunk.

Fragile as it is, paper seems to be the only thing left in the end.

Just before I took Katako to the Biwa Mansion to present her to the dowager empress, this reply came from Lady Kaga:

Naki hito wo shinoburu koto mo itsu made zo kyou no aware wa asu no waga mi wo
For how long should we grieve those now gone? Today's grief tomorrow is our own.

For Katako's sake, I tried to shake off these glum forebodings, for she was fairly bursting with excitement at the prospect of her court debut. I felt confident that entering service at her tender age she would adapt much more easily to the currents of court life than her mother had. I had been too old, unprepared, and set in my ways by the time my summons came. I had also been filled with unrealistic expectations that I made sure my daughter did not have.

We prepared Katako's wardrobe from fabrics contributed by my late husband's main house. None of Nobutaka's other daughters had shown any aptitude for royal service, but the rest of the family enthusiastically supported Katako.

—Do you remember when you were little and my dresses were being made, you wanted to come with Mama to visit the empress? I asked her. I told you your time would come, and now here we are, sewing yours.

She nodded happily, running her tongue over newly

387

blackened teeth. She looked like a doll, and I imagined how delighted Shōshi would be with her.

Putting Katako into the dowager empress's service was like releasing a fish into its natural element. From the very beginning she made friends with the younger girls and was looked upon fondly by the older women. My spirit lightened, and I felt that I had amply discharged my duty to Shōshi by giving her my daughter in my stead.

I was ready to ask Kerria Rose for help in gathering the seven herbs and aromatics I needed for a *goma* ceremony. Ginseng, milkwort, and asparagus I had; fir-root fungus and aspen I could obtain; but for the licorice root and Solomon's seal, one had to know the peasants living deep in the mountains.

When everything was assembled, Kerria Rose met me at the temple, bringing scissors. My hair was still thick and the cut ends flew up as if surprised by their sudden release. We piled the aromatics in bowls before a frightfully realistic image of the fierce Fudō, and lit a small fire of sumac wood by the altar. When the flames were high, in went the pungent herbs, sending up crackling spurts of fire and smoke. In, too, went letters and poems and old manuscripts. Clouds of smoke wreathed Fudō's wrathful countenance as the fire consumed the passions and illusions of my insignificant life. I had engaged a priest to chant the appropriate formulae, and my sins seemed to waft away, buoyant on his resonant voice.

Inexplicably I thought of the thin plume of smoke on the plain at my mother's funeral – the smoke that had deluded me into thinking I could shape reality by my writing.

I emerged from the temple light-headed and giddy. My short hair bounced around my shoulders in a strange and almost humorous way on the path back to the Gossamer Heritage. Mountain cherries stretched out branches of pale bloom in the soft spring air of evening, and I sat in meditation for the remainder of the night. Perhaps it would have been better had I climbed to the clouds on that day. My soul was purified, and I held no regrets for anything. Had Amida Buddha suddenly appeared to me then, I'm sure I would simply have floated straight up to Paradise.

But life rarely stops at these transcendent moments. I settled into routine in my hermitage. My pace became the quiet slow meander of the striped tree snail waving its delicate horns instead of the frenetically chirping cicadas we all resembled back at the palace. I took up my brush and went back to the nunnery where I had left Ukifune. Now I could imagine, without pressure or distraction, how my tale should end. I finished it, but felt no need to show it to anyone but Kerria Rose.

Tying off this last thread, I should have been at peace, but strangely, something still nagged at the edges of the tranquillity I strove for. I recalled the story of the old man who one day simply had to dig a hole and talk into it because "one feels flatulent when there is something inside one needs to express."

Thus I took up my brush and my leftover paper and wrung out what remained to be expressed. By this endeavour I have gradually come to realize that I was deluded into thinking truth was ever the goal of my writing merely because I tried to avoid magical tricks. Reality was neither the subject nor object of the tales, for Genji created his own reality.

Amazingly, I find after all this that I still have some paper left – but I think I have written enough.

KATAKO

Your grandmother simultaneously and methodically prepared me for court duty as she wrapped up her worldly affairs. I guess it would be more truthful to say that I was her main worldly concern at that point, and she put me in order just as she did her poetry. She copied out a collection of all her poems, public and private – many of them from her diary – excising them from their passionate contexts and supplying bland headnotes. This collection she sent off to her father in Echigo.

Years later when I was with Sadoyori, I happened to see one of the letters she was in the habit of writing to Tametoki during his tour of service in the provinces, and it brought tears to my eyes. Although she berated herself in her journal, she was in fact a most filial daughter. The letter I saw ended with this poem, praying for my grandfather's continued health:

Yuki tsumoru   toshi ni soete mo   tanomu kana   kimi wo shirane no   matsu ni soetsutsu
The snow piles up like the count of years, and thus I pray:
may you live as long as the Shirane mountain pines.

What a powerful talisman it proved to be. My grandfather felt almost embarrassed by his longevity in the end, for he outlived all three of his first set of children.

When my mother retired permanently to her Gossamer Hermitage in the spring after my court debut, Grandfather felt he had better return to Miyako to watch over me. He gave me her poem collection for safe keeping, but I confess I did not look at it very thoroughly at the time. I was utterly caught up in the affairs of court, including the attentions of Sadoyori, who taught me much about love and etiquette. I was single-minded in my goal of making a success of my court career, my mother's voice echoing in my ears.

During my first year in Shōshi's service I hardly came back home at all. Of course I returned to greet my grandfather, but since my mother was away at her Gossamer Hermitage, there was little reason to stay. I did visit her retreat twice, but it took a long time to get there, and there were always duties demanding my quick return to court. She never pressed me to stay.

I was a little surprised she made no mention of Michinaga's fiftieth-birthday celebration, which took place at the end of the following year, nor did she write of the terrible fire that destroyed over five hundred great houses in the capital, including the Tsuchimikado Mansion and her own house on Sixth Avenue. Old and weary, Tametoki retired to the temple called Miidera after this horrible conflagration, but my mother made no note of that, either.

She, along with her old friend Kerria Rose, joined a group of once-worldly people who had become disillusioned. They left their elegant dwellings and high positions in the capital to live in simple retreats near temples – near, but not in them. Their disillusion extended to the Buddhist priests and monks, and they were wary of being entangled in those religious hierarchies. They put their trust in Genshin, who preached the way for all souls, even women, to be saved directly by the mercy of Amida Buddha. Their days were spent in meditation. The notion that contemplating the transience of the world could be a path to enlightenment must have been congenial to Murasaki, for she had been writing about it in her Genji tales, in her journal, and in her poems throughout her life.

Separate from the long meditation on her writing life, I found a fragment of a story that seems to belong at the end of her Uji chapters. I am hesitant to give it to the empress dowager because of her distaste for my mother's later writing. I entrust it to you to make public at the appropriate time.

When Murasaki died in the third year of Kannin, the same year Michinaga took religious orders, I was told she was so thin and light she had probably starved herself. I cannot pretend that I understood my mother at the end of her life. I was trying to follow the goals she had set me even though she had rejected them for herself. I took the following to be her death poem:

Yo no naka wo   nani nagekamashi   yamazakura   hana miru hodo no   kokoro nariseba
Why do we suffer so in the world? Just regard life as the short bloom of the mountain cherry.

Over the years, my opinion of this poem changed. At first I considered it another lament in the pessimistic mode she so often adopted. Then one day I realized it was actually joyous, and my entire understanding of her was transformed. In the end she had no more sorrow than does a cherry blossom at its falling.

EPILOGUE

THE LOST LAST CHAPTER
of MURASAKI'S

Tale of Genji

LIGHTNING

Inazuma

Muted snatches of male speech, sporadic as birds calling in the underbush, caused Ukifune to look up from her Buddhist text. She slipped her circlet of prayer beads over her wrist and listened. In the quiet between swells of clamoring cicadas she made out the sounds of a convoy. Ukifune fled to her room deep in the recess of the decrepit nunnery the moment she recognized the voices of Kaoru's men.

For the half year since she had persuaded the bishop to cut her hair and administer vows, Ukifune felt she had at long last managed to set foot on a firm shore, leaving the terrors and impossible entanglements of her former unhappy life behind. The nunnery in Ono was a safe haven where she could concentrate on reading the holy scriptures the bishop had given her. She read the Lotus Sutra and was amazed. Of course she had heard it intoned at numerous ceremonies during her life, but she had always been mesmerized by the rich overlapping sonorities without paying particular attention to the meaning of the sacred text. Now the story that even a dragon's daughter had attained buddhahood in a flash filled her with curiosity and hope, sustaining her through long passages where the import of the difficult text was far from clear. Even when she didn't understand, Ukifune still felt the words themselves brimming with the promise of peace and enlightenment. Methodically she prepared her ink. Hours passed as she lost herself in writing practice, copying the sutras.

The old nuns into whose quarters Ukifune had drifted noted with astonishment how this beautiful young woman's brittle reticence finally softened after she had been allowed to shed her bright plum-red robes and put on the drab gray dress of their own humble calling. Before her tonsure, a step the older women could not understand and lamented greatly, nothing the nuns said or did seemed to have the slightest effect on the strange girl's dazed and distant manner.

Ukifune's newly won serenity crumbled at the sound of the men's voices, but after fleeing to her room, heart pounding, she succeeded in calming herself by glancing down at these gray robes.

—After all, I am now a nun, she reminded herself. How could they dare pursue her or lay claim to passions that were now so clearly buried under the ash gray of her religious garb?

Ukifune would not have felt so confident in her drab disguise, Dear Reader, had she known of the reaction of the captain of the guards, to whom the old nun had given a glimpse of her. Knowing his love to be hopeless, the poor man had thought that by seeing the object of his ardor swathed in a nun's habit, he might thereby extinguish his passion. But when he peered through the chink in the wall to which one of the servants led him, far from damping his devotion, the sight of Ukifune's pale complexion set off by the rich fringe of short hair fanning over her shoulders produced such a shudder of passionate regret that he had to restrain a sudden impulse to rush into the room. The pale gray habit she wore over a burnt-yellow robe set off Ukifune's fragile figure in a way that was, perversely, even more elegant than royal reds. That such a flawless beauty had become a nun was almost more than the captain could bear.

Ukifune nervously smoothed her damp hands over the subdued damask, reassuring herself that it had not suddenly begun to change hue, and she reached up to finger the tips of her hair. Yes, it now stopped short at her shoulders, and had not mysteriously grown back as it was wont to do in her anxious dreams. This was a nightmare she had often – suddenly finding her hair restored to its full length, impervious to the scissors she tried in panic to apply to the long black fall.

—No, she told herself. She could not be forced back.

Yet she thought uneasily about the letter that had come from the bishop just yesterday. It seemed reproachful, she felt, as if someone had told the eminent cleric about her connection to Counselor Kaoru. Was it possible to undo the step she had taken with such sincere finality? She would never have thought so, yet this seemed to be what the bishop implied. That there was merit in spending even a day as a nun? That she should consider her half year of retreat sufficient and go back to the world? After enduring endless warnings that she was too young to take this step and that once taken, regrets would be hopeless – indeed that second thoughts would be more damaging to her karma than had she never taken vows at all – to now suggest that she could recross that floating bridge of dreams and step back into her former self was, Ukifune felt, an outrage.

She was resigned to the fact that her maids and nurses had in the past disregarded her wishes and made it possible first for Kaoru and later Prince Niou to gain access to her house, her room, and her body. The women were foolish schemers. Some of them probably believed that they had her interests at heart – although most were only thinking of themselves. They hoped to escape from Uji by allowing their mistress to be swept up by a handsome prince. If Ukifune herself were to be moored in an elegant palace in the capital, they reasoned, they would all be carried along happily in her wake. Bitter as the results of their schemes had been for Ukifune, she could not really blame her women. They had been depressed, even slightly deranged, by their isolation emphasized by the constant sullen roar of the nearby Uji River. Perhaps they had begun to believe the fantasies of the fairy tails and romances in which they so often immersed themselves. Hadn't Ukifune herself been caught up in that disastrous passion for Prince Niou, succumbing so readily to his sweet words and sweeter caresses? Even at the time it felt like a dream. How much more so now in her present state – Ukifune felt a shudder ripple over her skin.

It was harder to forgive the nuns, who, while offering refuge, at the same time seemed all too eager to play matchmaker and return her to the sordid world from which she longed to escape. But that the bishop, the most eminent Doctor of the Law who had taken her seriously and administered the vows, that even he had somehow been swayed by Kaoru to question her step was the most devastating betrayal of all.

Ukifune was beginning to think all their pious pronouncements amounted to nothing more than delusion. She recalled how Kaoru would ramble on about his desire to take holy orders, talking as if to set himself apart from ordinary human desires, but in fact as deeply consumed by them as anyone. Ukifune had noticed that it seemed to be the most restless and disturbed people who are always going on retreats, making a fetish of attaining Buddha's calm. Truly enlightened people did not need to chatter about the ineffable.

Just remembering Kaoru's pious speeches made Ukifune angry, and she found a certain strength in this surge of hard feeling. Yes, it may even had been Kaoru himself who had gone to see the holy bishop and managed to coax the full story from him. Why couldn't he simply have left things alone? She had been presumed dead, drowned in the Uji River – there had even been a mock funeral, bodiless to be sure, but truer in fact that any of them could have supposed. *That* Ukifune was gone as surely as if she were dead.

Wearily Ukifune swept the back of her hand across her forehead and glanced out at the green hills, folded one beyond the other like a rumpled swath of soft green fabric. It was growing dark and the men had lit torches. The lights bobbed and disappeared then reappeared behind the leafy hills as the procession passed by. They reminded her of fireflies. Relieved, Ukifune saw that they were heading back to Miyako without stopping at the nunnery.

Ukifune could not even bring herself to lie down that night. She knelt at her small table, forcing her eyes over the script of the sutra until the characters swam together in the flickering light and eventually skipped right off the paper. She realized with a start that it was only that the dim light of the lamp had finally guttered out. She felt quite sure that she could depend on no one now to support her desire to be left in solitude.

With the faint light of morning, Ukifune returned to her writing practice. Growing up in the provinces, she had not received a wonderful education, but her mother had made sure she at least developed a decent hand. Now she wished she had memorized more poetry so that she would have more material to work with. Sometimes it helped to take a break from copying the prickly Chinese of the sutras to relax one's brush in the familiar cursive runs of a poem. She dipped into the ink and this slipped effortlessly onto the paper:

Ware kakute   ukiyo no naka ni   meguru tomo   tare ka wa shiramu   tsuki no miyako ni
That I still exist, floating in this sad world, can anyone in moonlit Miyako know?

Her fears were realized the next morning when a messenger from Kaoru appeared at the door of the rambling old mansion where the nuns lived.

The old abbess was aghast at this new evidence of Ukifune's connection to a personage of the importance of Counselor Kaoru. She had always known, of course, that Ukifune was no country girl, but that she should have been involved with people at the highest level of imperial society gave her a shock. Tearfully she reproached the girl for keeping her past a secret and begged her to receive Kaoru's envoy. Her entreaties only hardened Ukifune's resolve to be silent. Finally the old nun, who was, after all, the bishop's sister, convinced the recalcitrant young woman to at least look at the boy who had come bearing letters from the capital.

Peering from a hidden window, Ukifune saw only a handsome young page boy kicking at a pebble. He turned his head. She drew in her breath sharply, as if stung, for the boy was certainly her younger half brother. Kaoru had no doubt taken him into his service hoping to find clues as to her whereabouts. Ukifune's heartache upon seeing the boy (of whom she had once been fond) grew even more painful when she realized Kaoru must have sent him as a spy to confirm whether Ukifune was in fact still alive and whether she had really taken refuge as a nun. He knew the boy would be able to recognize her.

Ukifune was not wrong. Counselor Kaoru was of such suspicious frame of mind that he actually suspected Ukifune had gone through the charade of staging her own death merely to throw him off the track. He secretly believed she was being supported in some out-of-the-way place by Prince Niou – or perhaps even by some other lover.

—Yes, that must be it, he thought to himself. He was not so naive as to believe that Ukifune had actually shut herself off from the world. If such a serious student of the scriptures as he himself had been unable to disentangle his life from the concerns of society, how was it possible to suppose that a languid butterfly like Ukifune could have managed to do so?

But he would be magnanimous. Lord Counselor Kaoru lost himself in a reverie imagining Ukifune's embarrassment when prodded out of hiding, and then her gratefulness when he offered to take care of her despite these lapses. He was the steadfast one, after all. Everyone knew his sober reputation.

But what if she actually had become a nun? The thought bothered him until it gradually dawned that the situation might be even better that way. No one else would concern himself over her, and he alone would visit, all with due propriety, of course, and they could talk about religious matters and exchange poems of exquisite regret. If she was a nun, he needn't feel any compunction about pulling aside her screens, even holding her hand. In this way, dare he hope, he might yet find the ideal subject upon which to fasten his long-frustrated yearnings. He would have her, yet not in the way a sullied philanderer like Niou had his women. Best of all, he would never have to face the disappointment of becoming sated with her.

The more Kaoru thought about this outcome, the more he liked it. Even someone as debauched as Prince Niou, he reasoned, wouldn't dare pursue a romantic relationship with a nun. That, surely, would dash the prince's chances of being named next heir apparent. The emperor already grumbled a good deal about his son's flightiness.

Back at the palace, Prince Niou had also gotten wind of the rumor that Ukifune was still alive. She had disappeared when the throes of their passion were at their height. Niou had been devastated. Society misjudged the depth of his love for the mysterious lady in Uji merely because his way of recovering from the grief of her loss was to furiously engage himself in a half dozen fresh seductions.

Ukifune refused to reveal herself to the young page, but when the boy passed Kaoru's letter inside, the old nun herself noticed a family resemblance between the beautiful lad and the melancholy young woman she had nursed back to health.

—Come, come, she coaxed Ukifune. I can see the boy is related to you. Look how dejected he is that you refuse to even speak to him.

Ukifune felt like crying "Leave me alone!" She pressed her face into her sleeve. Finally, raising her eyes, she whispered to the nun,

—I don't mean to be furtive but I truly have nothing to say. When you found me, you know I was practically dead, my mind possessed by some sort of evil spirit. Somehow everything that happened before in my life was erased. Every now and then something brings back a distorted fragment of memory – but as if revealed in a brief flash of lightning.

The abbess shook her head. She would never understand this maddeningly shy creature.

—It's true I may have known this boy when I was younger, said Ukifune. But it is too painful to force myself to remember now. Please send him away. Tell him he has made a mistake.

With a sigh the nun summoned the boy and explained matters. He was most disappointed, as she knew he would be.

Back at her writing table, Ukifune sat with Kaoru's letter unfurled in front of her. It gave off the strange rare fragrance that always clung to him and whatever he touched. Even more than the pleading content of the letter, filled with his usual anguishings, the fragrance pierced deeply into her brain, awakening memories she felt no longer rightly belonged to her.

It was said that the Shining Genji was a master blender of scents, famous for the wonderful fragrance that always hung in the air about his person. In the palace there were old

401

women even now who swore that the perfume emanated from his body itself. Ukifune knew that Kaoru's exotic fragrance came from special sachets he tucked in his clothing, and she was inclined to doubt the stories of Genji's natural perfume. But what did she know of someone like Genji? He was already a legend, his radiance even more enhanced after his death, especially in comparison to the descendants Ukifune knew all too well – Prince Niou and Counselor Kaoru. Niou, of course, was also distinguished for his perfume. Ukifune had at one time or another been accused by each of them of harboring the lingering scent of the other.

—How strange, she thought to herself, that this one particular aspect of the Shining Genji should have been perpetuated by his heirs. Of his reputed radiance, she could discern no trace. Kaoru was as gloomy and morose a character as one was likely to come across, and as for Prince Niou – well, he could be charming, to be sure, but if he had any sort of brilliance, it was but the shimmer of a candle reflected on silver. There was nothing clear and steady about him at all.

Such were the musings the fragrance of Kaoru's letter set off in Ukifune's mind. The other nuns had gathered around to admire the lovely paper and Kaoru's elegant calligraphy. They annoyed Ukifune greatly by speculating on how she would answer him. She had not intended to reply at all.

Why was it, she wondered, that try as she might to be inconspicuous, she seemed to attract the attention of these men the way a tall tree invited a bolt of lightning? And not only the men. The abbess who adopted her when Ukifune had been found unconscious considered her a replacement for her own dead daughter, a gift sent by the merciful Kannon in answer to years of prayer. Certainly the old woman had been kind, patiently nursing her till her health and senses were restored – and Ukifune was not unmoved by her evident care. But, in the end, was this not yet another attachment that Ukifune had neither sought nor welcomed? Could not the old nun have simply left her under the sweet oak where she had been discovered? Indeed, in the opinion of a number of the servants who had been present that misty spring morning, leaving her would have been the proper thing to do – assuming as they did that any creature found in such a situation was most likely a fox spirit in disguise and ought not to be touched at all.

One night not long after her recovery, she had been asked by the others whether she played an instrument, and, embarrassed by her poor upbringing, Ukifune had to demur. She excused herself from the gathering and returned to her writing practice. Another poem slipped off her brush:

Mi o nageshi   namida no kawa no   hayaki se o   shigarami kakete   tare ka todomeshi
Though I flung myself into the torrent of tears, someone wove a net to catch my fall.

Ukifune had crept out of the house that stormy night fully intending to step off the bank into the treacherous currents of the Uji River, swelled by torrents of spring rain. She clearly remembered lifting the latch and easing her way outside onto the narrow verandah that ran around the edge of the building. The sky was utterly moonless and a chill wind whipped her hair about her face and arms almost as if it had come alive. She hesitated. Unable to see her way forward, yet she could not turn back. How long she stood there, agonizingly frozen, she had no idea. She seemed to recall the ghostly figure of a handsome young man taking her in his arms, and then she lost consciousness. The next thing she remembered was opening her eyes in a desolate spot steaming with morning mist, under a gnarled chinquapin tree. She was damp and clammy, chilled to the very core.

Had she somehow been dredged out of the river? At first, Ukifune truly could not tell whether she might not have actually succeeded in drowning herself and was now in some spectral stage of existence brought on by the headstrong sin of taking her own life. The chattering of a perfectly normal squirrel scolding from the safe distance of another oak convinced her that she had failed and was in fact still alive. Thus was she found, weeping bitterly, by the bishop's servants who had taken temporary refuge in the deserted mansion on whose grounds Ukifune had somehow been deposited.

She had made every effort to will herself to die. She refused food. But the willful spark of life proved tenacious. It was nursed along by the bishop's sister, who persisted in seeing a replacement for her lost daughter in this strange and beautiful foundling. She had even, to Ukifune's dismay, tried to interest her in the man, a guard's captain, who had once been engaged to her daughter before that girl's untimely death.

Ukifune knew that Kaoru was not likely to be deterred by her simply declining to reply to his letter. She was equally sure that if Kaoru had located her, Niou would only have to watch Kaoru's behavior to deduce for himself where she now dwelt. Soon she would be in exactly the same predicament that drove her to such desperation once before. Despite the entreaties of all the nuns, she refused to write a word to give to the boy, who had to return empty-handed to the city, wondering glumly what he was to tell his master.

More and more, Ukifune discovered, she liked to write. It was a pity she found herself having to resist so often. She had been pulled into circumstances where she was forced to give everything so often, that now, writing was the one thing she felt was hers to withhold.

She returned to her writing practice. The countryside visible outside her window seemed oppressively green in the heavy air. The young rice plants were just coming into flower. Next to a hedge that had been untended for some time, she noticed a single pink-fringed dianthus – a "bedflower" – blooming alone. She slowly rubbed her inkstick into a tiny puddle of water, turning it rich black. A roll of distant thunder signaled the approach of a summer storm. Ukifune knew the other nuns were excitedly whispering about the visitors from the city who would soon come hovering around their rustic abode. She continued to rub the smooth tablet of hard ink until her puddle was impossibly thick. She added more water.

Kakiho are   sabishisa masaru   tokonatsu ni   tsuyu oki sowamu   aki made wa miji

The rough hedge makes the bedflower appear even lonelier – it will not last to see the autumn dew, let alone for you to tire of it.

The poem slipped off her brush before she had a chance to think, as if the brush were connected to her inner thoughts. If she went over things in her mind too much, it was difficult to put anything on paper; but if she let her attention wander slightly, a tiny crack might appear and her feelings slide through. She was getting better at this oblique technique of trying not to try. There were many things she dared not admit directly to herself.

Ukifune smiled when she read what she had written. She could hardly send Kaoru a poem mentioning a bedflower without him getting the wrong idea. And there was that tired pun on *aki* – no, this was not a very good specimen. Ukifune would have crumpled the poem in her fist were that not a waste of paper. She glanced out at the small feathery pink flower beginning to tremble as the wind picked up. The sky had become quite dark and Ukifune could hear the nuns scurrying about closing shutters. A heavy drop of rain exploded on the verandah.

Perhaps I ought to go out and pick that flower, she thought on impulse, rinsing her brush. It was entirely unreasonable, of course, but Ukifune was seized with the notion that it would be too bad if the delicate blossom were to be pounded into the mud in the imminent storm. The tiny flower was the sole point of color amid the suffocating green outside her window. She did not mind getting a little wet.

A crack of thunder rumbled through the sky, throwing the nuns into a nervous panic. They imagined great muscular storm gods riding the winds, hunkering in the clouds, tossing balls of crackling fire over their heads. Crowding together in the main room where a statue of Amida Buddha looked down peacefully in the dim candlelight, the women all began clicking their prayer beads, invoking noisy mantras of protection. Without warning, a tremendous crash ripped the air. The nuns were all sure the building had been smitten, and fell to the floor wailing and covering their heads.

The thunder cracked again, but farther away this time, and again, farther still. After a while the rain seemed to follow, dwindling finally to a gentle drizzle. During the fright of the storm, the old nun hadn't noticed that Ukifune had not joined them. She now remembered the girl had been upset by her half brother's visit that morning. It was normal for people to band together when they were afraid, thought the nun, but this girl was not normal. Would she be ensconced in her room, too terrified to move? The worried nun ventured toward the rear of the building to see how Ukifune had managed during the storm.

The room was empty. The old nun stood there puzzled, then, experiencing a sudden chill, called for the others. Had anyone seen Ukifune? she demanded. They scattered through the rooms of the nunnery, opening shutters, calling her name. Ukifune's writing brushes, ink, and paper lay neatly on her low table, but of the girl herself, there was no trace. The old nun collapsed in an agony of remorse. Her worst fear had been realized – the vile spirit who had originally snatched this girl away and stolen the memories of her earlier life had returned under cover of thunder to reclaim her. Why had she not immediately rushed to Ukifune's side at the first gust of unlucky wind? The old nun berated herself and would not be comforted. If only she had brought the girl under the gaze of the statue of Kammon, this would not have happened. The other nuns were quite at a loss as well.

Just before dusk, as the slanting golden rays of the setting sun broke through the clouds, a gardener who had gone out to assess the storm damage saw that the old oak tree by the abandoned hedge had been struck by lightning. The tree had been split practically in two, the ground strewn with branches, leaves, and charred bits of wood. He shook his head, then his attention was drawn to a gray heap near the shattered trunk.

Ukifune was, if not dead, quite unconscious.

The abbess assumed the worst, but numbly had the frail body brought inside and laid onto some soft coverlets. Up until that very morning she had envisioned Ukifune restored to a position of grandeur by the powerful people who had loved her in her previous life. It had been impossible to take seriously Ukifune's own resolute refusal to acknowledge these connections. The nun attributed her stubbornness to the lingering effects of the evil spirit. She now began to see that her own actions in coaxing the girl to reestablish those ties had led directly to her being snatched up and broken by this thunderous evil. How could she have been so blind?

Ukifune lay in a coma for three days, during which the abbess was constantly by her side, watching for faint signs that the young woman's spirit still inhabited her traumatized body. The old woman felt deeply responsible and vowed to Kannon that if the girl could be saved from death one more time she would do her utmost to help her keep her vows. She carefully dripped water from a twisted cloth into Ukifune's mouth, rejoicing to see the girl's throat work to swallow the drops.

On the morning of the fourth day Ukifune opened her eyes. She heard the abbess's exclamation of delight and she felt smooth dry hands touch her face. She smelled the familiar scent of sandalwood incense mingling with the smell of pickles on the old nun's breath. Yet her senses were in a jumble. Though she had the sensation of moving her eyelids, all was dark. Ukifune fumbled for the old woman's hand, and in her relief and joy to see her patient respond, the nun did not notice till that afternoon that Ukifune was blind.

Over the course of the summer Ukifune slowly regained a sense of her shattered self. Only her eyes refused to function, while her other senses were, if anything, sharpened by the fierce flash of light that had coursed through her body. She could still recall the strange heavy smell in the air just as she reached to pluck the flower under the oak tree. She knew that Prince Niou had managed to find his way to the nunnery because she detected the faint echo of his perfume one afternoon. Perhaps he had convinced the nuns to grant him a glimpse of her – she didn't know, but in any case he did not speak to her, nor did he write anything. And then the fragrance faded away.

Niou was impatient to follow his instincts after that conversation with Kaoru. The counselor may have thought he had successfully concealed any hint of his knowledge of

Ukifune's whereabouts, but it had been easy for one of Niou's retainers to follow Kaoru's man over the hills to Ono. Once there, he had but to chat up one of the serving girls at the nunnery to get the whole story. So now the prince knew where she was. The only real difficulty was thinking up an excuse to offer the emperor and empress for a day's absence from the palace. They watched him like parental tigers these days. Finally at the beginning of autumn Niou proposed a reasonable-sounding excursion to a temple nearby and managed to get himself to Ono.

The abbess of the nunnery was uncommonly adamant in refusing his request to see Ukifune, and, usually skilled at getting sympathy from women like this, Niou was surprised to find himself so utterly rebuffed. Pretending to leave, he turned his charms on one of the younger nuns and convinced her to lead him to a corner of the garden where he could get a clear peek into Ukifune's room.

It was good that he had taken the trouble, Niou told himself later. Otherwise, he might had pined uselessly for something that no longer existed. He was taken aback at the young nun's story of how Ukifune had been struck by lightning and blinded. If he had not seen for himself, he might not have believed it, thinking it a tale concocted by Kaoru to keep him away. The gaze of those sightless eyes made his skin crawl. He would creep away quietly. No use to send in a poem, because she wouldn't be able to read it. Better if she never knew of his visit.

Kaoru, of course, heard of Ukifune's disaster right away through his connection with the bishop. He was talked out of an immediate urge to rush to Ono, and then with one thing and another, and all the official duties pressing on him, he did not actually make the trip himself until autumn was half over. He stopped on his way to visit the bishop in his mountain retreat.

—Give what's happened, the bishop had said to him, it's probably for the best that she has already taken her vows.

—Even so, Kaoru responded, it couldn't hurt for me to visit her now, could it?

408

Kaoru couldn't bring himself to ask, but he assumed Ukifune had been terribly disfigured by the accident. Would he still love her? he wondered.

Ukifune sat on the verandah next to the garden, feeling the cool autumn breeze blowing past her face. It was the day before the equinox, so all the nuns were busy preparing for the services of the morrow. No one was available to read to her. She listened to the bell crickets, the weaverbug, and the *kirigirisu*. It had all been an autumn soundscape of undifferentiated insects in years past, but now she could make out subtle differences in their cries and chirps. She noticed that when the temperature dropped, the insects became more shrill.

A kitchen maid had brought her a bundle of chrysanthemums that Ukifune lifted to her face now and then, inhaling their bracing bittersweet odor.

—What color are they? she had asked the girl.

—Oh, there's white ones, and yellow ones, and white ones with yellow eyes, and bronzy-red ones, and white ones with purple backs . . .

The girl placed Ukifune's hand on each one as she described it.

—I've heard tell the dew from these buds is very good for you, she said shyly. Maybe you could rub some on your eyes, my lady.

Ukifune smiled at the country girl.

—Maybe so, she said. Thank you.

They heard a carriage and horses arrive at the gate.

—That must be the priest who's come to lead the sutra chanting, said the girl, who just at that moment was summoned away by an irate serving lady hunting for rags to wipe the ash from the censers on the altar.

Laying the chrysanthemums in her lap, Ukifune told the girl to hurry off. She brushed her fingers over the petals, some tight, some soft and trailing. Gradually she became aware of another scent, a complex blend of musk and aloe, a hint of clove, so familiar she thought she must be dreaming. The faint fragrance pulled memories from her mind. Then she heard voices – the abbess almost hysterical, but who was the other, low and urgent?

Kaoru. Of course, the fragrance.

They stopped outside her room. The old nun realized Kaoru was determined to see Ukifune no matter what she said, and had no choice but give in. It was most irregular, and she would speak to her brother, the bishop, about this behavior. Even if he was an influential man in Miyako, there were limits, after all. At least she would not leave the girl alone with him.

Scandalized as she was, it did occur to the nun that perhaps the meeting was not such a bad idea in fact – let the counselor see her, talk to her even. He would finally see for himself that Ukifune was no longer the person he had once apparently been so hopelessly in love with. Then he would leave her alone, and the girl would finally be at peace.

Talking thus to herself, the abbess opened the door. Ukifune remained as she was, holding the chrysanthemums, her face profiled by the garden. Kaoru drank in her image. She didn't look at him. Of course not, he reminded himself. She can't see. He beheld her boldly, paying not the slightest attention to the old woman sitting fiercely at his elbow. Yes, she had that blank unwavering gaze of the blind, but otherwise her beauty had not been touched. Kaoru was relieved. He spoke softly to her, telling her not to be afraid, that he felt their spiritual kinship now more than ever. Ukifune appeared to be listening, although her responses were minimal.

What on earth can the counselor be going on about? wondered the abbess as she watched this strange scene. Whatever is the karmic connection between these two souls?

It grew late, and the old nun had to join the priest for chanting sutras. The cleric had arrived right after Kaoru and was waiting patiently to begin services. She begged the counselor to leave now, and somewhat to her surprise he meekly followed her out.

—Now you see how it is, sir, the abbess said. There really can't be much point in your trying to coax the girl into anything. Things have gone much too far.

—Yes, replied Kaoru. I do see how it is. But I am very fond

of her nonetheless, and I'm sure you won't object to my looking in on her from time to time.

Too rushed to argue, the abbess bowed to Kaoru and excused herself to join the other nuns. Kaoru took his leave, feeling inexplicably buoyant. He liked this new Ukifune very much. A little guiltily he enjoyed the fact that he could look at her without feeling self-conscious as he usually did around women at the palace. She couldn't see him watching her. And she was a good listener. Yes, he looked forward to visiting the nunnery in Ono in the future. He relaxed, enjoying the spectacular color of the maple-clad hills all the way back to the capital.

In her darkness, Ukifune had been almost suffocated by Kaoru's perfume. Ever since her encounter with that searing flash of light her senses sometimes became confused by strong stimuli. The counselor's fragrance was so loud she could barely concentrate on what he was saying in the trickle of words that lapped her ear without cease. Words unmoored, she thought. Wild, floating words. Kaoru's problem was mistaking words for reality. It was the sort of thing one couldn't explain with – well, words. In consequence, she had mostly remained silent. Protected by her impenetrable black screen, she no longer felt hounded, and indeed almost felt sorry for Kaoru. He was the one groping in the dark, not she.

It had become dark outside. Ukifune could feel dusk by listening to the insects modulate from the day singers to the night singers. Night air felt different as well. She groped toward the door of her room and pushed it open, letting the autumn breeze rush through, sweeping out all traces of lingering scent.

411

AUTHOR'S NOTE

I first read Arthur Waley's classic translation of the romantic novel centering on the figure of the Shining Price Genji when I was sixteen. I read it slowly over the course of a summer, and each time I opened the book I was transported from a humid backyard gazebo in Indiana to the Japanese imperial court of a thousand years ago, a world refined and shaped by poetic sensibilities. I was swept away by the powerful ability of this fiction to create a compelling world utterly removed from the reality of my twentieth-century, mid-western teenage life. Since then, I have reread the *Tale of Genji* numerous times, in each English translation, as well as in modern Japanese.

Over the years I became increasingly fascinated by Murasaki Shikibu. Legend has it that she wrote about Prince Genji in a frenzy of inspiration prompted by gazing at the full moon during a religious retreat to Ishiyama Temple. Indeed one may see the "Genji Room" at this very temple, complete with a life-size mannequin of Murasaki sitting at her writing table, with an appealing little girl meant to be her daughter, Katako, peering out from the background. This is a fiction, of course, but Japanese have an irrepressible urge to fix the place – for homage if nothing else – by asserting that this is where her *Tale* was created. The historical Murasaki Shikibu is glimpsed through the fragments of her diary that still exist and, in refraction, through her work, the *Tale of Genji* – yet unless some long-lost manuscript should happen to come to light after a millennium of obscurity, there is nothing else that can be established about her.

Who knows why some parts of her diary survived the centuries and some did not? Perhaps Murasaki destroyed

412

parts of her journal and her letters, or perhaps her heirs did. Or perhaps the fragile notebooks were consumed in one of the many fires that swept through ancient Kyoto, a city built largely of wood and paper. The tantalizing notion that she probably recorded much more of herself during her remarkable life gave me the impetus to imagine her story.

Thanks to a grant from the Japan Foundation, I returned to the city of Kyoto for two months in the autumn of 1998 in order to search out traces of eleventh-century Miyako. I took flowers and incense to Murasaki's grave and visited the temple Rōzanji, situated on the plot of land where it is claimed she was born. Here were Murasaki's poems, by now so familiar, inscribed in stones set about the courtyard. Hidden in the temple's inner precincts is a garden called the *Genji no tei*, consisting solely of raked white pebbles and pines on islands of moss. For one month alone there is color: the *murasaki* purple of bellflowers, blooming only in September.

I bicycled along the Kamo River to its northern reach. Snowy egrets and great blue herons waded the shallows spearing fish; iridescent black dragonflies darted about. Just once I spied a blue jewel, a migrating kingfisher, perched on the reeds. I reached the Upper Kamo Shrine, so important to the people of Murasaki's world, still a sacred Shintō religious center today. On the night of the full harvest moon, the night Murasaki was said to have begun writing Genji, I went to the Lower Kamo Shrine to view a performance of *bugaku* dance and music – precisely the sort of entertainment Murasaki may have enjoyed. Wisps of cloud raced across the face of the full moon.

The imperial palace and grounds lie in a great, open rectangle at the center of the modern city of Kyoto, shifted eastward from the configuration of the palace of eleventh-century Heian-kyō. There I toured the replicas of Heian buildings by permission of the Imperial Household Agency.

I retraced my heroine's journey to Echizen, boarding a tour boat at the southern tip of Lake Biwa, transferring to train at the eastern edge of the lake, proceeding by local across the

Shiozu Mountains, over the Hokuriku Road to Tsuruga and on to Takefu City, where Tametoki had been posted as governor. Back in Kyoto, I visited the western hills of Arashiyama, and the eastern hills where Kiyomizu Temple is located. And I went to Uji, to Ishiyama Temple, and to Suma.

I discovered the Murasaki Shikibu Appreciation Society of Kyoto, which sponsors various Genji-related activities, and was able to attend several of their lectures on aspects of Heian culture, as well as a talk by Setouchi Jakuchō on her new translation of *Genji* into modern Japanese. Searching out the dim outlines of Murasaki's Miyako, I have had the good fortune to discover the old city of Kyoto more deeply. The shadows still exist, if one but knows where to look.

ACKNOWLEDGMENTS

While *The Tale of Murasaki* is fiction, it contains large chunks of Murasaki's historical diary and practically all of the *waka* from her poem collection. A scholarly and fascinating English translation and study of these works has been done by Richard Bowring: *Murasaki Shikibu: Her Diary and Poetic Memoirs* (Princeton University Press, 1982), also available in his revised translation without the poems as *The Diary of Lady Murasaki* in a 1996 Penguin edition.

Readers familiar with Heian literature will notice many echoes of the *Tale of Genji* reverse-engineered into my version of Murasaki's life. They should refer to Edward Seidensticker's magnificent translation, which is considered the English standard for the *Tale of Genji*. They will also see insights borrowed from Sei Shōnagon's *Pillow Book* (translated by Ivan Morris); the diary and poems of Izumi Shikibu (translated by Edward Cranston); and the *Gossamer Diary* by a woman known to history only as "the mother of Michitsuna" (translated by Edwin Seidensticker, and more recently by Sonja Arntzen). Much of the historical information has been gleaned from *A Tale of Flowering Fortunes (Eiga Monogatari)*, translated by Helen and William McCullough. This remarkable work has been characterized as the historical counterpart to the fictional *Tale of Genji*. I am deeply indebted to the work of all these eminent scholars.

In addition, I have drawn on studies by specialists in the field of Heian literature: Doris Bargen, Karen Brazell, Norma Field, Aileen Gatten, Thomas Harper, G. Cameron Hurst, Edward Kamens, Donald Keene, Earl Miner, Joshua Mostow, Andrew Pekarik, Esperanza Ramirez-Christiansen, and Haruo Shirane. In Kyoto, Ohara Kiyoko graciously allowed me to accompany her Genji study group to tour the famous spots of Uji. In most Genji-like fashion, Professor Ike Kōzō of Chubu University sent me a sweet flag root after I had asked him what that botanical specimen looked life. Gaye Rowley provided the translation of the one *waka* in the book not from Murasaki's era. It is by Murasaki's first great twentieth-century translator, Yosano Akiko, on page 121.

For helping me understand what readers wanted to know about Murasaki, I am grateful to Margaret Corrigan, Marie Dalby, Jennifer Futernik, Arthur Golden, Carolyn Grote, Kathy Kunst, Gaye Rowley, Cathleen Schwartz, John Stevenson, and Nan Talese.

Professors H. Mack Horton, Helen McCullough, Joshua Mostow, and Patricia Fister kindly read early drafts, offering encouragement and substantial advice, and Professor Doris Bargen has been a thought-provoking intellectual companion throughout. As always, my husband, Michael, has been unstinting in his love and editorial assistance.

Liza Dalby
Berkeley, California, 1999